THE NEW MELVILLE STUDIES

What does Melville studies look like after a phase of intense critical activity? This book addresses that question by analyzing Melville as a writer who was keenly interested in the pleasures, limits, and possibilities of various reading practices. It collects and assesses all of the major new trends in Melville studies. Essays, written by some of the leading scholars in the field, test out emerging critical methods. They explore Melville's centrality to American literary studies and consider the full range of Melville's career, connecting his poetry to his prose. This collection reimagines Melville as a theorist as well as a writer, approaching his works as philosophical forms in their own right. It shows how scholars are changing Melville studies not only by reorienting the texts upon which those studies are based, but also by incorporating new approaches that unsettle prior assumptions and interpretive claims.

CODY MARRS is Associate Professor of English at the University of Georgia. He is the author of *Nineteenth-Century American Literature and the Long Civil War* and the co-editor of *Timelines of American Literature*.

TWENTY-FIRST-CENTURY CRITICAL REVISIONS

This series addresses two main themes across a range of key authors, genres, and literary traditions. The first is the changing critical interpretations that have emerged since *c.* 2000. Radically new interpretations of writers, genres, and literary periods have emerged from the application of new critical approaches. Substantial scholarly shifts have occurred too, through the emergence of new editions, editions of letters, and competing biographical accounts. Books in this series will collate and reflect this rich plurality of twenty-first-century critical energies, and wide varieties of revisionary scholarship, to summarize, analyze, and assess the impact of contemporary critical strategies. Designed to offer critical pathways and evaluations, and to establish new critical routes for research, this series will collate and explain a dizzying array of criticism and scholarship in key areas of twenty-first-century literary studies.

Forthcoming Books in this Series:

VICTORIA AARONS
The New Jewish American Literary Studies

JEAN-MICHEL RABATÉ
The New Samuel Beckett Studies

MICHELLE KOHLER
The New Emily Dickinson Studies

JOANNE FREER
The New Pynchon Studies

MARK BYRON
The New Ezra Pound Studies

MATT COHEN
The New Walt Whitman Studies

JENNIFER HAYTOCK & LAURA RATTRAY
The New Edith Wharton Studies

KIRK CURNUTT & SUZANNE DEL GIZZO
The New Hemingway Studies

DOUGLAS MAO
The New Modernist Studies

THE NEW MELVILLE STUDIES

EDITED BY

CODY MARRS

University of Georgia

CAMBRIDGE
UNIVERSITY PRESS

CAMBRIDGE
UNIVERSITY PRESS

University Printing House, Cambridge CB2 8BS, United Kingdom

One Liberty Plaza, 20th Floor, New York, NY 10006, USA

477 Williamstown Road, Port Melbourne, VIC 3207, Australia

314–321, 3rd Floor, Plot 3, Splendor Forum, Jasola District Centre, New Delhi – 110025, India

79 Anson Road, #06–04/06, Singapore 079906

Cambridge University Press is part of the University of Cambridge.

It furthers the University's mission by disseminating knowledge in the pursuit of education, learning, and research at the highest international levels of excellence.

www.cambridge.org
Information on this title: www.cambridge.org/9781108484039
DOI: 10.1017/9781108646383

First published 2019

Printed and bound in Great Britain by Clays Ltd, Elcograf S.p.A.

A catalogue record for this publication is available from the British Library.

Library of Congress Cataloging-in-Publication Data
NAMES: Marrs, Cody, editor.
TITLE: The new Melville studies / edited by Cody Marrs.
DESCRIPTION: Cambridge, United Kingdom ; New York, NY : Cambridge University Press, 2018– | Includes bibliographical references and index.
IDENTIFIERS: LCCN 2018031738 | ISBN 9781108484039 (v. 1)
SUBJECTS: LCSH: Melville, Herman, 1819–1891 – Criticism and interpretation.
CLASSIFICATION: LCC PS2387 .N47 2018 | DDC 813/.3–dc23
LC record available at https://lccn.loc.gov/2018031738

ISBN 978-1-108-48403-9 Hardback

Contents

Notes on Contributors

JOHN BRYANT is Professor Emeritus of English at Hofstra University. He is the author of *A Companion to Melville Studies*, *Melville and Repose*, *The Fluid Text*, *Melville Unfolding*, and over 60 articles. He is the founding editor of *Leviathan: A Journal of Melville Studies* and has published print editions of *Typee*, *The Confidence-Man*, *Melville's Tales, Poems, and Other Writings, and Moby-Dick*, as well as the electronic edition *Herman Melville's Typee*. He is founder and director of the online critical archive and scholarly edition *Melville Electronic Library* and of Hofstra University's Digital Research Center. In 2015, he received the Distinguished Editor Award given by the Council of Editors of Learned Journals. Currently, he is working on a comprehensive biography titled *Herman Melville: A Half Known Life*.

ELIZABETH DUQUETTE is Professor of English at Gettysburg College. She is the author of *Loyal Subjects: Bonds of Nation, Race, and Allegiance in Nineteenth-Century America* and the co-editor of *Elizabeth Stuart Phelps: Selected Tales, Essays, and Poems* and Phelps's *The Gates Ajar*. Her work has appeared in journals such as *American Literary History* and *Arizona Quarterly*, and in collections such as *Melville and Aesthetics* and *The Oxford Handbook of Nineteenth-Century American Literature*. She is currently writing a book on tyranny, ubiquity, and Napoleon Bonaparte's nineteenth-century American empire. With Stacey Margolis, she edits *J19: The Journal of Nineteenth-Century Americanists*.

CHRISTOPHER FREEBURG is Conrad Humanities Scholar and Professor of English at the University of Illinois, Urbana-Champaign. He is the author of *Melville and the Idea of Blackness* and *Black Aesthetics and the Interior Life*. His work has appeared in journals such as *American Literary History* and *South Atlantic Quarterly*, and in collections such as *The Cambridge Companion to James Baldwin*. He is currently completing a book titled *Slavery: Art and Counterlife*, which focuses on slave texts across a variety of media.

JENNIFER GREIMAN is Associate Professor of English at Wake Forest University. She is the author of *Democracy's Spectacle: Sovereignty and Public Life in Antebellum American Writing* and the co-editor of *The Last Western:* Deadwood *and the End of American Empire*. Her work has appeared in journals such as *Postmodern Culture*, and in collections such as *The New Cambridge Companion to Herman Melville* and *Melville and Aesthetics*. Her article on Melville and Tocqueville, which appeared in *J19: The Journal of Nineteenth-Century Americanists*, was awarded the Hennig Cohen prize for the best essay or chapter on Melville. She is currently writing a book on aesthetics and democracy in Melville.

PAUL HURH is Associate Professor of English at University of Arizona. He is the author of *American Terror: The Feeling of Thinking in Edwards, Poe, and Melville*. His work has appeared in journals such as *Nineteenth-Century Literature, Style*, and *Novel*, and in the collection *Melville's Philosophies*.

MICHAEL JONIK is Senior Lecturer in American literature at the University of Sussex. He is the author of *Herman Melville and the Politics of the Inhuman*. His work has also appeared in journals such as *Leviathan* and in collections such as *Melville's Philosophies, Thoreauvian Modernities*, and *A Political Companion to Herman Melville*. He is a founding member of The British Association of Nineteenth-Century Americanists (BrANCA).

ROBERT S. LEVINE is Professor of English and Distinguished University Professor at the University of Maryland, College Park. His most recent books are *The Lives of Frederick Douglass* and *Race, Transnationalism, and Nineteenth-Century American Literary Studies*. He is the editor or co-editor of a number of volumes, including *The Cambridge Companion to Herman Melville, Frederick Douglass and Herman Melville: Essays in Relation*, and a Norton Critical Edition of Melville's *Pierre*. He is General Editor of *The Norton Anthology of American Literature*. In 2014, the American Literature Section of the MLA awarded him the Hubbell Medal for Lifetime Achievement in American Literary Studies.

CODY MARRS is Associate Professor of English at the University of Georgia. He is the author of *Nineteenth-Century American Literature and the Long Civil War* and the co-editor of *Timelines of American Literature*. His work has also appeared in journals such as *American Literature, American Literary History*, and *J19*, as well as in edited volumes such as A *History of American Civil War Literature* and *The New Dickinson Studies*.

DOMINIC MASTROIANNI is Associate Professor of English at Clemson University. He is the author of *Politics and Skepticism in Antebellum American Literature*. His work has also appeared in *Comparative Literature, ESQ, Studies in American Fiction*, and in the Norton Critical Edition of *Pierre*. He is currently writing a book on attention in Thoreau and Emerson.

JUSTINE S. MURISON is Associate Professor of English at the University of Illinois at Urbana-Champaign. She is the author of *The Politics of Anxiety in Nineteenth-Century American Literature* and the co-editor of special issues of *American Literary History* and *Early American Literature*. Her work has appeared in journals such as *American Literature* and *Atlantic Studies*, and in collections such as *Timelines of American Literature* and *The Neuroscientific Turn*. She is currently writing a book on privacy, political hypocrisy, and the secularization of the body, and editing a volume titled *American Literature in Transition, 1820–1860*.

GILLIAN KIDD OSBORNE is Lecturer and Research Associate for Poetry in America courses at the Harvard Extension School and co-editor of *Ecopoetics: Essays in the Field*. From 2015 to 2017, she was a postdoctoral fellow at the Harvard Center for the Environment, and her work has been supported by fellowships from the American Antiquarian Society and the Emily Dickinson International Society. She is at work on a book about the flowers in American poetry from its beginnings to the present.

SAMUEL OTTER is Professor of English at the University of California, Berkeley. He is the author of *Melville's Anatomies* and *Philadelphia Stories: America's Literature of Race and Freedom*, and the co-editor of *Frederick Douglass and Herman Melville: Essays in Relation* and *Melville and Aesthetics*. He is the editor of *Leviathan: A Journal of Melville Studies*. His work has appeared in journals such as *American Literature, American Literary History*, and *Representations*, and in collections such as *The New Cambridge*

Companion to Herman Melville and *Melville's Philosophies*. He is currently writing a book titled *Melville's Forms*.

ELIZA RICHARDS is Associate Professor in the Department of English and Comparative Literature at the University of North Carolina at Chapel Hill. She is the author of *Battle Lines: Poetry, Media and the US Civil War* and *Gender and the Poetics of Reception in Poe's Circle*, and the editor of *Emily Dickinson in Context*. Her work has also appeared in journals such as *ESQ*, *Victorian Poetry*, and *Amerikastudien/American Studies*, and in collections such as *Whitman Among the Bohemians* and *A History of Nineteenth-Century American Women's Poetry*.

EDGWARD SUGDEN is Lecturer in American Literature at King's College London. He is the author of *Emergent Worlds: Alternative States in Nineteenth-Century American Culture*.

BRIAN YOTHERS is the Frances Spatz Leighton Endowed Distinguished Professor of English at the University of Texas at El Paso. He is the author of *Reading Abolition: The Critical Reception of Harriet Beecher Stowe and Frederick Douglass*, *Sacred Uncertainty: Religious Difference and the Shape of Melville's Career*, *Melville's Mirrors: Literary Criticism and America's Most Elusive Author*, and *The Romance of the Holy Land in American Travel Writing, 1790–1876*. He is the editor of *Billy Budd, Sailor: Critical Insights*, and co-editor of *Above the American Renaissance: David S. Reynolds and the Spiritual Imagination in American Literary Studies* and *Visionary of the Word: Melville and Religion*. He is associate editor of *Leviathan: A Journal of Melville Studies*, co-editor with Wyn Kelley of the *Moby-Dick*/Travel section of the *Melville Electronic Library*, associate editor of *Melville's Marginalia Online*, and editor of the series "Literary Criticism in Perspective."

Acknowledgments

This volume would not exist without Ray Ryan's guidance and encouragement. *The New Melville Studies* also benefitted a great deal from Edgar Mendez, and everyone else at Cambridge University Press who helped bring this book into the world. I am grateful to Robert S. Levine, who not only read and responded to the book in its entirety but also provided crucial feedback on the volume's organization. To Samuel Otter and Christopher Hager, who read the introduction and helped me figure out ways to reframe and refine it: thank you so much. Last but not least, I wish to thank the volume's contributors, all of whom worked very hard on these essays and responded to my editorial suggestions – no matter how tangential or obsessive – with grace and equanimity.

—

Parts of Gillian Osborne's chapter, "Melville and His Flowers," previously appeared as "Herman Melville, Queen of the Flowers," *Leviathan: A Journal of Melville Studies* 18.3 (October 2016): 129–148. Those passages are reprinted here with permission of Johns Hopkins University Press.

Abbreviations for Texts Cited

BB	*Billy Budd, Sailor*
CL	*Clarel*
CM	*The Confidence-Man*
IP	*Israel Potter*
J	*Journals*
L	*Correspondence*
M	*Mardi*
MD	*Moby-Dick*
OM	*Omoo*
P	*Pierre*
PP	*Published Poems*
PZ	*The Piazza Tales and Uncollected Prose*
RB	*Redburn*
TY	*Typee*
WJ	*White-Jacket*
WW	*Weeds and Wildings*

CHAPTER 1

Introduction: Melville Studies, Old and New

Cody Marrs

The world is forever babbling of originality.

—Melville, *Pierre* (1852)

About halfway through *The Confidence-Man* (1857) – Melville's wonderfully odd, unnerving novel about belief in the modern age – the narrator discusses the near-impossibility of inventing something new. Every story, he says, has already been told. Every genre is ancient, and every character is based on the personalities we find in the world around us. Even in those rare instances in which an artist seems to have created something utterly and shockingly unique – an unprecedented plot or character – it often turns out to be "singular, or striking, or captivating," but not wholly *original*. Nor is such newness theoretically possible, since it is "as true in literature as [it is] in zoology, that all life is from the egg" (CM 239).

Why, then, try to produce anything at all? Melville was sometimes troubled by that question. He was a relentlessly experimental writer with acute traditional inclinations; an author who worked within highly established genres while twisting them in distinct ways. For Melville, writing tapped into a basic human impulse: an irrepressible will to create even if everything has been created – to reinvent, in lieu of inventing. Scholars who work on Melville tend to find themselves in a similar situation. Almost everything that critics are now examining, from Melville's materialism to Melville's aesthetics, was already examined, to one degree or another, generations ago. There is also an inherent traditionalism to the very idea of "Melville studies": it foregrounds a single, highly canonical author; indicates a distinct career and set of works; and it suggests that the principal subject of literary studies is imaginative writing. Yet there have undoubtedly been important turns and advances. We now know far more about Melville's life, ideas, and contexts than we previously did. Scholars have unearthed writings that had been forgotten or overlooked. And Melville criticism has always occupied a central place in the evolution of literary studies: there is hardly a single method or theory that has not been applied to Melville's works – or originated in Melville studies then migrated outward.

This volume captures the dualistic nature of Melville studies and shows why this pull between the old and the new, instead of presenting a problem to be overcome (or innovated out of existence), is responsible for the field's enduring power. All of these essays are "singular, or striking, or captivating" in their readings and approaches. Moving between the postcritical, the posthuman, and the postsecular, *The New Melville Studies* addresses many of the theoretical questions that are currently redefining literary studies. The following essays also address a wide range of topics – the slipperiness of genre and sexuality, the vicissitudes of belief, the relation between form and feeling – and offer fresh accounts of Melville's writings. Yet this volume converges around a single, influential author and a scholarly tradition that has a long, layered history.

In other words, the "new" Melville studies is both new and not-so-new. Let us look first at what is distinct, and then at what is not.

What Is New in *The New Melville Studies*

"Every generation," writes Christopher Castiglia, "needs a new 'Melville' suited to that generation's assumptions and needs."[1] The history of Melville's reception bears out this point. Ever since the Melville Revival of the 1920s, Melville has proven to be a crucial voice, an author to whom we repeatedly – indeed, almost obsessively – return. It is difficult to think of another writer who has become such a cynosure for literary critics: regardless of how the field morphs, or which theories rise or fall, interest in Melville never seems to wane. However, the nature and terms of that interest *do* change, sometimes quite dramatically, in response to new events and ideas. Melville continues to anchor our sense of the field, but the shift that Castiglia announced – the making of a new Melville, and a new Melville studies, suited to a different set of assumptions – is undoubtedly occurring.

For a long time now, scholars have been accustomed to reading Melville against the grain. With the flowering of New Americanism in the 1980s and 1990s, Melville's writings came to be seen as texts shaped in complex ways by their discursive and historical circumstances. Approaching literature as a means of cultural diagnosis and political critique, New Americanism reinvented Melville for a scholarly generation influenced by the political upheavals of the 1960s and 1970s. New Americanism disclosed the intricate capillaries of Melville's world, showing us how his writings stage subtle dialogues with racial discourses, class formations, and sexual practices. It elevated neglected works, such as *Pierre* and *Benito Cereno*. It pulled Melville out of the Cold War era that had either disguised or obscured some his political commitments. And it linked Melville to an array of developments in American history, from the development of jurisprudence to the *longue durées* of colonialism and imperialism.

The field is now undergoing a transformation, and scholars are searching out alternative interpretive frames for Melville's formal commitments, philosophical entanglements, and cultural exchanges. The new Melville studies grows out of a keen awareness of the fact that every interpretation – as the New Americanists showed us – bears as much on the present as it does on the past, and the institutional and intellectual circumstances that scholars inhabit in the twenty-first century are quite different from the circumstances that prevailed 30 years ago. As Robert S. Levine noted in his *New Cambridge Companion to Herman Melville*, this change was already afoot in 2014. "Melville," Levine points out, "could understand and critique his culture as well as any" modern-day literary critic.[2] *The New Melville Studies* extends Levine's claim. These essays ask: What might it mean – and what would it look like – to read Melville *with* the grain?

Something you will not find, in any sustained or robust form, are readings predicated on the notion that the critic occupies a position outside or above Melville's works that allows them "to diagnose texts' allegiances as the product of a bounded historical moment."[3] (Edward Sugden's essay comes closest, but he is less interested in Melville's implication within structures of power than in the dynamics of nineteenth-century border zones, dynamics to which Melville himself was quite attuned.) If New Americanism tended to approach literature vertically, viewing texts in terms of surfaces and depths (a paradigm that recent calls for "surface reading" retain), these essays are oriented along decidedly different axes.[4] They read Melville from positions within or next to Melville's works. Although they differ in their interests and emphases, these essays all tend to read adjacently and position themselves alongside Melville as he writes.

Two modes of reading come into focus here. Part I, "Feeling with Melville," focuses on the moods, tones, and sentiments that vitalize Melville's works. Gillian Osborne shows how, in *Weeds and Wildings*, Melville approaches flowers as both a literary conceit and a vehicle of homosocial attachment. Justine S. Murison emphasizes a different but no less defining feature of Melville's writing: its sly, raucous humor, which often scrambles the way we read Melville's stories. As Murison points out, "Melville not only anticipates our current debates about the efficacy of critique . . . but also points us to what is definitively left to the side of these debates: the depths of surfaces and the perversities of a joke." Other essays recover a wide range of felt experiences that are released by Melville's writing: feelings of marginality (Edward Sugden), racial acoustics and performances (Christopher Freeburg), and senses of belief and unbelief (Brian Yothers).

The essays in Part II, "Thinking with Melville," take the well-established tradition of using a theory to read Melville and flip it on its head, disclosing how Melville's writings *themselves* advance numerous theories – about language, the body, even matter itself. These essays recover Melville's mind at work, showing how his ideas bubble up, descend, circle back, and leap forward. Elizabeth Duquette elucidates the analogies that hold together Melville's poetry and prose, while Samuel Otter retraces the verbal and ideational movements that mark Melville's style. Other essays in Part II have a different focus – Melville's materialism (Michael Jonik), perfectionism (Dominic Mastroianni), fascination with paranoia (Paul Hurh), interest in consciousness (John Bryant), understanding of poetic networks (Eliza Richards), and his view of literature as a vehicle for theorizing (Jennifer Greiman) – but the "egg of suggestion" (CL 294) is that Melville saw practicing philosophy and writing literature as mutually constitutive acts. Poetry and prose are for Melville ways of testing out ideas, exploring concepts, and examining the relation between the mind and the world; and philosophy, in turn, is a creative process that always involves acts of writing, reading, and interpretation. As Jennifer Greiman aptly puts it, "Melville proposes that philosophy and fiction share a common world of figures and conceits, fables and counterfactuals, so why not read accordingly?"

Despite the volume's bifurcated structure, it is best to read these essays together. Almost everything Melville wrote, from *Typee* through *Billy Budd*, suggests that feelings are ideational and that ideas have psychic and emotional dimensions. This is one of the major insights of Melville's art: it reveals – and finds both joy and terror in – the incessant intermingling of thought and feeling. In reading *The New Melville Studies*, one should take a cue from Melville and approach Part I and Part II as critical diptychs – scholarly versions of "The Two Temples," or the Stonewall Jackson poems, or "The Paradise of Bachelors and the Tartarus of Maids." For Melville, the mutuality demanded by diptychs has a twofold effect: it both accentuates and reveals, disclosing overlaps and clarifying differences.

When read alongside one another, many of the essays have precisely that effect. The unsettling of perspective that, according to Samuel Otter, anchors Melville's style also has a political dimension that Edward Sugden captures in his essay; and Otter's essay suggests that Sugden's "border zone" – which is filled by "recalcitrant . . . points of blockage, erasure, and duress" – might have distinct linguistic features (and, for Melville, aesthetic consequences). There is also a great deal of continuity, even a shared energy, in the essays by Jennifer Greiman, Justine S. Murison, and Paul Hurh. (So the volume has at least one triptych, too.) All three critics approach Melville as a kind of theorist in his own right, as a writer who was deeply and passionately interested in the pleasures, limits, and complexities of various reading practices. All three essays also take up Eve Sedgwick's model of "reparative reading" in an effort to place Melville vis-à-vis recent debates about the role of suspicion in literary criticism.[5]

Reading these essays together clarifies other shared concerns as well. One of the signal changes in Melville studies over the past twenty years is the renewed interest in Melville's poems.[6] This volume both responds to and reflects on this turn in the field, with Melville's poetry playing a prominent role in several of the essays. But to my mind, the focus on Melville's poetry is less notable than what these critics *do* with it: they each read Melville's poetry with and through Melville's prose, approaching the poems not as disparate experiments but as a vital part and connective force in Melville's broader career. As Gillian Osborne demonstrates, Melville did not merely write *Weeds and Wildings* and *Billy Budd* around the same time; these books are aesthetically, erotically, and textually entangled. Samuel Otter shows that *Clarel* and *Typee* share a common approach to landscapes, language, and the relation between them, while Elizabeth Duquette links *The Confidence-Man* to *Battle-Pieces* through their joint interest (which is formal as well as philosophical) in analogy. And for Brian Yothers, Melville's lifelong fascination with belief, his "complex dialogue with the secular and the sacred," animates his poetry and prose alike, tying *Timoleon* to *Typee*, and *Clarel* to *Omoo, White-Jacket*, and *Moby-Dick*.

These essays also join the ongoing conversation about whether critique, in Bruno Latour's words, "has run out of steam." In recent years, many scholars have claimed that the common practice of treating literary works as ideological symptoms – an approach through which the scholar probes texts for what they conceal or repress – has reached an endpoint. According to Rita Felski, literary studies has been overly reliant on a "style of interpretation driven by a spirit of disenchantment," a style grounded in the assumption that a critic's aim is "to expose hidden truths and draw out unflattering and counterintuitive meanings that others fail to see." In a similar vein, Joseph North argues that the rise of the "historicist/contextualist paradigm" did not merely coincide with the ascendance of neoliberalism; it was a direct result of that ascent and the accompanying retreat of the radical left.[7] These critiques of critique, as it were, have yielded robust replies and counterarguments. As Justine S. Murison points out, these responses often fall into one of two different camps: "articulations of what their theory omits in their account of symptomatic reading, and attempts to proliferate approaches to literary history beyond the hermeneutics of suspicion." Carolyn Lesjak reminds us that symptomatic reading is not as uniform or monolithic as its detractors would believe: it is not a fixed "hermeneutics of suspicion" but an eclectic array of interpretative methods which only in their most reductive, watered-down forms treat literary works as mere cultural containers. Timothy Bewes claims that what is actually being reconsidered is not critique as such but the spatiality of the act of reading. The challenge of twenty-first century literary studies, according to Bewes, is to rethink the "topographical conception of the literary text" as well as "the scene of the critical encounter," in "full acknowledgment that the notion of critical distance, and the innocence it implies, can no longer be regarded as a given – or at least that the current problems faced in literary methods arise with the persistence of this notion."[8]

Although these essays situate themselves in diverse ways in relation to this debate, some shared claims do emerge. Melville's writings (and interpretations thereof) indicate that the choice to critique or not to critique is a bit of a false choice. Jennifer Greiman makes a similar point in her essay, which recasts *Pierre* as a narrative *about* the failure of critical theory. That, of course, is the situation in which Melville's protagonist finds himself: in the wake of his "great life revolution," Pierre has taken up reading, writing, and philosophy only to discover, to his almost catastrophic disappointment, that such heady pursuits never succeed in remaking the world (P 225). Melville, however, is less interested in the mere failure of critique than in what it tells us: "Rather than indicting philosophy, theory, and criticism for not remedying the world, as his protagonist does, Melville instead subjects these to the figures, fables and conceits of *Pierre*'s fictive universe and discloses their explicitly literary enterprise." Literature and criticism, she writes, both tend to fail, and "fail in precisely the same way," yet they persist, propelled as they are by our endless will to construe. The inexorability of literature and critique is embodied, Greiman suggests, in Plotinus Plinlimmon's pamphlet, which "puts into practice the very work of literary criticism," revealing that "the fallacy of criticism" lay not "in the belief that subterranean political content can be mined through symptomatic reading, nor in the assumption that [literature] can perform, in its very literariness, political acts. Instead, criticism fails when it does not recognize that it shares a common hermeneutic plot with literature itself – a plot in which the very thing we try to read slips between a surface and a lining to be unwittingly carried everywhere."

That is elegantly stated. But if we flip Greiman's conclusion, inverting it like Hawthorne's moonlight, we can see the positive claim it implicitly forwards: criticism *succeeds* when it recognizes that it, too, is a creative process that is constantly adjusting, adapting, and weaving conceits. That is one of the benefits of reading Melville adjacently: it neither mistakes the critic's position as transcendent nor abandons the ethics, politics, and aesthetics afforded by critique. Instead, it sees criticism as an act of reconstruction – a means of retracing an author's ways of thinking, feeling, and writing – which requires both critical *and* postcritical modes of reading.

To guide their reconstructions, many of the contributors turn to Melville's own reading, as well as his thoughts about reading, as a model. Few writers were so ardently, even compulsively interested in the phenomenology of interpretation. This is partly (though not entirely) a result of Melville's philosophical bent. As Branka Arsić observes, Melville is a "thinker of genuine philosophical significance for current agendas," a writer who "used every resource of thought and language of the time in order to make philosophical contributions that belong to all time." Those contributions are finely assessed in Corey McCall and Tom Nurmi's *Melville Among the Philosophers* (2017), Branka Arsić and K.L. Evans's *Melville's Philosophies* (2017), and Paul Hurh's *American Terror* (2015), which examine Melville's elaborate engagements with posthumanism, new materialism, and philosophical traditions from ancient Greece, Renaissance Europe, and the wide, rolling Atlantic world of the eighteenth and nineteenth centuries.[9] What makes Melville's philosophies possible – indeed, what engenders his motley speculations about art, nature, history, language, violence, and knowledge – is the way his writings think about thinking. Melville routinely puts thinking on display in diverse and intricate ways, unraveling how thoughts flit, moods fluctuate, and beliefs advance or retreat.[10]

Melville's imagined worlds are worlds populated, first and foremost, by thoughts, and those thoughts suggest that critique is an essential mode of experience, an almost primal human endeavor with distinct delights, disappointments, advantages, and insufficiencies. Melville's writings also illustrate an important axiom: how we interpret something – including whether and to what extent we critique it – depends on one's perspective, and the best interpretations are based on multiple, juxtaposed perspectives that are capable of wrestling with life's paradoxes. Both of these points – i.e., the nontranscendent yet inexorable nature of critique and the value of using, while not collapsing, different hermeneutic viewpoints – unfold across Melville's works, animating everything from the cultural disorientation in *Typee* to the philosophies of knowledge in *Moby-Dick*; the proliferating perspectives in *Battle-Pieces, Clarel*, and *John Marr*; the aesthetic investments of *Timoleon*; and the many "ragged edges" in *Billy Budd* (BB 128). These essays follow Melville's lead and try to inhabit, to the degree that it is possible, the myriad viewpoints that Melville provides in, across, and between his works.

What Is Old in *The New Melville Studies*

These scholars are not the first Melvilleans to make that leap. Some version of this method, in different forms, can be found in Melville studies ever since its inception. C.L.R. James's luminous book, *Mariners, Renegades, and Castaways* (1953), is perhaps best known for what we might call its thoroughgoing critique: *Moby-Dick*, according to James, limns the origins of state capitalism. That fateful fusion of capitalism with state governmentality is embodied by Ahab, with his fanatical soul and insatiable desire to have men – ideally, "manufactured men" – under his thumb (MD 212). Nonetheless, what so interests James about Melville is not his symptomatic evocations of nineteenth-century American culture; it is Melville's astounding creative and critical vision, his ability – much like Toussaint L'Ouverture in *The Black Jacobins* (1938) – to not only see the shape of modernity but also explore everything it unleashes.[11] How, James wonders, did Melville do this? How did he somehow anticipate so much of what was to come?

> The best answer is given by Melville himself. He once explained how great writers wrote great books. A character like Ahab is an original character, . . . a type of human being that had never existed before in the world. Such characters come once in many centuries and are as rare as men who found new religions, philosophers who revolutionize human thinking, and statesmen who create new political forms. Melville mentions three: Satan from Milton's *Paradise Lost*, Hamlet from Shakespeare's play and the Don Quixote of Cervantes. That is how rare they are. According to Melville,

> many a gifted writer can create dozens of interesting, sprightly, clever, intriguing characters. But original characters? No. A writer is very lucky if in his lifetime he creates one.[12]

James, riffing on *The Confidence-Man*, puts his finger on Melville's method, which is at once literary, sociological, historical, and artistic. In describing these original characters, James is also, in a way, describing Melville himself: such artists only come along very rarely, and they are as consequential as the founders of religions and philosophies. Though contemporary scholars tend to shy away from such grand claims (as well as the gendered language in which James pitches his assessment), James centers his book around Melville's capacious imagination, which James brilliantly reprises and reexamines.

The temporal modifier in this volume's title is therefore a bit misleading. The "new" Melville studies is not wholly or entirely new; it is also the result and outgrowth of previous scholarship, and some of the newest approaches echo some of the earliest studies. The recent swelling of interest in Melville's ties to science and materialism was anticipated by Elizabeth Foster's "Melville and Geology" (1945) and Walter Bezanson's seminal work on *Clarel*.[13] Similarly, the philosophical qualities of Melville's writings have been a perennial focus of Melville studies, from F.O. Matthiessen to Charles Olson. And what are books such as William Braswell's *Melville's Religious Thought* (1943) and Ronald Mason's *The Spirit Above the Dust* (1951) but works – to invoke a much more recent term – of "postsecular" criticism? Critical shifts tend to be pitched as agonistic battles or revolutionary displacements, but in reality, and in practice, they tend to resemble musical performances. Melville studies is a kind of song being passed from one set of players to another (or, in some cases, back to a seasoned musician who is now taking up a different style).[14] The notes and arrangement may differ, but in many cases the song is the same.

One of the songs that has been played almost on repeat has to do with the range and resonance of Melville's imagination. I do not simply mean the Romantic notion, with which Melville was of course familiar, that the imagination is an elevated and distinctive form of thinking, a version of Thoreau's claim that he'd never "met a man who was [fully] awake."[15] Nor do I mean that that all politics are imaginative and we access the world by constructing and reconstructing it in our minds – though that is certainly true, and it is on display throughout Melville's works. Rather, what we take from Melville –

and from Melville studies, when it is done well – is that the imagination is the richest and most wide-ranging resource not only for writers but also for critics. It is what enables us to envision worlds beyond our own, and it is what allows us to read with – or better yet, next to – Melville, following his thoughts as they rise, fall, ripen, or jolt, even now, after all this time.

PART I

Feeling with Melville

CHAPTER 2

Paranoid Reading, Surface Pleasures, and Deadpan Humor in The Confidence-Man

Justine S. Murison

> What is a joke to me can be just a comic story to someone else. But if a joke admits of this doubt, it can only be because it has one side for show, a façade – in our instances a comic façade – which will satisfy the eyes of one viewer, while another may try to look behind it. The suspicion may begin to stir that this façade is meant to dazzle the probing eye, that stories of this kind have something to hide.
>
> —Sigmund Freud, *The Joke and Its Relation to the Unconscious* (1905)

> I relish a good joke too well to spoil it by letting on.
>
> Herman Melville, *The Confidence-Man* (1857)

If there is one thing that critics of Herman Melville's *The Confidence-Man* (1857) agree on, it is that the novel is not one of deep psychology. As Elizabeth Renker has trenchantly shown, in *The Confidence-Man* "the word character appears repeatedly but has no enduring substance – no essential meaning – beneath its changing surfaces."[1] The novel, indeed, presents character as an "epistemological problem," as Maurice Lee notes, and "[w]hat characterization there is in the book is largely accomplished through eccentricities of body and dress, demographic stereotyping, as well as long dialogues that, given the ever-present potential for dissimulation, cannot be trusted to indicate deeply held feelings or thoughts."[2] Scholars have interpreted these surface characterizations as tied to a historical context of Barnumesque fraud and theatrical culture; of race, minstrelsy, and charity; or arising from a culture promoting liberty and social mobility.[3] But all seem to assume, as Jennifer Greiman puts it, that the novel's surface of theatricality is part of the "text's gradual erosion of authenticity, consistency, continuity, and identity, as conceptual bases for an understanding of character as private, interior, and continuous."[4]

Critics in Melville's own day, as well, took issue with the way characters in this novel seem only to be made of surfaces. The novel received more positive notices than had *Pierre* (1852) before it, but across these reviews, a consistent complaint about the characters and the plot emerges: namely, that there is "no there there." "The Confidence Man goes on board a Mississippi steamboat and assumes such a variety of disguises, with an astonishing rapidity," summarizes the *New York Dispatch,* "that no person could assume without detection, and gets into the confidence of his fellow-passengers in such a way as would tend to show that the passengers of a Mississippi steamboat are the most gullible people in the world."[5] The *Literary Gazette* called it "a book professing to inculcate philosophical truths through the medium of nonsensical people talking nonsense," and the London *Illustrated Times* admits that "after reading the work forwards for twelve chapters and backwards for five, we attacked it in the middle, gnawing at it like Rabelais's dog at the bone, in the hope of extracting something from it at last."[6] Scanning these, it's apparent that a telling disjunction lies between the contemporary reception of *The Confidence-Man* and our current fascination with it: what was considered a philosophical or aesthetic "problem" with the novel became a sign of its power to deconstruct, and, in particular, its ability to call into question liberal notions of private selves and narrative coherence.

The consensus that *The Confidence-Man* is a novel concerned with surfaces rather than something we might call "deep" or "private" character certainly precedes Stephen Best and Sharon Marcus's recent call for literary study to develop a method of "surface reading," which they define as paying attention to "what is evident, perceptible, apprehensible in texts; what is neither hidden nor hiding; what, in the geometrical sense, has length and breadth but no thickness, and therefore covers no depth. A surface is what insists on being looked *at* rather than what we must train ourselves to see *through*."[7] Set against the "hermeneutics of suspicion" (as Paul Ricoeur famously termed the similarity in approach of Marx, Freud, and Nietzsche), "surface reading" would embrace the apparent and the descriptive rather than seeking out the latent and the hidden. Best and Marcus's theory of surface reading has attracted a lot of criticism in recent years, coalescing into two general camps: articulations of what their theory omits in their account of symptomatic reading, and attempts to proliferate approaches to literary history beyond the hermeneutics of suspicion.[8] Carolyn Lesjak, in her critique of "surface reading," shows how the two responses can come together, arguing that "what is needed is a better way of reading surfaces as perverse rather than as obvious, as never identical to themselves in their 'thereness,' and always found within and constitutive of complex spatial relations, both seen and not seen, deep and lateral, material and figural – all of which requires a more rather than less expansive reading practice."[9]

Following Lesjak's suggestion that we attend to the way surfaces can often be perverse rather than obvious, I argue that Melville not only anticipates our current debates about the efficacy of critique – no surprise for a novel obsessed with the same market capitalism that would inspire Karl Marx – but also points us to what is definitively left to the side of these debates: the depth of surfaces and the perversities of a joke. Put differently, there is nothing obvious about a surface in *The Confidence-Man*, but to approach these surfaces with an eye toward symptoms likewise misapprehends the novel. And this is due, first and foremost, to the way Melville wields humor in the novel.[10]

As it turns out, while the recent examination of the hermeneutics of suspicion has spawned numerous responses, they rarely take up the question of humor in relation to the questions of surface/depth and paranoid reading/reparative reading. This is a surprising turn of affairs considering how the debate can be traced to a very funny essay, Eve Kosofsky Sedgwick's "Paranoid Reading and Reparative Reading." Peppered throughout Sedgwick's argument are laugh lines: from the subtitle ("or, you're so paranoid, you probably think this essay is about you") to her joke about Frederic Jameson's dictum to "Always historicize" ("It reminds me of the bumper stickers that instruct people in other cars to 'Question Authority'") to her satiric asides about the revelatory power of paranoia in our current era ("How television-starved would someone have to be to find it shocking that ideologies contradict themselves, that simulacra don't have originals, or that gender representations are artificial?") and, finally, to her *tour-de-force* parody of "Comes the revolution" jokes ("Comes the revolution, Comrade, you'll be tickled pink by those deconstructive jokes; you'll faint from ennui every minute you're not smashing the state apparatus; you'll definitely want hot sex twenty to thirty times a day. You'll be mournful *and* militant. You'll never want to tell Deleuze and Guattari, 'Not tonight, dears, I have a headache.'")[11] Sedgwick's humor is more than leavening: it models the "reparative" work that she presents as an alternative to the pervasive nature of suspicion in critique. Revisiting D. A. Miller's *The Novel and the Police* allows Sedgwick to highlight what is often overlooked about this exemplary text of paranoid reading: "a wealth of tonal nuance, attitude, worldly observation, performative paradox, aggression, tenderness, wit, inventive reading, obiter dicta, and writerly panache."[12]

This list not only reflects Sedgwick's own writing style but is also a fair summary of *The Confidence-Man*. While it would seem that Melville's novel invites a strong paranoid reading – Who is the confidence man? Is it one man or a team of men? Are we, or the man's interlocutors, being duped? – these questions, in the end, prove red herrings. Instead, it is the incidental and the local that make the reading experience an intense pleasure. And that pleasure, I would like to suggest, is rooted in the novel's particular form of deadpan humor. *The Confidence-Man*'s humor depends on a different metaphor than the spatial one that Best and Marcus promote and this difference is instructive. Melville is concerned less in this novel with the spatial arrangements of paranoia than its temporal pacing. Filled with temporal misdirections and cues to reread previous chapters, *The Confidence-Man* both invites and thwarts the paranoid reader. How the jokes on paranoia and confidence unfold only becomes clear if one takes a second look ("peers behind" the comic façade, in Freud's words). Above all, to find the "joke" at all in *The Confidence-Man* is to reconsider the role of pleasure in our own hermeneutics of suspicion. As I will elaborate, Melville's deadpan is about the pleasure of discovery in a way akin to but distinct from the hermeneutics of suspicion: for a deadpan joke is neither a demystification nor a revelation of a deeper structure but, instead, a new view of the surface itself. Put differently, deadpan makes surfaces perverse and "deep." In what follows, I will consider both how Melville's deadpan humor questions the paranoid structure of the novel form and then how Melville's local stagings of paranoia, in turn, opens out to a better articulation of pleasure's relation to interpretation and politics.

Melville's Deadpan

The Confidence-Man is a funny novel, but it is rarely comic. As Sianne Ngai has argued, while *The Confidence-Man* may be "[t]alky, noisy," it is "essentially atonal."[13] Rather than thinking of its humor as "atonal," I would suggest that this is one effect of the overall work of deadpan in the novel. Sacvan Bercovitch places it at the beginning of a tradition of American deadpan humor.[14] Deadpan, as Jennifer Greenhill explains, "works hard to conceal its mechanics," a method elaborated on by Mark Twain in "How to Tell a Story" (1897).[15] Citing Artemus Ward as a key example of this type of deadpan humor, Twain writes: "Very often, of course, the rambling and disjointed humorous story finishes with a nub, point, snapper, or whatever you like to call it. Then the listener must be alert, for in many cases the teller will divert attention from that nub by dropping it in a carefully casual and indifferent way, with the pretense that he does not know it is a nub."[16] According to Twain, deadpan depends on tonal and bodily control – the comic's face remains unmoved or registers surprise that anyone in the audience finds the joke funny.

Though deadpan is best known for the way surface and meaning do not align, it is also a humor of misdirection. Misdirection, in Twain's description, has to do with pacing and rhythm: the comedian drops in the "nub" in a "carefully casual and indifferent way" but doing so successfully, Twain explains, depends on timing: the pause preceding the nub "is a dainty thing, and delicate, and also uncertain and treacherous; for it must be exactly the right length – no more and no less – or it fails of its purpose and makes trouble."[17] Deadpan humor cannot be mapped via surface and depth; its coordinates, if we follow Twain's logic, are about diversion (looking here when the joke is happening over there) and its "dainty" and "delicate" temporality requires one to pause and look backward for the joke.

But this does not mean that deadpan offers itself up as the corrective to suspicion, as a perfect vehicle for, in Best and Marcus's words, "what, in the geometrical sense, has length and breadth but no thickness, and therefore covers no depth." To the extent that deadpan humor undoes the surface-depth model, it does so through a complicated relation of temporality to pleasure. Jonathan Elmer points out in his reading of "Bartleby, the Scrivener" that critics tend to be "suspicious of pleasure," treating it as "an index of unreflectiveness, or of lingering investments in demystified ideological categories" but that by "tabling or quarantining our pleasure, we also forget the processual nature of literary experience; we take the text as an object that might be 'unpacked' or 'placed' in an appropriate context, when in fact it is a record of *attempts* to make meaning, full of lucky hits and dead ends, a foray into deep water."[18] Elmer's description of a "processual" text is also a useful way to consider how a deadpan novel like *The Confidence-Man* does not open out to either the hermeneutics of suspicion or to surface reading. Deadpan is not about hidden depths or factual surfaces; yet it is also a "foray into deep water" in that the goal of the joke is quite often a serious affair, but one that is, to paraphrase the words of Charlie Noble in the novel, too good to be spoiled by letting on.

If the novel offers no characters of psychological depth, as its critics continually note, it does provide metacommentary on the project of producing such characters. In chapters 14, 33, and 44, the narrator memorably pauses the action to reply to imagined objections to his characters ("How unreal all this is! Who did ever dress or act like your cosmopolitan? And who, it might be returned, did ever dress or act like harlequin?" [CM 182]). These chapters confront questions of novelistic realism and reader expectations. In doing so, they produce a complicated joke that rebounds backward and forward in the novel. After the narrator suggests in chapter 33 that he sides with readers who expect fiction to "evoke scenes different from those of the same old crowd round the custom-house counter, and same old dishes on the boardinghouse table, with characters unlike those of the same old acquaintances they meet in the same old way every day in the same old street" (CM 182), he includes the following hedge:

> If, then, something is to be pardoned to well-meant endeavor, surely a little is to be allowed to that writer who, in all his scenes, does but seek to minister to what, as he understands it, is the implied wish of the more indulgent lovers of entertainment, before whom harlequin can never appear in a coat too parti-colored, or cut capers too fantastic. (CM 183)

On the surface, this narrative intervention uses the atonal mode that Ngai so correctly identifies. As deadpan, these jokes do not reveal themselves readily. While the narrator sides with the desire for comic amusement that those "more indulgent lovers of entertainment" seek, neither this scene – the drinking scene between the boon companions that dead-ends when Frank Goodman, the Cosmopolitan, asks for a friendly loan – nor *The Confidence-Man* as a whole provide just such "antics." In fact, the narrator here describes exactly the kind of humor that the novel refuses to provide – in Twain's terms, this is a description of the "comic," that style in which the joke is shouted at you.[19]

In other words, in his defense of the type of novel he is presenting, the narrator fully mischaracterizes its tone and effect. The joke is, first, on readers who rationalize the paradoxical desire for escapism with a taste for realism. Yet while the narrator seems to align with readers who love the fantastic and the comic, he surreptitiously undermines that sympathy as well – after all, they are not reading a *comic* novel. In the end, the joke ricochets on the writer, who, it seems, is trapped in a paradox produced by the form of the novel itself: a demand for realism in a "work of amusement." Hence the tautological title of chapter 33 – "Which may pass for whatever it may prove to be worth" – which might be boiled down to the contemporary slang phrase, "It is what it is." As Elizabeth Renker explains, "The mirror effect of tautology" in *The Confidence-Man* "suspends language at the level of its own materiality – that is, of itself as language – refusing to penetrate its surface in order to 'mean' something."[20] If we recur to Elmer's description of the suspicion of pleasure, we see Melville staging just such a suspicion, and showing that pleasure, unlike suspicion, seems to move in a circle; it does not drill down.

Therefore to delve "below" this mischaracterization of the novel as comic – to attempt, perhaps, to psychologize it or to read it for its historical context and ideological import – would be to flatten and misread the joke. We don't drill down to get it; instead, as the joke suggests, we need to move backward and look at previous chapters. Chapter 33 ends with a recommendation that the reader return to chapter 14, "where some similar apparent inconsistency in another character is, on general principles, modestly endeavored to be apologized for" (CM 183). The joke in chapter 33 depends upon *rereading*, returning to a previous portion of the book. Yet a return to chapter 14 hardly resolves the joke's meaning. For if readers return to chapter 14, they are greeted with the opening line, "As the last chapter was begun with a reminder looking forwards, so the present must consist of one glancing backwards" (CM 69). And if we flit further back, to chapter 13, to recall this "reminder looking forwards," we see an anecdote about an American visitor in London (a "savant") incorrectly judging Sir Humphrey Davy as an inconsequential fop because of an "absurd ribbon in his lapel," with the second paragraph commenting that "[t]he above anecdote is given just here by way of an anticipative reminder to such readers as, from the kind of jaunty levity, or what may have passed for such, hitherto for the most part appearing in the man with the traveling-cap, may have been tempted into a more or less hasty estimate of him" (CM 64).

The main thrust of the joke in chapter 13 seems to be, of course, on the preening self-pretension of the "American savant" who has not had his worldview undermined by this revelation. However, the "nub" of the joke, again, lies in the temporal sleight of hand going on between these chapters. The narrator warns readers not to, like this "savant," mistakenly be "betrayed" into a "surprise incompatible with their own good opinion of their previous penetration" (CM 64). Like the phrase "anticipative reminder," this joke operates on a complicated scale: the narrator's advice is to ward against being surprised into reconsidering our previous sense of our abilities to penetrate. If ever there was a good description of Sedgwick's account of paranoid reading, *avant la lettre*, it is this. After all, as Sedgwick puts it, "paranoia requires that bad news be always already known."[21] The joke plays out Sedgwick's point: readers guard against surprise and, in doing so, reestablish their own (mistaken) good opinion of their penetrative abilities. And thus the joke is on the paranoid, those who would never be surprised or betrayed.

Even as the joke about paranoia starts to take form, these chapters remain temporally vertiginous. What is an "anticipative reminder," after all, but yet another direction for us to follow, going forward while looking backward? The chapters and references keep pointing to each other, and then pointing further away. Yet they all coalesce on the same message to the reader and on reading in general: Do not judge a book by its cover, to give the clichéd version of it. Since the novel primarily encourages readers to judge books by their covers, we might call this yet another joke, a moral that purposefully misses its mark. All we have as readers for any logical coherence is the ability to judge a character to be the confidence man based on his clothing. Thus, the moral of the anecdote about Davy returns us to the opening of the novel itself, to the list of men who will vouch for "Black Guinea" (the second of the Confidence Man's avatars):

> "Oh yes, oh yes, ge'mmen," he eagerly answered, as if his memory, before suddenly frozen up by cold charity, as suddenly thawed back into fluidity at the first kindly word. "Oh yes, oh yes, dar is aboard here a werry nice, good ge'mman wid a weed, and a ge'mman in a gray coat and white tie, what knows all about me; and a ge'mman wid a big book, too; and a yarb-doctor; and a ge'mman in a yaller west; and a ge'mman wid a brass plate; and a ge'mman in a wiolet robe; and a ge'mman as is a sodjer; and ever so many good, kind, honest ge'mmen more aboard what knows me and will speak for me, God bress 'em." (CM 13)

How do you know a man? How do you go and find him? At the opening of the novel, we glimpse how objects and clothing index identity: the gentleman with the weed; the gentleman in the gray coat; the gentleman in a yellow vest, in a violet robe, in a soldier's uniform; the gentleman holding a big book, a brass plate, bottles of herbal medicine. While the metacommentary chapters propose that we not judge a man by his clothing, or that we do not look for consistency if we want realism, the deadpan joke of it all is that we indeed do. And must. Or we risk losing the thread of the narrative entirely.

Gender and the Joke

Crucially, though, the story of the American savant and Humphrey Davy comes at a particular moment in the novel: following directly the "touching" story of Goneril. Therefore, while the deadpan humor and metacommentary play between the chapters point first to readers' contradictory expectations about novelistic realism and character development, the later chapters deliver us back to this embedded story. The story of Goneril is told by the man with the weed, John Ringman (a confidence man avatar, ostensibly her husband) to Henry Roberts, the merchant; it is then told by Roberts to the agent of the Grand Rapids Coal Company, the next confidence man to appear; and finally told directly to the reader via the narrator. Implying the multiple voices of the differently clothed avatars of the Confidence Man (including the narrator), this story is heavily mediated. Moreover, while the tale unveils a private difference between a husband and wife, its original version is also kept completely secret from the reader: Ringman pulls the merchant aside and speaks in low tones, words the reader does not overhear; all a reader registers are the increasingly large bills Roberts takes out of his pocket to give to the man with the weed. The tale hits its mark – the bills exchanged indicate its affective power.

On the surface, the story is the tale of a poor, innocent man suffering at the hands of a wife with a nature "anomalously vicious," one that would "almost tempt a metaphysical lover of our species to doubt whether the human form be, in all cases, conclusive evidence of humanity" (CM 60). In other words, this story opens with the question of whether you can judge someone as human via their form alone, and then it plunges into a misogynistic account of a family torn apart by a women's monstrous nature. Goneril, the man's wife, has a style of beauty "rather peculiar and cactus-like." Her personality, so the story continues, partook of the cacti: she preferred criticizing over complimenting, and she inwardly chuckled when "she saw frankness and innocence tyrannized into sad nervousness under her spell." The narrator goes on to recount the charge that Goneril had a "strange way of touching, as by accident, the arm or hand of comely young men":

> Needless to say what distress was the unfortunate man's, when, engaged in conversation with company, he would suddenly perceive his Goneril bestowing her mysterious touches, especially in such cases where the strangeness of the thing seemed to strike upon the touched person, notwithstanding good-breeding forbade his proposing the mystery, on the spot, as a subject of discussion for the company. In these cases, too, the unfortunate man could never endure so much as to look upon the touched young gentleman afterwards, fearful of the mortification of meeting in his countenance some kind of more or less quizzingly-knowing expression. (CM 61–2)

What is so fascinating about this description of Goneril in company is just how tacit it is, even as it is conveyed in Melville's typical verbosity. Beneath the baroque wording, the bare fact is fairly unalarming: Goneril touches the arms of men as they converse. That's all. At most, this gesture implies a breaching of a personal zone of privacy – bodies not already intimately related touching in public – and (again implied) that Goneril gains pleasure by breaching this zone.

However, it is readily apparent that the indecorum of this supposed breach of privacy is all from Ringman's point of view: "the strangeness of the thing *seemed to strike upon the touched person,* notwithstanding good-breeding forbade his proposing the mystery, on the spot, as a subject of discussion for the company"; "the unfortunate man *could never endure so much as to look* upon the touched young gentleman afterwards." While the first example floats freely from the narrative voice – "seemed to" being a very common way not to locate the response to a subject – when coupled with the next sentence we begin to see that the reactions and indecorums all arise from Ringman's perspective (whom the narrator calls the "unfortunate man," already stacking the deck against other interpretations). And the tale sparks the merchant's charity precisely because his donation will help reconfirm a zone of privacy. The man with the weed (in proper mourning clothes for Goneril's death, even after she had divorced him and taken their daughter) seeks to reconstitute his private family without this monstrous woman.

In this way, the story of Goneril hitches the metacommentary of surface and depth to a different dialogical pairing, that of public/private, with the gendering of those spheres very much central to this moment in the novel. Thus, this heavily mediated story reinforces what Lauren Berlant and Michael Warner have argued about the function of privacy in the modern United States: that privacy is a product of heterosexism and ultimately protective of it.[22] If we keep in mind the novel as *deadpan* here, we also see something else: delving too deeply into this symptomatic reading risks losing touch with a basic fact about the story. It's a con. The spinner of the tale already knows that he is playing on a suspicious character and in order to induce him to fork over money, he provides a tale of disorder and misfortune wrought by a woman on the heterosexual family, and it works.

It is notable, though, that Goneril has, within the embedded story, actually "won" the contest with her husband, using the court to grant her custody and a separation, as Beverly Hume points out. However, although (as Hume also suggests) Melville recognizes "that the most troubling, if not deepest, levels of cultural oppression have historically been reserved for women," the Goneril story does not exactly offer us insight into that history.[23] In fact, it does not go "deep" at all. Rather, the metacommentary chapters point and direct us to Goneril, and we might therefore surmise that this story is central to the entire question of character depth in the novel. And to be sure, a doubt about the story is expressed almost immediately by the Confidence Man – in the guise of the transfer agent for the Grand Rapids Coal Company – when he suggests that "the description of the lady, charity could not but regard as more or less exaggerated, and so far unjust. The truth probably was that she was a wife with some blemishes mixed with some beauties" (CM 65). While the merchant objects to this interpretation, what makes it so persuasive is actually how it accords with the other chapters about characterological *fictionality* – it's an appeal to realistic conventions, an appeal, in other words, to the very aspects of character construction we see the narrator objecting to in chapters 14 and 33. After they drink together a little more, the merchant bursts out with an expression of deep suspicion that wine cannot even ease. And here we return to the endpoint of all of the vertiginous metacommentary on novel writing. In chapter 14, the narrator pauses to expand upon the inconsistency of the merchant's character, which "may be thought inconsistent, and even so he is. But for this, is the author to be blamed?" After all, as the narrator goes on to ask, how does an author balance readers' desire for character consistency with "another requirement – equally insisted upon, perhaps – that, while to all fiction is allowed some play of invention, yet, fiction based on fact should never be contradictory to it; and is it not a fact, that, in real life, a consistent character is a *rara avis*?" (CM 69). While this extended joke on the paradoxical nature of fictional realism refers to the change in character of the merchant when drunk, it rebounds onto the embedded story of Goneril, for as the transfer agent points out, she is too thoroughly and consistently vicious to be true, too much like a licentious vixen in a city mystery novel to be a realistic woman.

While all signs point to our seeing the story of Goneril as not realistic because too consistent, I want to trace a different meaning for the story that brings us back to surfaces, pleasures, and the often perverse nature of a deadpan joke. This story is not just about heteronormative privacy but also about nonnormative private pleasures. According to the narrator, Goneril reaps a "secret delight" in producing an effect on the men she touches. And as the narrator describes it, the man with the weed cannot confront what he sees in other men's facial expressions, namely, their "quizzingly-knowing expression." Both of these phrases invoke "secrecy," which is not the same thing as privacy. Privacy is marked by the drive to transparency, and is therefore always in some sense public.[24] Secrecy, on the other hand, is what symptomatic reading seeks to uncover – the hidden meaning beneath what is apparent and discernible. And the story of Goneril is definitely about secrecy and how we read for it on surfaces, and it is Ringman (and the merchant, who offers him charity) who ostensibly seeks to correct secret pleasures and turn them back into heteronormative privacy. Just as Goneril's delight must be revealed from its secret place, Ringman perceives but never confirms that the other men *secretly know* that she has touched them and that it was inappropriate. Their "quizzingly-knowing" faces prompt a paranoid reaction in him, which we see in the double meaning of "quizzing," at once both detecting through interrogation *and* teasing.

The man with the weed as he appears within this heavily mediated tale is perhaps one of the first paranoid readers we encounter in the novel. He reads for secret knowledge, and he attempts to wield it to his advantage:

> Now Goneril brooked no chiding. So, at favorable times, he, in a wary manner, and not indelicately, would venture in private interviews gently to make distant allusions to this questionable propensity. She divined him. But, in her cold loveless way, said it was witless to be telling one's dreams, especially foolish ones; but if the unfortunate man liked connubially to rejoice his soul with such chimeras, much connubial joy might they give him. (CM 62)

Clearly an expert symptomatic reader herself, Goneril "divines" his meaning out of his "distant allusions," but turns it around on him. She suggests that these allusions reveal his own secret pleasure in suspecting her ("connubially to rejoice his soul with such chimeras"), and if that's the case, he's welcome to them. But he must admit that they say more about *his* secret pleasure than hers, and his sexual delight in secret intrigues and imagined plots. What's more, these distant allusions become fodder in the lawsuit when he attempts in court to "reveal in self-defense those eccentricities which had led to his retirement from the joys of wedlock," and he "had much ado in the end to prevent this charge of derangement from fatally recoiling upon himself – especially, when, among other things, he alleged her mysterious touchings" (CM 63). The court, following Goneril's lead, suspects that Ringman's symptomatic reading actually reveals his own perversities. From the center of the Goneril story, we find her deadpan (cold and loveless) jokes on Ringman's intensely earnest obsession with her "touchings." In fact, Goneril is actually a deadpan artist and Ringman the paranoid reader, something difficult to see when women are continually cast (and still perceived today) as not having the capacity for comedy.

Goneril's centrality to the overall humor of the novel also helps us understand the novel's inconclusive ending, for it replays and amplifies the way paranoia, surface, and pleasure all circle each other. The other deadpan artist in the novel (outside of the narrator, of course) is Frank Goodman, the Cosmopolitan that the novel follows for its final third. Goodman is distinct from the other confidence men in the novel, for he never seems to be making any money. At most, he gets a haircut for free and checkmates Charlie Noble, another confidence man, by asking directly for a loan. But otherwise, he appears to be engaged in a long joke, amusing himself by interacting with the suspicious passengers. Goneril and Goodman are likewise linked via the metacommentary of the novel, for the final metacommentary chapter is a reaction to the barber's reaction to the Cosmopolitan ("Quite an original!"). Chapter 44 observes that, in fiction, it is impossible to imagine an original character, because the form, as the narrator has already extensively joked about in relation to Goneril and Roberts, inspires in readers a desire for consistency. The final chapter follows this deadpan about character and realism, pleasure and paranoia, to its end. In the chapter (aptly named "The Cosmopolitan Increases in Seriousness"), Frank Goodman converses with an old farmer with a "hale look of greenness in winter" (CM 238) as he buys several detection devices from a ragged boy reminiscent of Charles Dickens's Artful Dodger. In this scene, deadpan jokes abound, and many of them underscore how paranoia makes one blind to what is in plain sight. Drawn in by devices to stop thieves and root out counterfeit bills, the old farmer not only invests in trash like a lock for a door and a "money-belt," neither of which will work if the thief sells them to you or is the one to escort you to bed (CM 241). He also spends his time inspecting the surface of bank bills he has picked up in St. Louis. Using the counterfeit detector, he scrutinizes every inch of the surface of one bill for a goose that should indicate its authenticity. When he asks Goodman if he can see the goose, Goodman's reply is pure deadpan: "Can't see the goose? why, I can; and a famous goose it is" (CM 249). Goodman then escorts the old farmer to his bed, not without handing him a commode as a life preserver first.

As this innocently paranoid character exits the stage with Goodman, the novel ends with the line "Something further may follow of this Masquerade," a promise that disappointed many of Melville's first reviewers. While we may read it as a final reminder that the novel's narrative – much like its characters – refuses to conform to generic expectations, it also makes sense as the ultimate deadpan gesture. This last image of the old man with his commode and money belt risks being ludicrously comic, but the final line resolves that comedy into a promise of more to come. This promise, like the rest of the narrative pronouncements, is ultimately temporal. While suggesting a future sequel, it gestures back to the repetitions of the narrative itself. It returns us again to the fact that deadpan depends on both timing and tone; rather than offering a final revelation about the confidence games of the novel, the end defers it. We get another "anticipative reminder," a return to the center of the novel and a prompt for reconsidering the surfaces that delivered us to the final promise of more to come.

This final gesture thus culminates the deadpan humor of Goneril, Goodman, and the narrator's metacommentary. Taken together as a method, we might call it "deadpan reading." While surface and paranoid reading depend on spatial metaphors – surface and depth, horizontal and vertical – deadpan reading depends on the metaphor of time to understand interpretation and pleasure. Though time and space are interlocking concepts, the emphasis makes a difference. Temporality suggests patience and a willingness to revise, a generosity when a reader doesn't "get it" because a joke can always be reread. Deadpan reading can also be cutting and critical in its processual nature, as it is in the hands of Goneril. Melville's deadpan thus ultimately suggests a route out of the impasse that the surface reading critique raised: an interpretive method that counters the paranoia of depth without becoming blind to the work of power. And the ability to take a joke for whatever it may prove to be worth.

CHAPTER 3

Melville and His Flowers

Gillian Kidd Osborne

Others have read *Weeds and Wildings Chiefly: With a Rose or Two* as a collection of love poems for Melville's wife, Elizabeth Shaw – Lizzie as she was known to family and friends.[1] And the manuscript's opening section, "The Year," does explore the domestic pleasures of the household and reproductive life that the Melvilles may have shared, celebrating the "lowly" Clover as representative of that life. But there are roses in the manuscript, too, and these are not for Lizzie. Instead, the rose poems, and the reworking of Washington Irving into "Rip Van Winkle's Lilac," offer further examples of Melville writing through his reading of and relationship to Nathaniel Hawthorne. *Weeds and Wildings* is continuous with Melville's earlier work in its examination of what literature makes of life. But *Weeds and Wildings* also shows Melville writing *toward* life, imagining what it might mean to write for and with: to write for oneself as a practice of almost (though flowerier) monastic devotion; for and with a fellow writer and "dear fellow-mortal" (L 192). In this sense, *Weeds and Wildings* is an important companion volume to *Billy Budd*, which Melville labored over around the same time, and which has been interpreted as resistant to readers, as not written "for" us.[2] In contrast, *Weeds and Wildings* is a book whose central theme is dedication: what it means to devote oneself to love, labor, craft, and how writing vivifies those commitments, even when what one writes goes unread, or becomes misread.

One reason why critics have thus far overlooked these features of the manuscript, including Hawthorne's centrality, is that in *Weeds and Wildings*, Melville adopts the floweriness of nineteenth-century American women's writing: he writes *like* a woman. This has seemed to indicate the presence of a preferred, and gendered, reader: writing for his wife. However, this interpretation takes style as more essential than it is – the result of being or desiring a particularly gendered body, rather than a flourish, a performance, or a choice. In an 1855 letter to William Ticknor, Hawthorne griped about the "d[amne]d mob of scribbling women" who dominated the literary marketplace by writing "like emasculated men" only distinguishable "from male authors by greater feebleness and folly."[3] This letter is often cited as proof of Hawthorne's misogyny, but the idea of women as unmanly men complicates his dismissal by implying that some men do not write like men and that women writers are defined by the surface qualities of their writing rather than their natures. Recent critical work on nineteenth-century American women's writing has drawn attention to the destabilizing powers of these "highly wrought" qualities of style,[4] the influence of women writers on their male peers,[5] and the importance of the poetess as a representative, depersonalized type.[6] While such studies contribute to understandings of nineteenth-century women's writing, they also offer valuable insight into the instabilities of feminized qualities in nineteenth-century writing by male authors, including Melville.

Weeds and Wildings adopts a common practice within nineteenth-century women's writing: disavowing the effort and accomplishment of authorship. In her "Preface" to *Fern Leaves from Fanny's Portfolio*, for example, Fanny Fern forswears her success as an author: "I never had the slightest intention of writing a book," she begins, equating her sketches and stories to "leaves" "gathered at random."[7] This gesture of dismissing the products of authorial labor by claiming them as synonymous with the verdure of a tree, or a fern, is a feature of Romantic organicism – like the "Leaves" John Keats suggested should come easily to a poet's tree, or the *Leaves of Grass* Walt Whitman loafed among.[8] But while the ease of Keats's tree and Whitman's leaves is testimony of an author's power – vital enough to convert nature into verse – Fanny's ferns grow irrespective of her abilities or intentions (or so she claims).

We see a similar disavowal of expertise in many manuals to the language of flowers. E. W. Wirt, publishing her *Flora's Dictionary* anonymously as "A Lady," variously cast off her work as a "*petit jeu*," "a trifle," a "little *divertissement*," "an *embryon* bud," and "a *bagatelle*," without "any serious consequence." Sarah Hale, who contributed original poems to her *Flora's Interpreter*, called the collection a "trifling production," comparing the work of "[m]aking a book (*not writing it*)" to domestic labors "like preparing a dinner." For Hale, roses epitomized this minor making. Contrasting the poems gathered in her book to the "evergreens of our literature" commemorated in Cheever's *The American Common-Place Book of Poetry*, and to the utilitarian value of "corn and cotton, the tobacco and potatoe," Hale offers merely "roses."[9] By collecting his poems under the trifling title *Weeds and Wildings*, and tossing in *A Rose or Two*, Melville similarly diminishes his aspirations, a stance that offers us a Melville nearly unrecognizable from the author striving after monument in works such as *Moby-Dick*.

Yet, as with flower language, this diminishment could be liberating: freeing a lover, or an author, to perform confessions – erotic, or aesthetic – that seem to belong to language alone. Flower-language, stylistic ornamentation, and generic convention had emancipatory effects for women writers because these were means of self-expression disguised as self-abnegation, a public form of discourse whose central feature was the semblance of privacy and discretion.[10] While these features of women's writing were dismissed by generations of critics as aesthetically uninteresting, the canon of Melville's work has largely been built around claims for aesthetic achievement. Alex Calder, who explores what he calls Melville's "bad" writing, identifies experiential effects that others have found in nineteenth-century women writers: Melville's writing can be "vitalized" by a "psychic insulation." While Calder attributes these effects to Melville's "disregard" for audience, a carelessness that is not the same as making space for readers by figuring authorship as circumstantial and surprising,[11] these features also comprise a "feminine" quality in Melville's writing that can be traced from the not-so-secret messages conveyed in the flowers of *Mardi*, to the hyperbolic gothic-sentimentalism of *Pierre*, and the plants in *Weeds and Wildings*.[12]

I read such moments as expressions of homosexual desire, just as others have read the eroticized female characters of Isabel in *Pierre* or the philosopher Urania in "After the Pleasure Party" as ciphers for men.[13] In this reading, *Weeds and Wildings* should be considered a collection of love poems for Hawthorne. But what interests me most about this is that as Melville is writing, Hawthorne is dead, and has been dead for over twenty years. Hawthorne will never read these confessions as confession. Unlike *Moby-Dick* or *Pierre*, which qualify as veiled conversations, or invitations to converse, with Hawthorne, *Weeds and Wildings* lacks at least one of its primary interlocutors. Rather than simply substituting Hawthorne for Lizzie, then, I suggest that we also attend to this quality of the text, reading *Weeds and Wildings* as a mode of confessional poetry that navigates a relationship between literature and life different from exposure or revelation. Unlike the inward gazing performance of authority and pain that characterize the work of twentieth-century confessional poets like Robert Lowell or Sylvia Plath, Melville's late flower poems perform pleasure and invitation while also being, in some ways, a solitary performance, lyric at its most insular, so quiet that they have evaded even effective overhearing.

Critics have long sensed a "privacy effect" in *Billy Budd* that is also an "open secret."[14] In *Weeds and Wildings*, we can trace the inverse of this: an intimacy effect. The intimacies are real, and so are the textual effects that invoke them. *Weeds and Wildings* thus comprises an important final movement in Melville's complex and career-long exploration of how literature draws from and serves life itself. As we will see, the uniquely intertextual and private nature of *Weeds and Wildings* also invites us to think about the uses of the most basic technologies of literary study and craft: why write; why read; for what and for whom.

Melville and His Mosses

The persistence of life into literature is invoked in the title of Hawthorne's *Mosses from an Old Manse*, in which moss signifies history's persistence into the present and its power over individual lives. The opening essay describes the Manse itself: an already historic house, flanked by Revolutionary battlefields and the Concord River, previously inhabited by several generations of ministerial Emersons, including Ralph Waldo as he further defected from that tradition while drafting *Nature*. This was where Sophia and Nathaniel Hawthorne lived as newlyweds. The mossy roof and the moldering books in the study of their rented home are symptoms, for Hawthorne, of the intractability of history, reminders, amid the expansiveness of love and life, of how individuals are subsumed in the accumulations of time. How moss, which appears from a distance a singular swath of green, is a host, slowly growing. Just as the manse manse absorbs, and thereby conceals, history, Hawthorne lets his work absorb and shield him: "I have appealed to no sentiment or sensibilities save such as are diffused among us all," he summarizes. "So far as I am a man of really individual attributes, I veil my face." Disappearing, he denies readers access to "the inner passages of [his] being."[15]

Responding enthusiastically to his first encounter with Hawthorne as an author and a man, Melville, in his ecstatic, anonymous review "Hawthorne and His Mosses" (1850), claims an intimacy with Hawthorne by converting the symbolism of his mosses. Rather than signs for history's stranglehold on the present, moss becomes, in Melville's reading, expressive of Hawthorne's resistance to equating life with literature. Combining moss with Hawthorne – "this sweet Man of Mosses," this "Mossy Man" – Melville conveys his own desire as an author: that literature mingle symbiotically with life (PZ 241). Melville rewrites Hawthorne's mosses to be more continuous with other expressions of

Romantic "vegetable genius."[16] Like Whitman, Melville makes his organic metaphors embodied and sexual. In the same review, Melville describes how Hawthorne's vegetal quality infiltrates him, turning his "Southern soul" to "hot soil" under the influence of a spray of "germinous seeds" and the drive of "strong New-England roots" (PZ 250). Later on, Melville associated Hawthorne with still other plants, from the tumultuous pastorals and hyperbolic forests of the first half of *Pierre*, set in the Berkshires of Massachusetts, where Melville and Hawthorne met, to the vine and grape imagery associated with the Hawthorne-based character of Vine in *Clarel*.[17] In this early review, and again in *Weeds and Wildings*, the mingling of moss and flowers is central.

Melville depicts his discovery of Hawthorne's writing as a transition from the pleasure he takes in flowers and fruits, epitomized by a woman who is an allegorical "Cherry" to plant-life that is mossier, more literary, and Hawthorne-specific – alluring, but harder to digest. One morning, this "mountain girl, a cousin, who for the last two weeks has every morning helped [him] to strawberries and raspberries," offers her cousin a book. She has seen him reading "Dwight's Travels in New England" in the "hay-mow," and gives him something "better." The substitution of Hawthorne for Dwight swaps fiction for non-fiction, "raspberries" for "moss." Though Melville fixates here on Hawthorne's mossy difficulty, he also transfers Cherry's fruity and flowery loveliness onto the book, and the man, she hands over. "'Yes,' said cousin Cherry, 'yes, it is that flowery Hawthorne.' – 'Hawthorne and Mosses,' said I, before taking the book" (PZ 240).

Weeds and Wildings represents Melville's attempt to reconcile the forms of literary labor and expression that flowers or mosses might represent: the trifling flowers of a feminized poetics designed for its time and place, and the monumental mosses of a literature designed to last. Melville draws both on particular passages from Hawthorne's *Mosses* and on a more generalized language of poetic and flowery practice, from which Hawthorne draws as well. Writing off the efforts of authorship, Hawthorne dismisses *Mosses* as a collection of "trifles," a set of "tales and essays which had blossomed out like flowers in the calm summer of my heart and mind," as well as "old, faded things, [. . .] flowers pressed between the leaves of a book." Hawthorne's flowers combine the living and the dead, the vitality of imaginative literature and the bookishness of history. Hawthorne qualifies the first of these in terms of the latter: not simply roses or lilacs, but "idle weeds and withering blossoms," flowers impinged upon by the slightness of aesthetics, and the predictability of time.[18] At the end of the century,

Melville takes up these weeds, converting withering into "wilding," idleness to ideality, marrying the past to the present, mosses to flowers, and Hawthorne to himself.

Rose, Moss-Rose

There are several reasons – both biographical and textual – for reading the complex romantic impulses of the rose poems of *Weeds and Wildings* in relation to Hawthorne rather than Melville's wife Lizzie. The most literal of these is Hawthorne's name: the hawthorn shrub (Genus *Crataégus*) belongs to the Rose family (an expansive tribe that includes many of the commonest edible fruits and other flowering shrubs).[19] In contrast to this literal affiliation, Lizzie suffered for years from an allergic reaction to roses, though she did eventually recover enough for Melville to begin cultivating roses at their house in the 1880s.[20] Secondly, the primary piece of textual evidence linking Melville's wife to the manuscript is tenuous: a handwritten note, "Lizzie," beside a dedication "To Winnefred" placed at the beginning of the book (WW 60). The handwriting is not clearly Melville's or Lizzie's – the two hands otherwise most visible throughout – and Melville's dedication to a fictional name indicates the striking of a pose. Elsewhere, he took dedication as a literary space in its own right, capable of absorbing irony as easily as sincerity, as in his extravagant dedication of *Pierre* to "His Majesty, Mount Greylock." Indeed, "To Winnefred" is not the only dedication included in the manuscript. The third section of the manuscript, "Rip Van Winkle's Lilac," begins with an address to Washington Irving, "a Happy Shade." Reading Lizzie as the only meaningful interlocutor across the manuscript interprets "To Winnefred" too literally.

To write of the rose is also to invoke centuries of literary history, including the works of Hawthorne himself.[21] Roses feature centrally in two of the stories from *Mosses from an Old Manse*, "The Birthmark," and "Rappacini's Daughter," as well as *The Scarlet Letter, The Blithedale Romance*, and *The Marble Faun*. In each of these episodes, Hawthorne's pallet is a striking red and white. In "The Birthmark," Hawthorne compares the red of Georgiana's birthmark to "a crimson stain upon the snow," "a bas-relief of ruby on the whitest marble," and a red rose on the white rose of her cheek.[22] In the opening pages of *The Scarlet Letter*, roses appear beside the prison door through which Hester walks. When Hester's daughter Pearl tells a minister that she may have sprung from this very rose bush, he questions the aptness of her name, mingling red and white again, the red of Hester's letter and Pearl's matching clothes with Pearl's name: "Pearl? – Ruby, rather! – or Coral! – or Red Rose."[23] In *The Blithedale Romance,* this white and red imagery returns with Zenobia, whom Coverdale finds to be a "perfectly-developed rose" and who drowns herself in a white gown for want of Hollingsworth's love.[24] In *The Marble Faun*, the virginal painter Hilda repeatedly tosses "a single rosebud" at her admirer, Kenyon.

These reds and whites are conventional, a feature of almost any literary flower-scape, including others Melville may have encountered. Although critics have been particularly intrigued by Melville's encounters with more broody authors during his late years – Arthur Schopenhauer, Matthew Arnold – the books he read or owned during this period also include more flowery fare.[25] Several of these books were gifts from Melville's wife. Lizzie gave Samuel Hole's *A Book About Roses* to Melville on his sixty-fifth birthday.[26] During the same period, she gifted him several books of poetry, each with many rose-poems: Rossiter Johnson's collection of *Poems Narrative* and Thomas Aldrich's collected *Poems*.[27] Johnson's anthology reprints Shelley's "Sensitive Plant," with its imagery of "rose-leaves, like flakes of crimson snow, / Pav[ing] the turf and the mosses below." In the next line, lilies embody the actual color of snow, "white, and wan," and metaphorically extend the sickliness of these wintry features from the garden to "the head and the skin of a dying man."[28] This transposition of the flowery onto the human is central to the conventionality of flower language, and to roses in particular as the most conventional of flowers. Even without binaries of red and white, roses invoke poles of innocence and experience coded as sexual (think of Blake's "Sick Rose" with a worm in her bosom). In one of Aldrich's poems, dead children clutch roses while a "virginal" rose shrinks in the "tangles of a harlot's hair." In another, the speaker compares his heart to a rose, whose "fragrant soul" is wafted by a wind he wishes "could tear [his] heart."[29]

Melville believed that Hawthorne had "a secret" (L 186), and when he turns to roses in *Weeds and Wildings* he explores Hawthorne's language of flowery secrecy from the inside out.[30] Hawthorne routinely connects roses to secrets and to desire, so that the inclusion of a rose in a scene can seem like a confession of something otherwise unsaid. When Hilda lobs another rosebud at Kenyon in *The Marble Faun*, he feels the tap melt away "his own secret sorrow."[31] Elsewhere, roses exacerbate rather than relieve. The "terrible secret" of "Rappaccini's Daughter" is that she "has been nourished with [plant] poisons from her birth upward, until [. . .] she herself had become the deadliest poison in existence." Her breath smells "richer than a garden of Persian roses" but would kill with a kiss.[32] Making flowers themselves a source of sexual threat, Hawthorne disrupts a nineteenth-century floral language that could assert illicit desires, including same-sex desires, without perverting the inherent innocence of flowers.[33] In "Rappaccini's Daughter," roses, and the woman they have become, take the fall.

Even as they take up convention, however, the reds and whites of Hawthorne's roses resist the stark oppositions of life and death, virginity and harlotry. More often, they represent entanglements, the inextricability of the beautiful and pure from all the realities of earthly life. Georgiana cannot be the beauty she is without her birthmark; when her husband attempts to strip red from her cheek, he kills all of her. Pearl is the child of neither innocence, nor betrayal, but of both. Hawthorne uses the conventionality of literary roses like a minister's veil, a suggestive surface to lurk behind. We sense guilt, but the actual effect of a rose is to obscure origins, to invoke a vast referential history that absorbs and effaces the particularity of any individual's desire, choice, or failing. Hawthorne's boldly colored roses obscure the murkiness of origins – Pearl's paternity is a fog compared to the rosy blaze of her clothes, and the rose bush outside the courtroom door may or may not have sprung from Ann Hutchinson's steps. In this regard, Hawthorne's roses extend a central trope in his work: literature gesturing at life, but resisting an equation of literature and life that would be reducible to personal exposure or confession.[34]

By taking up this imagery of white and red, snow and fire, roses and deathliness, Melville explores the secrecy of Hawthorne's desire from the inside out. In "Amoroso," one of the rose poems of *Weeds and Wildings,* two lovers ride together in a sleigh "o'er the snows," alongside "ice-bound streams enchanted," and guided by the red star, "Arcturus," a "huntsman ever ruddy." Though bundled together, the lovers are "a plighted pair" in whom "Frost makes with flame a bond." Their love is transcendently inhuman, like ice or fire, yet also "spousal," embodied and earthly. These opposites zoom together across "Arctic Paradise" (WW 38). The poem is an exploration of how opposites attract, and the one opposition the poem successfully reconciles is not of fire and ice, red and white, or the difference between genders, but a vegetal union: moss and rose.

The poem emphatically begins, "Rosamond, my Rosamond / Of roses is the rose." Yet roses are not the only plants in the poem. The lovers are "mossed in furs all cosy," an unusual choice of verb, particularly when any number of others would work just as well metrically and descriptively. Moss returns in the final line, as "Rosamond, my Rosamond" migrates into

"Rose Rosamond, Moss-Rose!" (WW 38). Melville would have known the moss rose as *Rosa muscosa* – one of the commonest of garden roses,[35] and yet one connoting "Superior Merit" (WW 83) according to nineteenth-century guides to the language of the flowers.

A poem that circulated through several of these flower guides relates how the moss rose combines "nature's simplest weed" with all that is "fairest" in a rose,[36] as well as "the fanciful origin" of this winning amalgamation.[37] A grateful "angel," waking from a nap in a rose's "sweet shade," offers to grant his favorite flower a wish. With "deepen'd glow," she asks simply for "another grace." The angel "throws" a "veil of moss" over her blush, alleviating the rose's suggestive boldness.[38] Moss roses are identifiable by the green fuzz covering their unopened buds. As the moss is transformed from the real green at the angel's feet to a metaphorical veil, the moss rose becomes representative of a mingling of the real and the metaphoric, the literary and the lived. In an earlier version of "Amoroso," this "Moss-Rose" was even more central to Melville's imagination; the original title for the piece was "Amoroso sings his Moss-Rose" (WW 83). In this version, the final line might have read, "Queen Rosamond, Moss-Rose" (WW 251–52).

Melville celebrates this "Queen of the Flowers" in two other poems. The first of these extends the reconciliations of the moss rose between humility and regality from a single flower to all plants. This poem appears at the end of the manuscript's second section, "This, That, and the Other," which, as a section, marks the first divergence from the domestic themes of "The Year." In this section, a vine – a plant Melville associated with Hawthorne in *Clarel* – attempts to intercede with the Queen on behalf of the clover, the central plant figure of "The Year." The vine asserts connections across plant-life based on shared materials: "O Rose, we plants are all akin, / Our roots enlock; each strives to win / The ampler space, the balmier air" (WW 24). But by the end of the poem, the Queen remains aloof. She will have to be supplicated again.

The second Rose Queen poem, "The Devotion of the Flowers to their Lady," comes at the end of the primary sequence of Melville's rose poems, "As They Fell." Here, the Rose is unquestionably Queen: the other flowers confess their subservience in a collective third person. This poem, rather than claiming commonality across plants, addresses the rose as a symbol of all flowers, whose earthly transcendence rescues the other flowers from the life and death consequences of sexual reproduction. The flowers introduce this drive to reproduce as a "nothing." "What nothing has happened?" they rhetorically ask the Queen, "Begetting things hateful – / Old age, decay, and the sorrows, / devourers of man?" (WW 9–12, 41). Reproduction – so expected as to not even count within this poem as an event at all – propels both flowering and decay. Melville extends an allegory of flowers as exiled natives of paradise in which mere reproduction and nothing further signals a loss of Eden. In Melville's rendition, the Edenic bower of heterosexual love is already a fallen space. Afterward, we see Adam, alone with his "impulse / disordering all" and flowers "[l]anguish[ing] with secret desire" (WW 19–20, 42).

The poem ends rosily, however, as the flowers celebrate their Queen. They are "blessed in banishment" because the "Rose" represents them. As a "voucher of Paradise" and "visible pledge," the Rose's representative nature turns it into the "Flower" that transcends reproductive cycles of birth and death, enduring in "spite of the Worm" (WW 38, 40–41, 42). In this poem, flowers are united not by materially interlocking roots, but by their transfiguration into literature. Melville takes up the language of flowers – "We the Lilies whose pallor is passion, / We the Pansies that muse nor forget" – to emphasize just how over-written these material transmigrations are (WW 30–31, 42). Standing for flowers more broadly, as well as the literary practices that invest them with meaning, the Rose represents a literary encryption of life.

Melville addresses this quality of the rose most directly in "The Rose Farmer," one of two final poems set apart from the rose sequence, but which comment on many of their themes. The poem seems to contrast life and literature, as the farmer grapples with whether to appreciate living flowers, or to press them into perfume. This is also the poem that directly takes up the Persian origin of flower language, and of rose worship in particular. During his final years, Melville read and returned to works of Persian poetry, including Sa'di's *Gûlistân* and *The Rubáiyát of Omar Khayyám*.[39] Roses are a primary convention in these texts, and poets like Shelley and Aldrich, as well as the authors of guides to flower language, drew from the rose imagery of this tradition.[40] In the introduction to Edward Fitzgerald's translation of *The Rubáiyát*, Melville marked a passage in which the translator comments on the feelings of intimacy produced by reading. Fitzgerald describes how he is drawn to "Omar," whom he "cannot help calling" by his "familiar name." In Khayyám's work, the translator elaborates, "we seem to have the Man – the *Bonhomme* – Omar himself."[41] From *Typee* onward, Melville had been interested in how writers appear "really" present, as Fitzgerald puts it, through textual performance. Yet as Melville experienced in his early readings of Hawthorne, this authorial presence – even when producing a "shock of recognition" (PZ 249) – is apparitional, already always a ghost. Fitzgerald only *feels* as if he is at the table with Khayyám.

In "The Rose Farmer," roses are no longer singular queens but seas of flowers, and the backdrop to an exchange between two pairs of men. First, the narrator of the poem remembers a deceased "friend," "Whose kind good will to me began / When I [. . .] Prepared a chowder for his feast." In compensation, this friend has left the narrator "A brave bequest, a farm [. . .] Forever consecrate to roses." This friend is almost certainly Hawthorne, to whom Melville offered *Moby-Dick*, and the roses of *Weeds and Wildings* are Hawthorne's bequest. Wondering what to do with these texts and memories – whether to convert them into profit for a literary audience or appreciate their evanescence – the narrator happens upon a second rose farmer, a mirror of himself. There is an insularity to each. The farmer tells the narrator, circularly: "I flourish I." He counsels him to take his roses as they are, "In mossy pots, or bound in posies," without seeking to make them more consumable by others. The roses respond to the farmer, "turn[ing] their heads like ladies, when / They hear themselves discussed by men." In this collective form, they are feminized, but the farmer also distinguishes between these flowers and "Eve's fair daughters." It was not women that "lured the sons of God below," he tells the narrator, but something far "Less fugitive in charm," more cliché and hardy: "It was the rose."

Writing of moss and roses at the end of his life was a way for Melville to return to his early reading, and to reading and writing as expressions of intimacy and the preservation of that intimacy through time. The contradiction between roses and attar, life and its compression into literature, which the old Rose Farmer grapples with, is a false contrast. Hawthorne's roses are symbols marred in earthliness, yet torn up without their roots. Melville was still feeling Hawthorne's roots at the end his life, and, in response, constructed a living memorial.

Mossy Lilacs

Hawthorne's presence is most evident in "Rip Van Winkle's Lilac," the prose-poem at the center of *Weeds and Wildings*. This is not immediately obvious because Hawthorne is costumed in Washington Irving, himself a master of disguise. Irving's *Sketch Book* makes authorship an elaborate performance: Irving attributes the volume as a whole to Geoffrey Crayon, and further fictionalizes the authorship of particular pieces by claiming to have "found" them "among the papers of the late Diedrich

Knickerbocker."[42] "Rip Van Winkle" is one such tale. In his rose poems, Melville mimics this authorial self-styling, attributing his second Rose Queen poem to a Provençal monk, Clement Drouon, a former troubadour. Hawthorne makes a similar move – down to the specificity of the nationality of his assumed identity – at the beginning of "Rappaccini's Daughter," when he introduces the tale as a translation of M. de l'Aubépine (Hawthorne in French). In "Rip Van Winkle's Lilac," Melville plays Irving playing Crayon playing Knickerbocker, making substitution itself a central trope.

After stepping into Irving, Melville next transposes landscapes, swapping his Western Massachusetts with Rip's Hudson River Valley. Wandering homeward after his long sleep, Rip comes across "a view deeply stamped in his memory": a vista of a mountain, whose silhouette, "the head of one distant blue summit peered over the shoulder of a range not so blue as less lofty and remote," resembles Mount Greylock, the mountain Melville could see from the window above his desk at Arrowhead while he was writing *Moby-Dick.* Disoriented by the strange sense that his memory is not his own, Rip comes upon a lilac, a flowering tree that he does not remember, but that grows beside his old house in "the very spot which he could only recall as occupied by an immemorial willow" (WW 78–9).

For this imagery of willows and lilacs, Melville likely drew from Hawthorne's sketch in *Mosses from an Old Manse,* "Buds and Bird Voices." In his review of *Mosses,* Melville calls this sketch "a delicious thing," and quotes from Hawthorne: "Will the world ever be so decayed, that Spring may not renew its greenness?" (PZ 241). In *Mosses,* however, Hawthorne lingers over decay, beginning with a willow covered with moss: "The moss-grown willow-tree [. . .] is almost the earliest to gladden us with the promise and reality of beauty [. . .] and the last to scatter its yellow, yet scarcely-withered, leaves, upon the ground [. . .] Our old house would lose a charm, were the willow to be cut down, with its golden crown over the snow-covered roof, and its heap of summer verdure." Moss contributes to the willow's appeal, as Hawthorne discerns a picturesque quality in the tree's decrepitude as well as its yearly rebirths. Because the willow is not particularly beautiful to begin with, Hawthorne resists allegory in his description. Not so the lilac, whose floweriness invites aesthetic equivocation:

> Old age is not venerable, when it embodies itself in lilacs, rose-bushes, or any other ornamental shrubs; it seems as if such plants, as they grow only for beauty, ought to flourish in immortal youth, or, at least, to die

> before their sad decrepitude. Trees of beauty are trees of Paradise, and therefore not subject to decay, by their original nature, though they have lost that precious birth-right by being transplanted to an earthly soil. There is a kind of ludicrous unfitness in the idea of a time-stricken and grandfatherly lilac-bush. The analogy holds good in human life. Persons who can only be graceful and ornamental – who can give the world nothing but flowers – should die young, and never be seen with gray hair and wrinkles, any more than the flower-shrubs with mossy bark and blighted foliage, like the lilacs under my window. Not that beauty is worthy of less than immortality – no; the beautiful should live forever – and thence, perhaps, the sense of impropriety, when we see it triumphed over by time.[43]

In the language of the flowers, lilacs could signal youth, love's first flush, and sometimes, fastidiousness.[44] In his mossy lilacs, Hawthorne sees a refutation of all these attributes, uncovering the disappointments of experience in these "grandfatherly" "flower-shrubs." Part of the allure of lilacs, and of literature for Hawthorne, is an enduring transcendence, a floweriness so effusive that it leaves the earth behind. Moss mars this escape.

In "Rip Van Winkle's Lilac," in contrast, Melville celebrates a flowery old age in which life and literature are dependent on one another. Rather than opposing mossy willow and mossy lilac, Melville figures these trees as substitutions: the lilac merely stands where a willow once grew. On Rip's lilac, moss flourishes along with flowers. Melville explores this interdependence of flowering and decay as a relation between art and life in the middle section of the piece, in which "a young artist" comes upon "the pink Lilac relieved against the greenly ruinous house" while Rip is off sleeping his long sleep (WW 30). Here is Melville's version of "The Artist of the Beautiful." While painting, the artist is accosted by yet another Hawthornian type, a "gaunt, hatchet-faced, stony-eyed" minister who rides by on a horse and attempts to direct the artist's attention to the "new tabernacle," freshly painted white on the hill. The painter rejects the church, which, he says has been "sufficiently painted already," as a suitable object for artistic attention. In the argument that ensues, Melville responds directly to Hawthorne's claim that "[o]ld age is not venerable, when it embodies itself in lilacs, rose-bushes, or any other ornamental shrubs." The minister begins:

> "You will stick to this wretched old ruin, then, will you?"
>
> "Yes, and the Lilac."

> "The Lilac? and black what do-you-call-it – lichen, on the trunk, so old it is. It is half-rotten, and its flowers spring from the rottenness under it, just as the moss on those eaves does from the rotting shingles."
>
> "Yes, decay is often a gardener," assented the other. (WW 30–1)

In "Buds and Bird Voices," Hawthorne claims, "there is no decay" even as he describes with relish his weathered house and musty books. Signs of outward decay are counteracted by the "renewing power of the spirit."[45] Rather than negating decay through these transmigrations of spirit, Melville considers dependencies and coexistences.

"Rip Van Winkle's Lilac" ends – like *Billy Budd* – in a poem. Both these lines of verse, and "Billy in the Darbies," break from third to first person, and from past into present tense. Through these turns, Melville negotiates the relationship between the literary and the personal, the remembered and the lived. Rip speaks; Billy speaks. Both stutter: "Ay, ay, all is up," Billy sings; "No, – ay! – Bless me, it is the same!" crows Rip (BB 132; WW 33). Realizations proceed chattily, blow by blow. Rip's repetitions – "Dear, dear me!" "Lilac? – a lilac?" and "My head! – whose head? – Ah, Rip (I'm Rip)" – unfold within a protracted present (WW 7, 17, 25), while Rip's courtship and marriage, the artist and his critic, and the rest of the final poetic section, employ a past, or, in the last stanza, a future tense. This same dizzying sense of plant-life concludes Billy's soliloquy, as Billy senses the man coming to hang him – "Sentry, are you there?" – and his own sailor's death – "I am sleepy, and the oozy weeds about me twist" (BB 132). The time of these weeds is the same time as Rip's lilac: plant-time, which, Melville suggests in *Weeds and Wildings*, can be literary time as well, transpersonal and transhistorical.

For Melville, writing and reading take place in a perpetual present tense, even when memory is involved. Faced with his lilac, Rip's memory "crack[s]" (WW 18). Within these fissures, Rip finds – or perhaps invents – a new memory: of himself, finding the lilac: "I found it – dear me – well, well, well." Rip remembers not only that he was responsible for planting the lilac, but that he planted it so "that it might thrive and come / To plead for [him] with wife, though dumb" (WW 21–23, 33). The lilac "speaks" for Rip; its speech recasts his life. With Rip's realization of the lilac as a floweriness belonging to both life and literature, Melville introduces his retelling as a performance. Why, he asks, should one "rehearse" the "good fellow's resurrection" when Irving, "[n]ever from genial verity swerving," has already told the tale (WW 29–31, 33)? Or when "Jefferson," an actor whom Melville saw play Rip in a staged version of

Irving's story, has already "acted true to life" (WW 33)?[46] Melville's choice of the verb "rehearse" frames storytelling as performance rather than transcription. Both acting and writing have an element of truth; Irving's written version sticks to "verity," while Jefferson's performance brings the story back to "life." In his dedication "To a Happy Shade," Melville may have acknowledged a "happy" quality in Irving's staid fictions – a happiness of completion, art-making sealed off from the uncertain impulses of memory and feeling – but he aligns himself in this stanza with the actor (WW 25). In dressing his life in the writing of others, Melville again demonstrates the degree to which, for him, life and art inform one another. Hawthorne is an *hors-texte* and an intertext. The personal becomes depersonalized, and the textual is opened to materials and experiences beyond the words on a page.

These flowery confessions directed toward yet performed in the absence of a particular reader are the work of *Weeds and Wildings*. In nineteenth-century manuals of flower language, including one owned by Melville's wife, while the full bloom of the moss rose connotes "superior merit," its unopened bud bespeaks "confession," the expression of "many a feeling that long seem'd effac'd," or a "*token*" of "things that words can ne'er disclose."[47] In the final stanza of "Rip Van Winkle's Lilac," Melville invites a generic reader to visit the land Rip's lilacs have transformed in some future June, where "his heart flowers out confessed" (WW 73–74, 34). By taking up Hawthorne's imagery, Melville both revises and reconnects. His moss-roses and mossy lilacs are revisions to Hawthorne's love of the aesthetic and reticence of letting literature absorb too much of the muddiness of life; they are expressions of old age as true to youth, still desirous and decadent. Documenting a flowery old age through poetry, Melville adopts the conventions of his century, which were also Hawthorne's conventions: the fantasy of flowers as showy throwaways, a means of dismissing desire or an ambitious literature while continuing to practice either or both. When, in "The Rose Farmer," Melville "arrest[s]" his "line," he participates in a feminized projection of the "flower of a subject" as "enough" (WW 190): simple, almost invisible, fine.

CHAPTER 4

Pip and the Sounds of Blackness in Moby-Dick

Christopher Freeburg

When thinking about Melville's *Moby-Dick* (1851), ideas about power, nature, and the dark sides of romantic reverie all come to mind. What doesn't come to the forefront in Melville scholarship are the religious rituals, music, and moral vitality of black expressive culture.[1] Scholars of African American history, with a few exceptions, also overlook the workings of black culture in Melville's *tour de force*. One glaring exception to this is Sterling Stuckey. Stuckey has been working on connections between Melville's fiction and black expressive culture for decades. In *African Culture and Melville's Art* (2008), Stuckey made a compelling case for the presence of African art forms in works such as *Moby-Dick* and "Benito Cereno," documenting Melville's exposure to black singers and performers.[2]

Yet we have only begun to measure the depths of Melville's engagement with black culture. The moral and artistic influence of black culture resonates in many of *Moby-Dick*'s defining moments, anchoring the novel's ethical conundrums and sense of existential angst. With this in mind, I begin with the question: what is the relationship between black expressive culture and the existential disruption that blackness signifies in *Moby-Dick*? This essay claims that not only is black expressive culture present in *Moby-Dick* but that its presence is integral to Melville's boldest aesthetic strokes, central themes, and characters. My purpose here is to demonstrate the profundity of black culture in *Moby-Dick* and to encourage further inquiry into this neglected aspect of Melville's blackness.

Moby-Dick's Pip is one of the most compelling figures of black culture. Melville depicts him as a symbol of blackness itself, a living emblem of joy, music, and festive camaraderie – so full of life that he is removed from the drudgery of whaling. Pip's improvisational scats, tambourine playing, and relationship to eternity connect him to the religious and moral dimensions of black culture. In several pivotal chapters – "The Castaway," "A Squeeze of the Hand," "Queequeg in His Coffin," and "The Deck" – Pip amplifies

Melville's inquiry into the tension between individual and communal interests. Through Pip, Melville suggests that what fuels the ambition for power are feelings of individual powerlessness and the intensities of loneliness, which, if left unaddressed, can turn into psychic and physical violence.

The exchanges between Pip and Ahab near the closing moments of the novel revolve around the moral challenges that spring from the violent pangs of isolation. Viewing Pip as an exemplar of black culture also gives us a chance to take seriously a hidden gem C. L. R. James offered readers in *Mariners, Renegades, and Castaways* (1953). James wrote about Pip: "The most abased of the crew … will be hailed as the greatest hero of all." While I am not interested in Pip's traditional heroic qualities, Pip's importance to *Moby-Dick* as a figure of black culture points critics to the "tragic graces" (MD 117) and moral insight that even James did not fully attend to in his interpretation of the novel.

Studying Pip as a figure of black culture has implications for black performance studies as well. Melville cast a voiceless coward in the very antebellum moment that slave narratives and other progressive presentations of black people relied on ideals of social uplift, education, or antislavery violence. Pip does not fulfill any of these tropes. In fact, Pip epitomizes the opposite. I conclude this essay by discussing how Melville's presentation of Pip's inarticulate impossibility encourages critics to think beyond key tenents of voice, agency, objectification, and subjectivity that define ongoing discussions of black performance. Pip, physically and metaphorically, sits "in the break," where Pip's *sonic semblance* – his utterances, percussive intensity, and improvised gestures – creates meaning without articulation, sociomoral impacts without cogent speech.[3] By analyzing Pip's sonic semblance, I uncover black culture's centrality to *Moby-Dick*'s most crucial moral and philosophical questions.

Black Culture and Melville

If there is one thing that Toni Morrison, Ralph Ellison, and David Bradley have in common, other than their shared interest in black culture, it is their fascination with Melville. Morrison's musing on blackness and whiteness found the locus of whiteness as an ideology in *Moby-Dick*.[4] Despite these writers' interest in Melville's racial entanglements, they did not see the impact of black culture on Melville's seminal fiction as Stuckey saw it. Stuckey, a historian of West African culture and its presence in the USA, was quite specific in identifying Melville's reliance on African and African

American art forms, particularly the ring shout movement that emerges in *Moby-Dick*'s "Forecastle – Midnight" chapter. There is a link between the ring shout, Pip's contribution to it, and the foreshadowing of violent disarray on the *Pequod*. The ring shout allows readers to see the stakes of maintaining a diverse social collective in the face of violence. What appears as a playful song and dance before a coming storm actually forecasts the novel's central concerns with existential angst and the moral necessity of human connection.

How did one of the key examples of black culture appear in Melville's fiction? Where Melville lived, one did not have to go very far to be exposed to black culture. Publications like the *New York Statesman*, the *New York Gazette*, and the *New York American* reported on black people celebrating and performing in music, dance, and marching. In Albany and New York City, many festivals, clubs, parades, funerals, and minstrel shows featured black people dancing with ritualistic movement. In *Moby-Dick*, Melville describes black people as festive and celebratory. Stuckey depicts these acts as a frivolity rich with religious and artistic meaning that comes directly from West African culture. While Stuckey sought to demonstrate that this culture is in fact African and not "mere minstrelsy," my focus here is on identifying and analyzing how Melville produced a distinct view of moral value through Pip and black expression.[5]

Melville's interest in the moral and philosophical possibilities of blackness erupts in "Forecastle – Midnight." The chapter begins with sailors expressing their farewells to the land through song and dance. Pip enters the scene at the call of the French sailor: "Pip little Pip! hurrah with your tambourine." Pip cannot find his tambourine and the sailor says playfully, "beat thy belly, then, wag thy ears." More calls to dance by the sailors immediately follow: "Form, now, Indian file, and gallop to the double shuffle" (MD 174). The men move together with orgiastic intensity, pushing themselves to their limits and entering a state of mystic elevation. "[T]ear yourselves," a sailor implores. "Rig it, dig it, stig it, quig it, bell-boy," says another (MD 175).

Pip's tambourine is the foundational beat for the dance. Stuckey identifies this scene as constituted by black culture for specific reasons: phrases such as "jig it" and "quig it" are associated with the ring shout and other black improvising movements. The sailors themselves, moving in "double shuffle" and "Indian file," resemble the participants in a ring shout, the most influential slave dance in nineteenth-century America. When whites attended black funerals, worship services, and organized dances, they sometimes described the movement as "Indian file." The "double shuffle" was similarly central to black dance expression.[6] When discussing Pip and the ring shout, Stuckey is most interested in making connections between African rituals and Melville's fictional expression, and his analysis demonstrates vital connections, but Stuckey leaves out what I think is most relevant about black culture in *Moby-Dick*: its tie to Melville's moral philosophy and ethical worldview.

The ring shout contains strong moral underpinnings. In West Africa, the ring shout appealed to the ancestors and the gods. Participants took an oath, testifying that they shared their life with "the dead below the river or the sea."[7] Their energetic leaps in the air expressed reverence for the divine and consecrated a social space through ritualistic movement. In North America, the ring shout is not only about reverence and joy but also about committing to a life where one lives for God and for others in God's name – to stake the meaning of one's life on the beauty, challenges, and responsibility of community.[8] The ring shout brings the ancestors into the circle and produces a spiritual connection that reaches across individuals. The circle symbolizes and actualizes eternity: by concretizing social bonds, it elevates collectivity over individual alienation, and this is a key theme in the novel.

The revelry in "Forecastle – Midnight" comes to a head precisely along these lines.[9] While the men dance, they appear to triumph over adversity and alienation, making manifest the value and ebullience of community. Melville doubles down on this moral affirmation when the ring is broken and the men fall into violent disarray. When the dancing ceases, the men split into groups and a storm appears on the horizon, which creates fear and disunity. The ring of men and the ringed horizon from the coming storm blur and blend. The merriment turns dark with a potential fight between the Spanish sailor and Daggoo. The Spanish sailor grips a knife and the men prepare to square off. With murder in the air, their prior link is severed. The Old Manx sailor recalls Cane and Abel: "In that ring Cain struck Abel. Sweet work, right work! No? Why then, God mad'st thou *the ring*?" (MD 178). In Genesis, Cain murders Abel out of envy and their brotherhood is split by this bloodshed. Melville underscores the significance of linked merriment and implicitly disavows the violence (which has no apparent cause other than a few insults), lamenting the lost social connection and suggesting the need for intimate collaboration.

At the end of "Forecastle – Midnight," Pip cries out to "God aloft somewhere" to protect him from men who do not fear the consequences of their wrongdoing (MD 178). When beating his tambourine in the circle, Pip had no need to for this protection, but now the anxiety of impending doom encourages violent tribalism between the groups. Pip plays a key role in constituting the space of moral possibility and even a sense of conversion for the reader, underscoring the strength of social bonds forged between men of different origins. Melville is not duplicitous or ambiguous here: Pip helps him affirm that there is a right side of the fence. The difficulty is getting men to see it in moments of crisis that bring out their selfishness and impatience.

At the chapter's close, Pip stands as the innocent, the small, the uplifter who sits alone. Pip's presence is indelible. Lamenting the loss of their prior merriment, Pip says, "there goes the jib-stay... and there they go all cursing?" Pip prays, pleading with God to save him from "all men who have no bowels to feel fear" (MD 178). Though his tambourine is quiet, he is a source of narrative insight: the ringed horizon is completeness or eternity, and the chapter pushes the reader to think about the meaning of brotherhood in the midst of violent peril. Pip feels the danger of the dark storm, the sin of men's action, and the sense of existential limits with great intensity. The ring shout, with Pip as its tambourine player, enables Melville to reveal the moral crux of what makes a life worth living, even in the face of death.

Pip's Eternities

Pip's music returns in "The Castaway" chapter, which, like "Forecastle – Midnight," points toward the *Pequod*'s calamity. In "Midnight," Pip plays music and the crew participates in a black cultural moment. In "The Castaway," Pip symbolizes black culture in a different way: he crystallizes the moral value of social equality and empathy. "The Castaway" may not produce another ring shout, but it deepens our sense of Pip as a festive performer from a jubilant people. In "The Castaway," Pip provokes moral dilemmas illuminated and accentuated by his connection to black music and performance. Pip's tambourine-playing creates something that is utterly good, innocent, and communal, and all of this is at stake in his alienation from and mistreatment by the crew. Pip thereby embodies the moral crux of the novel and clarifies its account of why black cultural expression matters.

Pip almost drowns because he jumps from a boat in pursuit of a whale. To teach him a lesson, Stubb and the rest of the crew leave him behind. But there is purposeful ambiguity in Melville's orchestration of the scene that enhances the chapter's moral and spiritual conviction. Stubb was shorthanded on his boat and Pip had to fill in. Pip jumps from the whaling boat not once, but twice. Stubb warns Pip the first time and says he's going to let him drown if he jumps again. Stubb clearly does not plan to carry out the threat, assuming that the fear of death is enough to keep Pip on task. But Pip jumps a second time anyway. Why? Is Pip attempting suicide? Or protesting the hunt? Or expressing cowardice? If Pip is truly a coward, why doesn't he fear Stubb enough to fall in line?

There is a conflict between Pip's identity and the whaling business that Pip feels overwhelmed by. His jumping is neither a courageous attempted suicide nor an expression of cowardice but the result of an irresolvable contradiction between the violent business of whaling and Pip's "peaceable securities" (MD 412). There is little indication that Pip really means to jump; when he does, despite Stubb's warnings, Melville writes, "we are all in hands of the Gods" (MD 413). If "we are all in the hands of the Gods," there is no answer for what happens, or why, but the community still must confront Pip's near drowning. Despite Stubb's best efforts, no one had control of Pip. No one could stop him. The crew was powerless and Pip's actions stand in their way. The facts are that Pip *did* jump and Stubb instructed the crew to leave him. Because Pip can't swim, when Stubb choses to go after the whale instead of Pip the situation becomes life threatening. Stubb assumed Pip would finally learn his lesson and realize that the business of whaling was serious, that Stubb was a man of his word, and that Pip must play his role.

The fact that something altogether different happens tells us something important about Pip, and about Melville. As Ishmael asserts in the chapter's introduction, Pip is an "evil-blazing diamond" and the artist is a jeweler who takes careful attention to transform the least admired and most admonished character to make him shine – not just with idyllic beauty but with the sublime glow like that from a "crown jewel stolen from the King of hell" (MD 412). To do this, Pip nearly drowns, sees something divine underwater, then absorbs its power and loses his mind and speech. He embodies "Heaven's sense," which the crew sees as madness. Melville writes: "The sea had jeeringly kept his finite body up, but drowned the infinite of his soul . . . Pip saw the multitudinous, God-omnipresent, coral insects, that out of the firmament of waters heaved the colossal orbs. He saw God's foot upon the treadle of the loom, and spoke it" (MD 414). The reader is confronted by the infinite force of eternity thrashing within Pip's finite body. Instead of linking the community with the divine through dance and song, Pip now embodies the tragic destruction of social bonds.

Pip's near-death experience and its aftermath are quite serious. Melville approaches the gravity of the event in three ways. Pip loses himself, becomes increasingly isolated from the crew, and Pip's descent into divine madness underscores the immorality of Stubb's choice to chase the whale rather than rescue Pip. Perhaps Stubb was justified in his decision and Melville wants his abandonment of Pip to seem challenging, but in the end it is Stubb who Ishmael asks the reader not to blame but to have sympathy for. "Blame not Stubb too harshly," says Ishmael: Stubb's whale was "dearly purchased" (MD 415).

We know the price for Pip, but what about the price for the crew? Stubb and the crew excoriated Pip in the moment of his worst fears. Stubb told Pip the whale was worth more than he could get for Pip at a slave auction in Alabama. Stubb left him, and Pip nearly drowned. Pip paid a price and Melville intimates that the crew felt guilty for it, or at least looked guilty in the eyes of Ishmael. The crew violated a higher code even when they felt justified by the violation. Pip's near drowning is a moral failure. Success would have made their actions and bond more sacred. Instead, they left Pip to die, Pip paid the price, and the men must live with it.

What exactly the crew must live with is not easily smoothed over, which makes the chapter that follows "The Castaway" pivotal to understanding Pip's abandonment. That chapter, "A Squeeze of the Hand," is where Melville depicts the soothing, sensual, and spiritual capacity of social bonds. Whiteness, which mostly appears as evil in the novel, here materializes an ethereal social ideal. The men cannot fix Pip but they can find reprieve from the blood oath that drives them. Ishmael explains the magic of the spermaceti:

> I forgot all about our horrible oath; in that inexpressible sperm, I washed my hands and my heart of it; I almost began to credit the old Paracelsan superstition that sperm is of rare virtue in allaying the heat of anger: while bathing in that bath, I felt divinely free from all ill-will, or petulance, or malice, of any sort whatsoever. Squeeze! squeeze! squeeze! all the morning long; I squeezed that sperm till I myself almost melted into it; I squeezed that sperm till a strange sort of insanity came over me; and I found myself unwittingly squeezing my co-laborers' hands in it, mistaking their hands for the gentle globules. Such an abounding, affectionate, friendly, loving feeling did this avocation beget; that at last I was continually squeezing their hands, and looking up into their eyes sentimentally; as much as to say, – Oh! my dear fellow beings, why should we longer cherish any social acerbities, or know the slightest ill-humor or envy! Come; let us squeeze hands all round; nay, let us all squeeze ourselves. (MD 416)

Squeezing one another's hands all around forms another ring, another concrete link to the sense of eternity that Pip embodies. The materiality of the moment is important: their joyous, fleshy connection restores the bond that abandoning Pip had severed. Pip does not sing here but he makes this whole scene possible.

Edouard Glissant's musing about what links disparate members of the black diaspora is helpful for thinking about Pip's role. Glissant argues that strong communal bonds are forged through the experience and memory of shared affliction. Glissant writes: "For though this experience made you, original victim floating toward the sea's abysses, an exception, it became something shared and made us, the descendants, one people among others. People do not live on exception. Relation is not made up things that are foreign but of shared knowledge. This experience of the abyss can now be said to be the best element of exchange."[10] The exchange is complete in the spermaceti. Pip is visually absent but present in the moral imperative and necessity of the moment. The men embody ideal connections that, like the feeling of community in the ring shout, can be physically expressed but not verbally communicated. The squeezing "all around" represents rings of eternity, identified in Pip, that reveal the force of socio-moral amelioration.

If Pip's music can only be heard in the background of "A Squeeze of the Hand," it is very much in the foreground of "Queequeg in His Coffin." Here, Pip sits beside Queequeg, who lies in his coffin dying from illness. The magnitude of the coffin cannot be overstated; this is the coffin that turns into a lifebuoy for Ishmael at the novel's end. The meaning of *Moby-Dick* is focalized in this chapter, and Pip, yet again, is at the center. Pip takes Queequeg in one hand and his tambourine in the other. Black music, pulsating rhythm, and touch, come together and Pip finally speaks, his repetition at once intensifying and consecrating the moment. "Rig-a-dig, dig, dig!," Pip utters. Then, more loudly, he calls out, "Rig-a-dig, dig, dig! huzza!" (MD 419). "But ere this was done," adds Ishmael,

> Pip, who had been slyly hovering near by all this while, drew nigh to him where he lay, and with soft sobbings, took him by the hand; in the other, holding his tambourine . . . "Rig-a-dig, dig, dig! Now, Queequeg, die; and I'll beat ye your dying march." "I have heard," murmured Starbuck, gazing down . . . "that in violent fevers, men, all ignorance, have talked in ancient tongues . . . So, to my fond faith, poor Pip, in this strange sweetness of his lunacy, brings heavenly vouchers of all our heavenly homes." (MD 479–480)

With his scatting style and tambourine pulses, Pip elevates the mournful tone and imparts a sense of the divine. In the nineteenth century, enslaved

Africans and free blacks were known to beat drums and percussive instruments at funerals, singing and dancing in rhythmic movements that climaxed in heightened states. Vincent Brown explains that Africans used last rites to affirm value in the face of a culture that devalued them.[11] Here, at the threshold of earth and heaven, of life and death, Pip beats his tambourine like in a funeral worthy of a general. His music makes the moment sacred, creating holy meaning and a noble send off. Pip's physical and spiritual presence affirms the value of social belonging and the potential for eternal connections to assuage feelings of earthly disarray.

Melville's portrayal of Pip not only reveals just how enmeshed black culture is in *Moby-Dick*; it also reveals something about the character to which Pip is most directly linked, Captain Ahab. Near the closing chapters, both Ahab and Pip are bonded in their madness (Pip even imagines himself as Ahab's missing leg), yet they oppose one other in size, stature, race, and attitude. Notably, when Ahab and Pip appear together, Ishmael does not mention Pip's verbal syncopations or his relation to other crew members. Ahab does not want to be close with anyone in his cabin other than Pip. Pip is indeed special. Ahab says, "he sucks wondrous philosophies from" Pip (MD 529). Ahab continues: "some unknown conduits from unknown worlds must empty into thee." Yet while Ahab dwells in Pip's "unknown conduits," that very connection becomes a problem, since Pip might be able to cure Ahab's spiritual affliction. Their social bond provides Ahab with the companionship he otherwise rejects, a companionship that draws his attention away from the white whale that consumes his every waking (and sleeping) thought.

About Pip, Ahab says, "there is that in thee . . . which I feel too curing to my malady" (MD 534). Ahab acts on his intuition and shortly afterward tells Pip: "And now, I quit thee. Thy hand!" The abrupt withdrawal of Ahab's hand severs his relationship with Pip, echoing the violent dissolution of the ring shout in "Forecastle – Midnight," and enables Ahab to turn back to the white whale. Scholars tend to see Starbuck as the novel's character of possible yet failed salvation – it is Starbuck, after all, who contemplates pulling a gun on Ahab and, in "The Symphony," elicits Ahab's final moment of humanity. Yet the development of Ahab's madness and its fateful consequences are just as bound up with his relationship with Pip. Through Pip, Ahab sits on the edge of changing the way he relates to himself and others. It is when he finally breaks away from Pip that the *Pequod*'s fate is sealed. The entire voyage of the novel is at stake in Ahab's relationship with Pip.

When Ahab abandons Pip, we are reminded of Pip's mad scatting in his absence: "Pip! Pip! Ding, dong, ding! Who's seen Pip?" (MD 535). Melville hints that when Pip communicated with Ahab, he did so through the same rhythmic shouts and expressions that he uses throughout the rest of novel. When Ahab withdraws from Pip, he leaves behind the possibility of social life, the incarnation of social bonds, and the musical expression of eternity, as well as the potential to alleviate Pip's sense of exclusion. Ahab reneged on their bond, leaving Pip alone with his sonic semblance. We know how the novel ends for both of them, and that end is made possible by Ahab's abandonment of Pip and everything he represents.

Black Objects

It is no accident Pip that is defined by rings of men in anguish. The ring materialized eternity, a wrestling with life, death, the pleasures of God's beneficence, and the anguish of God's indifference. Pip is enacting and calling upon the tradition of enslaved Africans, free blacks, festival dancers, and church worshipers who communed in circular movement with various strategies of revelation and conversion. If the evil that flows through *Moby-Dick* is marked by vengeance, greed, and domination, Pip's voice and presence represent an alternative, maybe even an antidote. For Melville, black cultural expression, exemplified by Pip, offers an occasion to think about one's choices and the consequences of those choices.

Critics still tend to see Pip as an anti-social character. Most recently, Donald Pease reads Pip as figure of social death because after Pip nearly drowns he can no longer cogently speak. Pease contends, Pip's "drowning involved his becoming flooded by too much to be processed as speech." Pease continues, "Pip, who has been part of the crew up to this point, now feels himself so completely cut off from the crew that his alienation has assumed the status of the social death productive of the slave."[12] It is true of that in terms of normative speech, Pip's tragic incident cuts him off from his crew. He can certainly be called socially dead in this register. Pip possesses no eloquence, nor does he deliver commanding speeches like Ahab; he is discursively inarticulate, and almost entirely incoherent.

But Pip is a social, moral, and spiritual vessel that encourages the crew and readers to recommit to a life lived for others. In the novel, black culture represents moral and spiritual elevation in ways that differ from how most scholars understand the social force of black performance and expression. If Frederick Douglass, the gifted orator and writer, symbolizes the strident black political performer, Pip is quite the opposite. Pip does not manipulate older scripts or re-objectify himself to become a subject. Nor does he achieve self-mastery.

Pip's absence of voice is telling. Pip makes manifest black cultural tropes based on race. Slave narratives, from Harriet Jacob's to William Wells Brown's, produced the most erudite interlocutors, whereas nineteenth-century black performers tended to improvise and signify against racist ideas. One can look at Pip, whose performances are almost always improvisational, as a figure most critics in black studies would call an object. Even if Pip bears the residue of one of slavery's objects, Fred Moten contends that objects resist through the "complexity of their interiority."[13] Pip is Melville's object (like all the characters) but he bears a special shallow burden because we can know nothing of his interiority other than its sublime beauty. Yet that is precisely the point, one that has often been lost in Melville studies as well as black studies. Pip's relation to other characters houses the highest moral and spiritual affirmation the novel offers, but his interiority comes through only in the impressions he makes upon others. Melville confronts the reader with Pip's sense of tragic loss while Pip chases after the self he appeared to lose. Despite this lost self, Pip, endowed with a heavenly but unknown interiority, nourishes life itself and seizes the meaning of loyal companionship that Melville champions.

No doubt, Pip is paradoxical and vexed – though in refreshing ways. As a figure of black culture, song, and performance, Pip presents the reader with an opportunity to confront the meaning of spiritual brotherhood in the face of violence and death. These tropes are indeed romantic, but no less inspiring and fulfilling. Pip's participation in the ring shout and in makeshift funerals contributes to Melville's layered symbolism and reinforces Stuckey's claim that Melville was shaped by black culture. Placing Pip at the center allows us to realize that black culture is lodged in the very heart of the novel, animating its entire moral philosophy. Melville's blackess, of course, is quite different from anti-racist or abolitionist counter-discourse. Pip is blackness without agency or voice, yet he provides a forceful way to reenvision what it means to be black, radical, and American in art. His presence constitutes the greatest value of the novel; he is a symbol of social equality and a catalyst for altruistic insight. Through Pip, Melville creates an embodied blackness that asks: what type of life is worth living – or, for that matter, worth dying – for?

CHAPTER 5

Melville after Secularism

Brian Yothers

Herman Melville's Bible is its own sort of revelation. Markings, annotations, erasures, even excisions show the pages of Melville's personal copy of *The New Testament and the Book of Psalms* to be a curious sort of intellectual battleground, in which Melville wrestled for decades with a text he found both compelling and unsettling.[1] Melville could be unabashedly antagonistic in his relationship to the Christian scriptures, as when he carefully crossed out the very verses in the Book of Revelation that condemned those who failed to preserve "the words of this book of prophecy." Meanwhile he could attend carefully to the ethical precepts of the Sermon on the Mount with a precision that seems to suggest that his narrator's praise for that passage in *Pierre* might accord with Melville's own views. He could also reveal that he was an attentive reader of historical criticism of the Bible, one of the great secularizing influences in the intellectual sphere during the nineteenth century, as when he noted Paul's appropriation of pre-Christian philosophers in the Acts of the Apostles and the epistle to Titus. He could suggest that the Jesus of the Gospels is a compelling literary figure whose use of irony contributes to the richness of his character, as when he glossed Jesus' admonition to the disciples to "sleep on, and take your rest," with the laconic remark, "This is ironical." Centrally, what Melville's Bibles reveal about him is that he valued both the secular society that resists religious dogmatism and the transcendent yearnings that undergird religious belief.[2] To read Melville "after secularism," is to consider him as at once utterly secular in his suspicion of the coercive power of religion and deeply religious in his valuation of the interpersonal ties and transcendent aspirations that religious belief enables. Reading Melville in this way enables us to reach a richer understanding of our own moment, which may seem well after secularism even as the project of secular democracy seems tenuous.

Melville's ambivalent annotations to the Bible and his increasingly complex treatment of religious belief and secular society over the later portions of his career can serve as a key to what secularism meant and did not mean to Melville in the nineteenth century, and to what an approach to Melville's political theology – one that is both shaped by Melville's own impulses toward the secular and his own impulses toward older modes of religious discipline and community – might look like in the twenty-first century. When we consider how secular and post-secular approaches might shape, and indeed alter, our present understanding of Melville, we must consider how Melville himself was an author in a complex dialogue with the secular and the sacred throughout his career. This essay, then, considers not just how critical approaches might function after secularism – in a moment that is sometimes described as post-secular – but also how Melville has always been a writer whose work probes the possibilities and the limits of the secular.[3] It is easy for readers who are suspicious of secularism to construct a Melville who resists secularism; it is likewise easy for readers who are suspicious of religious orthodoxy to see Melville as an early prophet of an emerging secular age. New approaches to the question of Melville in relation to the religious and the secular must contend with the degree to which both of these aspects are intertwined in his work.

To understand Melville's biblical marginalia, his journal and letters, and his published fiction and poetry, we should dispense with twenty-first century assumptions about the privacy of religious belief. Melville's writing about religion and how religious belief was being altered in his increasingly secular era was in one sense deeply personal: the marginalia appear in his own books, the journals were not published during his lifetime, the letters are sent to his closest friends, and in his fiction and poetry he buries any sort of manifesto on the meaning of religious faith and doubt in layers of narrative framing and irony. For a thoughtful person living in the nineteenth century, however, the weight of responsibility associated with religious choices was perhaps heavier than for even the most conflicted of souls in our own century. Melville frames this responsibility in a way that shows the interpenetration of the secular and religious in his approach to moral questions:

> Yet though all this be so, nevertheless, in our own hearts, we mold the whole world's hereafters; and in our own hearts we fashion our own gods. Each mortal casts his vote for whom he will to rule the worlds; I have a voice that helps to shape eternity; and my volitions stir the orbits of the furthest suns. In two senses, we are precisely what we worship. Ourselves are Fate. (WJ 320–1)

The concept of a deity who is voted upon is saturated in assumptions that are at once highly religious and profoundly secular. In this brief phrase, Melville nods toward both the sovereign deity of Calvinist theology, presiding over the cosmos as an absolute monarch bound by neither time nor space, and the deity as candidate for high office in a democracy in which election is the matter of human, rather than divine, choice. The ruler of the world, understood in the Calvinist terms that Melville inherited from his mother's Dutch Reformed faith, is beholden to no one, and makes choices regarding eternal salvation and damnation according to his own sovereign will. The recipient of a vote, by contrast, must submit to the choices of others, and derives standing from the verdict of the sovereign people. The fact that we have our own "vote" provided by secularism does not necessarily mean that we will choose a secular world. Melville's own lifetime predated the rise of religious fundamentalism in its various forms, but based on this passage, we can safely doubt that it would have come as an utter surprise to him. This capacity to "antedate" unsettling developments is something that Melville attributes to literature itself in one of Melville's most telling poems from *Battle-Pieces*, "The Coming Storm." In this brief poem he reflects on the tragic case of Edwin Booth, the famous Shakespearean actor and Union supporter who was brother to Lincoln's assassin, John Willkes Booth, that "no utter surprise can come to him/ Who reaches Shakespeare's core./ That which we seek and shun is there,/ Man's final lore" (PP 106). Melville's journey into the interpenetrating relationship between the religious and the secular sheds considerable light on that which we seek and that which we shun. Melville's capacity to "antedate" means that when we explore his work in the post-secular framework suggested by Charles Taylor and others, we are still struggling to bring the newness of our readings up to date with the prescience of his insights.

After Secularism in the South Pacific

Melville's evolving treatment of the secular begins with an invocation of the liberating power of skepticism in his first published book, *Typee.* Melville was an advocate for religious diversity and a critic of religious certainties right from the start of his career as a writer, and indeed, he was already beginning to probe in *Typee* what the end of a broad Protestant consensus in American society might mean. His secularism is that of a pluralistic society, one that sheds its own idols even as it refuses to sack the temples of its rivals. Early in *Typee,* Melville offers a critique of the missionaries who are attempting to win converts to Protestant Christianity in the Marquesas, and he concludes the novel with a blistering critique of Protestant missionaries in Hawaii, a move that parallels his later anti-missionary satire in *Omoo*. Meanwhile, Melville presents indigenous Marquesan and Tahitian cultures as alternatives to American capitalism and Christianity. Rejecting the missionary imperative means that Melville embraces a this-worldly measure for evaluating religion: he is less concerned with the question of whether the eternal souls of Pacific islanders are saved or damned than with the concrete results of religious belief, stability, and happiness in this life. Most memorably, he praises Marquesan society for the absence of "those thousand sources of irritation that the ingenuity of civilized man has created to mar his own felicity," borrowing biblical language to reproach North American civilization for its devotion to money, and to praise the Marqesans for the absence of money as a source of conflict (TY 126). In this, Melville suggests the treatment of religious belief in Benjamin Franklin's *Autobiography*, where religious dogma is subordinated to moral virtue.[4]

Even as Melville points clearly toward a this-worldly secular response to religious dogma, he finds religiously framed moral judgments to be useful in *Typee*, as when he parodies and denounces missionaries by contrasting their behavior with the moral demands of the Sermon on the Mount. A missionary woman, for example, is said to be "not sufficiently evangelized" (TY 7) in *Typee* when she fails to forgive islanders who have humiliated her. *Typee* both affirms basic ethical principles from the Sermon on the Mount and suggests that there is no obvious connection between these principles and orthodox Christianity. This suggestion is reaffirmed in *Omoo*, where Melville satirizes the implication of missionaries in specific nationalist agendas when a British missionary delivers a sermon denouncing the French. In *Mardi*, Melville explores the implications of this tension between ethics and dogmatism in more depth, as his allegorical archipelago is shaped by a reverence for Jesus' ethics that is combined with skepticism toward religious institutions through the philosophical ruminations of Babbalanja.

After Secularism in *Moby-Dick*

A memorable set piece early in *Moby-Dick* consists of a skeptical reaction to a sermon – and a sermon that is, in its own terms, quite compelling. Father Mapple delivers a sermon that, like the "vote" for the world's ruler suggested in *White-Jacket*, offers a curious amalgam of theocracy and secular democracy. Father Mapple calls for an absolute submission to the Christian deity, but he frames his story within the context of working-class seafaring culture, imagining Jonah as a stowaway, and voicing a bitter critique of the privileges of wealth. Ultimately, his prophetic voice is at its fiercest when he calls for "senators and judges" (MD 48) to be exposed for their hypocrisy. The most salient crime in Father Mapple's sermon is not blasphemy against a vengeful deity but a secular sin against democratic values. Father Mapple's eloquence has little effect on the one non-Christian member of his congregation, however: Queequeg wanders out of the Whaleman's Chapel well before Mapple's peroration.

The most famous instance of Ishmael's religiously infused secularism in *Moby-Dick* is, of course, his decision to worship Yojo with Queequeg. As is evident to every reader of *Moby-Dick* who has even a passing familiarity with the Hebrew and Christian scriptures, Ishmael's choice to commit idolatry is a decision to violate a central command in both the Old and New Testaments. Ishmael shows that this violation of an absolutely essential element of doctrinal orthodoxy can be justified in religious terms through recourse to Jesus' command to "do unto others" as one would wish to be done by. Ishmael thus reasons his way to a wholly secular conclusion – that the proscription of idolatry can be voided in the service of temporal human relationships – through a religious mode of reasoning, even as Father Mapple and the narrator of *White-Jacket* can make secular democracy and theological absolutism mutually illuminating.[5]

Similar complexity appears in the sexual improprieties of "The Cassock," in which Melville includes recondite biblical references to Canaanite phallus-worship alongside a jocular account of the size of the whale's penis and the uses of its skin. "The Cassock" provides a fine example of the way in which Melville balances wickedness and religious reflection: it feels sacrilegious, but it achieves its sacrilege in a manner that requires substantial biblical literacy on the part of both author and reader. It is highly secular and profoundly religious at once in the sense that it operates in a context in which one can arguably blaspheme without civic consequences, but in which complex allusions to sacred texts can inform even a fairly crude joke.

When Ishmael floats on his coffin at the conclusion of *Moby-Dick*, he is a religious orphan on a secular sea – or a secular orphan borne up by a sea of faith. Everything about the scene is biblically infused: the sharks that decline to attack him are reminiscent of the lions who spare Daniel, the *Rachel* calls to mind the slaughter of the innocents by King Herod, and, as countless critics have pointed out, Ishmael's three days lost at sea correspond to Jesus' time in the tomb before his resurrection. The scene is saturated with the Christian mythos, but events themselves are fully explainable in quotidian terms. The secular and sacred here meet and intermingle on the open sea.

After Secularism in North America

If *Moby-Dick* constitutes a climax of sorts for Melville's acknowledgment of the liberating qualities of the secular, his next move is to dive more deeply into questions of ethical responsibility. In *Pierre*, he weighs Plotinus Plinlimmon's humane secularism against the absolutism of the Sermon on the Mount, and finds neither to be entirely satisfactory. If the Sermon on the Mount seems unworkable, Plinlimmon dodges the fundamental questions that it raises more than he answers them, and his advice and influence cannot save the title character from catastrophe. In *Israel Potter, The Piazza Tales*, and his other magazine fiction of the 1850s, Melville tests the boundaries between moral convictions conventionally associated with religion and the practical requirements of life in a capitalist nineteenth-century society and finds no decisive resolution to their competing claims. In *The Confidence-Man*, he plays with the boundaries between faith and fiction, a poignant move in a novel dedicated to "the victims of auto da fe." By the time Melville published *Battle-Pieces* in 1866, he was fully capable of writing poetry immersed in biblical language and allusion that reflected self-consciously on the declining power of this language to compel assent. The very fact that biblical exegesis from the perspective of a shared Protestantism could not even lead northern and southern white Christians to agree in condemning slavery, a system that Melville described in the Supplement to *Battle-Pieces* as an "atheistical iniquity" (PP 185), meant that the ethical authority of the Hebrew and Christian scriptures did not resolve fundamental questions, but amplified disputes.

That scriptural authority could no longer compel consensus finds parallels in Pierre's declining belief in his own father's moral virtue, and in his declining confidence in the institutions of Christianity. Pierre's crisis of faith means that he is able to consider options that fall outside the usual range of religious possibilities for a young Protestant, and in this he mirrors the expanded array of religious possibilities that an increasingly secular nation afforded.

Pieces from Melville's magazine years as different from each other as *Israel Potter*, "The Piazza," "Bartleby, the Scrivener," and "The Paradise of Bachelors and the Tartarus of Maids" continued this narrative of secularization. The narrator of "Bartleby" finds that the Sermon on the Mount is inconsistent with the values of Wall Street, and while he appears to prefer Christ to Mammon, he nonetheless is incapable of loving Bartleby as himself in a way that Bartleby will accept. Israel Potter, upon reading Benjamin Franklin's *Poor Richard's Almanac* concludes that "Poor Richard ain't a Dunker" (IP 154), a rich remark given both its acknowledgment of Franklin's distance from the unworldliness of the Dunkers, and its implicit reminder that Franklin himself admired the Dunkers for their openness to new forms of truth as a result of their non-creedal religious structure.[6] The narrator of "The Piazza" reflects ruefully on "fading faith and failing knees" in a secularizing society (PZ 2). In "The Encantadas," Melville provides a picture of the Galapagos Islands, intimately connected in history with Charles Darwin's discoveries and their secularizing effects, in which God is absent but moral urgency persists. "The Paradise of Bachelors and The Tartarus of Maids," "Rich Man's Crumbs and Poor Man's Pudding," and "Cock-a-Doodle-Doo," all interrogate wealth and poverty relative to biblical injunctions to love one's neighbor.

The Confidence-Man is remarkable in its acknowledgment of what Charles Taylor called the "nova effect" – the proliferation of varieties of religious belief and experience, not just in opposition to secularism, but as a predictable outcome of the rise of the secular.[7] Early on, Melville provides a taxonomy of "that multiform pilgrim species, man" (CM 9) that includes Americans from a rich array of religious traditions on board a Mississippi steamer named the *Fidele*. As the novel progresses, Melville shows the emergence of alternatives to traditional religious observance in a variety of heterodox communities, from New England Transcendentalism to frontier utopian communities. Melville's shows, in his final full-length novel, that the secular and the religious – skepticism and confidence, to put it another way – remain fluid categories.

Battle-Pieces continues Melville's development as a complexly secular thinker. Repeatedly, Melville finds ways of connecting the events of the American Civil War with events from the Hebrew Bible and John Milton's adaptation of these narratives in *Paradise Lost*. As Cody Marrs has shown, Melville's deft use of these references is suggestive of a circular view of history.[8] It is also suggestive of Melville's developing sense of the interdependence of the secular and the religious and how this interdependence can be both empowering and threatening for religious diversity, and religious diversity in its turn adds urgency to emerging secular trajectories. In "The Battle for the Mississippi," Melville claims that "God appears in apt events" (PP 47). Melville balances the victorious Mosaic refrain from Exodus 15:13, "The Lord is a man of war," with concrete, this-worldly details about naval warfare and thus heightens the tension between secular and providential readings of the war. The poem concludes on a note that points to the uneasy truce between secular and more conventionally religious readings of the war: "There must be other, nobler worlds for them/ Who nobly yield their lives in this" (PP 48). The "nobler worlds" imply a Christian heaven, but stop well short of orthodox certainty.

After Secularism in the Holy Land

By 1876, Melville's Holy Land poem *Clarel* showed that his developing conclusions from 1851 and 1866 had become still more complex and uncertain. Melville's 1856–1857 journal from his travels in Europe and the Holy Land show his consciousness of the contradictions between spiritual and psychological interpretations of religious phenomena, as when he attributes the Hebrew conception of God to the physical dimensions of the Egyptian pyramids, or when he deflates the religious pretensions of Jerusalem with mundane references to coffee. Growing out of this experience, *Clarel* is a poem that persistently presses the boundaries between the secular and religious.[9] Most characters are doubters, and most characters are suspicious of their own doubts, some so much so that they revert to an intensified version of their earlier faith, and others more moderately so, maintaining tenuous balances between the secular background against which they view the world and religious impulses that threaten to redefine that background.

Melville was fully aware that fundamentalism (the phenomenon, if not the term) could loom on the other side of profound doubt, and that extreme religious controversy could paradoxically resolve itself into the destruction of religious belief. Nathan, the Jewish convert from Christianity who becomes an Arab-hating settler in Palestine, is the sort of figure who can only arise against a backdrop in which secular tolerance of religious pluralism and sectarian religious fervor coexist. He begins as a Calvinist, understanding the world as the province of a sovereign deity, loses that faith to a secular deist understanding of the world, and then investigates the Mormon faith as a new absolutist religious alternative. He dismisses the Mormon faith based on his continuing adherence, in practice, if not in theory, to broadly Protestant norms, and he then marries a Jewish woman, Agar, and takes her faith as his own with a convert's fervor. Nathan's fanaticism, which ultimately not only costs him his own life, but also leads to his wife's and daughter's untimely deaths, is representative of one possibility after secularism: the rebel shades into the extremist enforcer of religious dogma, and the structures provided by religious institutions no longer hold his nascent fanaticism in check.

The same paradox plays out in an opposite direction with the Elder, whose delight in religious controversy is such that he ultimately loses his Calvinist faith to his own polemics against Catholicism, and with Mortmain, whose disillusionment as a young, secular revolutionary leads him to embrace a religious suspicion of human goodness without a tempering sense of human connection. With the impassioned evangelical missionary Nehemiah, a reaction against his initial loss of faith carries him, like Nathan, into extreme forms of religious observance, and he confronts Clarel with an embodiment of the conflicted yet interdependent relationship between the religious and the secular. Nehemiah's saintly devotion to his own faith challenges Clarel, even as his evident folly leads adherents of Islam in Jerusalem to regard him as a holy fool, whose tracts aimed at converting Jews and Muslims ends up being food for camels.

Rolfe, Vine, and Derwent, in one way or another, offer a third approach to the dialectic between the religious and the secular. Each of these three figures, in his own way, walks a fine line between the possibility of an utterly secular existence and the possibility of absorption into religious orthodoxy, and each negotiates this dichotomy in a different manner. Vine approaches the question in aesthetic terms, maintaining an ironic distance from the affective side of faith and doubt. Rolfe, often read as the nearest counterpart to Melville himself, shares the impulse toward irony, but tempers the irony with a touching earnestness. Derwent has often been dismissed as a satirical target, yet his religious liberalism offers a genuine alternative to Rolfe's and Vine's detached position, one which retains the benefits of religious institutions while declining to submit to untenable orthodoxies.

Melville considers one other alternative to the tension between religious community and secular individualism: the possibility than an older, more authentic, religious tradition could offer an alternative to a secularized Protestantism. Melville entertains this possibility through figures like the Dominican and Ungar (Roman Catholic), the Syrian Monk (Eastern Orthodox Christian), Abdon (Jewish), Djalea (Druze), and Belex (Muslim), and he gestures toward Hinduism and Buddhism as well during Clarel's vision of global pilgrimage, but ultimately he suggests that each of these traditions has their own secularizing trajectory and their own repressive qualities. Conversion ultimately provides no alternative to the necessary task of defining the contours of a secular world. If, for the early Melville, secularism and pluralism figure as varieties of spiritual liberation, by the 1870s they carry the weight of profound intellectual and ethical responsibility. Melville in 1876 is alive to the ways in which pluralism – Taylor's nova effect – can evoke danger as well as exaltation. As Melville's second major published poem, *Clarel* also helps to illustrate what poetry provided Melville in his evolving treatment of the religious and secular: a form in which apparent contraries could be balanced using compression and controlled irony.

After Secularism in *Billy Budd* and the Late Poetry

The earliest responses to *Billy Budd*, the novella that Melville left in manuscript form, tantalizingly close to completion, suggest that Melville had arrived at a kind of resolution to his life-long interrogation of the meaning of secularism for American society and for the moral and spiritual quests of nineteenth-century individuals. E. L. Grant Watson defined *Billy Budd* as a "testament of acceptance" in the 1930s, and Phil Withim and Joseph Schiffman responded by defining it, respectively, as a "testament of resistance" and a "testament of irony" in the 1950s, with Lawrance Thompson presenting an acerbic amalgam of defiantly secular irony and resistance as the real meaning of *Billy Budd*.[10] The novella's treatment of religion and the secular may be better understood as part of a final development of Melville's complex understanding of the interpenetration of religion and secularity. *Billy Budd* compresses, to a remarkable degree, a series of biblical allusions from the creation story and Abraham's near-sacrifice of Isaac in Genesis to the crucifixion of Christ, and it does so in a way that acknowledges the power of the biblical narrative even as it resituates it within the time of modern secular governance, when mortals facing fraught decisions cannot assume a knowledge of the mind of God. Captain Vere gains mythic significance through his association with Abraham, even as he takes the decision to execute Billy out of timeless theological debates over divine justice and resituates it within the context of contemporary law. The complex reaction that Vere's judgment and his rationale for that judgment have elicited from critics points to Melville's ambivalence regarding the relationship between the religious and the secular: Vere may be right in bracketing out ultimate questions from his judgment, but something is still lost when he does so. Thus Vere's admonition to the drum-head court that although Billy may be "innocent before God," the court's duty is "to the King" dramatizes powerfully the contingencies of secular justice and what is lost when ultimate questions must be suspended (BB 110).

Melville's final volumes of poetry shed some light on the quandaries posed by *Billy Budd*, as numerous critics have recognized.[11] "Shelley's Vision," from *Timoleon*, is an especially profound statement of secularism's religious potential. The poem tracks the emergence of the spiritual consciousness of a man, the Romantic poet Percy Bysshe Shelley, whose lack of traditional religious belief is required for "self-reverence" to "awake." At the same time, Shelley's awakening to "self-reverence" emerges by way of a religious metaphor: assaulted by religious censors whose "Hate" "pelted" him with metaphorical stones, he casts a stone at his own shadow and sees it transformed into the image of St. Stephen, the first Christian martyr (PP 283). Shelley's vision enables his acceptance of his own unbelief by placing it in the context of Christian redemption, thus making a case for the secular in terms taken from the sacred, and his status as a poet means that he is well placed to articulate the fraught relationship between secular substance and sacred language.

Melville's unpublished verse in *Weeds and Wildings, With a Rose or Two*, is especially suggestive in its treatment of secularism, given that it takes as its model Edward Fitzgerald's free translation of the *Rubaiyat of Omar Khayyam*, a text that employs the voice of a skeptical Muslim and offers both religious diversity and secularism. The rose poems show that Melville had confirmed his earlier suspicions in *Clarel* that the interdependence of the religious and the secular is utterly ecumenical, as he presents his readers with urbanely secular speakers who partake of both Islam and Catholicism in their use of imagery. Most notably, the poem "Rosary Beads" makes use of a devotional tool used in both Catholic and Muslim devotions, in order to reflect on actual, physical roses. He complicates matters still further when he uses the language of Protestant revivalism in the lines "Adore the Roses; nor delay / Until the Rose-fane fall / Or ever their censers cease to sway: / Today the rose-priests call."[12] Islam, Catholicism, and Protestantism all come together in Melville's late poetry in illustrating his reverence for beauty.

Melville's engagement with religious questions, so often undertaken with a note of skepticism, complicates any easy drawing of boundaries between the secular and religious. Melville was not, even at the end of his career, a religious conservative seeking to turn back the movement toward secular standards of meaning and value in American culture. He was also not, even at his most irreverent in the earlier portion of his career, a thinker who imagined that religion was drifting toward a preordained obsolescence that would entail no necessary loss. Rather, he consistently considered how mythic narratives and ethical codes derived from religious sources could be recombined and transformed in an increasingly pluralistic, secular cultural context, providing sources of meaning that were deepened, not obliterated, by fearless intellectual inquiry. Early scholars of Melville who saw him as a youthful rebel who was ultimately reconciled to the Christian deity through the final "testament" of *Billy Budd* were overly hasty in drawing this conclusion, but they were right to note that Melville's religious and secular identities were fluid over the course of his career. Perhaps the greatest resonance that readers from our own times can find in Melville's treatment of secularism and religious belief is his clear-eyed acknowledgment that spiritual quests, whether enabled by secularism or in revolt against it, often do not have happy resolutions.

Perhaps nothing captures Melville after secularism more elegantly than his late engagement with Buddhism. In the poem "Buddha," from *Timoleon*, Melville draws a direct parallel between Christian doctrine and Buddhist philosophy, with Melville's reading of Arthur Schopenhauer on Buddhism hovering in the background. "Buddha" begins with an epigraph from the Epistle of James 4.14, "For what is your life? It is even a vapor that appeareth for a little time and then vanisheth away," and the substance of the poem, broadly a statement of the Buddhist doctrine of nirvana, echoes the biblical passage's emphasis on evanescence:

> Swooning swim to less and less,
> Aspirant to nothingness!
> Sobs of the worlds, and dole of kinds
> That dumb endurers be–
> Nirvana! absorb us in your skies,
> Annul us into thee. (PP 281)

The poem is among Melville's most compressed works, but he spells out what may be the reasoning behind his juxtaposition of James with the Buddha in "Rammon: A Fragment," where he suggests parallels between the wisdom of Solomon and Buddhist ideas imported by the Queen of Sheba. For the Rammon of Melville's title, a younger son of Solomon, both the insights of his father and those of the Buddha point in a direction that we would readily recognize as secular, in that he embraces the "cessation of being" as the crucial idea that draws him to Buddhism, and his father's own wisdom leads him to the secular in leading him to contact with Buddhism:

> Solomon a very lax Hebrew did not altogether repel foreign ideas. It was in his time that reports of Buddha and Buddhistic belief had, along with the recorded spices and pearls, been conveyed into Palestine by that learned Indian dame, not less communicative than inquisitive, the Princess of Sheba[.] Through her it was that the doctrine of the transmigration of souls . . . came to flourish among a people whose theocratic lawgiver was silent as to any life to come.[13]

Melville's secularism here, as is so often the case, is leavened by an exploration of religious difference. Solomon's laxity – his status as a secular presence in a central religious text – leads him to open the door for a richer array of religious possibilities than were previously available for the Israelite people. The movement, then, from rigor to laxity within one religious tradition, offers the opportunity for an increased interpenetration with another tradition, and this interpenetration suggests that the synthesis of these traditions need not, in itself, fall outside of the everyday secular world. Moreover, the concluding sentence suggests that the most supernatural of Christian doctrines, the resurrection, could owe its existence to secular trade.

For Melville, writing after secularism meant writing in a world ineluctably changed by the secular, in ways that could be both exhilarating and discomforting. He tracked the ways in which an emerging secular world foreclosed old sources of consolation and opened up new ones, and he saw both the possibilities and the dangers posed by the emerging religious configurations that were enabled by secularism and in some cases reacted against it. He knew, as we must, that the secular is by definition embedded in time. As such, it carries within itself the meaning that, to paraphrase the concluding words of *The Confidence-Man*, "something further" may always follow (CM 251).

CHAPTER 6

Marginal States: Herman Melville in the Marquesas, 1842

Edward Sugden

The Border Zone

Borders are hard to cross. Within the border zone, humans and their worlds run against barriers that are both physical and cultural. Some buckle within the zone, crushed and transformed by the pressure, while others emerge diminished. To enter a border zone is to change on privative terms: less through the free and permeable interplay of different social formations than through collisions with recalcitrant, almost unyielding, points of blockage, erasure, and duress. Herman Melville learnt these lessons from bitter experience, for he chose to place them front and center in his first published book, *Typee* (1846).

In 1842, he (or his narrative surrogate Tommo) and bosom pal Toby decided to abandon ship upon their arrival in the Marquesas Islands. After months at sea, they were both disenchanted by the ship's grim exploitative materiality and the relentless, repetitive monotony of life at sea. These circumstances had all but totally deflated the romantic fantasies that impelled them to ship in the first place. Yet the Marquesas Islands offered them a glimpse of a different world, a catalyst that quickened, once more, their almost disregarded youthful dreams of exploration. "I felt as if floating in some new element" (TY 28), reflected Tommo, upon bathing in the waters of the islands, and, with similar hopes of reinvention upon contact with this still mostly unknown Pacific world, Toby and Tommo headed to land with no intention of returning to their ship. Upon arriving, they quickly realized that they would have to cross over the mountains to escape the attentions of the locals who might try to return them to their loathed whaling ship. This journey was to take them from the port of Nukuheva, where their vessel was harbored, across an extended and contested border zone, and into either the territories of the seemingly peaceable Happars or else the feared and ferocious Typees. With these thoughts in mind they started climbing the mountains, and so their border crossing began . . .

The world within this border zone could not be more indifferent or resistant to their presence. This is a place not of cultural intermixing but rather one in which motion was always slowed or forestalled. While in it, Tommo and Toby collide with obstacle after obstacle, obstruction after obstruction, never seeming to get any closer to their destination in spite of their agonized motion. As they do so, they experience all manner of privations, from hunger to thirst and physical debility. They come against a thick, almost immovable "mass of tall yellow reeds," and find themselves "stopped" when trying to get through them, for they are "as tough and stubborn as so many rods of steel" (TY 37). They have to cross an interminable number of deep gulches and ravines, each one steeper and more inhospitable than the last, and thus see "[n]othing but dark and fearful chasms, separated by sharp-crested and perpendicular ridges as far as the eye could reach" (TY 53). There are waterfalls, raging rivers, torrential rains, rocky debris, cliff edges, and sheer falls, and they experience fever, insomnia, and the shivers on their way. As Tommo has it, "in our present situation it was in vain for us to think of ever overcoming the obstacles in our way, and I gave up all thoughts of reaching the vale which lay beyond this series of impediments" (TY 54). Even the local peoples in the lands below do not dare to enter this imposing region, leaving Tommo and Toby utterly isolated and sealed off from culture, confronting only nature in its most indifferent, overwhelming form. If all this seems excessive, that is because it is: at every step of the way, the obstacles repeat and enlarge, making progress towards their still unknown destination seem ever more impossible for the weary travellers.

Keeping Toby and Tommo's experience in mind, this essay proposes to use it as a starting point for rethinking transnational theorizations of the border zone in the nineteenth century. For many critics, the border is a place of permeable interchange between different cultures, a region of mixing in which once separate traditions and peoples come together and merge. And it certainly is that in some of its iterations. However, what the start of *Typee* suggests is that this conception of the border is incomplete and elides more problematic and resistant formations in which these sorts of interchanges are patently disallowed. After surveying contemporary renderings of the border, the essay will use *Typee* to propose an alternative configuration for the border: the marginal state. The marginal state, as we will see, is an extreme version of a border, insofar as it marks the point between the edge of the world-system and an area as yet unincorporated into it; which is to say, a space between two qualitatively different trajectories of historical development at a moment in time when they are coming into collision. I suggest that *Typee* generally, and the above experience of curtailed crossing in particular, offers a paradigmatic example of a marginal state of this sort, as Pacific cultures come into contact with the emergent, capitalistic imperial world in the region. Charting the marginal state not only alters our understanding of transnational discourse in the nineteenth century and now, but also reframes Herman Melville from being a transnational writer *par excellence* to someone who is more invested in the ambivalences of the border and the globe.

Transnational Borders

After all, Melville's version of the border in *Typee* is difficult to reconcile with those proposed by theorists of transnationalism and scholars of the nineteenth-century Americas. In spite of their many differences, transnational theorists such as Gloria Anzaldúa, Michael Hardt and Antonio Negri, Arjan Appadurai, Gilles Deleuze and Felix Guattari, Paul Gilroy, Mary Louis Pratt, Homi Bhabha, and others, have all envisaged the border zone to be a place of cultural permeability and dynamic exchange. For them, the border is a place where the essentialisms of national traditions, racial formations, and other cultural monads break apart through organic and unpredictable interaction: languages become polyglot, identity becomes hybrid, histories become plural. The boundaries that separate here from there dissolve in the border zone as different cultures freely interact, mingle, and fuse with one another. Insofar as there is constraint in the border zone, it comes from the outside, from the half-remembered shibboleths of nation, state, race, and gender. These formations nonetheless break apart in these spaces of exchange. And out of these exchanges, new non-national collectivities are born that tear apart the power structures of the nation in a newly egalitarian polis predicated on mutually recognized but non-hierarchical difference.[1]

The transnational turn in nineteenth-century American literary studies (a turn which ran for about a decade from the early 2000s onwards and which continues insofar as its precepts have been almost totally internalized by the field), drew extensively on these theorists and their models for culture. Whether interested in the transatlantic, hemispheric, trans-Pacific, planetary, or world traditions, this turn proposed a similarly permeable model for borders in nineteenth-century America in order to track the ways in which different nations, traditions, and peoples traversed the globe. On this basis, they created what we might term "hyphenated cultures": Anglo-American, Spanish-American, Franco-American, right through to Polar-American. Borders functioned like the hyphen that brought together these diffuse traditions into a single syntactic unity. The US nation-state, insofar as it existed for these critics, was at most a conflicted and incoherent entity or, at its most ideological, a social fiction for manufacturing order that masked the structural ways in which culture always travels across borders. Within these interpretive frames, the ideal citizen was a mobile and nomadic cosmopolitan figure whose personality was a composite of these international strains and who actively sought to create culture out of transnational polyphony and to deconstruct settled identity categories. As Paul Giles phrased it, the interest of the field was in "the ways in which geographical consciousness enters subliminally into American cultural narratives, evoking tensions and crosscurrents that destabilize the reproduction of a self-authenticating literary subject."[2] The border in this set-up is an almost totally transparent membrane through which individuals and cultures move. Transnationalism was thus buoyed by a spirit of political utopianism as it sought to rescue political subjects and communities for whom national and racial difference ceased to matter, even when they had to deal with the excesses of nationalism and imperialism.[3]

Nineteenth-century America proved fertile historical ground for these studies. It was not until the end of the Civil War that the United States became much more than a loosely and casually federated collection of states. The effect of the Civil War's conclusion was to hypostatize a sense of the naturalness of the nation's "united-ness" in such a way that made the existence of, say, a Confederate States of America appear almost impossible. To speak of the American nation-state before this time is inevitably to invite some measure of anachronism, notwithstanding the various nationalisms that did circulate in the first half of the century. In this sense, the nineteenth-century United States was transnational by definition (though, perhaps, pre-national might be more accurate) and its borders accordingly fluid and contingent.[4]

Moreover, the historical and geographical proximity of the United States to the colonial world-system meant that it was still inevitably caught up in the web of power relations that had organized the continent up until the nineteenth century. Its own anti-colonial struggle only concluded in the late-eighteenth century and so it was inevitably imbricated in the sort of postcolonial pushes and pulls with the Atlantic world that normally define the relationship between recently independent societies and their old colonial rulers.[5] At the point of its independence through the first thirty years of the nineteenth century, it found itself surrounded by colonial cultures, whether the French-British empire to the north, the Russian empire to the west, the British and French empires in Caribbean, or the Portuguese and Spanish empires to the south. In this sense, the nineteenth-century United States might best be conceived as a proto-national formation within a colonial gestalt – a burgeoning, would-be nation whose borders only make sense within the context of a larger structure of international relations.[6]

Yet even with the downfall of the colonial system in the Americas (with the thirty years spanning from the Haitian Revolution of 1791 to Mexican independence in 1821 forming the outer parameters of this history), the USA remained transnational. The move from mercantile colonialism to free trade industrial capitalism liberalized the international markets and encouraged an era of global expansion, interaction, imbrication, and invention.[7] This new phase of capitalism exploded centrifugally and relentlessly transformed all that stood in its way into its own image: as Marx noted, capitalism at this juncture possessed a "feverish velocity" with "its constant flinging of capital and labor from one sphere of production into another and its newly created connections with the world market."[8] Accordingly, new spheres of production and technologies to support them emerged: most importantly for Melville, the American shipbuilding industry underwent a period of massive expansion. Faster and safer ships carried slave-produced cotton from the Eastern ports into Liverpool, whaling vessels brought back oil from the Pacific, and boats carried middle-class tourists and working-class and rural immigrants back and forth between Europe and the Americas.

Herman Melville was simultaneously a product and the foremost observer and theorist of this transnational world. He sailed on each of the aforementioned ocean routes that were catalyzed by the shift from colonial to capitalist rule. This disposition and autobiographical circumstance means he is something of an emblem for the critical turn towards the global. Uniquely among writers of the mid-nineteenth century, he occupied two of the major new roles that came into being in this era: the proto-industrialized, proto-globalized sailor and the dilettantish middle class traveller-tourist. In the former role, he saw the fringes of South America, journeyed into the whaling grounds of the Pacific, took in the Atlantic trade between the east coast of the United States and Liverpool, and, seemingly, went to places not strictly down on any maps at all. In the latter role, he travelled through the literary circles of London, soaked up the classical magnificence of Rome, and journeyed to the Middle East. From *Typee* through *Timoleon,* his literary work bears the impress of these labors and travels, roving across borders both spatial and temporal. This world catalyzed and transformed his intellect, his writing, and his politics into inclusive, permeable, and relativistic forms. Although this is an obvious point to make, we can say with almost total certainty that had Melville not gone to sea he would not have been a writer, or, at least, not the one that we know of today.

All of which is to say, not only was the nineteenth century a demonstrably interconnected era, but also, should it need a poster child, there would be no one better than Melville to fill that role. Which leads to the question: why, in his first extended piece of writing, does he focus on the utter intransigence of a border zone? In what is undoubtedly an international configuration, Melville does not think about exchange or permeability, the characteristics of the transnational version of the border, but about physical and mental degradation and geographical obstruction. This dissonance implies that transnational critique has something yet to tell us about the border and that, indeed, Melville is directing our attention towards this elision. All of which leads to the question: how can it be that this most transnational of writers so forcefully configures the border as a zone of resistance? That we can ask this question means there must be a different way that exchange worked at the borders, a difference that ultimately impacts upon our sense of how the transnational might relate to geography, history, identity, and politics.

A rethinking of the border zone is timely given the simultaneous if uneven rise of ultra-right-wing nationalist movements around the world. At the heyday of transnationalism in the first decade of the 2000s, the political theorist Wendy Brown could write that border walls arose from "the weakening of state sovereignty, and more precisely, the detachment of sovereignty from the nation-state," yet in a world where crass ideologues such as Rodrigo Duterte, Victor Orbán, Geert Wilders, Marine le Pen, and Donald Trump are in the ascendant, we might need to think about borders in a way that renders them more than inversely symptomatic of a suddenly borderless world.[9] We must deploy a model that acknowledges, in short, that borders are real, traumatic for those seeking to cross them and, sadly, not going away any time soon. Indeed, in partial response to these contexts, transnationalism has come under increasing pressure in recent years from scholars such as Jeremy Adelman, Jared Hickman, and Nan Z. Da.[10] In what follows, I deploy what I call "marginal states" as a means of thinking transnationally while also, simultaneously, acknowledging the resistances embedded within such a mode of thought. The marginal state is a global form, yet it is a recalcitrant and problematic one that often forestalls the sort of utopian exchange that once seemed possible at the border. In other words, to think about the marginal state is to accept that it is necessary to use global frames for reading nineteenth-century culture but to qualify the sort of political claims that have arisen on the basis of using such a mode. Out of limiting the claims of transnational discourse, certain potentially ameliorative forms of political being emerge. Given the current political exigencies of the world, transnationalism needs to consider the obstacles and blockages that fail to bring about utopian, global exchange, and Herman Melville acts as a guide into one specific zone and heuristic that does something of this work.

Marginal States

The marginal state provides an alternative rendering of the border zone. It is not a space of exchange, heterogeneity, and permeability. It is an extreme form of a border as the term denotes the space between two proximate, but as yet untouching, forms of historical reality: namely, the *terra incognita* in between the edge of the emergent zones of the world-system and societies that are soon-to-be but not yet incorporated into them. Two alternative orders of historical development slowly and tectonically move towards one another. The marginal state is the space that becomes legible and partially traversable in the moments prior to the collision. They occur at the geographical edges of the world-system. It is only there, at the peripheries, where the collocations of empires, nations, markets, colonies, and tribes can come into close contact and, through that nearness, have their power structures strained to the limit. At propitious, fleeting moments of history in which these marginal states occur, new markets, trade routes, and technological innovations provide the material basis for individuals to gain access to them. As they are simultaneously outside the world-system and those societies which soon will enter into it, it is a blank political space, radically open and uncategorizable even as it is about to be erased. The meanings of the "marginal" in the marginal state are thus stacked upon one another. The "marginal" signifies a geographical position, as they are located on the edges of the world-system and the brinks of the societies that came before it. It indicates a historical position as both the world-system and the societies outside of it, by dint of their proximity, are on the verge of a qualitative historical transformation, as is the marginal state itself. It connotes a political state of mind, too, insofar as anyone within it, by definition, regardless if they exist in a structural position of power elsewhere, becomes marginalized through it.

The zone between Nukuheva and the Typee Valley that Tommo and Toby traverse is an exemplary marginal state. This marginal state lay at the unoccupied intersection between an emergent French empire, proto-globalized US-led industrial capital, and disintegrating tribal communities. In the years after Melville's stay on the island, these forces would coagulate to subsume the South Pacific islands (including the Marquesas and Tahiti) under the power relations of imperial-capitalist rule. However, Melville arrived at a historical transition point in which this process had yet to play out. Although the Rear-Admiral Dupetit Thouars had declared the island a French possession – as indicated by the "tri-colored flag of France trailing over the stern of six vessels" (TY 12) that Melville claimed to have witnessed in the bay of Nukuheva – their imperial rule had yet to solidify in the region, and would not until the French victory at the conclusion of the Tahitian War of Independence in 1847.

Meanwhile, the energies of US capitalism were spreading outward across the Pacific through the gory profit that characterized the whaling industry. This growth meant that many South Pacific islands had developed a sort of dock culture, where whaling vessels could trade for provisions. However, unlike Tahiti, which had become an important thoroughfare and marketplace, the Marquesas were comparatively unchanged by the withering touch of capital when Melville came to them. As he reflects, although the "inhabitants have become somewhat corrupted, owing to their recent commerce with Europeans," they nonetheless "retain their original primitive character," and there are "hostile clans" which "are in every respect unchanged from their earliest known condition" (TY 11). Yet the appetites of capitalism are voracious. Accumulation begets more accumulation, production ever-greater production, and profit knows of no natural limits. In Melville's account of the Marquesas, we get a glimpse into what Marx called "primitive accumulation": the shift that, usually through violent, physical force, incorporates individuals and communities into the capitalist system, changing them from free independent proprietors of the land, mainly working for subsistence purposes in self-sustaining local communities, into wage-slaves, dispossessed of the means of production and enmeshed in a global web of unequal capital relations. The local communities of the Marquesas were on the precipice of transformation, as the world-system encroached further and further into the Pacific, incorporating everything into its almost totalizing grasp: not yet wage-slaves but able to see the gathering clouds of exploitation on the horizon.[11]

Empire and capital were the winds that directed Toby and Tommo to the Marquesas. US ships had journeyed deep into the Pacific in the wake of the War of 1812 that wrested markets from British control and the Latin American independence movements that loosened the grasp of Spanish colonialism on the ocean. As a result, empires competed with one another to gain control over the eastern fringe of the Pacific, running from Chile up to modern-day Canada and the islands that speckled the South Pacific and Australasia. Representatives of Russian, British, French, Spanish, and US imperial interests circled in their ships around the ocean, taking military control of islands from Hawaii to Tahiti, going to war in China, and setting up trade agreements with Japan. US commerce in particular exponentially expanded, trading mostly in whale oil. Tommo and Toby are agents of this world-system. Yet, in travelling through and across it they arrived at its limit, in the zone beyond Nukuheva Bay.[12]

Thus, in the Marquesas, empire, capital, and tribal community were all strained to their very limits at this point in time, simultaneously at the geographical margins of empire and capital. The marginal state between Nukuheva Bay and the Typees is poised between these changing worlds. In this way, the border zone that Tommo explores is a border in an intensified form, a chasm not just between nations but between different orders of historical reality. Perhaps all borders were once like this. Uncodified and definitionally a free zone, there is no crystallized sense of what the marginal state is or will become, where it is, or what relation it has to the globe. It is an "open space" with "unknown regions" (TY 37). Indeed, the region appeared so open to Tommo that "the interior of the island" seemed to be "untenanted since the morning of the creation" (TY 44).

This vision of an empty, unchanged space represents more than just a tactical colonial unwillingness to see the visible appurtenances, traces, and evidence of non-western society. Instead, this marginal state is out of reach of the sovereign grasp of western imperialism and capitalism and, one footprint aside, even the local communities of the island. Toby and Tommo do not possess a definitional social superstructure with which to describe, categorize, define, or homogenize the world they see before them. The normal orders of power are suspended. While in the marginal state, unyoked geographic descriptors index the definitional amorphousness of this bubble of power-empty space. Melville emphasizes that throughout his time in the zone, he was unable to orientate himself in relation to any known point: the "great height" of the aforementioned reeds "completely shut us out from the view of surrounding objects, and we were not certain but that we might have been going all the time in a wrong direction" (TY 38); as he descends a slope, he remarks, "I scarcely knew whether I was helplessly falling from the heights above, or whether the fearful rapidity with which I descended was an act of my own volition" (TY 53); similarly, he invokes a sense of cartographical indistinctiveness while lost, reflecting that "[t]he remotest idea of returning to Nukuheva, unless assured of our vessel's departure, never once entered my mind, and indeed it was questionable whether we could have succeeded in reaching it, divided as we were from the bay by a distance we could not compute, and perplexed too in our remembrance of localities by our recent wanderings" (TY 54). There is no scale or point of reference with which to render this location comprehensible. He is adrift in a world outside of the forms of social organization that had defined his existence up to that point.

As I have argued elsewhere, the superstructural forms of political, historical, and geographical organization of "states" percolate downwards to permeate into individual political subjectivity.[13] They create a stage upon and within which people move or think. When an individual lives in a "state" in this sense of the word, they therefore register its historical being in local forms of affect, perception, and expression. To move through a marginal state, this raw form of the border zone, was to share its political indefinability. Detached from the matrix of historical and power relations provided by the world-system, Toby and Tommo lose the capacity to define themselves according to an already known set of categories of political being. Tommo describes this process as being "almost unmanned." He recalls how one night of heavy rain and purgatorial cold, whose "accumulated horrors" included "the death-like coldness of the place, the appalling darkness, and the dismal sense of our forlorn condition," very nearly "unmanned me" (TY 46). As they cross the marginal state, Toby and Tommo undergo a larger process of "unmanning": they lose the political dimension of their being and so experience a human reality that is stripped of all its social excesses. What is left is simply life, and life alone. The realities of the marginal state erode and almost erase their existence entirely. Indeed, it is a space defined by negations – chasms, coldness, and darkness – and bodily states of privation and lack: hunger, thirst, debility.

If we follow Aristotle and ascribe the political element of man's life to the capacity for speech, then it is significant that language almost breaks down entirely in the marginal state. Voicelessness and inarticulacy indicate the loss of the political element of man's life. Toby and Tommo tend to communicate in shapeless sounds, silent glances, truncated syllables, and elemental instincts (although, at times, a more picaresque tone infuses their interactions). Some examples: early on in the crossing, Melville tells us how "[s]ince leaving the canoe-house we had scarcely exchanged a single syllable with one another" (TY 37); on reaching a place of stunning beauty, he reflects that "[o]ver all the landscape there reigned the most hushed repose, which I almost feared to break lest, like the enchanted gardens in the fairy tale, a single syllable might dissolve the spell" (TY 49); on meeting with another seemingly insurmountable physical obstacle, he tells us how "[w]ithout exchanging a syllable on the subject, Toby and myself simultaneously renounced the design which had lured us thus far" (TY 54); on deciding to take a risky action, he recalls that "[a]fter I had signified my assent, Toby, without uttering a single word, crawled along the dripping ledge until he gained a point from whence he could just reach one of the largest of the pendant roots" (TY 60); and finally, at a point where everything seems hopeless, he describes how "my companion, whose spirit at last was a good deal broken, scarcely uttered a word during the whole night" (TY 65). Moreover, there is an overall pattern of dissolution in the marginal state: food becomes scarce, bodies dissolve with hunger, and selfhood breaks down.

Toby and Tommo thus undergo a gradual process of self-erasure that erodes the political dimension of their being. They are reduced to a state similar to what Hannah Arendt calls "the abstract nakedness of being human."[14] For Arendt, this category refers to what it means to be a human without rights, outside of political communities, and without any legitimizing structures of power. All that is left is the biological fact of being alive, with man assuming the status of living animal rather than political human. Melville's constant recourse to animal metaphors and similes to conceptualize their acts of crossing and journeying through the resistant geographies of the border zone suggest that a similar process occurs in the marginal state. He describes how Toby "bound like a young roe"; how, when stuck amongst the reeds, their chances were equivalent to that of "a bull-frog" trying "to work a passage through the teeth of a comb"; how they were hidden "screened from observation by the grass through which we glided, much in the fashion of a couple of serpents"; how, after entering into a particularly difficult part of their journey, they make "a snail-like progress of an hour or more"; and that Toby, feeling a certain ecstasy in nature, "was as blithe and joyous as a young bird" (TY 37–39, 52, 55). Unloosed from their prior political categories of identity, these citizens of nation-states, with clear settled socio-political and socio-economic roles, find that all they have left is the naked fact of animal biology.

As such, in the marginal zone, Toby and Tommo's senses and bodies become extraordinarily sensitive. The physical reality of their bodies stands out in starker relief and expands now that they are not burdened by political existence. Intense sensory and tactile experience, whether of cold, wetness, taste, hunger, pain, thirst, or fever characterizes their crossing through the mountains. On eating a miniscule, watery, pulpy piece of almost dissolved bread, Melville recalls how "[t]here was a flavor and a relish to this small particle of food that under other circumstances it would have been impossible for the most delicate viands to have imparted." Similarly, his experience of fever and the almost totally unexplained (and unexplainable) swelling of his leg indicates this switch from political to solely embodied life: "Cold shiverings and a burning fever succeeded one another at intervals, while one of my legs was swelled to such a degree, and pained me so acutely, that I half suspected I had been bitten by some venomous reptile" (TY 47–48). Like his senses, his body, his flesh, grows in size and receptivity. There are times when sense perception almost totally overwhelms his mind, orienting all of the world on the axis of its insatiable and impossible demands: "I am aware of no feeling, either of pleasure or of pain, that so completely deprives one of all power to resist its impulses, as this same raging thirst" (TY 52). In the marginal state, Toby and Tommo are bodies without political life, senses without minds, and they experience the vertiginous and dizzying feeling of being outside of a power structure, outside of a community, outside of a polis.

This loss of political rights is traumatic, for it aligns these two middle-class white men, both of whom are only temporarily enmeshed in the semi-global maritime industrial working-class, with the most vulnerable citizens of the world. Their reduction to mere biology means that they share their status with the internationally vulnerable – the stateless, slaves, and others – who are explicitly excluded from having a political existence by exclusionary and violent forms of juridical and social power and hegemony. Indeed, one hears in Melville's account of their crossing the slightest echoes of slave autobiography. In the reeds, he writes of how their "limbs" were "torn and lacerated with the splintered fragments of the broken canes" (TY 38) in a moment that recalls scenes of plantation punishment with the whip. Similarly, in a scene that recalls both the precarious, naked visibility to power that slaves experienced when escaping through enemy territories, he says they feel the need to escape the local people in case they are captured and forced to return to ship. At one point, they hear "the distant shouts of the natives, who had just descried us, and to whom our figures, brought in bold relief against the sky, were plainly revealed" (TY 39). Obviously, such a reversal can only be partial given that Toby and Tommo ultimately remain in a position of comparative structural power – they are, after all, agents of the world-system, on an island about to be torn asunder by empire and capital. Nonetheless, these moments provide an insight into the fluidity of political life in the marginal state and the sorts of surprising congruences and overlaps that might arise between those separated and hierarchized by the identity categories of modern power. An exchange of a diminished sort does occur.

However, there is also a radical freedom at play in the marginal state for Tommo and Toby. A dialectic is in operation. By virtue of having their political life taken away and so reduced to almost nothing, they explore what it is to live outside the constraints of power. For to be almost nothing at all is also to live without the web of modern power structuring their being. Accordingly, they can, briefly, become anything. Melville expresses this strange, ambivalent, and counter-intuitive freedom through numerous scenes of falling. Among the many repeated set-ups that occur in the marginal state are moments when they jump into chasms, fall down cliffs, and miraculously escape unscathed from death-defying acts of daring across vast deep empty valleys. These leaps into the air provide an allegorical rendering of the freedom the marginal state can create: the moments where Toby and Tommo hang suspended in the air, without anything to hold or support them, leaping across a void, allow an insight into what it would be like to be totally and only human, outside of the domain of power, without definition framing life. "My brain," reflected Tommo after one such leap and near fall, "grew dizzy with the frightful risk I had just run," showing how it is that his subjectivity began to slip away in these emptied out political spaces (TY 61).

The marginal state tells us about what it means to exist outside of power in a world prior to the official formation of geopolitical borders. If we circle back around to where this essay began, we can ask one final question: why is it that, in the marginal state, Toby and Tommo come up against so many physical obstacles that offer resistance to their crossing? My speculation would be this: that these obstacles allegorize the difficulties of moving through a space that does not possess shared structures of history or power to render both actual and cultural contact legible. The lesson learnt for those who crossed them, and for critics now, is that a transnational world creates barriers to exchange at the same moment in which it develops spaces where such exchanges might take place. These barriers qualify the politics of the border, by making it as much a space of incommensurability and resistance as it is of cultural permeability. And while modern borders are ostensibly mere mediating zones between shared formations, in an era of walls, actual and figurative, being built, of refugees and immigrants being kept rightless, stripped of their political life, in holding pens in airports and extra-judicial border prisons, it is quite possible that there remains a trace of the old marginal states that once existed on the edges of the world-system in them. It is just that now we might be witnessing the recrudescence and enlargement of their most terrifying features.

PART II

Thinking with Melville

CHAPTER 7

Perfectionist Pierre

Dominic Mastroianni

In the introduction to *Conditions Handsome and Unhandsome* (1990), Stanley Cavell places *Pierre; or, The Ambiguities* (1852) tantalizingly in a list of texts that "might have been mentioned" in another list of texts (including *Republic* and *Walden*) that develop an outlook he calls perfectionism.[1] As far as I know, Cavell has not printed another word about *Pierre*.[2] A signature term of Cavell's, perfectionism is difficult to introduce, because he pointedly abstains from defining it. As Cavell understands it, "there is no closed list of features that constitute perfectionism"; instead he offers "an open-ended thematics."[3] Perfectionism, the kind Cavell calls Emersonian, involves the pursuit of, or attraction to, what Emerson calls the "unattained but attainable self."[4] But Emersonian perfectionism is not a doctrine for achieving perfection. As Cavell explains, such perfectionism "does not imply perfectibility" or embrace what he elsewhere calls "a foreseeable path to a concluding state of the human."[5] Nor is such perfectionism a theory of the best form of life, in part because it rejects the moralism that would impose a single conception of a best form of life, and in part because perfectionism is not a theory, but rather "an outlook or dimension of thought embodied and developed in a set of texts spanning the range of Western culture."[6] Perfectionism is not separable from the work of examining such texts, which themselves examine, in view of changing, their cultures' ways of conceiving and valuing everyday life.

Working out what Cavell calls "a concept of truth to oneself," perfectionism "places tremendous burdens on personal relationships and on the possibility or necessity of the transforming of oneself and of one's society."[7] Perfectionist attention to possible transformations of self and world entails a "devotion to the discovery of false necessity" in everyday understandings and modes of life. The actual shape of everyday life may be found to be contingent, replaceable, though it may impose itself forcefully, or seem not to impose itself at all. If a daily living saturated with false necessities is ordinary to us, so, we may see in clearer moments, is a different life turned to what Cavell names truer necessities. As he explains, "The everyday is ordinary because, after all, it is our habit, or habitat; but since that very inhabitation is from time to time perceptible to us – we who have constructed it – as extraordinary, we conceive that some place elsewhere, or this place otherwise constructed, must be what is ordinary to us."[8] One site for considering *Pierre* as perfectionist writing is its musings on the ordinary, especially its appeal to an idea of the ordinary mind and its diminishment of comparative intellectual giftedness, made to confront what Cavell describes as perfectionism's liability to snobbery. More on this later.

Cavell observes that Emerson, in "History" (1841), "is claiming to be a path to one's unattained self."[9] Does the writer of *Pierre* claim to be such a path? In what follows, my hope is less to answer the question than to show the importance of asking it. The idea that *Pierre* could be a path to one's attainable self may seem ludicrous, even repugnant. I can hardly deny the book's power to elicit derision and disgust. But perfectionism relies on finding the self's present position, together with the shape of its world, laughable or repellant. Then the question is when, if ever, do we find that *Pierre* addresses our present positions?

Sharon Cameron seems to identify a perfectionist bent in Melville when she asserts that what is "elicited" in *Moby-Dick* is "that we could be more than what we are or less than what we are – that, more or less, we could be different from what we are."[10] Colin Dayan aligns Melville with perfectionism when she says "he used his writing to transform how we think, which meant how we position ourselves in the world."[11] *Pierre* is a study of how we position ourselves, a book preoccupied with posture, and especially with gait. In *Pierre*, gait models thinking, while also modeling the self's way of inhabiting the world. Forms of thinking, Melville suggests, are not separable from forms of, let's say, the journey of life. Whereas perfectionist writings often emphasize walking, climbing, and leaping – taking steps – *Pierre* is much concerned with a state prior, or inhospitable, to stepping. So Melville thinks of gliding, floating, and sliding. If *Moby-Dick* is consumed with the question "of what are bodies made?", as Cameron argues, the question *Pierre* stresses is: how do bodies move?[12]

Asking how bodies move, in *Pierre*, is related to asking how minds move; Melville makes it hard to tell whether the two questions are different or the same. Driven in part by interest in new materialism and posthumanism, much has been written about Melville's blurring of categorical boundaries between the human and the nonhuman. His meditation on thinking in *Pierre* emphasizes human bodily movement, while suggesting such movement is continuous with the movements of nonhuman bodies. The book's inquiry into motion is not just a matter of physics; physics alone cannot describe every way a human life can be said to move. It is equally true that *Pierre* does not restrict questions of movement to a rarefied spiritual realm. One might say that the movements of *Pierre* are made to produce dissatisfaction with the divide between physics and metaphysics. Melville's slides, glides, floatings, steps, and falls cumulatively strain distinctions between body and mind, matter and the immaterial. It is tempting to say that *Pierre* portrays the mental as material, or blurs, even deletes, the boundary between mind and body. But reading *Pierre* – coming to terms with its dizzying show of what Nancy Ruttenburg calls Melville's "relentless specificity" – makes us wary of easy appeals to blurred or deleted boundaries.[13] Such appeals seem empty when they fail to produce a picture of what something is, or is like. A specific concern of Melville's in *Pierre* is to consider how the postures and gaits of human bodies afford pictures of human minds (Wittgenstein: "The human body is the best picture of the human soul").[14]

What follows is, in a part, an invitation and an attempt to reconsider Melville's relation to Emerson. In *Pierre,* Melville appears less as a ridiculer or rejecter of Emerson's thinking than as a collaborator, say a strong friend. Obviously Melville does not celebrate Emerson at every turn, but, as I will argue, he embraces central concerns of the work Emerson published in the early 1840s. Its sustained engagement with Emerson's thought is one reason to take *Pierre* seriously as philosophical writing, or as writing that rewards the philosophically interested attention demanded by Emerson's essays.

From Sliding to Toddling

The portrayal of thinking as self-positioning, and specifically as taking difficult steps, is familiar in the Western philosophical tradition. A philosopher as sober and modest as Emmanuel Levinas can still describe his thinking as a strenuous climb toward a point to which "access . . . is as steep as in ancient times."[15] The image of a philosophical climb hearkens to Plato's *Symposium,* where philosophical labor is pictured as stepping up a ladder whose rungs are called "the things of this world."[16] And in *Republic*, of course, the sedentary prisoner's release and ascent from the cave begins when he is "suddenly compelled to stand up, turn his head, [and] walk."[17]

A memorable philosophical slide appears in Ludwig Wittgenstein's *Philosophical Investigations* (1953), which depicts distance from everyday life as a layer of ice between our feet and the ground. When "we examine actual language," Wittgenstein claims, we find ourselves in a conflict with what he calls our "requirement" for "the crystalline purity of logic." Wittgenstein describes a moment when this requirement begins to seem unnecessary: "The conflict becomes intolerable; the requirement is now in danger of becoming empty. – We have got on to slippery ice where there is no friction and so in a certain sense the conditions are ideal, but also, just because of that, we are unable to walk. We want to walk; then we need *friction.* Back to the rough ground!"[18] Cavell takes Wittgenstein's claim that we are unable to walk as "signifying something about our inability to move ourselves in accordance with our apparent desires," adding that Wittgenstein is "mythologizing our requirement for an ideal order of language as a wish to inhabit a medium other than one with human grounding that supports the human gait of walking."[19]

Characters in *Pierre* are sometimes found in a medium other than one that supports a human gait of walking. We might think of the novel's elements of sliding and gliding and floating as expressing a wish to become what Melville calls "earth-emancipated" (P 347). Centrally, Melville's images of frictionless movement answer to the condition in which Emerson says we find ourselves in the first section of "Experience," an essay that Melville likely read in 1849.[20] There Emerson says we "wake and find ourselves on a stair," thus positioned for a climb, or a descent. But we are evidently unable to take a further step, finding no surface capable of producing friction. Emerson describes a "lubricity of all objects," and laments that "there is at last no rough rasping friction, but the most slippery sliding surfaces."[21] To glide upon such surfaces is to be both out of place and dead to the world ("Ghostlike we glide through nature, and should not know our place again").[22]

Pierre imagines what it would be like to pass beyond the slippery conditions described in the beginning of "Experience." The titular Pierre is a wealthy young man who comes to be convinced that an enigmatic, impoverished woman named Isabel Banford, to whose beauty and suffering he is attracted, is his long-lost half-sister, the daughter of his late father. With the thought of preserving his father's image from disgrace, Pierre pretends to have secretly married Isabel, or actually marries her, breaking off his engagement to the mother-approved Lucy Tartan.[23] Pierre moves from rural New York to the city, is disinherited, and tries to write a book that will change the world. In reading of Pierre's early education, what Melville calls his "breeding" and his "culture," we learn that he advances by gliding: "Thus ... did this Pierre glide toward maturity." In this glide, Pierre is said to be "thoughtless of that period of remorseless insight" that,

Melville hints, is to come (P 6). Pierre's early thoughtless gliding is called, two paragraphs later, an insensible sliding process: "[A]s to Pierre had descended the numerous other noble qualities of his ancestors; and as he now stood heir to their forests and farms; so by the same insensible sliding process, he seemed to have inherited their docile homage to a venerable Faith" (P 7). Noble qualities and forests and farms alike slide to Pierre, who himself slides through the world, moving in a fashion indistinguishable from that of inherited qualities and properties. His cultivation, his way of living, is by the thoughtless glide and the insensible slide.

It is not clear that Pierre's sliding way sets him apart from others, or is due to anything peculiar to himself. Other characters slide too, including Isabel and Lucy. Isabel enters Pierre's world not just "slidingly," but, somehow, intensely slidingly. "For an instant," writes Melville, Pierre "almost could have prayed Isabel back into the wonder-world from which she had so slidingly emerged" (P 129). Late in the novel we read that Lucy seemed "to be somehow inexplicably sliding between" Isabel and Pierre, "without touching them." Isabel perceives this sliding to be, or result from, something called an "untraceable displacing agency" (P 338).

Pierre slides, and things slide into him. Such things are seemingly immaterial. For instance, a thought can enter Pierre slidingly, as when "the sweet unconditional thought of Lucy slid wholly into his soul, dislodging thence all such phantom occupants" as the "weirdnesses" said to haunt him (P 50). Similarly, a form can slide into Pierre. Think of a snake: "[N]ow finally, to top all, there suddenly slid into his inmost heart the living and breathing form of Lucy. His lungs collapsed; his eyeballs glared; for the sweet imagined form, so long buried alive in him, seemed now as gliding on him from the grave" (P 181).[24] A form buried "in" Pierre exits him only to slide both "on" and "into" him. This form does not erase boundaries. Pierre's boundaries remain, but Lucy's sliding, gliding form seems capable of existing on both sides of a boundary at once. Sliding bypasses any barriers to Pierre's heart and soul. The inmost self is pervious to thoughts and forms with a strange heft, capable of dislodging occupants and collapsing lungs. As in *Moby-Dick*, "Melville displaces ideas from an explanatory status and confers on them the status of immediacy or palpability."[25] In sliding movements Melville confounds distinctions between form and matter, self and other, the animate and the inanimate.

As particular thoughts and forms slide, so do the principles, philosophies, and religions promising to guide lives. Echoing Emerson's idea of "the transitions by which virtues and vices slide into their contraries," Melville evokes a "rarefied atmosphere" in which "the most immemorially admitted maxims of men begin to slide and fluctuate, and finally become wholly inverted" (P 165).[26] Sliding describes the departure of protections afforded by philosophy and faith. Such sliding is precipitated by a turbulence in Pierre: "All his Faith-born, enthusiastic, high-wrought, stoic, and philosophic defenses, were now beaten down by this sudden storm of nature in his soul." Melville's narrator claims that under the pressure of this storm, this "test," "all the fair philosophic or Faith-phantoms ... slide away and disappear as ghosts at cock-crow" (P 289). Melville here lumps philosophy and faith indiscriminately together, as though philosophy's value were nothing but the value of faith, as if philosophy's teaching were no more than indoctrination.

But it is not only selves, forms, thoughts, maxims, and philosophic defenses that slide. Seemingly inanimate matter slides: the expected, as when in Isabel's story we are told of the "slidings of rocks undermined"; and the less expected, as when Melville writes of the "first light that slides from the sun" (P 110, 85). Sliding describes the motions of objects within the world, but also the movement, the loss, of the physical world itself. That world departs when Pierre is in a trance: "On all sides, the physical world of solid objects now slidingly displaced itself from around him" (P 85). Melville presents a pervasive sliding unbound by distinctions between thought, form, self, other, particular material thing, and the entire physical world.[27] One might say that the book rejoices in disrespecting such major philosophical distinctions. Or it presents a life for which such distinctions are empty: they no longer, or don't yet, provide a way onward. It is not that such distinctions don't matter; they matter to the degree that Melville's slides disturb his reader. Perhaps the book aims to disorient readers, to sow confusion concerning where things belong, where we belong – or to show us our confusion, to make us capable of asking, with Emerson, a question that may easily fail to hold our attention: "Where do we find ourselves?"

How does friction begin in the lubricous world *Pierre* describes? Returning late in the novel to the idea of Pierre's culture, Melville likens him to an "orange-tree of the Floridas" that has been "transplanted to northern Maine"; as winter nears, Pierre has not produced the "fruitage" of a mature book. The new ground in which Pierre has been planted seems, strangely, to provide the friction required for taking steps. Melville reveals that Pierre has changed from an insensible slider to what he calls a soul-toddler. Immediately after describing Pierre the author as a tree struggling to bear fruit, Melville describes Pierre the soul as a toddler struggling to stand and walk unsupported: "Watch yon little toddler, how long it is learning to stand by itself!" Melville adds: "There now, do you see the soul." I grant that it is possible to portray Pierre consecutively as a tree and as a toddler, without blending the two figures. But still: How does a treelike person take steps? By pulling up roots? Again? Pierre has already been transplanted. Then is each step to be imagined as an uprooting? Called a "fruit . . . born from the world-husk," the soul – Pierre's, and anyone's in his position – "still clamors for the support of its mother the world, and its father the Deity. But it shall yet learn to stand independent, though not without many a bitter wail, and many a miserable fall" (P 296). Miserable falls result not from any slickness of terrain, but from the toddler's weak limbs and poor balance. Slippery ground, it seems, may be left behind; but the leaving is involuntary.

A year after the publication of *Pierre*, Frederick Douglass emphasized the violence of frictionless motion: "What a world of inconsistency, as well as of wickedness, is suggested by the smooth and gliding phrase, AMERICAN SLAVE TRADE."[28] In *Pierre*, sliding involves thoughtless violence: to slide, Melville repeatedly insists, is to displace someone or something ("more and more did [Lucy] seem, hour by hour, to be somehow inexplicably sliding between them . . . Isabel was alive to some untraceable displacing agency"; "the physical world of solid objects now slidingly displaced itself from around him"; "the sweet unconditional thought of Lucy slid wholly into his soul, dislodging thence all such phantom occupants" [P 337, 85, 50]). By contrast, to toddle in Melville's sense is to be newly exposed to the pain foretold in Emerson's call for "rough, rasping friction." Emerson sees a need for friction to make us sound: we are like silent violins awaiting the bow's rasp, or incompletely crafted blocks of wood, awaiting the rasp that will smooth and shape us, scraping away our excess. (Thoreau: "Before we can adorn our houses with beautiful objects the walls must be stripped, and our lives must be stripped."[29]) As one might expect, Melville emphasizes the roughness of Emerson's friction.[30] According to Dayan, "What is most striking about the method in Melville's hyperboles and hesitations, his imprecision and fragmentations, is his emphatic denial of a supernaturalism emptied of what harrows: the wounds, the wear and tear of daily life."[31] To become a soul-toddler is to shift from an easy slide to a living acutely exposed to the wear and tear of daily life. To soul-toddle is, in part, to wail bitterly and fall miserably.

Prior Steps

Melville's interest in sliding and stepping seems particularly alive to Calvinist language concerning salvation and damnation, and to

Immanuel Kant's view of Enlightenment.[32] Melville's soul-toddler is a near relation of the toddler who figures centrally in Kant's essay "What is Enlightenment?" (1784). On a transatlantic voyage in 1849, Melville had discussed Kant in long conversations with George Adler, a scholar of German idealism.[33] On multiple occasions, *Pierre* invokes Kant by name; for instance, the motley collection of thinkers and artists living at the Church of the Apostles is devoted "to the proper digesting of the sublimated Categories of Kant"; and Pierre's comically enthusiastic friend Charlie Millthorpe encourages him to "Stump the State on the Kantian Philosophy" (P 267, 281). I do not know if Melville read "What is Enlightenment?", but when he wrote *Pierre* it was available in two English translations, the more recent published in 1841 in Sarah Austin's *Fragments from German Prose Writers*, where it is distinguished by appearing in its entirety, "almost the only thing in the volume to which the name 'fragment' does not apply."[34] Kant defines enlightenment as the capacity for unaided thought: "A man is enlightened when he emerges from a state of self-imposed pupilage. Pupilage is the inability to use one's own understanding without the guidance of another."[35] Kant pictures intellectual immaturity as an inability, specifically an unreadiness, to walk. Enlightenment is achieved in taking "the step to majority." Kant claims that most people are non-enlightened, an "unthinking, unreasoning mass" of what he goadingly calls quiet creatures and domestic animals.[36] Kant writes of "guardians" – e.g., priests, doctors, rulers, and books – that have "carefully prevented the quiet creature from venturing to take a step without the go-cart [*Gängelwagen*] into which they have put it." A go-cart or Gängelwagen is a wheeled enclosing frame that supports toddlers' attempts to walk. Coming to think without guidance is like learning to walk without a baby walker.

Melville's toddlerhood differs from Kant's in a few respects. Kant's toddlers vigorously free themselves from bondage. In preparation for an unsupported step, they "extricat[e] themselves ... by their own efforts," "throw[] away" their "gyves," and "throw[] off the yoke."[37] Melville's toddler, by contrast, suffers a moment when "cruel father and mother have both let go his hand"; the withdrawal of parental support is felt as "utter loss" (P 296).[38] And whereas Kant's toddler is restrained by instruments, "mechanical tools," Melville's is supported by intimate flesh, the warm hands of "both father and mother." The struggle in Kant is to release the self from its subordination to tools and to its own animal nature; the struggle in Melville begins after the self is released from the care of human kin. Kant presents mental toddlerhood as a debased starting point, whereas Melville suggests that toddlerhood is an achievement – there is worse, or rather, there are states further from the mental condition, or form of life, he portrays as unaided walking.

Melville disagrees with Kant's evaluation of the risks of falling. Kant claims that most people, and all women, have been led to view the passage to unaided thinking "not only as laborious and difficult, but also as extremely dangerous." Writing of the go-carted toddler, he continues: "Now in truth this danger is not so very great; it would learn to go alone at the expense of a few tumbles." Kant's "few tumbles" become Melville's "many a bitter wail, and many a miserable fall" (P 296). Moreover, Kant claims that "one fall generally makes" a toddler "timorous, and frightens it from any further attempt," suggesting that unabated despair is the likely outcome of trying to think independently. Melville's toddler, by contrast, makes many attempts to stand independently; in the suffering of many wails and falls, Melville presents a hope, even a confidence, that a new standing can be achieved.

Adducing the passage in which Melville names the "insensible sliding process" by which ancestors' qualities, forests, farms, and faith pass to Pierre, Emory Elliott writes: "Although the narrator is necessarily vague about how exactly this generational transmission of attitudes occurs, he assures the reader that the nineteenth-century youth is intellectually, culturally, and spiritually linked even to his earliest Puritan ancestors."[39] One spiritual ancestor of *Pierre* is Jonathan Edwards's "Sinners in the Hands of an Angry God" (1741), whose text is "Their foot shall slide in due time." Consider some of the sermon's closing words: "Now . . . the axe is in an extraordinary manner laid at the root of the trees, that every tree which brings not forth good fruit, may be hewn down and cast into the fire."[40] Edwards's threat of damnation becomes, in Melville, a description of Pierre's transition to rough ground, and of the stakes of his authorship, the generation of his fruit: "Though transplanted to northern Maine, the orange-tree of the Floridas will put forth leaves in that parsimonious summer, and show some few tokens of fruitage; yet November will find no golden globes thereon; and the passionate old lumber-man, December, shall peel the whole tree, wrench it off at the ground, and toss it for a fagot to some lime-kiln" (P 296). Elsewhere *Pierre* presents a "Calvinistical view of humanity, " one that takes us to be bad enough to be an easy slide from hell, as itself something into which one "slide[s]" (P 232).[41]

Edwards emphasizes that the slide to hell is always intensely possible, even when it does not seem to be. His sermon tries to reconstruct his auditors' sense of the ordinary, to make ordinary the risk of immediately sliding to hell. For example, he argues: "It is no security to wicked men for one moment, that there are no visible means of death at hand . . . [T]here is nothing to make it appear, that God had need to be at the expense of a miracle, or go out of the ordinary course of his providence, to destroy any wicked man, at any moment."[42] In Edwards, persons stand on "slippery declining ground" but, held up by God, are not yet sliding.[43] In Melville, by contrast, persons are already sliding, and the loss of divine support occasions no ultimate fall, but rather the many falls that accompany the soul-toddler's transition to unassisted standing. Moreover, in Edwards one slides to another place, while in Melville the slide is through this place, as if there is no other: thoughtlessness and insensibility are the hell from which escape is imagined.

Melville's concern with steps, together with stages and degrees of transition, echoes sixteenth- and seventeenth-century Reformed theological discourse, especially the terms of preparationism. Perry Miller observes that "covenant theologians . . . early began to speak about a stage of 'preparation,' a period in time when a saint . . . would suffer preliminary motions which sooner or later would eventuate in conversion."[44] For instance, the English theologian William Perkins claimed that "the [sic] conuersion of a sinner is not wrought all at one instant, but in continuance of time: & that by certaine measures and degrees."[45] The standing of Melville's soul-toddler is wrought by degrees: "[L]ong time it is ere by degrees this child comes to stand without any support" (P 296). Similarly, Melville says that "God" helps a person "illy prepared" to encounter "his soul" in its "immensity," by slowing and dividing that encounter into degrees: "Only by judicious degrees, appointed of God, does man come at last to gain his Mont Blanc and take an overtopping view of these Alps" (P 284). Instead of salvation there is height and an "overtopping view": a view recurrently sought by the Emersonian perfectionist, the kind of thinker unsettled by the "continual effort to raise himself above himself, to work a pitch above his last height."[46]

Melville portrays Pierre in a series of stages of movement toward a new element, something groundlike, capable of accepting transplants: "While Pierre was thinking that he was entirely transplanted into a new and wonderful element of Beauty and Power, he was, in fact, but in one of the stages of the transition." How close are these stages of transition to the "stages toward salvation" marked in preparationism?[47] Melville says the stages head toward an ultimate element: "That ultimate element once fairly gained, then books no more are needed for buoys to our souls; our own strong limbs support us, and we float over all bottomlessness with a jeering impunity" (P 283). Melville here seems to endorse a perfectionism that looks to a final state of perfection. (But his next page, after describing the achievement of an overtopping view, states that "even then, the tithe is not shown; and far over the invisible Atlantic, the Rocky Mountains and the Andes are yet unbeheld" [P 284].) Note the bizarreness of the ultimate element – the incoherence, or irony, of Melville's vision of support by one's own strong limbs, when such limbs float rather than stand. What then is limb strength? Perhaps Melville's point is that the kind of thinking portrayed as walking is not achieved once and for all. The frictionless world remains a standing threat to the perfectionist thinker, as well as, perhaps, an animating condition.

Ordinary Minds

Cavell remarks that "Plato's and Aristotle's perfectionisms, however different from each other, are for the privileged," and claims that their "concession" to privilege is "combatted" in Emersonian perfectionism.[48] Is it combatted in *Pierre*? Introducing his account of Emersonian perfectionism, Cavell notes: "Since the (secular) perfectionist outlook I am sketching is concentrated within the position of the relatively advantaged (which I am taking to exclude the most disadvantaged and also the most advantaged), anyway those in positions for which social injustice or natural misfortune (to themselves) is not an unpostponable issue, the perfectionist may be variously subject to snobbery."[49] When the novel begins, Pierre is one step, so to speak, from counting among the most advantaged. A physically and mentally gifted white man born into a prominent family, he is poised to inherit a fortune. All he lacks is unmediated access to the wealth he stands to inherit, a point of obvious importance to the novel's plot.

Melville retroactively portrays the juvenile Pierre as unable to stand, as a soul that has not yet attained its toddlerhood. Are we prompted to think Pierre's transformation from slider to toddler anomalous, or extraordinary? Only for the few, the lucky or the unlucky? *Pierre* entertains the possibility that every human being has a capacity, usually undetected, for the extraordinary. After his first conversation with Isabel, Pierre asks himself whether the unremarkable daily life of any human being may be seen to be vastly mysterious: "Is it possible then, thought Pierre, that there lives a human creature in this common world of everydays, whose whole history may be told in little less than two-score words, and yet embody in that smallness a fathomless fountain of ever-welling mystery?" Rather than separating the elite from the common, Pierre thinks of commonplaceness, together with the wonderful surpassing of the commonplace, as a shared human condition: "Is it possible, after all, that spite of bricks and shaven faces, this world we live in is brimmed with wonders, and I and all mankind, beneath our garbs of common-placeness, conceal enigmas that the stars themselves, and perhaps the highest seraphim can not resolve?" (P 139).

Potential aside, Pierre's mind actually surpasses the common. Melville writes of "[t]hat amazing shock of practical truth, which in the compass of a very few days and hours had not so much advanced, as magically transplanted the youthful mind of Pierre far beyond all common discernments" (P 166). And Melville presents Pierre's mind as having grown profound: "[I]n Pierre, was presented the apparent anomaly of a mind, which by becoming really profound in itself, grew skeptical of all tendered profundities" (P 354). And yet, ordinary minds may harbor profound ideas: Melville writes of "profound ideas, which at times atmospherically, as it were, do insinuate themselves even into very ordinary minds" (P 196–197). So when Melville writes of "a mind fitted by nature for profound and fearless thought," it is not clear whether he means Pierre's singular mind, or a class of extraordinary minds exemplified by Pierre's, or some broader set of ordinary minds, or very ordinary minds – whatever those might be (P 165).

Melville's novel categorizes minds. We hear of "unhealthily critical minds," and "a steady philosophic mind," and "very unoriginal minds," and the "bluff-minded," and the "unscrupulously infidel-minded," and the "naturally strong-minded," and "[a] mind less naturally strong than Pierre's," and "the best human intellects" contrasted with "minds comparatively inferior," and "earnest minds" contrasted with "enviable dunces," and the "random but lynx-eyed mind" that Pierre seems to embody (P 221, 175, 259, 221, 222, 226, 246, 258, 227, 283). Melville can describe minds as if they are gradable like gems, as when he says Pierre's mother has "a fine mind of medium culture" (P 4). He also can write of the human mind in general, as when he describes "that certain strange infatuation of fondness, which the human mind, however vigorous, sometimes feels for any emotion at once novel and mystical" (P 63).

If an ordinary mind is one without remarkable talents, then Pierre's mind is not ordinary: it is said to be comparatively delicate and poetical and strong and profound and advanced. But part of the novel's teaching is to prompt an assessment of the value of comparative intellectual power. What Melville calls a "thinking man," he defines as "any sincere man of ordinary reflective powers, and accustomed to exercise them at all" (P 166, 165). Now it may be the case that, in *Pierre*'s view, sincerity is harder to come by than extraordinary reflective powers. A thinker seems to require what Melville calls "an ear for Earnestness" – strange pun – a way of listening that he suggests is rare (P 264).

What I seem to make out is this: Melville supposes some minds more gifted than others, but when it comes to the task of thinking, comparative giftedness is beside the point. Melville writes:

> For it is only the miraculous vanity of man which ever persuades him, that even for the most richly gifted mind, there ever arrives an earthly period, where it can truly say to itself, I have come to the Ultimate of Human Speculative Knowledge; hereafter, at this present point I will abide. Sudden onsets of new truth will assail him, and overturn him. (P 167)

What is clear is that "the most richly gifted mind" is an ordinary mind: ordinary minds are exposed to sudden onsets of new truth, which may look for all the world like sudden nonsense. Pierre's mind is in this sense ordinary. The mistake is to overvalue, or misinterpret, a distinction between the ordinary and the extraordinary. This point seems to me central to the idea that *Pierre* is philosophically engaged writing, a view shared by many critics and expressed even in F. O. Matthiessen's claim that in *Pierre* "Melville's scorn had begun to spread from transcendentalism to all philosophy."[50]

Readers of *Pierre* are pressed to answer an awkward question: Is this a book for us? Can its words, strange and demented as they may sound, be said to address our condition? Can we say of *Pierre* what Cameron writes of *Moby-Dick* – that its "demented strangeness seems to implicate us in the understanding of it"?[51] Can we tell ourselves what Cavell tells readers of Emerson: "Your work now . . . is the reading of his page, and allowing yourself to be changed by it"?[52] *Pierre* seems calculated to prompt fierce resistance to being changed by it. Yet Melville suggests that his novel utters his readers' unutterable thoughts. His narrator announces: "I am more frank with Pierre than the best men are with themselves." He continues: "He who shall be wholly honest, though nobler than Ethan Allen; that man shall stand in danger of the meanest mortal's scorn." Minus the choice of Ethan Allen, the sentence might appear in *Walden*, where Thoreau admits: "I never knew, and never shall know, a worse man than myself."[53] Something the writer of *Pierre*, like the writer of "Experience," seems to want to teach is that in the world as we find it, we may be most unfree, and inflict harm most thoughtlessly and insensibly, most casually, just where it feels easiest to move.

CHAPTER 8

The Confidence-Man *between Genres*

Elizabeth Duquette

For a book that frustrates interpretation, seemingly by design, there is surprising unanimity in readings of *The Confidence-Man* (1857), particularly centering on the book's purported formal deficiencies. Scholars generally agree that Melville's last full-length novel lacks all of the genre's definitive features, including a conventional plot, fully developed characters, clearly delineated action or dialogue, and accurately realized settings. Given its rejection of these most basic conventions, readers have asked since its initial publication if it is correct to call *The Confidence-Man* a novel, proposing alternate terms, like romance or "novel-length prose fiction" or "a version of the fictional anatomy," to denote this "masquerade."[1] Still, even if the "sensuously constricting" and "intensely privative" world Melville depicts on the *Fidèle* fits uneasily into generic parameters, critics concur that it represents the culmination of "Melville's quarrel with fiction," to borrow Nina Baym's enduring phrase, the final outburst of an embittered author.[2] Nor is it just the work's style that critics maintain is characterized by absence and deficiency. Even as they draw productively on contextual information to explain, or explain away, aspects of this difficult work, critics regularly acknowledge that Melville satirizes all of the era's norms – religious and moral, intellectual and political – with little in the way of a positive message to mitigate the withering satire of established epistemological, ethical, and political beliefs. Given its many oddities, that critics will often register a personal evaluation is no surprise: for many, *The Confidence-Man* is "a masterpiece of irony and control" even though it "leaves . . . some Melville enthusiasts cold."[3] As a novel, in other words, it is a tedious but important slog.

After noting one further commonplace, nearly as old as the book itself, this essay will attempt to diverge from some of these established critical practices by bracketing, to the extent possible, investigation into the meaning of *The Confidence-Man*. In 1857, the reviewer for the London *Literary Gazette* wondered

> who will meddle with a book professing to inculcate philosophical truths through the medium of nonsensical people talking nonsense – the best definition of its scope and character that a somewhat prolonged consideration has enabled us to suggest. A novel it is not, unless a novel means forty-five conversations held on board a steamer, conducted by personages who might pass for the errata of creation, and so far resembling the Dialogues of Plato as to be undoubted Greek to ordinary men.[4]

The comparison is a just one: Melville, like Plato, presents characters in conversations that seem designed to uncover the fallacies associated with their most deeply held beliefs. Indeed, when one recalls that in *Apology* Socrates begins by stressing his confidence in his cause's justice and continues to insist the he has been sent "to perform the office" of a "stinging fly" for a city that has become "lazy" in its habits and principles, an office that often includes questioning the relationship between goodness and wealth, it is impossible to deny the similarity.[5]

Nor do I want to. As familiar as the connection to Plato is, there remains something to be gleaned from it: *The Confidence-Man* is full to bursting with analogy. Much like Plato's elenctic method, Melville's characters persistently rely on analogy to forward their arguments, buttress their claims, and establish likeness or kinship between people, places, and things. Often these analogies are pedestrian, but they can also be outlandish and far-fetched. From its opening paragraphs, the book's prose is saturated with figures of similitude, including analogy, simile, example, parable, fable, and pun. In this excess, the characters are joined by the narrator, who likewise proliferates these rhetorical devices. The book begins, for example, with a crowd gathered around a reward poster "as if it had been a theatre bill" and preyed upon by charlatans hawking money belts and thrilling narratives of bandits or pirates, "one and all exterminated ... like the hunted generations of wolves in the same regions" (CM 2). A mute circulates among them, "shield-like bearing his slate before him" (CM 3). The slate itself inspires comparison – thanks to its changing definitions of charity it is "not unlike the left-hand numeral of a printed dated" (CM 3) – and, although it stresses identity over similitude, the serial meanings of charity pithily replicate the rotation of meanings the text insistently invokes. On the boat's "long, wide, covered deck," which has "shop-like windowed spaces" akin to "some Constantinople arcade or bazaar, where more than one trade is plied," the barber opens his shop with "business-like dispatch" (CM 4). Increasing in "tired abstraction and dreaminess," the mute's "lamb-like figure relaxes" "as some sugar-snow in March" and he sleeps "like some enchanted man in his grave" (CM 5, 6). The "huge *Fidèle*" is "like any small ferry-boat" in its progress down the Mississippi and the constant supply of strangers it gathers is "like [a] Rio Janeiro fountain, fed from the Cocovarde mountains, which is ever overflowing with strange waters, but never with the same strange particles in every part" (CM 7). Were I to continue, it would become clear that analogies appear in more iterations than the mercurial confidence man himself.

This abundance leads me back to the problem of genre *The Confidence-Man* presents. What if "Melville's most formally innovative novel" is *not* a novel but only analogically akin to a novel?[6] Critics agree that Melville played with form across his career – how else can we explain *Pierre*? – but we tend to consider these experiments by genre: first he played with prose forms and then he turned to poetry. But what if that's not the best way to think about his career? What if a neat distinction between narrative fiction and verse misrepresents not only Melville's works, but also his aims as a writer? In "Hawthorne and His Mosses," Melville observes that poets, those who are "painters of Nature," write in "prose or verse" (PZ 249). As William Spengemann notes, such a view rejects form as poetry's definitive trait, focusing instead on "the verbal apprehension and expression of otherwise ungraspable truths." The idea that a "poet" could work in prose is not a position unique to Melville – F.O. Matthiessen stressed the importance of the "transcendental denial of distinction between prose and verse," more a practical than a theoretical position – but it may be particularly applicable to Melville's works. If, as Spengemann argues, "poetry in this very large sense" was Melville's "main business, the thing he felt both called and most inclined to do," then there is little reason to think of his works as falling into clearly demarcated categories like verse or prose.[7] Since the superfluity of analogy in *The Confidence-Man* thematizes the problem of differentiating people and things as they slide and glide into one another, I propose that we think of Melville's relationship to genre as having a similarly fluid quality. Put differently, if we consider not what the many analogies in the book mean, but instead what Melville means by including so very many of them, a different kind of book emerges, one in which "the indefinite privileges of the poet" are part of its prose (CM 224).

While Melville's previous novels often contain bursts of analogical excess – "The Whiteness of the Whale" provides an excellent example, although there are equally good instances in *Mardi, White-Jacket*, or *Pierre* – the relentlessness of analogy in *The Confidence-Man* culminates explicitly and pointedly in the question, "But is analogy argument?" (CM 165). This is a query asked with renewed vigor across the nineteenth century, in both established and emergent disciplines, and it is a central question for Melville as well. Tracing Melville's reply in *The Confidence-Man* will not tell us what the book means, but it may get us closer to understanding how it works, its relationship to both philosophy and poetry, and the relationship between philosophy and poetry that Melville was developing. If we divorce readings of the book from (reasonable) assumptions about Melville's career (and the ways it made him feel), what remains may not be a novel, but neither is it a failure.

While critics have not been particularly interested in the role of analogy in *The Confidence-Man*, mine is not the only argument taking up the topic. Although I frame my intervention by sketching the figure's history, I draw on the compelling analysis previously forwarded by Sianne Ngai. Detailing the connections – formal and thematic – between affect theory and mid-century market capitalism, Ngai pursues the "semblance of feeling" (confidence) that is the "basis of all transactions in the social world of the novel." Moving from the writings of psychologist Silvan Tomkins, Ngai uses *The Confidence-Man* to consider the status of tone in literary analysis through a deft reading that explores the perverse affective formulations of fiduciary money across its many transactions. Most strikingly for my own analysis, Ngai suggests that anaphora "overtakes" analogy as the book's definitive figure, introducing a degree of anaphoric noise that "*drown[s] out*" analogy through the amplification of ceaseless repetition. Diverging from her claim that "analogy becomes engulfed by anaphora,"[8] I demonstrate instead how analogy's many forms organize the book's generic slipperiness, associating its sometimes "lyric mood" (CM 220) with its tacit acknowledgement of a position Melville will articulate later in "Art," that "form" must "lend" coherence for "unlike things to meet and mate" (PP 280).

- - -

"What we know we know only through analogy," Johann Herder asserted in 1778.[9] He was neither the first, nor the last, person to identify in analogy a fundamental element of human cognition; the subsequent recognition that analogy is key to nonhuman cognition as well has expanded the implications of Herder's plural pronoun. At least since Aristotle, thinkers have argued about analogy, struggling to explain its powers while simultaneously positing its central role in the development of philosophy, law, religion, aesthetics, ethics, politics, and the natural sciences.[10] No wonder, then, that Novalis, Herder's contemporary, referred to analogy as a "magic wand" ["*den Zauberstab der Analogie*"], capable of generating fascination and enchantment with its magical connections. Simultaneously pedestrian and mysterious, analogy transforms the disparate into the similar. A conjunction usually announces its presence, a syntactical addition that has come to distinguish it from metaphor. Analogy wins popularity contests – Hugh Blair admits that nothing delights the fancy more than "resemblances of objects," which is why "some relation or analogy between one thing and another" is the basis of "all Tropes" – not only because of its rhetorical flexibility, but also because its range of applications is incredibly broad.[11] Terminological imprecision also accounts for its comprehensive applicability. Indeed, as an omnibus concept, analogy denotes a variety of operations. As Paul Bartha notes,

> An *analogy* is a comparison between two objects, or systems of objects that highlights respects in which they are thought to be similar. *Analogical reasoning* is any type of thinking that relies upon an analogy. An *analogical argument* is an explicit representation of analogical reasoning that cites accepted similarities between two systems in support of the conclusion that some further similarity exists.[12]

The distinctions between the layers of analogy's application usually flatten in non-technical use, contributing to both its magic and its confusions. Indeed, Bartha points out, despite centuries of effort, "We have no substantive normative theory of analogical arguments."[13] That is to say, no one has ever articulated an adequate set of rules to account for the validity of analogy or its arguments. In all cases, local knowledge, familiarity with both sides of a proposed comparison, is the only way to evaluate an analogy's precision. This limitation notwithstanding, analogy can be programmatic in that it helps to establish and maintain particular perspectives on the world which we might call philosophies; it can be justificatory or descriptive (examples and parables and similes), in which capacity it helps to clarify perception; and it can be heuristic, leading to startling discoveries and surprising insights.[14]

Intellectual historians have long held that analogy reached its zenith in the medieval era, when the twelfth-century "recovery" of Aristotle allowed it to emerge as an important tool for navigating pressing issues of signification in logic, theology, and metaphysics. Across the writings of Boethius, Aquinas, and Duns Scotus, analogy provided the scaffolding for an ambitious hermeneutic program that explained the otherwise unfathomable links between the human and the divine. This program was subsumed by the "allegorizing of Scriptures," "the prevailing medieval procedure" for reading, but analogy was nevertheless the tool that bound the different forms of interpretation together.[15]

Rejected, even derided, by early modern thinkers, analogy's influence waned – or so it seemed. In truth, however, while analogical argument was superseded by induction, analogical reasoning continued to be fundamental to law, philosophy, and the sciences. In religion, analogy also proved its ongoing utility; "by the eighteenth century analogy became the immanent method of natural theology and displaced allegory and other interpretive methods as the definitive test of Christian doctrine," Devon Griffiths explains.[16] Just as analogy provided "a key to the scriptures," it also "put into [human] hands the key of nature," thus showing "us a new correspondence or analogy between the word and works of God." David Hartley's *Observations on Man* (1749) was particularly expansive about the infinite combinations analogy permitted, observing "For the more any one looks into the external natural world, the more analogies, general or particular, perfect or imperfect, will he find every where."[17]

By the early nineteenth century, analogy could simultaneously serve as a cultural marker of an "antiquated" orientation to the world while its nearly magical ability to create links between disparate historical moments, cultures, and scientific facts made it indispensible to the development of the descriptive and laboratory sciences. Note, for example, that "the first four chapters of *On the Origin of Species* are devoted to an extended analogy between what breeders do when 'selecting' for specific characters and what happens in the state of nature," a clear indication of analogy's importance to nineteenth-century thought.[18] Yet, despite changing evaluations of analogy's powers, its prior theological use as a means of "posit[ing] the adequacy of all relational perception within the perfectly created cosmos" lingered, haunting these new discourses. John Stuart Mill did not exaggerate when he said "There is no word . . . which is used more loosely, or in a greater variety of senses, than Analogy."[19]

The Confidence-Man employs all the loose variety of analogy – and the result is chaotic. In addition to the rhetorical senses of the word, evident in the consistent use of analogy for description, emphasis, and elaboration, Melville explores the role of analogy as a form of argumentation and the implications associated with analogy as a "doctrine," harkening back to its place in theological debate (CM 173). The book's investigation of analogy and argument is the more familiar of these two approaches, because it has been read as forming part of Melville's engagement with skepticism, most persuasively by Maurice Lee. Nevertheless, Melville cannily cycles through all of analogy's functions – in argument, in doctrine, in rhetoric – and its magic organizes *The Confidence-Man*. My analysis of the book focuses on the central arc of episodes with Pitch, a misanthropic bachelor from Missouri, where analogy is most thoroughly interrogated. One of the few named characters, Pitch encounters three versions of the confidence man or men: the herb-doctor, the representative of a Philosophical Intelligence Office (P.I.O.), and the cosmopolitan. Stubborn Pitch has not fared well in the critical literature; in a recent reading, Rachel Cole contends that he is "humiliated" by the P.I.O. representative, becoming emotional and "ridiculous," "a fool" who "somewhat hysterically" repeats himself.[20] Still, he is the only interlocutor the text takes seriously enough to engage in three different ways. Other characters talk their way through a greater number of chapters – the stranger (later Charlie Noble) appears in eleven – but they do not meet as many different iterations or avatars of the confidence man. The vehicle for Melville's examination of analogy as argument (Pitch explosively asks "But is analogy argument?") *and* as doctrine ("The doctrine of analogy recurs"), Pitch may be less a fool than a victim of analogy's imprecision (CM 173). Put differently, if Pitch is a fool, then, as in Plato's dialogues, so are we all.

Initial bluster and offensive conclusions notwithstanding, Pitch presents the P.I.O. representative with an argument to support his position that a machine will be more reliable than a human employee. Drawing on "fifteen years' experience" with "twenty-nine boys," Pitch concludes that "boyhood is a natural state of rascality" (CM 155). The "boys" in this sample hailed from nations around the world ("American, Irish, English, German, African," as well as Chinese, Indian, Causasain, and Mongol) and demonstrated an array of personal qualities ("polite," "saucy," "white," "black," "smart," "lazy" [CM 157]). Still, each had "some wholly unforeseen species of viciousness peculiar to that one peculiar boy" (CM 156), which led to his dismissal. The similarities in the cases ("rascality") override the differences ("wholly unforeseen") as Pitch moves inductively from evidence to conclusion. While there are certainly problems with Pitch's method – his misanthropy makes it easy to imagine that he manufactured the outcome of these trials, as does his claim to represent the position reached by "all thinking minds" (CM 154) – he is nevertheless in good company in relying on empirical experience and experiment to reach a conclusion: induction is key to the modern scientific method. Because the order of the narrative introduces Pitch's personal biases *before* the way in which these beliefs took shape, it is easy to mistake the induction here for deduction, a confusion that seems to fit with Melville's general design across the episode.[21] The "empirical modes of analysis" Pitch (problematically) deploys in his study of the character of boys do not differ substantially from the practices of the era's natural scientists, works Melville knew.

Shocked by Pitch's misanthropy, the P.I.O. representative sets out to rebut his position with an analogical argument, drawing parallels between different systems in order to establish constructive similarities. He explains that his office is devoted to the "careful analytical study of man" and, to accomplish this end, they have developed a "quiet theory" which "teaches us to proceed by analogy from the physical to the moral." This process, he admits, may seem "peculiar" but is "strictly philosophical" (CM 160). Given its similarity to Plato's practice across his dialogues, it is hard to disagree. Juxtaposing physical attributes, like the succession of teeth or the ability to grow a beard, with moral qualities including reliability and efficiency, the P.I.O. representative posits the natural (although often belated) appearance of human potential. A boy may not yet have a beard, he observes, but this absence does not preclude its eventual presence; so, too, the present absence of "any noble quality" cannot be taken as evidence that such a trait will never emerge. Thus, even if markers of moral potential are missing, "the trust of perfect confidence," vouchsafed by analogy, should be granted. Although he initially only "hint[s]" at his analogies (CM 163), the P.I.O. representative ultimately deploys their full "force" (CM 165) to dislodge Pitch from his intransigence. Pitch thus seems a later-day Thrasymachus, the blustering interlocutor from Book I of the *Republic* who complains about Socrates's "loose way of speaking."[22] By the end of their protracted conversation, Pitch is willing to entertain the P.I.O. representative's position – although he refuses to decide on these "new views" "in the concrete" – and assents to "try that boy" (CM 171).

Across the chapter, Pitch's harrumphing interruptions tether the conversation to philosophy, although the debate itself turns to rhetoric when the frustrated Missourian likens the P.I.O. representative's argument to the pun (a term that appears at least 39 times in the novel):

> "—Your analogy," like a snapping turtle.
> "Yes, respected sir."
> "But is analogy argument? You are a punster."
> "Punster, respected sir?" with a look of being aggrieved.
> "Yes, you pun with ideas as another man may with words." (CM 165)

Here Pitch, supplanted by analogy ("like a snapping turtle"), lodges the book's clearest comment on its own formal obsession. Like analogy, the pun, one of the earliest rhetorical figures (*paronomasia*), works via similitude. Mining the resonances that can emerge from the "similarity of form and disparity of meaning," puns evoke "disparate meanings in contexts where each differently applies."[23] To "pun with ideas," then, would also be to slip between different meanings, relying wrongly on similarities of form to produce flawed conclusions. That something like a "pun with ideas" was one of the regular concerns about analogy is conveyed by David Hartley, an author Melville read in 1848.[24] After a dizzying list of possible connections, between different kinds of bodies, minds, occupations, disasters, structures, and systems, all of which "afford endless instances of analogies natural and artificial," Hartley warns: "For the mind being once initiated into the method of discovering analogies, and expressing them, does by association persevere in this method, and even force things into its system by concealing disparities, magnifying resemblances, and accommodating language thereto."[25] Persevering in its method, *The Confidence-Man* never shies away from forced similitudes or submerged disparities, particularly in its central pun-like maneuver, taking a single word – *confidence* – and insisting, through a series of formally similar dialogues, on the recognition of its uneven application and disparate connotations.

Likening analogy to pun, underscoring the potential violence of superficial or discordant similitudes, Pitch's ferocious responses enact the violence George Campbell associated with analogy in his *Philosophy of Rhetoric* (1776):

> Nevertheless, when the analogies are numerous, and the subject admits not evidence of another kind, it does not its efficacy. It must be owned, however, that it is generally more successful in silencing objections than in evincing truth, and on this account may more properly be styled the defensive arms of the orator than the offensive. Though it rarely refutes, it frequently repels refutation, like those weapons which, though they cannot kill the enemy, will ward his blows.[26]

Despite its familiarity and ubiquity, analogy is a figure, and a form of argument, that inflicts pain, especially when used indiscriminately.

Although it is the mourning man who actually strikes the confidence-man ("a sudden side-blow all but felled [the herb-doctor]" [CM 115]), Pitch comes to share Campbell's views on analogy's efficacy. Shortly after the P.I. O. representative disembarks, Pitch begins to suspect he has been "betrayed into being an unphilosophical dupe" (CM 172). Blaming his "too indulgent, too artless and companionable nature," he commits to a more "splenetic" approach for the future (CM 173). As part of this reversion, and slipping into free indirect discourse,

> The doctrine of analogies recurs. Fallacious enough doctrine when wielded against one's prejudices, but in corroboration of cherished suspicions not without likelihood. Analogically, he couples the slanting cut of the equivocator's coat-tails with the sinister cast in his eye; he weighs slyboot's sleek speech in the light imparted by the oblique import of the smooth slope of his worn boot-heels; the insinuator's undulating flunkeyism dovetail into those of the flunkey beast that windeth his way on this belly. (CM 173–4)

Now a "doctrine" rather than a theory, rhetorical device, or argumentative tool, analogy shifts associations yet again, a change aided by Melville's use of religiously inflected imagery. The brevity of the sentence – "The doctrine of analogies recurs" – obscures a simple question: recurs from where? Neither Pitch nor the P.I.O. representative invokes a "doctrine of analogies"; nor does this "doctrine" appear in earlier episodes. This is not to suggest that a "doctrine of analogies" did not exist as a possible antecedent. To the contrary, the central place of analogy in both Scholastic thought and eighteenth-century arguments for natural theology presupposed the correlation of divine and material realms, making analogy central to, if not a component of, religious doctrine. Melville's own familiarity with the association of doctrine and analogy is made clear in *Moby-Dick*, although Ahab invokes the Romantic reworking of its principles, characteristically placing the human in the place of the divine: "O Nature, and O soul of man! how far beyond all utterance are your linked analogies! not the smallest atom stirs of lives in matter, but has its cunning duplicate in mind" (MD 264). As David Simpson suggests, "there was a lingering theological version of analogy" positing "the adequacy of all relational perception within the perfectly created cosmos" which "post-Enlightenment philosophers sought to displace." That they were only ever partially successful, that the correlation of analogy with Christian doctrine persisted even as the descriptive sciences embraced analogy's creative and expansive powers, is suggested here as Melville shifts from an argument about best business practices, through philosophy and rhetoric, to religion. Eased by the sibilance of "sleek" and "sinister" "slanting," the "doctrine" eases Pitch along yet another route between the physical and the moral which allows him to reach a new (and contradictory) conclusion. As Sianne Ngai points out, Melville's "sibilant excess . . . demonstrates how analogical 'coupling' intensifies through the multiplication of analogies to a point at which it might be said to hiss or feed back, enabling Pitch to detect the presence of a separate, snaky element within the analogies the confidence-man has already produced."[27] At the same time, the rational sense of analogy yields to the leaps of faith of Scholastic interpretation, as this "magic wand" uncovers similarities between the P.I.O. representative and the tempting serpent of Old Testament fame.

There is more to be said about the multiple forms of similitude in the text, the numerous ways analogy and its "appendages" "glide about," "serpent-like," defying reason and belief, but I did propose to bracket what these figures might mean in place of how they worked (CM 159). Were I to transgress my own boundaries and venture a guess about what Melville seeks to communicate concerning the *Fidèle*'s world, I would note that his concern with analogies – the confusions and contradictions they introduce, the ways they "glide" – underscores their prevalence in American thought. Analogies provide the basic mechanism for sympathetic identification and create the equality celebrated in the nation's framing documents. If they can be easily perverted and manipulated, as Melville relentlessly demonstrates across *The Confidence-Man*, if the pairings they wantonly create can be handily demolished or replaced, where can a safe mooring be found? Is there a way around Pitch's claim that "the entire ship is a riddle" (CM 159)?

A brief glance at the book's infamous twenty-sixth chapter, "Containing the Metaphysics of Indian Hating, According to the Views of One Evidently Not so Prepossessed as Rousseau in Favour of Savages," will indicate that the answer to the above question must be no. Metaphysics is the study of first principles and the chapter presents a "philosophy" that takes hatred, irrational and unrelenting, as its motivating premise. In 1857, as well as today, the chapter provides a chilling commentary on the dangers of sectional and racial antagonisms. But it is also an acknowledgement that philosophy is shaped by the prejudices and assumptions of philosophers; indeed, Melville's representation of the "Metaphysics" confuses principle and example in a way that recursively presents one of the basic dilemmas of analogy. Racism, or any other belief system, will create first principles to posit its conclusions and then select comparisons to support both. As Hartley noted, humans may take intellectual pleasure in uncovering similarities between objects or experiences, but the analogies thus created can go wrong in multiple ways. Our perception might be skewed, such that the subsequent analogy would point to the wrong objects or experiences. Alternatively, we could be attached to a particular theoretical model that encourages us to look at the world in a warped way. Because we value the order that the confirmation of our beliefs brings, it is nearly impossible to convert people from their fixed positions.

Given the far-reaching powers of analogy – loose and magical, scientific and theological, non-human and human – it would be more surprising had

Melville *not* been intrigued by its potential. In *The Confidence-Man*, Melville mines analogy's implications so ceaselessly that this investigation may be the only consistent feature of an otherwise inconsistent work. The book foregrounds "a throng of functionally analogous characters" presented in "a series of analogous encounters."[28] That *The Confidence-Man* does not resolve into a unified message may be as much a feature of its form as a result of its content. As Goethe observed, "We mustn't scorn thinking that proceeds by way of analogies" for it "has the advantage of not closing doors or in fact aiming at any ultimate solution."[29] Its obsession with analogy, in other words, makes it formally impossible for *The Confidence-Man* to forward "any ultimate solution" to the social issues its repetitive episodes repetitively explore. The allegorizing move of interpretation, already implied by analogy's history, is blocked by complicated layers of Melville's perverse formal commitment across the text. But, as the turn to the puns hints, there is another way to think about what the book is doing, one that remains faithful to its obsessions and that responds to Pitch's question about argument. What if *The Confidence-Man* is "a kind of poetry but in a form which stands in something the same relation to blank verse which that does to rhyme. A sort of free-and-easy chant with refrains to it" (CM 221)? As the book itself demonstrates, this "kind of poetry" is, in fact, prose, but one that enjoys "indefinite privilege."

- - -

Reading *The Confidence-Man* in 1979, Nina Baym concluded that Melville had decided that the novel was a "mendacious medium," one in which the only "sort of truth" that could be expressed concerned "fiction and language."[30] In the final section of this essay, I will build from Baym's influential claim, expanding its reach to include Melville's explicit turn to poetry.[31] In *Ornamental Aesthetics* (2016), Theo Davis argues that Henry David Thoreau's *Journal* – which is "so strange" that it forestalls normal interpretative strategies – develops a "poetic form, grounded in ornamental notation rather than symbolism or verse." "Attending to what calls for notice and snagging briefly onto a beautiful object are, then, ways that Thoreau's *Journal* is a poetic work," Davis contends.[32] Developing her position from Thoreau's engagement with Greek poetry and his sustained attention to the natural world, Davis proposes a means of thinking about literary form that diverges from our more usual attention to generic features, preferring instead the mental qualities, actions, or responses, like attention, that particular forms encourage.[33]

Melville's project in *The Confidence-Man* is more conventional in all senses of the word. His book solicits, but does not reward, attention. Nevertheless, I think its pressing formal strangeness is productively, even appropriately, approached by placing it on a trajectory toward poetic form, defined by a focus on limitation and repetition rather than "ornamental notation." This, too, is what poems do. Through his fascination with the possibilities of formal constraint, his obsessive engagement with analogy as figure and argument, and his repudiation of established novelistic conventions, Melville aligns *The Confidence-Man* with poetry, broadly construed. This is not to say that the chapters are a series of prose poems, but rather to suggest that the work explores problems inherent to the poetic process as much as it rejects those associated with the narrative one. In short, I think we should read the book not as a failed or problem novel, but as an experiment in form and its possibilities. To use the book's own idiom, *The Confidence-Man* glides "serpent-like" between genres.

Or between genres as they are defined today. As scholars working in the field of historical poetics have made clear, nineteenth-century "poetry" already existed between genres. The "intergeneric colloquy" of Melville's works captures one of the fundamental features of nineteenth-century genres: they were not discrete.[34] Indeed, "*in the nineteenth century, poetry is not a genre*," Michael Cohen explains; while "poems have operative functions for nineteenth-century readers and writers, poetry ... is a retro-projection." There are many things a poem *may* have – rhyme, meter, specifically designated lineation, concentrated language for aesthetic ends – but none of these can be deemed either necessary or sufficient – and they may not have mattered to nineteenth-century readers, adept navigators of the varied "formats, media, [and] modes of media and address" active at the time.[35] One critic maintains that "what makes a poem different from any other kind of composition is a species of magic" derived, in part, from "the way words lean upon each other."[36] On this account, a poem is like an analogy in its ability to wrest meaning from manufactured contiguity. Elizabeth Renker's reading of Melville's complicated verbal play about character offers a different sense of how words might "lean" together. Equally productive is the ("retro-projective") definition Cleanth Brooks and Robert Penn Warren provide at the start of *Understanding Poetry:* "Poetry is a form of speech, or discourse, written or spoken. ... In poetry, as in all other discourse, one person is saying something to another person." Parsing the context of this "discourse," particularly in terms of the information it does – or does not – communicate, Brooks and Warren stress that "the specialization of language" in poetry is an attempt to negotiate its "different character," one that does not rely wholly on the "communication of matters of fact."[37] Nothing in this definition excludes Melville's talky book. That *The Confidence-Man* often seems to prioritize sound over sense, as Ngai proposes, affiliates its verbal program with verse.

Rather than force *The Confidence-Man* into yet another genre, particularly one that did not exist, I will turn to *Battle-Pieces and Aspects of the War* (1866), Melville's subsequent book, likewise suspended between genres.[38] Thanks to its formal features – lineation, rhyme, rhythm, etc. – *Battle-Pieces* is more identified as a collection of poetry than *The Confidence-Man* is as a novel. Still, what Robert Milder identifies as its particular achievement – a remarkable "interplay of voices"[39] – harkens back to the many conversations that comprise *The Confidence-Man.* Not only does the volume include various prose features, including a preface, footnotes, and the "Supplement" appended at its end, but the poems themselves are dependent on prose. Instead of concluding that either or both of these books are deficient, I suggest we recognize that Melville experimented with forms that occupied a murky middle ground, both and neither verse and prose. The recent attention to, and appreciation of, Melville's poems changes what it is possible to understand about *The Confidence-Man* – and vice versa. If we recognize the formal play foundational to the text, it is also possible to recognize that it is as much an anticipation of verse as it is a repudiation of prose.

Two further observations underwrite the reorientation I suggest here. First, poetry before the Romantic era was not exclusively lyric; nor was it prized primarily for its originality. As W. K. Wimsatt explains, "the method, the bondage, and the main freedom of all English neo-classic and pre-romantic poetry" was "the principle of imitation or free-running parallel." Such poems were "relatively unoriginal," although subsequent redefinitions of freedom made them appear even less original than they may have been.[40] For these writers, poetic excellence was measured by the skillful manipulation of convention: formal constraint provided the conditions for creativity, a model of literary production well suited to a writer gifted with "eccentric craftsmanship."[41]

Nor was such engagement with convention only a practice of poets long dead. As Claudia Stokes demonstrates, "poetic conventionality" has emerged as an "active subject of recent scholarly inquiry" in nineteenth-century American literature because many poets, often but not exclusively women, relied on "stock poetic tropes and forms."[42] Stokes and others working on historical poetics have established that, for many poets, deploying a convention was a conscious decision, not an indication of limited creativity or talent. Melville may not have thought highly of these poets – the depiction of Pierre Glendinning's poetic fame suggests no small amount of contempt – but he also took a dim view of the uncritical celebration of originality (as *Pierre* again makes clear): Melville toyed with the limits of convention in prose too, both in the representation of a popular poet and in the creative engagement with the features of sentimental and gothic romance. In this regard, he had plenty of company across the antebellum period. Although our critical priorities prefer originality, recent attention to the importance of repetition, imitation, convention, and reprinting has established that, for many, "the importance of *not* being original" was key.[43] Like poems that rework classical or Biblical predecessors, individual episodes of *The Confidence-Man* are variations on a consistent theme, a set of "free-running" parallels that take up and enact the same principle. Drawing on the text's key term, one could even assert that fidelity to this central schema organizes the book as a whole: writing with a schema (con+fidelity) draws on an alternate way of assessing and enacting creativity.[44] The same can be said of *Battle-Pieces*. Not only did Melville draw on published accounts about the war, particularly *The Rebellion Record*, he also engaged carefully with popular "vernacular forms," like "hymn, ballad, song, and epitaph."[45] For this reason, *Battle-Pieces* was long dismissed by critics, who dismissed the collection as "versified journalism."[46] But such trivializing remarks misrepresent the social role of poems during the Civil War, when they provided assistance to readers seeking to understand events that regularly exceeded comprehension. In different ways, then, both *Battle-Pieces* and *The Confidence-Man* engage with the assumption that originality matters less than facility within a set of (variously rigid) conventions.

There is no need to wonder if Melville joined his peers in puzzling over the role of originality, for *The Confidence-Man* takes up the topic in three metacritical chapters: 14, 33, and 44. Each of the chapters explores the relation between originality, fiction, and reality, weighing fidelity to experience against narrative norms and readerly expectations. They circle around a shared concern, namely that the expectation that characters will be consistent and coherent fails to capture "real life" where "a consistent character is a *rara avis*" (CM 89). Novelistic conventions suffer, in Melville's depiction, from the problems that trouble analogy: "Experience is the only guide here; but as no one man can be coextensive with *what is*, it may be unwise in every case to rest upon it" (CM 90). As with analogy, in other words, reliance on partial (and likely biased) assumptions generates a desire for similitude that is structurally flawed (and illogical). Working against the desire for the familiar is a contradictory demand for originality, also misunderstood. Like the "worthy barber" and his friends, readers are too quick to dub a "queer customer" original, a kind of loose accounting that misrepresents literature and life. "A good fiction may be full" of characters that are "new, singular, striking, odd, [and] eccentric" (CM 318–319); it is an "impropriety" to think they are original, however (CM 319). Readers thus resemble Pitch when he notes that analogies are "not without likelihood" in supporting a position they prefer but "fallacious" in other instances; they prefer characters who support the views of the world they hold, and reject others who do not conform to these preconceptions. Arguing against these assumptions directly in the metacritical chapters, and indirectly across the rest of the book, Melville repudiates the demand for originality, preferring instead to repeat, recycle, and reuse figures and characters.

Melville's repudiation notwithstanding, the meager praise and ample opprobrium *The Confidence-Man* received from critics was associated with its purported novelty, and William Dean Howells famously deplored the display of the "negative virtues of originality" in his savage review of *Battle-Pieces.*[47] Although usually positioned on opposite sides of a generic divide, the two books share more than negative assessments of their putative originality. They cover similar thematic ground – the "Supplement," for example, explores the demands that "Christian charity" imposes on persons and communities while arguing against "contrition hypocritical" (PP 259) – such that when Melville writes "May we all have moderation; may we all show candor," he could be commenting on the world of the *Fidèle* as easily as the early years of Reconstruction (PP 242). As in *The Confidence-Man, Battle-Pieces* takes up the question of genre, from the figure of the Aeolian harp in the "Preface" to the "explicit statements of poetic theory" Timothy Sweet identifies in "Dupont's Round Fight" and "A Utilitarian View of the Monitor's Fight."[48] Most important for the argument here, however, is Melville's observation in "Supplement" that "literary scruples" are no match for historical events. But what is presented as a scruple might be better described as a convention, for it turns out that what history does not respect is narrative "symmetry," the expectation that "events" will be "rounded ... into completion" (PP 259). "To altered circumstances complicated adaptations are to be made," Melville suggests, a phrase that speaks simultaneously to individual assumptions about what it might mean that the war is over and the expectations that readers bring to texts. "There are difficulties great and novel" that arise from these changes, Melville concludes (PP 259). Given the volume's regular concern with what it means to write about and through the Civil War, "novel" resonates more broadly (and even counterfactually) than the narrow sense the sentence suggests.

But there is no suggestion in "Supplement" that Melville thought the novel would be an apt form for depicting the conflict or the circumstances that emerged in its wake. "Let us hope," he writes in the essay's final lines, "that the terrible historic tragedy of our time may not have been enacted without instructing our whole beloved country through terror and pity; and may fulfillment verify in the end those expectations which kindle the bards of Progress and Humanity" (PP 246). The reference to Aristotle's *Poetics* is explicit: through catharsis, tragedies expunged terror and pity from the *polis*, allowing it to function smoothly. It is not difficult, Melville hints, to understand the war in these terms, as "the terrible historic tragedy of our time," one that Sophocles, Aeschylus, or Shakespeare might have been able to write. But, although he reads the war as a tragedy, he does not suggest that it will be represented by tragic drama; the 1864 death of Hawthorne, the American writer he had judged best suited to claim Shakespeare's mantle, may have influenced this conclusion. Instead, Melville suggests a different genre will account for the war – poetry. The complicated temporality of the essay's concluding clause promises that the optimistic "bards of Progress and Humanity," the poets who sing of what is best in human nature and ingenuity, will prove to have been right in their optimism once the tragedy's instruction is complete. They will write the future. Shifting between genres, and implicitly claiming the mantle as one of these "bards" at the end of a volume of variations on the ballad, Melville muses on the relationship between genre and history, ending hopefully (or hopefully enough) with the eventual satisfaction poets and their readers may enjoy.

Literary scholars tend to use genre to organize what we think literary works both represent and do. But, like other forms of categorization, generic classification can also prevent us from appreciating complexity, nuance, and innovation. It is worth asking, in other words, what is to be gained from the consistent critical effort to make *The Confidence-Man* match the category 'novel'? If we read this work with other authors from the era experimenting with form – with Thoreau, with Walt Whitman, with Emily Dickinson – we might find that *The Confidence-Man* has more to offer than tedium, and that genres do things we have not yet begun to understand.

CHAPTER 9

Melville's Style

Samuel Otter

An "old" term for the "New" Melville studies, "style" continues to entice and confound. Although critics over the past generation assert that treatments of literary style have become unfashionable, and while it is true that the professional cachet of such approaches declined as many theorists and historicists came to associate the term negatively with individual signature and scholarly connoisseurship, interest in Melville's verbal textures has been continuous. Such interest includes the early biographies of John Freeman (1926) and Lewis Mumford (1929), whose authors metaphorically parsed the rhythmic sentences of *Moby-Dick*; F. O. Matthiessen (1941) on Melville's Shakespearean transformations; Newton Arvin (1950) on the experimental diction of *Moby-Dick* and the convoluted tetrameters of *Clarel;* Warner Berthoff (1962) on Melville's prose tenacity (his "unstinting exactness"); Eric J. Sundquist (1981) on the ironies bordering on tautology that convey the suppressed recognitions and revolutions of slavery in "Benito Cereno"; James Creech (1993) on the coded eroticism and explicit periphrasis in *Pierre*; Elizabeth Renker (1996) on the attenuation of letters, syllables, words, and characters in *The Confidence-Man*; Sharon Cameron (2007) on the agrammaticality distinguishing a range of phenomena in Melville's later novels and especially *Billy Budd*; William Spengemann (2010) on the deliberate obscurity, knotted allusiveness, equivocality, and impersonation in Melville's poetry; and Alex Calder (2011) on the improvised opacities and modal discontinuities that typify Melville's "bad writing" in works such as *Omoo, Mardi, Pierre,* and "The Bell-Tower." Whether formalist, historicist, phenomenologist, epistemologist, aestheticist, ethicist, or some amalgam, critic after critic has been impelled to articulate what is peculiarly Melvillean. We might say that, along with Henry James (occasional comparisons between the two writers appeared as early as 1919), Melville is among the foremost literary stylists in the nineteenth-century United States: a restless, experimental writer for whom words distinctively bear the weight of thought.[1]

Yet verbal style is hard to define and to describe, and stylistic accounts are not easily – or can be too easily – sutured to literary interpretations. The meanings of the word shifted in the eighteenth and nineteenth centuries from "style" as a register of decorum (associated with persistent classical views about hierarchy and appropriateness) to "style" as inseparable from content and as revealing individual character and aesthetic preference (style as choice). With this shift, questions raised by the term were amplified. What are the relationships between ornament and essence? Inheritance and inflection? Norm and deviation? Description and analysis? Writing about literary style can risk myopia and tautology. But the effort also holds the possibility for advancing our understanding of verbal knowledge, of the ways in which, as Susan Sontag puts it, "every style embodies an epistemological decision, an interpretation of how and what we perceive." Such attention can illuminate what Charles Altieri describes as writers' "complex and elaborate modes of individual purposiveness." Considerations of style help to explain the ways in which particular writers compel (or alienate) readers in specific contexts and also across time and place.[2]

Nelson Goodman suggests a connection between writing about style and writing about metaphor: "A complex and subtle style, like a trenchant metaphor, resists reduction to a literal formula."[3] For Goodman, the challenges in analyzing elusive verbal objects are inevitable, and the difficulties are commensurate with the perceptive achievements. Style and metaphor are not only analogous but often intimately linked: it is almost impossible to write about style without employing metaphor. The discerner of style, seeking to interpret arrangements of diction, syntax, rhythm, and figure in a register that exceeds the particular verbal line or literary text, makes comparisons and often employs figurative language. Metaphors of style seem inescapable, maybe even necessary, in the effort to impart significance to pattern. Such metaphors need to be judged by their aptness and explanatory force and by the textual, biographical, and historical evidence on which they are based.

Metaphors of style frequently draw on visual analogies, and some of the most influential treatments of style have focused on the visual arts, whose elements and media are more concrete than those in the verbal arts. Andrew Harrison, invoking Richard Wollheim, has called style a "direction of salience," in which the prominent formal elements in a work of art influence and even direct the attention of viewers, listeners, or readers. Alternatively, Richard Neer, invoking Wittgenstein, maintains that style involves an "aspect," a viewing from a particular orientation, "*saturated* with interpretation" (emphasis in the original). We do not need to choose. We can regard "style" as produced by the reciprocities of "salience" and "aspect": a recognition of meaningful patterns across an artist's career that emerge from the qualities and contexts of the work, assessed from the perspective of the critic and rendered shareable through evidence and argument. "Style" thus reveals the properties of both object and observers.[4]

In the pages that follow, I argue that across the years Melville was drawn to a verbal line – an articulation of discontinuity – that he repeatedly associated with the fissured landscape of the Marquesas, and in particular the island of Nuku Hiva, where he spent a month in 1842 after deserting the whaler *Acushnet* with his fellow crewmember Richard Tobias Greene. This argument may seem counterintuitive, given Melville's restless verbal experiments and the customary separation between his prose of the 1840s and 1850s and his poetry of the 1860s, 1870s, and 1880s. But from his first book *Typee: A Peep at Polynesian Life* (1846), a fictionalized narrative of his sojourn on Nuku Hiva, to the epic poem *Clarel: A Poem and Pilgrimage in the Holy Land* (1876), the account of a young protagonist's quest in the Levant, and the short lyric "To Ned," a reflection on Pacific encounters included in his late volume of prose and poetry *John Marr and Other Sailors* (1888), Melville portrays a trajectory of discrepancies: smooth lines of sight that turn out to be composed of ridges and gaps, whose traversal involves a strenuous, discontinuous, and often unexpected advance. Crucial to the aesthetics and epistemology of this verbal landscape are the dynamics of perspective, as Melville explores the distance between viewer and prospect and the relationships between position and interpretation. Colin Dayan, in her essay "Melville's Creatures," has called for a renewed scrutiny of Melville's prose: "Let us imagine what prose would look like if it were to become a perspectival phenomenon, a means of seeing otherwise or crosswise."[5] I respond to that provocation, tracking a characteristic verbal outlook from the early prose to the late poetry. The pattern I analyze is not the key to it all, nor is it the only conspicuous verbal design in Melville's career, but it is a revealing feature whose complex persistence may allow us to understand aspects of Melville's writing that we have not noticed before.

Critics rarely think of the lush island of Nuku Hiva in *Typee* as having any relation, other than that of a lost paradise, to the deserts of Palestine in *Clarel*. Melville distances himself from such a narrative of longing when, in an 1860 letter to his brother Allan, giving directions for the publication of his *Poems* (a volume that was never issued), he declares, "For God's sake don't have *By the author of 'Typee' 'Piddledee' &c* on the title-page" (L 343). The still dominant sense among many readers and literary critics, beyond devoted specialists, is that there is a split in Melville's writing career between the exuberant prose from *Typee* (1846) through *Moby-Dick* (1851), which largely draws on his Pacific experiences, and the later, supposedly exhausted poetry from *Clarel* (1876) through *Timoleon* (1891), deemed to have been composed in the abstract registers of theology, philosophy, or nostalgia. (The politics and prosody of Melville's 1866 Civil War collection, *Battle-Pieces and Aspects of the War*, have generated significant critical interest in recent decades.) Yet neither persistent critical narratives nor the author's weariness with his typecasting should obscure the importance of *Typee* for the epic reflections of *Clarel*, in which Melville rewrites his Marquesan encounters. When critics do avoid a narrative of loss in moving from *Typee* to the poetry, they tend to interpret Melville's Pacific allusions as retrieving a balance or repose that he associated with the South Seas.[6] I would like to suggest something different: that the Marquesas continue to disorient and surprise and that these effects are valued, maybe given the highest value, by the poet. In writing about his experience – bringing together what he saw on Nuku Hiva, what he read, and what he imagined he saw – Melville developed a characteristic verbal line and a set of images that become apparent across his career.

At the beginning of *Typee*, Melville's narrator and alter ego "Tommo" introduces the perceptual dynamics that will define his Marquesan landscapes:

> Those who for the first time visit the South Seas, generally are surprised at the appearance of the islands when beheld from the sea. From the vague accounts we sometimes have of their beauty, many people are apt to picture to themselves enamelled and softly swelling plains, shaded over with delicious groves, and watered by purling brooks, and the entire country but little elevated above the surrounding ocean. The reality is very different; bold rock-bound coasts, with the surf beating high against the lofty cliffs, and broken here and there into deep inlets, which open to the view thickly-wooded valleys, separated by the spurs of mountains clothed with tufted grass, and sweeping down towards the sea from an elevated and furrowed interior, form the principal features of these islands. (TY 12)[7]

Westerners in the Marquesas do not see what they expect. The islands are composed not of smooth plains but of jagged vertical coasts, high mountains, steep valleys, and a "furrowed interior." "Furrowed" is a curious word here. Melville's narrator uses it to compare the surface of the inner highlands to channels ploughed in the ground, but the adjective both implies and elides agency. The "interior" is "furrowed" – by whom or what? The term carries associations with the land and also with tracks in the sea and wrinkles in the brow. Etymologically, "furrowed" has a double reference to both trench and ridge.

Tommo further specifies the "principal features" of the Nuku Hivan landscape several chapters later. Having escaped from the whaling ship *Dolly,* he and his fellow deserter Toby reach the high plateau and hope to secure a commanding view of the two valleys they believe to be inhabited by vivid tribal alternatives: the Typee (cruel savages) or the Happar (gentle natives). Yet their expectations are unsettled by their perspective:

> But here we were disappointed. Instead of finding the mountain we had ascended sweeping down in the opposite direction into broad and capacious valleys, the land appeared to retain its general elevation, only broken into a series of ridges and inter-vales, which as far as the eye could reach stretched away from us, with their precipitous sides covered with the brightest verdure, and waving here and there with the foliage of clumps of woodland. (TY 41)

Like "furrowed" earlier, the word "inter-vales" here deepens the prospect. Webster and Goodrich's *American Dictionary of the English Language* (1851) notes a usage of "intervale," but asserts that the proper spelling was "interval," minus the "e" and without any hyphen. It includes among definitions for the word "a tract of low or plain ground between hills, or along the banks of rivers." The *Oxford English Dictionary* describes "intervale" as a rare variant or doublet for "interval," noting a New England custom, dating back to the seventeenth century, of using the term with its superfluous "e" to refer to "a low level tract of land, especially along a river."[8] Melville's use of "inter-vale" is uncommon and also, in the Marquesan context, inaccurate. He repurposes the word to emphasize the difference between New England and Nuku Hiva. The terrain he describes early, and repeatedly, in *Typee* involves not shallow expanses but abrupt depths and an apparently limitless vista of ridges and gorges. With "inter-vales," Melville draws on etymology both historical (*inter* + *vallum*: "the space between palisades or ramparts") and popular (*inter* + vale, invoking the actual "vales" or valleys in his scene). He was attached to the spelling and also, the evidence would indicate, to the hyphen, which offered a visual pun that cleaved the word itself. That hyphen, located at the end of the prose line in the first English edition (1846), was then removed in the first American printing of *Typee* when the word fell within the line, and finally restored as the clear marker of a compound word, likely at the author's direction, in the revised American edition, published later in 1846.[9]

The view of Nuku Hiva put forward early in *Typee* – the ascent that provides access to gaps, the line of sight that is ruptured – seems to have made a deep impression on Melville. He devotes four chapters to the trip over the ridges from Taoiha'e Bay, where Tommo and Toby jump ship, to the valley of the Typee. The improvised journey is described as lasting for five days, inordinately longer than the several hours it would have taken to travel across the established route. The chapters are repetitive – Tommo and Toby climb to summits and descend into ravines, moving from ridge to ridge in numerous "perpendicular episodes" (TY 52) that involve vigorous effort and scant progress – and also compelling in their humor, rhythm, topographical detail, and manufactured adventure. Attention is lavished on the pattern of ridges and gaps:

> At last we gained the top of the second elevation, the loftiest of those I have described as extending in parallel lines between us and the valley we desired to reach. It commanded a view of the whole intervening distance; and, discouraged as I was by other circumstances, this prospect plunged me into the very depths of despair. Nothing but dark and fearful chasms, separated by sharp-crested and perpendicular ridges as far as the eye could reach. Could we have stepped from summit to summit of these steep but narrow elevations we could easily have accomplished the distance; but we must penetrate to the bottom of every yawning gulf, and scale in succession every one of the eminences before us. (TY 53, repeating a scene described on 51)

The ridges that lie before the narrator stimulate his vision of a sublime advance from height to height and the achievement of mastery. But progress is complicated by ridge lines that contain depths. The narrator lingers on this terrain and its associated motions: a breach of perpendiculars, succession without success. The distance between two points on Melville's Nuku Hiva is not a straight but a broken line. The four-chapter sequence comes to a halt with an elision, as the narrator avoids relating how he and his companion descended the final precipice, an enormous sheer cliff of 300 feet: "I will not recount every hair breadth escape, and every fearful difficulty that occurred before we succeeded in reaching the bosom of the valley" (TY 65). The abrupt end to the journey and the residue of cliché leave the sequence unfinished, even open-ended.

Despite Melville's insistence, to his publishers and to his contemporary audience, on the veracity of his narrative, it is unlikely, given the topography of the parts of the island he reports having visited, that his account of the trip over the highlands to the Typee valley was accurate. While based on his Nuku Hiva sojourn, the journey blends experience, memory, reading, and imagination. As numerous scholars have demonstrated, Melville gave substance and context to *Typee* by drawing on other Pacific travel narratives. In the case of the journey over the mountains, he relied on U.S. Navy Captain David Porter's *Journal of a Cruise Made to the Pacific Ocean* (first published in 1815) and on Navy Chaplain Charles S. Stewart's *Visit to the South Seas* (first published in 1831). Porter details an arduous trip overland from Taioha'e Bay to the valley inhabited by the Happah (the tribe Melville will refer to as the Happar) in order to prepare for military action against the Typee. This expedition that followed guides "up and down the steep sides of rocks and mountains ... and by the sides of precipices which sometimes caused us to shudder." Stewart writes with a curiosity that Melville may have appreciated, an eye for local practices and island aesthetics (the chaplain often pictures himself sketching what he sees). He emphasizes the vertical rifts in the steep mountains that encircle the bay at Taioha'e: the "abrupt acclivities and precipices ... innumerable sharp ridges and deep glens [that] intersect the whole." Hiking overland with a guide to the valley of Hakahaa, which he designates neutral ground between the antagonistic Hapas and Taipiis (Melville's Happar and Typee), Stewart reports that "the hill is one of the steepest I ever ascended: in many places almost entirely perpendicular," and in *Typee* Melville echoes the details of Stewart's hand-to-hand climb. Melville likely acquired particular diction from Stewart, who portrays Nuku Hiva as "deeply *furrowed* with narrow glens, separated from each other by sharp spurs of mountain" and compares the "mild features" of the Hakahaa valley to familiar scenery: "the evenness and breadth of the *interval* or bottom land along the stream in its centre, and in the evident richness of the soil – it has a greater resemblance to a fine *vale* in America, than anything before seen" (emphasis added). As we have seen, Melville sets in motion a similar rural comparison but then, splitting and magnifying the provincial term "inter-vales," he distinguishes Pacific from American prospects.[10]

The different registers of *Typee* – curiosity, voyeurism, unease, exuberance, political commentary, and sexual responsiveness – are linked by the author's fascination with perspective, a regard for how stance and context shape the perception of detail and the understanding of relationships.[11] When Tommo and Toby, after descending into the valley, are inspected by their Typee hosts, Melville's terms multiply the frames of reference:

> They scanned the whiteness of our limbs, and seemed utterly unable to account for the contrast they presented to the swarthy hue of our faces, embrowned from a six months' exposure to the scorching sun of the Line.

> They felt our skin, much in the same way that a silk mercer would handle a remarkably fine piece of satin; and some of them went so far in their investigation as to apply the olfactory organ. (TY 73–74)

Surveyed and sniffed, Tommo represents to the Nuku Hivans what they will embody for him: the inexplicable object of curiosity and desire. "I saw everything," he hyperbolically confesses later in the book when he abandons his effort to make American sense of Marquesan religious practices, "but could comprehend nothing" (TY 177). In this sentence of bewilderment, Tommo echoes his earlier appraisal of his hosts' perplexity after handling his skin – "and in the end they looked at us despairingly, as if we were the receptacles of invaluable information; but how to come at it they knew not" (TY 75) – and he points toward the gap between seeing and knowing expressed in the fervent scrutiny of Queequeg's tattooed body at the end of the "Queequeg in His Coffin" chapter of *Moby-Dick*.

Comparing the Nuku Hivan interest in his skin to that of a textile merchant in an exquisite fabric, Tommo asserts familiarity (slotting the regard into a bourgeois frame of economic appreciation) but he also gestures toward the unknown. The simile conveys its interpretive limits. Whatever the islanders might mean by their attention, they mean more than the narrator's insular image of a silk mercer conveys. Such a comparison invites readers to speculate about the metaphors that the Nuku Hivan characters might enlist to understand Tommo and Toby. Figurative negotiations like these contribute to the humor, myopia, and insight of the book. The simile also literalizes racial ideas about the savor of white skin. The sensuousness in the encounter lends it a whiff of eroticism and suggests the alluring flesh, male and female, that the narrative will place on display.[12]

Likening Marquesans to silk merchants, Melville seems to be drawing the two positions together, comprehending the exotic in terms of the familiar. Yet the figure of speech, like Tommo and Toby's elevated view in the highlands, reveals its gaps. Much of the pleasure and the challenge of reading *Typee* and Melville's other prose and poetry involves the longing to "step from summit to summit" (as Tommo imagines his progress) and the experience of "inter-vales." Melville continually figures such interrupted rhetorical advances. In *Moby-Dick* (1851), the *Pequod* follows a complex path – forward, up, and side-to-side – as the narrator describes the course of the ship and also an experience of reading: "The strange, upheaving, lifting tendency of the taffrail breeze filling the hollows of so many sails, made the buoyant, hovering deck to feel like air beneath the feet; while still she rushed along, as if two antagonistic influences were struggling in her – one to mount direct to heaven, the other to drive yawingly to some horizontal goal" (MD 233). In *Battle-Pieces* (1866), in the poem "The Conflict of Convictions (1860–1)," one of the speakers, acknowledging the turbulence of the US Civil War, describes the "scheme of Nature" as it proceeds through time, using an image that also evokes Melville's often contrary poetics: "I know a wind in purpose strong – / It spins *against* the way it drives" (PP 10). Melville first marks these complicated forward motions in the vistas of *Typee*, and he continues to associate them, especially in *Clarel*, with his experience in the Marquesas.

To attend to Melville's verbal style is not to deny his interventions and implications in politics, theology, or sexuality but to insist that *how* these involvements play out in language is crucial for making sense of them. In *Typee*, Melville suggests the entanglements of language and politics when his narrator, explaining the hostility of the Typee to foreigners in the aftermath of David Porter's devastating attack on the valley three decades earlier, concludes, "Thus it is that they whom we denominate 'savages' are made to deserve the title" (TY 26). Melville's texts abound with such verbal inquiries: the giving of names, the histories and impacts of words, the disclosures of meter, the order – and disorder – of syntax: how meaning often spins against the way it drives. To attend closely to Melville's lines is to experience the distances and the depths that open unexpectedly between adjective and noun or adverb and verb, or between the tenor and vehicle of a metaphor, or across the sequence of subject, verb, and object. (Poetic enjambment offered Melville distinctive semantic opportunities.) Most readers expect a sentence or a line of poetry to extend smoothly. Melville's lines often contain chasms.

These gaps may be aporias in the Derridean sense, focusing attention on internal contradictions and excesses that reveal the impossibility of stable interpretation in language. (Melville makes such gestures in *Pierre, or, the Ambiguities* and *The Confidence-Man*.) The gaps may bring to mind the semiotics of Ferdinand de Saussure and especially Roman Jakobson, in which excluded verbal possibilities, understood as furnishing the vertical axis of language, help to define by contrast the horizontal meanings produced by syntax. Melville repeatedly figures such structures and dynamics, emphasizing the tension: the extravagant ascents and plunges of the highland journey in *Typee*, the shifting transit of the *Pequod* in *Moby-Dick*, the conflicted wind in *Battle-Pieces*. His errant diction often evokes alternatives. Melville's lines often display the "roughened, impeded language" (Viktor Shklovksy) and the "warping and twisting . . . qualifying and revising" (Cleanth Brooks) highlighted by poetic formalists and the "rifts and crevices" (Theodor Adorno) of defamiliarization stressed by Marxist formalists. From these perspectives, Melville's style involves an especially palpable reflection on the attributes of language, the experiences of reading, and the fractures of ideology. But in Melville's writing, these "vertical" features contribute to, rather than block, the "horizontal" drive to meaning, and formal properties are tied to a sustained intellectual project.[13]

What I have in mind is less structural than some varieties of literary theory would stipulate, or involves structure as inflected by position and history. I have in mind a peculiar verbal sensuousness and strenuousness evident across Melville's career. Decades ago, Warwick Wadlington, citing Kenneth Burke on verbal drama, outlined his goals for stylistic analysis:

> We can never totally capture the artistic motion and motive, of course; but we can try to identify how the real artistic thing moves and what its vital truth of motive is as it exists volatilely before us in the text. The ideal is to catch literature in the act, as it words itself out . . . It consequently demands a processual critical method, one alert to drives and counter-resistances, the moment-by-moment activity that betrays the processual force.[14]

This old approach, heeding both structure and duration and alert to specific writerly "drives and counter-resistances," seems oddly new. It seems echoed, for example, in Peter Coviello's call for a revitalized attention to literary style as a way of understanding a writer's relationship to historical context: "it is precisely at the level of words, in their smallest arrangements, that the deep particularity of any author's engagement with the salient languages of his or her day most meaningfully expresses itself." A "processual critical method" – then and now – offers an approach to style that combines deference and distance, yielding an intimacy, like the "closeness" of close reading, that can open into wider discursive fields.[15]

Several critics have sought to chart Melville's verbal motions. Warner Berthoff describes Melville's sentences as marked by a "thrust toward explication" that is "stamped with its urgency: an odd adjective; a defining participle; an unexpected sequence of verbs; circuitous and often distracting parentheses; imputations from all points of the compass as to cause and origin, category and probability, special feature and general law." Paul Lyons writes that in *Moby-Dick* "the movements from sentence to sentence are inherently dislocative" and the "tropes themselves annihilate their own calmness." Jennifer Greiman demonstrates how in *The Confidence-Man*, on the levels of setting, character, and sentence, "the appearance of continuity gives way to an essential strangeness." Alex Calder, applying Morse Peckham's notion of "modal discontinuity," examines the consequences in Melville's fiction "when an apparently inappropriate or affected or off-key style of writing invades and infects a host text," producing "a mode for discrepancies that feel right." These critics, proceeding from different assumptions and employing different methods, seek to catch the qualities of Melville's literature "as it words itself out," and they all point to a persistent, curious, unsettling passage across a discontinuous verbal landscape.[16] One can overstate such stylistic differences, but one also can understate them, and in doing so fail to appreciate the distinct contributions and complications a writer poses.

I mean to suggest that we can measure the impact of Melville's experience in the Marquesas, which unsettled his views about civilization, selfhood, politics, and sexuality, on both the matter and the method of his work, in both his prose and his poetry. I do not mean to argue that the four weeks on Nuku Hiva in 1842 or the almost four years at sea between 1841 and 1844 fundamentally changed him. Who knows about such things? One is wary of now-familiar narratives about Western travelers' conversions in the South Seas, the kind of story questioned by the author of *Typee* and its sequel *Omoo* (1847). But the literary evidence suggests that the Pacific encounters made a difference.

In "Fragments from a Writing Desk," a pair of sketches published in 1839, two years before he sailed on the whaler *Acushnet* and seven years before he published *Typee*, Melville tells the story of a sentimental male narrator drawn into a gothic quest. In the first sketch, the narrator outlines the charms of three local women to a male correspondent. In the second, he receives a note from an "Inamorata" carried by a female messenger, urging him to follow her. At the end of the second sketch, the desires that the narrator has limned in the first sketch are fulfilled, when he confronts an odalisque who turns out, to his shock, to be unable to hear or to speak. These sketches show a nice skill for parody of genre and tone and an irony at the expense of the narrator's fantasies, but there is little evidence of the critique or unease or the verbal intensity or irregularity that will distinguish Melville's first book. In *Typee*, the narrator's sense of having the ground under his feet open up and his prospects altered is conveyed through Melville's burgeoning interest in turns and histories of phrase, the shape of figures, and the intervals of syntax. Such verbal features can be discerned across his career and with notable prominence and Marquesan resonance in *Clarel* (1876), his long poem about a young man's disorienting pilgrimage through the Holy Land, his most ambitious literary effort since *Moby-Dick.*

In Part 3 of *Clarel*, Nuku Hiva's ridges and gaps reappear. Canto 29, titled "Rolfe and the Palm," begins with a series of landscape transformations. The American sailor Rolfe, one of the Holy Land pilgrims, meditates on a solitary palm tree extending over the Kedron gorge at the Mar Saba monastery in Palestine. In the cantos on the Mar Saba palm, which echo the staging of interpretations in the "Doubloon" chapter of *Moby-Dick*, individuals gaze at the same object and the writer reflects on their different perspectives. Rolfe, dwarfed on the ledges of the ravine, is compared to a storm petrel between the crests of ocean waves: "As Mother-Cary's bird in den / Of Cape Horn's hollowing billow-trough" (CL 371). Extending the simile, Melville magnifies and liquefies the Nuku Hiva prospect:

> Down, down, in bonds the seamen gaze
> Upon that flutterer in glen
> Of waters where it sheltered plays,
> While, over it, each briny hight
> Is torn with bubbling torrents white
> In slant foam tumbling from the snow
> Upon the crest; and far as eye
> Can range through mist and scud which fly,
> Peak behind peak the liquid summits grow. (CL 371–372)

The poet and the sailors look down into the ocean gorge at the "flutterer in glen" and also across a series of wave crests, a line of sight cleaved by deep ravines ("Peak behind peak the liquid summits grow"), an oceanic rendering of the parallel lines and vertical fissures on Nuku Hiva depicted in *Typee*. The final word – "grow" – suggests both the extended vista of crests and also the qualities of waves, continually in motion even as their size and rhythm create the illusion of stability. The sailors, at the crest of a wave and looking down, are on the verge of a trough they soon will inhabit. The simile offers a vivid example of what Hershel Parker describes as Melville's scenic memory, his recurrent portrayals of landscapes within landscapes.[17] The terrain of the Kedron gorge at Mar Saba reminds the poetic speaker of the crests and troughs around Cape Horn, the route from Atlantic to Pacific that sailors, including Melville, followed on their way to the South Pacific. These topographical correspondences prepare the reader for Rolfe's vision of the Marquesas in Palestine and his imagined communion with the undulating palm.

Rolfe imagines the Mar Saba palm gesturing to him: "Up, slow / He climbed for little space; then craved / A respite, turned and sat; and, lo, /

The Tree in salutation waved / Across the chasm" (CL 372). For Rolfe, this greeting is extended from the past and from his days in the Marquesas, "Where Eden, isled, impurpled glows / In old Mendanna's sea" (CL 372; the Spanish navigator Álvaro de Mendaña "discovered" the archipelago in 1595, bestowed the name "Marquesas," and engaged in violent conflict with the islanders).[18] Like Typee's narrator Tommo, and like Melville himself, the character Rolfe sojourned in a remote Pacific valley, was astounded by his experiences, and fled. Like the narrators of both *Typee* and its sequel *Omoo*, Rolfe mourns his renunciation. For all three characters, an under-articulated guilt tinges their sense of loss. The palm that salutes Rolfe across the chasm in *Clarel* echoes the solace given to the narrator of *Typee* at the end of chapter 33, just before the culminating spectacle of violence and escape. The older, narrating Tommo dramatically recalls three breadfruit trees: "Even now, amidst all the bustle and stir of the proud and busy city in which I am dwelling, the image of those three trees seems to come as vividly before my eyes as if they were actually present, and I still feel the soothing quiet pleasure which I then had in watching hour after hour their topmost boughs waving gracefully in the breeze" (TY 244). Yet, as in Rolfe's case, the beckoning trees offer Tommo a complex comfort. Tommo associates this memory with his most melancholy days on the island, when a severe pain in his leg rendered him immobile and he felt stranded and hopeless. When these breadfruit trees wave, what do they signify? The intimate contact with the Nuku Hivans? The lack of contact? The indelible experiences? The missed opportunities? The allure of escape? Escape to or from the island? Are the trees waving hello or farewell?

Critics, following Walter Bezanson, have too swiftly taken Rolfe as a surrogate for Melville, rather than an angle in his prism. The palm greets Rolfe "Across the chasm": to advance would involve a fatal plunge, with the interval underscored by the line break.[19] The ambivalent wave of the palm (and Melville's phrasing joins tree and hand, as they are joined etymologically) recalls the foliage that gestures at Tommo and Toby from ridges and valleys during their flight over the highlands in *Typee* (41, 64), and it augurs the "slow-swaying palms" whose "salute" lulls visitors into dream and possibly death in Melville's poem "The Enviable Isles" (PP 242), which appeared in *John Marr and Other Sailors* (1888). For Rolfe, the "chasm" is temporal (between past and present), geographical (between the Pacific and Palestine), and spiritual (the palm suggests the remoteness of both earthly paradise and Christian Resurrection). The diction that Melville gives to Rolfe cautions that remembrance is "tone[d]" by "pathos" and may be illusory: his is a "tricksy dream" explicitly linked with those that Puck induces in Shakespeare's *A Midsummer Night's Dream* (CL 373). Rolfe's many allusions in the canto to the classical features of the Marquesan landscape ("Indian Arcady," "Hesperian orchards," "Arcades of Iris," "threnodies of Pan") enable Melville to play up the artifice by redundantly embedding his character's Pacific idyll in Western literary tradition. Such allusions reinforce the insight of *Typee*, and many other of Melville's works, that there are no innocent landscapes. Rather than "a classic threnody to a retreating dream," as Bezanson affirms, "Rolfe and the Palm" offers Melville's goading of that dream.[20]

Rolfe savors his loss, indulges it, and Melville acknowledges the seductiveness of a conjured and evanescent Marquesan paradise. In the lyric "To Ned," published over twenty years later in *John Marr*, Melville extends the reflections on his Marquesan experience. "To Ned" shares with "Rolfe and the Palm" diction ("Typee-truants" in *John Marr* and "truant ship-boy" in *Clarel*), allusion (both invoke *A Midsummer Night's Dream*), and image (both compare the Marquesas to Paradise). Biographers and literary critics have suggested that the addressee in "To Ned" may be Melville's companion Richard Tobias Greene, the "Toby" of *Typee*, who jumped ship with him on Nuku Hiva in 1842.[21] The poetic speaker laments irrecoverable youth, vanished intimacy, and degraded Pacific islands, once "Edens" but now "over-run" (PP 238). The speaker envisions the late-nineteenth-century "pleasure-hunter" and "tourist," who seek but will not find a lost "Paradise" (the final word of the poem), and recalls the original travelers, himself and Ned, who, "years and years ago," discovered in the Marquesas "Authentic Edens in a Pagan sea" (PP 237).

Yet the two positions – then and now – open into one another. In "To Ned," the poet implies that he (not only the speaker who had sojourned in the Marquesas but also the author of the popular *Typee*) and his companion bear responsibility for the overwhelming of Paradise. The "Typee-truants" in the poem are the narrator and Ned, who escaped from their ship, and also the later runaways who flee to the valley, some of them, the diction forewarns, arriving with a copy of *Typee*. (The manuscript for *John Marr and Other Sailors* shows that while composing "To Ned" Melville had underlined the word "Typee" and at one stage had the book title, and not just the place, in mind; see PP 741.) "A legend urge the flight" (PP 237), the speaker reminds Ned: a mass-produced legend about Pacific authenticity intensified by Melville's first book, whose enduring popularity motivated readers, including literary tourists such as Robert Louis Stevenson and Jack London, to travel to the Marquesas.

The word "hollow" at the beginning of the poem – "Where is the world we roved, Ned Bunn? / Hollows thereof lay rich in shade / By voyagers old inviolate thrown" (PP 237) – suggests a more complicated temporality and memory than the speaker's partition between a bygone "Saturn's Age" (PP 237) and a vitiated present. The "hollows" of "To Ned" are topographical but also historical. The speaker's island appears bereft of inhabitants. In the decades between *Typee* (1846) and *John Marr* (1888), the population of Nuku Hiva had been devastated by infections transmitted in contact with Westerners, and especially by a smallpox epidemic in the mid-1860s. There is an eerily prescient aspect to the empty memories of Nuku Hiva in "To Ned," as though the negative consequences of European and American contact envisioned in *Typee* and fulfilled in actual catastrophe were then projected back onto the speaker's memories of his youthful experience on the island.

Stevenson and London, in Melville's wake, dramatically rendered the contrasts between the Nuku Hiva of *Typee* and the island they encountered. In the posthumously published *In the South* Seas (1896), Stevenson described the physical and psychological effects of depopulation he witnessed during his visit in the late 1880s. In *The Cruise of the Snark* (1911), London echoed Melville's humor but also, quoting from *Typee*, conveyed bitterness and disillusion at his own inability to realize visions of Marquesan beauty and romance that had been spurred by a boyhood reading of Melville's book. London occupies a position like that of the protagonist in Melville's *Redburn* (1849), who found that the sights catalogued in his father's decades-old Liverpool guidebook failed to match the altered mid-nineteenth-century city before his eyes. In *The Cruise of the Snark*, the Nuku Hivan paradise has become infected and disfigured. At the end of a chapter bearing the name "Typee," London pictured an exquisite moonrise in the valley: "all about us the dying islanders coughed in the night."[22]

The "hollows" in "To Ned," recalling the "hollowing billow-trough" in "Rolfe and the Palm" (CL 371), suggest the keen vacancy of nostalgia. And the placement of "To Ned" in *John Marr* alongside "Crossing the Tropics," a poem about Atlantic longing, and between two graphic poems of injury and casualty ("The Maldive Shark" and "The Berg") indicates the precipitous allure – the compelling fiction – of "Authentic Edens."[23]

Rolfe's "tricksy dream" of the Marquesas forms part of the intellectual and spiritual inquiries of *Clarel*. As Rolfe gazes at the Mar Saba palm, imagines that he receives its salute, and muses on his Pacific experience, the choice seems to be between a vital pagan past and a desiccated, fragmented Christian or post-Christian present, between a timeless Polynesia and a timebound, disenchanted modern Palestine. Yet the palm waving across the chasm signals to the reader, if not the character, a risky appeal. *Clarel* is the vast culmination of *Typee*, another encounter with difference – with, as Jenny Franchot suggests, the ultimate difference constituted by the divine. In *Typee*, the narrator searches for origins and alternatives in the far west; in *Clarel*, the protagonist searches for origins and answers in the Middle East. Both journeys end in estrangement. *Typee* and *Clarel* share a set of questions. What does it mean to see sights? To keep time? To encounter strangers? To possess territory? What are the relationships between the sensuous and the spiritual? Between form and faith? Do the quests in the Marquesas or the Holy Land represent a return? A recoil? Stasis, decline, or ascension? Clarel, a young theology student, hopes to find illumination and reassurance in the Holy Land. Yet the beliefs on display in the poem are often represented as deep but narrow. They provide an insular but illusive security for their adherents, like the steep valleys of Nuku Hiva as figured in *Typee*. At the beginning of *Clarel*, Jerusalem's Church of the Holy Sepulchre, carved into sectarian chapels, is described as though it were composed of Marquesan ravines: "shadowy spaces / Deep vistas where the votary paces" (CL 13).[24]

Poetry allowed Melville to explore his ideological landscapes with new types of verbal precision. He marshaled its resources to assess diction, etymology, syntax, and trope. In *Clarel*, he employs iambic tetrameter to evaluate – pair, split, and multiply – his characters and their positions. Writing reflexively, he describes Clarel, spurred by his dialogue with a monk at Mar Saba, brooding over questions about human sexuality and divine love in Christianity, approaching but then drawing back from thoughts of Mary's womanliness: "But came ere long profound relapse: / The Rhyme recurred, made voids or gaps / In dear relations" (CL 378). Here Melville conveys the oscillating qualities of Clarel's thought and the sense that the characters in the poem may be influenced by a spiritual cadence beyond their control or ken, and he also reflects on the poetics of *Clarel*, in which rhyme calls attention to "voids or gaps," establishing patterns that link but also skew.

Toward the end of the poem, in one of the longest cantos, titled "The Prodigal," the Marquesas reappear unexpectedly. Clarel is conversing with a young, worldly French salesman from Lyon of "mobile face" and "voluptuous air" (CL 468) with whom he shares a room in Bethlehem.

Melville associates the Frenchman, who remains unnamed, with the errant son in Luke 15.11–32. Clarel objects to the young man's apparent levity, and the Lyonese resists his roommate's studied gloom. As Clarel presses the austerity of the Palestinian landscape and the Lyonese seeks relief from his morbid importuning, it is hard not to discern in this scene an example of Melville's frequent staging of the relationship between the writer and his readers, here an acknowledgment of the melancholic extravagance of *Clarel*. Provoking Clarel, the Lyonese insists that the theology student should cheer up. Palestine is not the bearer of "Isaiah's dark burden" (CL 471), but a land of wine and revelry. It is the venue for the sensual pleasures lauded in the Song of Songs, a metaphor-laden sample of which the Lyonese quotes. Taken aback, Clarel replies, "Nay, pardon me, / But you misdeem it: Solomon's Song / Is allegoric – needs must be" (CL 473). It "needs must be," the antiquated syntax implies, because of Clarel's felt necessity to sublimate the Song's imaginative energies and his own desires. Here the poet is distant from the partial views of both the Lyonese and Clarel, since from *Typee* onwards Melville is responsive to the kind of polyphony represented in the Song, with its mixtures of voluptuousness and reticence, sensuousness and spirituality.[25]

The separation between Melville and his young protagonist, their strange intimacy, and the figurative pressure of the Song of Songs are all on display at the climax of Clarel's encounter with the Lyonese. Ridiculing the allegorical exegesis of the Song, the young Frenchman delivers a paean to Jewish women and their sensual charms. Clarel blushes. He continues: "Priests make a goblin of the Jew: / Shares he not flesh with me – with you?" (CL 474). Born Jewish, the Lyonese is uneasy with this aspect of his identity and conceals it from Clarel, while here intimating the affinity. And then, despite his imperative that Clarel read literally rather than allegorically or mystically – "Come, look at straight things more in line" (CL 473) – a scene unfolds between Clarel and the Lyonese in which Clarel's perspective is ruptured and the stanza is transfigured at its midpoint:

> What wind was this? And yet it swayed
> Even Clarel's cypress. He delayed
> All comment, gazing at him there.
> Then first he marked the clustering hair
> Which on the bright and shapely brow
> At middle part grew slantly low:
> Rich, tumbled chestnut hood of curls,
> Like to a Polynesian girl's,
> Who, inland eloping with her lover,

> The deacon-magistrates recover –
> With sermon and black bread reprove
> Who fed on berries and on love. (CL 474)

Here, again, the Marquesas make their appearance in *Clarel* through a series of transformations. Clarel's face turns red. Talk is replaced by silence and then vision and trope. The cypress, a Western symbol of mourning, insinuates itself into the palm, a symbol of luxuriance in South Seas fiction. The young French salesman, who has obscured his Jewishness, is beheld as a Polynesian and a girl. He is conjured through an extravagant metaphor – "Rich, tumbled chestnut hood of curls" – redolent of the lovers' comparisons in the Song of Songs. Describing Clarel's gaze, the second half of the stanza mixes locations, temporalities, genders, and desires, undermining the distinctions of allegory to which the young theology student is committed. As the Lyonese had suggested, flesh is and may be "shared," not only in the sense that all human beings are mortal but also in more carnal ways, as implied in the syntax and rhyme that halt the dialogue and prompt Clarel's vision: "The Jew / Shares he not flesh with me – with you?" When Clarel blushes after the Lyonese praises wine, flesh, and women, what stimulates his response? Clarel's desire for Ruth, the Jewish woman he met in Jerusalem and to whom he is betrothed? His attraction toward the Lyonese, whom Clarel suspects is a Jew (CL 475)? Either? Both? More?

Clarel's recollection and anticipation of the Lyonese as a Polynesian girl is an exorbitant moment. It belongs more to the writer and his imagined audience than to the character. As far as readers know, the inexperienced Clarel has never been to the South Pacific and has never seen a Polynesian. The vision evokes *Typee* and the unfixing of the narrator's desires on Nuku Hiva, when Tommo is drawn to both the lovely islander Fayaway and the handsome wanderer Marnoo. At the end of Clarel's vision, the poet alludes to a story of young island lovers who flee to the interior and are caught and punished by the authorities, and Melville's own *Omoo* may provide a source in its narrator's anecdote about fugitive lovers on Tahiti (OM 180). In one of the most fervent passages in Melville's Holy Land poem, his Polynesian narratives interpose in simile and example.[26]

In the Epilogue, when the poet imagines a possible future for Clarel, he mixes and escalates similes describing natural progression, individual discipline, and ineluctable disclosure. The speaker addresses the character directly, following imperative with subjunctive: do this and these things may follow. The poem draws to a close not in tetrameter, its dominant meter, but in pentameter. After almost 18,000 lines, the poet, in valediction, offers advice:

> Then keep thy heart, though yet but ill-resigned –
> Clarel, thy heart, the issues there but mind;
> That like the crocus budding through the snow –
> That like a swimmer rising from the deep –
> That like a burning secret which doth go
> Even from the bosom that would hoard and keep;
> Emerge thou mayst from the last whelming sea,
> And prove that death but routs life into victory. (CL 499)

The "whelming sea" brings us back to the Pacific, but so does something else. These last lines may appear straightforward, but they are not. The Epilogue to *Clarel*, like Tommo and Toby's vista in the highlands of Nuku Hiva, offers a prospect constituted by gaps. The impression of continuity is reinforced by the extended pentameter line and also by structure and poetics. This final octet contains relatively little enjambment and relatively few caesuras. Its opening couplet imperative is followed by four middle lines with suspended syntax and alternating end-rhyme and then a final couplet that indicates a possibility for "victory." Critics disagree about whether the last eight lines, in terms of theology, epistemology, and tone, follow or diverge from the monumental poem that comes before. And they disagree about whether the Epilogue provides a measure of resolution or continued ambivalence.[27] I would argue that these lines are the ultimate example of the poet's exploration of a fissured landscape of belief. The allusions here – to the Bible, to Hawthorne, to Melville himself – complicate the advance and the "victory." The syntax parallels and separates. The diction qualifies and gouges. The movement in these last lines is forward but also down and up.

The poetic speaker tells Clarel to "keep thy heart . . . the issues there but mind," echoing Proverbs 4.23 in the King James translation: "Keep thy heart with all diligence; for out of it are the issues of life." The phrasing also invokes Philippians 4.7: "And the peace of God, which passeth all understanding, shall keep your hearts and minds through Christ Jesus." Yet the echoes unsettle as well as seek to reassure. Describing a heart that should be "minded" and combining the two allusions, Melville complicates any elevation of the heart over the head. The similes give precarious shape to what might "issue" from the heart, and the series culminates not with "peace" but with a consuming emergence.[28]

First the poet tells us that Clarel may be like a small flower, a "crocus," pushing through the snow of winter to spring. If this were the only simile, we could view the Epilogue as endorsing a banal, if affecting, emblem of resurrection.

Then we are told that Clarel might rise, "like a swimmer," through the surface of the water to the air and the light. Another figure for resurrection, the swimmer indicates a different model for change, emphasizing individual effort rather than natural growth. Still, the gap between the two accounts seems traversable. We can imagine, in Tommo's words, stepping "from summit to summit" (TY 53).

The "burning secret" is harder to cross. How is a "burning secret" like a "crocus" or a "swimmer"? Unlike these, the secret "burns" – like spiritual fire, like desire, like sin. The path of the burning secret, "which doth go / Even from the bosom that would hoard and keep," resembles the route taken by Arthur Dimmesdale's "ever active tooth of remorse, gnawing from the inmost heart outwardly" in *The Scarlet Letter* (1850), a book (and author) that Melville knew well. As Stan Goldman suggests, Melville draws on Jeremiah 20.9: "But his word was in mine heart as a burning fire shut up in my bones." In the Epilogue to *Clarel*, the "issues of life" from Proverbs catch fire, as in Jeremiah, but the status of that fire is obscured. Moving through Proverbs, Philippians, *The Scarlet Letter*, and Jeremiah, Melville puns on "issue." First Clarel is told to mind the issues *in* his heart. Then he is told that secrets may issue *from* his heart, despite his body's efforts to contain them. Secrets that burn. And then this burning is tied through the verb "Emerge," which governs the series of similes, to a possible final "victory."[29]

Goldman, who cogently analyzes the links among religious inquiry, biblical intertextuality, and narrative technique in *Clarel*, argues that Melville endorses a "theology of the heart," a liberal Christianity annealed by skepticism that affirms the divinity within human beings as a counter to an absent God.[30] Goldman interprets the three similes in the last stanza of the Epilogue as each conveying such divine immanence. James Duban supplements this argument with a Unitarian reading of the Epilogue that hinges on mid-nineteenth-century exegeses of Proverbs 4.23 and on Melville's markings in his Bible. Duban's approach has some biographical support, given Melville's degrees of affiliation with the Unitarian Church during his residences in New York City. Goldman and Duban meet the interpretive challenges of Melville's Epilogue by invoking traditions of religious contradiction and poetic incongruity.[31]

But the "heart" in *Clarel* is associated not only with an almost Unitarian hope in the Epilogue but also with nearly Calvinist misgivings about interior mystery and iniquity in the "Prelusive" canto at the center of the poem: "The heart, with labyrinths replete" (CL 249). There is a discordance in the Epilogue that can be overlooked. The actions it depicts – unfolding, rising, and burning – are linked but also distinct, and readers are left to assess the sequence. At the end of the poem, syntax, figure, allusion, meter, and rhyme provide direction and also reveal disparity, exposing "inter-vales" (TY 41) and "voids or gaps / In dear relations" (CL 378). The path envisioned is strenuous and the outcome uncertain. If the Epilogue inclines toward Unitarianism, it does so with a peculiar edge.

The terminal "victory" in *Clarel* is qualified and enigmatic – "Emerge thou mayst from the last whelming sea, / And prove that death but routs life into victory" – especially when compared to the unmistakable triumph in Paul's "Death is swallowed up in victory" (1 Cor. 15.54) and Isaiah's "He will swallow up death in victory" (Isa. 25.8). The "victory" in *Clarel* may never arrive. As William H. Shurr observes, "prove" here might mean "to establish the truth of," but it also might mean "to test." To make this point another way, the archaic "mayst" might govern "prove" as well as "emerge," might suggest contingency or possibility as well as verity or ability. Here "prove" is not much proof. And what kind of "victory" grants death agency to "rout" life, as though scattering it on the battlefield? The final line is difficult to parse. It begins in regular pentameter bolstered by monosyllables, each corresponding to a beat: "And **prove** | that **death** | but **routs**." But then it proceeds less certainly. The word "life," matched with "**death**," rhetorically and lexically seems to call for stress, disrupting the meter. Do we hear the line as "And **prove** | that **death** | but **routs** | **life** in | to **vic** tory," with metrical substitution (the trochee of "**life** in") and a final unstressed elision? Or does the poem at its close extend into hexameter, a terminal alexandrine hitched by the inverted "life": "And **prove** | that **death** | but **routs** | **life** in | to **vic** | to **ry**"? Such a "victory," open to question, "spins *against* the way it drives," like the "wind in purpose strong" in *Battle-Pieces* (PP 10).[32]

Linked syntactically, the crocus, the swimmer, and the burning secret convey different kinds of advance. Together they form a discontinuous poetic landscape. The problem, or allure, of the Epilogue is not exactly the situation described by Edgar A. Dryden: "the surface meaning of the poet's lines fails to satisfy or convince."[33] Rather than a facile surface belied by depths, meaning in the Epilogue is generated by a disorienting movement across and into gaps. From *Typee* to *Clarel* to *Billy Budd, Sailor,* whose manuscript was left unfinished at Melville's death, readers can discern and are invited, even compelled, to experience such a literary phenomenology.

The Epilogue to *Clarel*, often read as indicating affirmation at the close of Melville's epic study of faith and doubt, resonates, surprisingly, with the debate between the Missouri backwoodsman Pitch and the Philosophical Intelligence Officer in *The Confidence-Man* (1857), Melville's satire on confidence and distrust, which is often regarded as a discourse on negation. The Philosophical Intelligence Office (P.I.O.) man, an employment agent, urges Pitch to hire a new boy to work for him. (He ultimately closes the deal.) When Pitch insists that "boyhood is a natural state of rascality," the P.I.O. agent responds by considering "the state of boyhood scientifically viewed" (CM 117, 120). He offers a series of analogies to persuade the Missourian that he should have confidence in the progressive development of boys, in spite of his unfortunate previous experience with them. (The exasperated Pitch already has hired and fired over thirty boys.) The P.I.O. agent insists that young men who may seem immature, unworthy, or corrupt are actually, or analogically, figures of great promise. He compares them to sketches that need filling out; lily-buds whose hidden beauties will flower; chins that will sprout noble beards; frail initial teeth that will be succeeded by exquisite permanent teeth; caterpillars that will turn into butterflies; sinners who will become saints (CM 121–126).

Like the trio of similes in *Clarel*'s Epilogue, the analogies in *The Confidence-Man* may appear to delineate smooth prospects (and the P.I.O. agent emphatically markets their coherence), yet the sequence, premised on the evidence of things not yet seen, conflates different agencies and impulses. (Melville's wordplay also invites double and triple entendres.) The Philosophical Intelligence Officer guarantees more than he can deliver, exhibiting the uncertainties of discontinuous progression. Those second teeth, which "follow, but do not come from, the first" (CM 123), seem particularly unnerving, since a boy with "leopard-like teeth," dressed in flame-colored rags and peddling door locks and money belts, makes an ominous appearance in the final chapter (CM 244). Across his writings, Melville is preoccupied with what lies between and what emerges. *Typee, The Confidence-Man*, and *Clarel* are filled with such rifts.

The characteristic patterns can be found not only in texts that explicitly reference the Marquesas but also in a range of Melville's works: in *Mardi*, the disorienting course from South Seas adventure to romantic quest to political and theological allegory; in *Moby-Dick*, the syncopated rhythms of the opening "Extracts," Ahab's sundered and seamed psyche (chapters 44, "The Chart," and 113, "The Forge"), Ishmael's periodic sentences that ascend and then turn or plunge (most conspicuously in chapter 42, "The Whiteness of the Whale"), and Moby Dick's spectacular breach (chapter 133, "The Chase – First Day"); in *Pierre*, the narrator's double-edged view in the opening chapters of the Glendinning family's ancestral manor as both paradise and tartarus, Pierre's later dream vision of traveling across an apparently level countryside abruptly torn open and upheaved, laying bare the amputated, writhing, reflexive figure of Enceladus the Titan (P 342–347), and the overburdened prose, in which it is often difficult to follow the movement across phrases and parts of speech ("Then they changed; they coiled together, and entangledly stood mute," the narrator reports, describing a vehement, possibly sexual, encounter between Pierre and Isabel, who may or may not be his sister [P 192]); in "Benito Cereno," the violence that has transformed the decks of the *San Dominick* into a surface of pitfalls, "every inch of ground mined into honey-combs" (PZ 115); in the paired transatlantic sketches "Poor Man's Pudding and Rich Man's Crumbs," "The Two Temples," and "The Paradise of Bachelors and the Tartarus of Maids," the intervals of correspondence and discrepancy, akin to prose enjambments, that involve geography, economy, class, and gender; in *John Marr and Other Sailors*, the complex motions – sinking and rising, forward and back, the "reverting turn" – of the voyage described in the lyric "Crossing the Tropics" (PP 239); in *Billy Budd*, the narrator's sinuous perusal of the master-at-arms Claggart's enmity – "To pass from a normal nature to him one must cross 'the deadly space between.' And this is best done by indirection" – and the dialectic of "forms, measured forms" and "ragged edges" put forward at the story's end (BB 27, 68–69).

In *The Confidence-Man*, when the philosopher Mark Winsome defends inconsistency, Melville provides readers with yet another image for his aesthetic investments and conceptual maneuvers, invoking an emblem of mid-nineteenth-century industrial development in the northeastern United States, as he cites and revises the journey in the highlands of Nuku Hiva:

> In a philosophical view, consistency is a certain level at all times, maintained in all the thoughts of one's mind. But, since nature is nearly all hill and dale, how can one keep naturally advancing in knowledge without submitting to the natural inequalities in the process? Advance into knowledge is just like advance upon the grand Erie canal, where, from the character of the country, change of level is inevitable; you are locked up and locked down with perpetual inconsistencies, and yet all the time you get on; while the dullest part of the whole route is what the boatmen call the "long level" – a consistently-flat surface of sixty miles through stagnant swamps. (CM 193)

Here are the features of Melville's style: the illusion of uniformity ("since nature is nearly all hill and dale"), the aversion to unbroken lines ("the dullest part of the whole route is what the boatmen call the 'long level'"), and especially the uneven verbal advance in which movement is fitful and horizontal prospects are vertically fractured ("you are locked up and locked down with perpetual inconsistencies, and yet all the time you get on"). Writing in the mid-1850s after the spectacular failure of his novel *Pierre* and his effort to refashion himself as a writer of short fiction and just before his shift to poetry, Melville points up and plays with the confinements of his enterprise, punning on the nautical and carceral senses of "lock."

Across Melville's literary career, the Marquesas appear. Something happened to Melville on the island of Nuku Hiva, or in his reflections on that sojourn, or in the attempt to convey his experience in words. He frequently renders that something in patterns of diction, syntax, figure, and image, constituting a distinctive verbal landscape. The ridges, gaps, and transits – which often are also epistemological trials – recur. Maybe it was the vistas. Maybe it was political awakening or racial encounter or sexual experience or friendship or cultural impasse. Maybe it was a sense of vulnerability or a discovery of the power of fiction or an acknowledgment of the reach and limit of words. Maybe it was all of these aspects. Beginning with *Typee* and for the rest of his writing life, Melville surveyed positions, altered perspectives, and inhabited chasms. He brought his readers along with him or lost them in the journey. The plunge between the ridges at the beginning of *Typee* and the transport envisaged at the end of *Clarel* display a strange symmetry. Both passages disorient, and they also imperil and exhilarate. Something happened to Melville on Nuku Hiva, and after that his lines could never quite hold together.

CHAPTER 10

Melville and the Conceits of Theory

Jennifer Greiman

1. Pierre's Pocket

Call it "critique," "symptomatic reading," or the "hermeneutics of suspicion," a genre of late twentieth-century literary criticism has been declared obsolete over the last decade, charged with the failure both to analyze a world in which power does not mask itself and to attend fully to the imaginative, temporal, and formal complexities of literary aesthetics. Extending Bruno Latour's 2004 appeal for "another powerful descriptive tool . . . whose import will no longer be to debunk but to protect and to care," scholars have argued that twentieth-century literary criticism reduced literature to its gaps, absences, and silences while turning criticism itself into the paranoid, suspicious work of negation.[1] With this indictment of their predecessors, contemporary literary critics might be said to suffer a mild version of the crisis that wrecks the moral and intellectual life of Melville's Pierre Glendinning as he grapples with the failure of philosophy to contend with nineteenth-century history. In Book XXII of *Pierre; or, the Ambiguities*, Melville's narrator peeps over the shoulder of his eponymous hero at his writing desk to witness Pierre's bitter assessment of his intellectual heroes – "ye chattering apes of a sophomorean Spinoza and Plato . . . thou inconceivable coxcomb of a Goethe" – as he declares "the end of Philosophy" (P 302–303). Pierre has turned to intellectual labor in the aftermath of his "great life revolution" (P 225), the renunciation of his name and fortune in a bid to recognize his supposed half-sister, Isabel. But rather than continuing the work of that revolution – or even sustaining the lives of Pierre, Isabel, and Delly – his reading and writing instead deplete and reduce him, leading him to accuse philosophy, theology, and literature of failing to alter or augment his world. "Is it creation or destruction? Builds Pierre the noble world of a new book? or does that Pale Haggardness unbuild the lungs and the life of him?" (P 306). "Civilization, Philosophy, Ideal Virtue! Behold your victim!" (P 302).

Melville's narrator is merciless as he details all of the ways in which philosophy has failed young Pierre, and Pierre's intellectual crisis is catastrophic. But if my analogy between the frustrations that have given rise to "post-critique" and the abyss into which Pierre plunges is, admittedly, a little strained, *Pierre*'s narrator may nonetheless have something to offer twenty-first-century critics more than a decade into the critique of critique. For even as Pierre lashes out at the philosophies that have failed him, Melville's novel demands of its readers a more complex and reflexive approach to such failures. Critical and speculative thinking may do nothing to remedy the catastrophes of the world; indeed, they may be, as *Pierre*'s narrator puts it, "more the excellently illustrated re-statement of a problem, than the solution of the problem itself" (P 210). But in spinning the conceits that "excellently" illustrate a world while having little or no impact on it, philosophy and theory fail in precisely the way that fiction does. In short, Melville proposes that philosophy and fiction share a common world of figures and conceits, fables and counterfactuals, and so why not read accordingly? Rather than indicting philosophy, theory, and criticism for not remedying the world, as his protagonist does, Melville instead subjects these to the figures, fables, and conceits of *Pierre*'s fictive universe and discloses their explicitly literary enterprise.

Melville develops one of the novel's more elaborate conceits for the persistence of a failed theory in one of its crueler – and funnier – passages. During Pierre's desperate pursuit of any philosophy that can answer his crisis, the narrator pauses "to anticipate," years after Pierre's death, the discovery in the lining of his surtout the very pages of Plotinus Plinlimmon's pamphlet, "Chronometricals and Horologicals" for which he has been searching.

> Pierre must have ignorantly thrust it into his pocket, in the stage, and it had worked through a rent there, and worked its way clean down into the skirt, and there helped pad the padding. So that all the time he was hunting for this pamphlet, he himself was wearing the pamphlet. When he brushed past Plinlimmon in the brick of the corridor, and felt that renewed intense longing for the pamphlet, then his right hand was not two inches from the pamphlet. (P 294)

Not content just to note the vexing proximity of the supposedly lost pages, the narrator also claims that they have become symbolic of Pierre's "self-supposed non-understanding" of the pamphlet's basic argument and conceit: "Could he likewise have carried about with him in his mind the thorough understanding of the book, and yet not be aware that he so understood it?" In the throes of his intellectual emergency, Pierre believes that he has failed twice, having lost the crucial pamphlet that he had earlier been unable to comprehend (P 293), but what he really doesn't understand is that neither of these things is true. Pierre has not only not lost the pages that envelope him wherever he goes, but he has also failed to misunderstand them. Rather than an illustration of his failure to grasp a theory that has, in turn, failed to remedy his situation, this wearing of the pages unknowingly in the lining of his coat instead becomes the very figure for a kind of comprehension that he cannot permit himself to know he has achieved. The perversity of this passage is not in the withholding of knowledge from Pierre that the narrator extends to the reader. Instead, the cruelty lies in the vision it provides of Pierre unwittingly clothing himself in the very thing he has regarded as useless and incomprehensible thinking – a vision that the narrator registers as literal and figurative at once.

As the narrator tells it, Pierre is literally wearing the pages, the wearing of which becomes the figure for his unknowing comprehension of them, all of which turns Pierre himself into a figure for his own knowledge, comprehension, and condition. Pierre slips through his own pocket to become the pamphlet's embodiment and the means of its circulation all the while the pamphlet, in William Spanos's words, "precisely theorizes the actual circumstances of Pierre's emergent occasion" as "one who cannot or refuses to accommodate his discourse and practice to the world."[2] Pierre's theory envelops him and eludes him, giving an account of his actions and his unknowing comprehension of them, while his coat pocket proposes a theory of that theory. Both literally and figuratively, Pierre's pocket registers his comprehension of and by a theory that describes the condition of one who will not accommodate himself to the world. But rather than giving Pierre any insight, his pocket turns him into another of the novel's memorable figures for speculative thinking – the mummy "buried in cloth" whose endless unraveling reveals nothing but "surface stratified on surface" (P 285) – all the while it taunts him with the impossible knowledge of the impotence of all his reading, thinking, and writing:

> Yet that knowing his fatal condition does not one whit enable him change or better his condition. Conclusive proof that he has no power over his condition. For in tremendous extremities human souls are like drowning men; well enough they know that they are in peril; well enough they know

> the causes of that peril; – nevertheless, the sea is the sea and drowning men do drown. (P 303)

Pierre's pocket is more than a metatheoretical figure in the narrative. It proposes a metatheory of the narrative – a theory of Pierre's repudiation of all the theory that he knows cannot alter his world or condition no matter how much he reads. A mummy and a drowning man who does not know that he is theorized by his own coat, Pierre is failed by both the surfaces and the depths of his reading – and yet, the pamphlet persists as the narrator generates more and more figures for this failure.

In this, the passage foregrounds reading in general as a practice of comprehensive failure, and it exemplifies the kind of self-reflexive involutions that have drawn critics and theorists to Melville's work. As Peter Szendy puts it, "to read Melville . . . is *to read what reading means*," and Pierre's pocket can clearly be numbered among the countless "scene[s] of reading" across Melville's corpus.[3] But what, exactly, constitutes reading in *Pierre*? Clearly, Pierre is not "just reading" (to borrow Sharon Marcus's influential phrase).[4] He is reading and writing with a critical vengeance to sound the foundations of a world he cannot abide, while keeping the knowledge of his powerlessness to change the conditions of that world at bay. He is, in other words, constantly reaching the limits of criticism and theory, all the while he is being read and written doing the work of criticism and theory. When Plinlimmon's theoretical tract slips through the tear in Pierre's pocket to rest beneath the outermost layer of his overcoat, the narrator's commentary anticipates the central questions around which critics of Melville's work have often divided: should such scenes be read literally or symbolically? for the thinking the work does or for the worlds it depicts? for the stratified surfaces or for the vacancies they conceal? Melville's conceit proposes that these are not choices a critic must make – between the literary, the philosophical, the historical, or the political – but the very boundaries across which reading operates. Against the post-critical assumption that attention to a literary surface comes only when one ceases to presume a structuring vacancy, Melville's figure of a theory lost in the lining of an overcoat is only legible as both. Surfaces and vacancies, like literature and theory, are inextricably bound together.

Similar to the advocates of post-critique who have privileged the category of the literary as something to disentangle from critique and context, the major critical theorists who have engaged Melville's work – "Bartleby" in particular – have sought to separate the literary from the philosophical.

Often, for these theorists, the literary connotes a mimetic, representational relation between text and world, while the philosophical force of Melville's writing is said to manifest the bare agency of language or the immanence in the text of "thinking" itself.[5] For theorists such as Giorgio Agamben and Gilles Deleuze, Melville's prose stands as exemplary philosophy precisely for the ways in which it is said to function "literally," to carry a particular force that either produces thinking or disrupts it. While assuming a split between literature and philosophy, this emphasis on reading Melville literally tends to treat the literariness of language as pure performance while devaluing the form of literature as mere mimesis. But if such generic distinctions as literature and philosophy do not survive Melville's writing, with its multi-form approach to form, style, language, silence, action, and history, then what of the distinction between the literal and the figurative?[6] As the fate of Pierre's pamphlet suggests, the literal is not opposed to the literary but instead bound up with one of the most conspicuously literary features of Melville's work – the proliferation of figures and analogies that function, like Pierre's pocket, as things, thoughts, and metaphors all at once. In what follows, I argue that Melville offers metatheoretical insight into the linked forms and methodologies of literature, philosophy, and critical theory precisely for the ways in which he plays with the entanglement of the literal and figurative. After examining a series of metatheoretical claims about Melville's "Bartleby," which hinge on the relationship of literature and philosophy, I return in the final section to a reading of Pierre's slippery pamphlet. The insight of Melville's fictional philosopher, Plotinus Plinlimmon, is that theory must be read as a literary enterprise, the work of fabulation and figuration, every bit as much as fiction is, and moreover, that the figures and fables of both must be taken literally.

2. Melville in Metatheory

In a recent essay tracking "Bartleby among the philosophers," Kevin Attell asks whether there is "a single short story of the American nineteenth century that has generated as much critical attention over the last half century, and from such a wide array of disciplinary perspectives as 'Bartleby the Scrivener.'"[7] (For that matter, is there a literary work of any century, with the possible exception of *Antigone*, that has?) Beginning with Maurice Blanchot's discussion of "Bartleby" in 1980 and continuing through Rancière's 2004 response to Deleuze's seminal 1989 essay, the theoretical cannon around "Bartleby" is now so capacious and established that it has spawned its own genre of metatheory: the Bartleby-in-theory essay.

In Attell's contribution to this genre, he offers a useful survey of the ways in which "thinkers' interpretations and appropriations of Melville's tale" are key to understanding the foundations of their work, providing "a series of Rorshach tests" with "Bartleby" serving as the inkblot into which each of them projects "the often obscure conceptual cores of their political ontologies."[8] Attell divides the Bartleby canon into French and Italian schools, with Blanchot, Deleuze, and Derrida reading the story as the confrontation of language with silence, and Agamben, Hardt, and Negri reading the story through the competing potentialities of human action and radical passivity. Where Attell places readings of Bartleby within distinct French and Italian lines of late-twentieth-century philosophy, both Nancy Ruttenburg and Michael Jonik set the European lineages against distinctly American ones. For Ruttenburg, the Americanist readings of Bartleby have been characterized by a focus on the "cultural-historical specificities of context," while Jonik weaves the debate between Deleuze and Rancière into more recent turns by Sharon Cameron and Branka Arsić towards Melville's expansion of character beyond the human in *Billy Budd* and "Bartleby" respectively – a turn that draws so deeply on Melville's European influences and readers as to blur the lines of strictly "Americanist" literary criticism.[9]

But more important than the national and methodological lineages these critics trace are the metatheoretical claims that Attell, Jonik, and Ruttenburg advance about what it is in Melville's work generally and "Bartleby" in particular that draws philosophers and theorists to it. Attell argues that "it is indeed at the point of political-philosophical first principles that Bartleby tends to intervene, appearing as it were, motionless on 'the office threshold the door being open' . . . as if he had always been there." As a site of "impassivity," "neutrality," and "negativity," Bartleby appears to Attell as a general opening for all philosophy.[10] For Ruttenburg, however, such an emphasis on Bartleby's neutrality tells only half of the story. She argues that "Bartleby" tends to force critics into a false choice between interpretive modes that are not only "mutually constitutive" but also explicitly thematized in the story by the scrivener and the lawyer. Whereas Melville's European readers have focused almost exclusively on Bartleby for the exceptional impassivity that Attell describes, she argues, Americanist critics have more often focused on the lawyer's narration to attend to "those cultural-historical specificities of context, which identify the aberration as such." Borrowing the Derridean image of silhouette and content, Ruttenburg argues that, in the lawyer and the scrivener, "mundanity and exceptionality exist in tense relation – the quintessential

Melvillean pattern of suspense."[11] In this, she says, the investment by philosophers in "Bartleby's" exceptionalism – whether as Deleuze's formula or Agamben's potentiality – misses what is essentially *literary* in both the character and the story: "the conversion of absolutes . . . into contingencies" and "the emplotment of contingency" in the local and the particular, in context and character.[12] Like Ruttenburg, Jonik takes up Rancière's critique of Deleuze to argue that Bartleby "presides" over a problem in which "both the philosophical uptake of literature and the literary uptake of philosophy" are essentially at stake. But for him, "Bartleby" is not the exceptional text in Melville's corpus for this problem – indeed, he suggests that there is no such text. Instead, Jonik draws on Deleuze's formulation of the "agrammatical" to argue that what is "unreadable" across Melville's work – murmurs, stutters, silences – also constitutes a theory of character as a process that continually moves across the human and the inhuman "to restructure the world, to make possible new configurations of affect and thought."[13]

Where Ruttenburg argues that philosophy and literature hang in suspensive tension in "Bartleby" and Jonik argues that they are always in excess of each other, both of these relations are in evidence in Deleuze's "Bartleby; or, the Formula." Arguably the most influential theoretical work on Melville's writing, Deleuze's essay is, in some sense, two essays: a theory of Bartleby's exceptional verbal performance as "ravaging" and "devastating" to mimesis, representation, and metaphysics on the one hand, and a taxonomy of Melville's major character types (demons, hypochondriacs, and prophets) on the other. If the first of these claims centers on the literal force of an utterance that destroys reference and representation, the second hinges on the capacity of Melville's art to produce "Original" characters of "primary nature" in their relations to those secondary beings who see them. At stake in these two claims is the very problem of reading that Deleuze foregrounds at the outset of his essay: "'Bartleby' is neither a metaphor for the writer nor the symbol of anything whatsoever. It is a violently comical text, and the comical is always literal . . . It means only what it says, literally." Opposing a literal reading of Melville to one that seeks to discern "anything whatsoever" as the ground of a metaphor, Deleuze introduces his formula by setting it against what he first characterizes as literary representation and later as mimetic identification and relation. To read Bartleby's formula literally, he argues, is to recognize that it functions beyond both constative and performative functions of language: it "excludes all alternatives . . . stop[s] reproducing words . . . [and] stymies the speech acts that a boss uses to command, that a kind friend uses to ask questions, or a man of faith to make promises." With its utterance, the formula thwarts both linguistic and identic mimesis to set in motion a procedure of "psychotic identification": the expression opens up an indeterminate zone where traits are exchanged and shared in the absence of subjects, all towards "a dream of establishing a function of universal fraternity."[14] All of this – the formula's function as an expressive trait that opens a zone of non-mimetic identification – ultimately secures Bartleby's exceptional status for Deleuze, which is to say that it secures his status as a "type" of the "great characters" of Melville's corpus.[15] Though Bartleby stands alone and without reference, neither general nor particular within the diegetic world of the story, he is nevertheless typical, existing in a relation of Originals across Melville's texts and among his characters. Deleuze draws his account of Melville's "Originals," of course, from the third metafictional chapter of *The Confidence-Man*, which implicitly links them to the duck-billed beavers and theatrical strangers through which Melville also figures fiction in chapters 14 and 33 respectively. The "Original" is thus an explicitly *literary* creature for Deleuze, as well as one who prefigures Pragmatist philosophy and emerges from the psychotic procedure of non-mimetic becoming that lies at the heart of Deleuzian ontology.

And so, as Deleuze traces the ways in which Melville's language, from Bartleby's formula to Isabel's murmuring in *Pierre*, initiates a process that opposes representation and yet yields types in a literary taxonomy, the literal is not in opposition to the literary but in strange collaboration with it. Indeed, for Rancière, Deleuze's insistence on reading "in its most literal sense" amounts to an absolute claim for literature that cannot hold. Rancière himself takes rather literally Deleuze's insistence that the comic force of Bartleby's formula is literal, arguing that Deleuze describes "a material operation that the materiality of a text produces," one that is almost mechanical in its pure operation and function. That function, Rancière claims, is to "lead the causal order of the world ... of representation to its catastrophe." In place of the "causal" view that is annihilated, Rancière argues, Deleuze substitutes an absolute and autonomous one. With this, Rancière places Deleuze's formula in a long history of claims for literature's autonomy, whether as the uniqueness of authorial genius, the absolute totality of the work, or "the pure power of language." In Rancière's account, the Deleuzean formula amounts to a latter-day version of literary autonomy: the insistence on the literal posits the materiality of style as an absolute way of seeing, in which no object is preferred, all matter is equal, and ontology is flat. Just as all earlier claims to literary autonomy rest on a specific heteronomy, so Deleuze's is no exception. Underneath all of these autonomies, Rancière claims, is the "heteronomy of thought," the assumption that thinking itself is, one way or another, made immanently present in the work. Deleuze's formula thus re-stages an old problem: "How to link in the form of the work the emancipated atoms of thought-matter?" Ultimately, Rancière argues, Deleuze cannot, and so he must collapse form into content and formula into symbol by focusing on those meta-literary "narratives that reveal, in their fable, what literature performs in its own work."[16]

On its face, Rancière's critique is a bit too easy: Deleuze claims that the literary formula mechanically transmutes material bodies, but – aha! – he can only point to fables of this metamorphosis as evidence.[17] However, what is really at stake concerns a more serious point of distinction, which Rancière develops over several essays, between how each of them understands literature's political and ontological claims.[18] In "Deleuze, Bartleby, and the Literary 'Formula,'" Rancière is less concerned that Deleuze cannot point to a text that "literally" disintegrates the world into atomic particles than he is by the ways in which the meta-literary fables that Deleuze privileges locate the process of becoming in exemplary characters – eccentrics and Originals – rather than in narratives that produce those characters and emplot the basic contradictions that they introduce. In Deleuze's readings, Rancière claims, such characters overtake all other aspects of the work, becoming "identical with the power of the author," as they condense within themselves the radically equalizing procedure of becoming. That is, they become, at once, "embodiments of literary production" and "mythic characters" who put Deleuzean ontology into practice, destroying fathers, models, copies, and mimesis itself.[19] Beyond what Rancière calls the basic "Deleuzean difficulty" – the simple substitution of one ground, the literal, for another, the mimetic – he argues that the literary formula fundamentally misconstrues the relationship of literature to equality and thus to its political efficacy: "What relationship does the molecular equality that grounds literary innovation have with the political community that can actualize it?" Although the force of the literal purports to produce material equality by annihilating the verticality of mimesis, it can only be wielded by exceptions and Originals who alone bear "the power of fictioning" through which the people come to appear as "a wall of loose uncemented stones, where every element has a value in itself but also in relation to others." Rancière concludes that the *aporia* of Deleuze's theory is in this erection of a wall at the very place where a passage is called for: "But this figure seems to block the mediating function of literature, to bar the road of shared fabulation, that of the people to come."[20]

Ultimately, Rancière takes Deleuze's figure of a wall literally in order to demonstrate the fallacy of the literal, and in catching Deleuze in his own conceit he ends up proving Deleuze's point that all figures have some force. Deleuze can no more articulate the stakes of the literal in Melville's work without introducing a figure than Rancière can avoid converting that figure into a literal impasse for Deleuze's philosophy. To be clear, I don't mean to suggest here that their respective theories of literature collapse: Rancière's emphasis on literature's perpetuation of contradiction and struggle between worlds obviously instills very different ways of reading than Deleuze's emphasis on the anti-mimetic force of becoming. However, when Rancière argues that "the artistic appropriation of the inhuman remains the work of metaphor," and Deleuze that "the mystery of formless, nonhuman life" appears only when "all referents are lost," both of them foreground a duplicity in figuration that is an essential feature of one of the works at the center of their competing readings: Melville's *Pierre*.[21] Throughout *Pierre* every figure is literal in the sense that the work of figuration is the principal achievement of a novel whose protagonist is, as Michael Snediker argues, "a figurative entity" and "ontologically stylistic."[22] Snediker's account of figuration offers a corrective to Deleuze's privileging of eccentrics and Originals in its claim that Pierre Glendinning must be read literally precisely because he is a creature of figuration – de-personified by the endless chains of metaphor and analogy that craft him. Pierre is not one of Deleuze's monomaniacs or hypochondriacs, nor does he belong to "primary nature." He is nonetheless a signal instance of the "power of fictioning" in Melville's work as a character whose impersonality and inhumanity are shown to be the work of literary art. At the same time, though, if Rancière insists that "metaphor" must be distinguished from "metamorphosis" in his critique of Deleuze, Snediker's insights into the primacy of figuration as "a process of verging on something else" suggest just how difficult this might be.[23] Throughout *Pierre*, the proliferation of metaphors, analogies, figures, and conceits exceeds the characterological to become central to the narrative's own fables of reference and representation. *Pierre* does not only spin a fable of "what literature performs in its own work," but it also makes literal the processes of figuration and fabulation that are central to both literature and philosophy.[24] This is nowhere more apparent than in Pierre's wayward pamphlet.

3. The Conceit of Theory

In considering the importance of Plotinus Plinlimmon's "Chronometricals and Horologicals" to *Pierre*, it's worth keeping in mind two fairly obvious points: first, both author and pamphlet are themselves works of fiction, and second, the fictional pamphlet is interpolated in the narrative as if being reproduced verbatim, so that "each person can now skip, or read and rail, for himself" (P 210). The invention of Plinlimmon and his philosophy is particularly strange, given that Melville inserts a sample of this philosophy after several pages dense with references to actual philosophers, from Spinoza and Goethe to (more obliquely) Carlyle and Emerson. But the only philosopher whose words we are invited to read literally is the fictional one. After detailing all of the ways in which "those imposter philosophers pretend somehow to have got an answer" from silence and to have found the "talismanic secret to reconcile this world with his own soul" (P 208), the novel embarks on its own philosophical pretense by inserting in the middle of the chapter a few pretend pages from a pretend philosophy whose title in Greek – "*EI*" – is the conditional conjunction "if" (P 210). Even though the pamphlet announces itself as nothing more than the "temporary Scaffold to the Portal" of a conditional philosophy, and even though Pierre's discovery of it is totally arbitrary, the narrator suggests that it might nevertheless pose a strong rejoinder to Pierre's general "life theory" if only he could comprehend it (P 209). Unfortunately, "[i]n this case, to comprehend, is himself to condemn himself, which is always highly inconvenient and uncomfortable to a man," and so Pierre immediately comes to believe "that he did not fully comprehend the strange writer's conceit" even though it is "one of the plainest in the world" (P 209–10). Unlike those real "imposters" whose pretenses cannot answer Pierre's crisis and whose words thus have no place in the narrative, the fictional Plinlimmon's arbitrarily found and conditional conceit is inserted into the narrative because it may "very palpably illustrate to him the intrinsic incorrectness and non-excellence of both the theory and the practice of his life" (P 209).

If critics have occasionally sought to unmask Plinlimmon as a caricature in order to find some satirized original under his mildly non-benevolent face and philosophy (P 290), the elaborate presentation of his theory as a "conceit" would seem to fly in the face of any such attempt. Any effort to discern a referent in "Chronometricals and Horologicals" stands in utter opposition to the theory itself, which installs its own referential system through a metaphor of reference as mechanical function. The pamphlet opens by drawing an analogy between God and the Greenwich Observatory that sets its conceit in motion, but the governing metaphor of the pamphlet hinges less on the mechanism of temporal reference – the chronometer's maintaining of Greenwich Mean Time throughout the globe – than on the imperfection of this referential relationship. Even "chronometers of the best make, and the most carefully treated, will gradually more or less vary from Greenwich time, without the possibility of the error being corrected by direct comparison with their great standard" (P 211). What is more, as chronometers imperfectly refer to Greenwich time while they roam around the world, they come to vary not only from their distant standard but also from the local time as measured by horologues. Doubly useless as a measure of standard time and local time, chronometers ultimately measure nothing but the absurdity of those who choose to live their lives in accordance with them – those who, referring to the imperfect instrument of Greenwich time while in China, eat lunch at midnight and go to bed at noon. But even as Plinlimmon's conceit argues the radical impracticality of all absolute standards, he insists that variance and relativism do not prove the absence of God, but that these are instead the proof of correspondence: "For he will then see, or seem to see, that this world's seeming incompatibility with God absolutely results from its meridianal correspondence with him" (P 213).

Predicated on the "organic inaccuracy" (P 211) of all referential mechanisms and the arbitrariness of the absolute grounds to which they imperfectly refer – the prime meridian, Greenwich mean time, year zero – Plinlimmon's conceit is "violently comic," and is thus quite literal. But what this means in *Pierre* is not quite what Deleuze says it means in "Bartleby." To read Plinlimmon literally is not to hear an echo of Bartleby's formula or Isabel's murmur. Instead, it is to read in the pamphlet the very processes of figuration and fabulation through which both theory and literature spin their conceits. If, as Spanos argues, Plinlimmon "precisely theorizes the actual circumstances of Pierre's emergent condition," I would argue that this is not because Plinlimmon has insight into a more general condition that Pierre shares and suffers, but because the pamphlet elaborates a complex metaphor for the narrative itself. It is Pierre's narrative in another form, voice, and genre. The narrator reveals the pamphlet's real function just before "reproducing" it in the chapter: "For to me it seems more the excellently illustrated re-statement of a problem, than the solution to the problem itself" (P 210). An excellent illustration that re-figures Pierre's story through an elaborate moral-temporal fable, the pamphlet exists entirely within the fictional universe of *Pierre* as an extension of its systems of figuration. In this, the pamphlet becomes something literal within the narrative – a fictional reference to which the novel returns as if it were a material fragment, a theory that works its way through a tear in Pierre's coat pocket to figure forth his comprehensive incomprehension of it.

Finally, in "excellently" restating the problem of the narrative itself, I would argue that Plinlimmon puts into practice the very work of literary criticism that, Rancière argues, best addresses the contradictions he details in his ongoing polemic with Deleuze – those between the "mute letter" and the "living body," metaphor and metamorphosis, interpretation and action. Arguing that literary theory and criticism have always shared the same system of meaning as literature, Rancière claims that both literature and theory rely on a duplicitous function of language – at once literal and representational – to "reconfigure the visibility of the common world."[25] The fallacy of criticism, that is, is not in the belief that subterranean political content can be mined through symptomatic reading, nor in the assumption that the letter can perform, in its very literariness, political acts. Instead, criticism fails when it does not recognize that it shares a common hermeneutic plot with literature itself – a plot in which the very thing we try to read slips between a surface and a lining to be unwittingly carried everywhere.

CHAPTER 11

Billy Budd*: Pessimism for Post-Critique*

Paul Hurh

Herman Melville's *Billy Budd* is about the loss of an earnest, non-ironic position within a world full of hidden motives and powers. One of the more remarkable effects of this theme is that criticism has itself followed a similar trajectory, yielding readings that are either rigorously ironist or thoroughly earnest. The earliest earnest interpretations considered the novel a "testament of acceptance," in which Vere's execution of Billy is a reluctant and tragic expression of submission to the necessity of justice.[1] Ironist readings, propelled by suspicions about Vere's and the narrator's testimonies, instead argued that the novel should be read as a "testament of resistance," in which Vere's execution of Billy is actually a reassertion of power, achieved through duplicitous manipulation that Melville ironically critiques. In recent years, the ironist readings seem to have carried the day, most notably in William Spanos's book-length "symptomatic" reading of *Billy Budd* as concealing a "radical indictment" of American imperialism.[2] Just as the naïve Billy Budd, for whom "[t]o deal in double meanings and insinuations of any sort was quite foreign to his nature" (BB 49), is lost to the pull of irony within the story, the earnest interpretations of the novel similarly become less viable – for Spanos, even impossible – in the drift of symptomatic interpretation in its critical history.[3] The interpretive dilemma that Barbara Johnson identified in the division between Billy, the "face value" reader, and Claggart, the "ironic reader" (BB 237), would seem to have spilled outside of its textual confines, reproducing itself in a critical history that veers from unsuspicious, face-value acceptance to suspicious, ironic resistance.[4]

In light of recent debates about the limits of critique and ironist reading, this interpretive divide takes on a new and altered form. For if the critical history of *Billy Budd* in the late twentieth and early twenty-first centuries tends toward ironic readings, it indexed the trend towards ironist interpretive practices – grouped together under the term "critique" – that became prevalent across multiple disciplines in the humanities and social sciences during the same period. The practice of critique begins with a suspicion of what cultural phenomena say they are doing, and instead looks to uncover the work that they *actually* do, which is always disguised or hidden and oftentimes malicious or unjust. Disclosing the hidden mechanisms of power becomes, for practitioners of critique, a form of political awareness that is both part and corollary to advocacy and activism. First occasionally, and then more frequently, scholars in recent years have voiced concern over the preponderance of critique within the disciplinary praxis. Bruno Latour, in "Why Has Critique Run Out of Steam?" worries that the very methodology of progressive critique, suspicious of any official narrative, has paradoxically been appropriated by conservative discourse to render all statements of "fact" suspect.[5] The call for imagining something variously called "post-critique" (Felski), "reparative reading" (Sedgwick), or "surface reading" (Best and Marcus), thus emerges at a moment in which the "weapons" (Latour's term) of deconstructive critique seem to have backfired.[6] The diversity of responses in *PMLA*'s 2017 forum on Felski's *The Limits of Critique* showed, however, that there is not yet consensus regarding what such practice would consist of and, more worryingly, what it would be good for.[7] Empowered by the rich political landscape of today's atrocities and horrors, critique can at least point to a political consequence as its aim. Felski's reply that "[r]eassessing critique, in this light, is not an abandonment of social or ethical commitments but a realization . . . that these commitments require us to communicate with intellectual strangers who do not share our assumptions" is more of a deferral than an alternative.[8] If post-critique's final aim is humility, then it might foster more communication between our disciplinary practice and intellectual strangers, yet the obligation towards the public sphere that considers such communication a goal is itself drawn from the set of ethical assumptions that underlie the practice of critique in the first place. It is within this discursive context that I would like to assign the stakes of a new reading of *Billy Budd*. For *Billy Budd* is not only adjacent to these critical questions by staging, in its story as well as its reception, the recession of earnest reading in the face of ironic interpretation; it is also the key text in the initial theorization of such reading practices in the first place. By returning to the novel as a tragedy of earnest reading, and noting the way that tragedy reproduces itself in its criticism, this essay finds in the novel a structural and historical account of the rise of ironist reading that implicates the liberal ideals that often justify our work, yet it offers a solution that doesn't require that we therefore abandon them.

In 1990, Eve Sedgwick undertook an ironist reading of paranoia in *Billy Budd*. Drawing from Robert Martin's recognition of the homosexual subtext, Sedgwick argued that the novel anatomizes a form of "homosexual-homophobic knowing" that she termed "[i]n a succinct formulation, paranoia."[9] Her exploration of the novel's manipulation of paranoid knowledge led her to a structural interpretation of its symmetrical form (the "fatal *symmetry* of paranoid knowledge") and an historical account of its possible extension ("the fantasy trajectory toward a life *after the homosexual*"). Claggart, Sedgwick argued, is a homosexual who activates the symmetry in paranoid knowledge which then becomes, through Vere's manipulations, the mode by which to ensure non-symmetrical, hierarchical, control: "Vere's discipline both requires and enforces the paranoid symmetry against which it is defined."[10] Sedgwick's chapter on *Billy Budd* ended by suggesting that Vere's asymmetrical relations to the doomed Billy "constitute the shining furrow of the disappearance of the homosexual" and aligned it with the story of Sodom and Gomorrah and other narratives of gay genocide. Towards the end of the essay, Sedgwick draws an even more apocalyptic conclusion, claiming that "the phobic narrative trajectory toward imagining a time *after the homosexual* is finally inseparable from that toward imagining a time *after the human*." Such a turn extrapolated the termination of human life itself and posited that "[t]he impulse of the species toward its own eradication must not [...] be underestimated." It would seem that Sedgwick's essay, beginning with the pairing of Billy's earnestness and Claggart's paranoia, illustrated not only how hierarchical modes of control may appropriate the power of such symmetrical structures, but also how the energies that they produce may recursively amplify, hurtling towards apocalyptic visions of the self-imposed extinction of the human. For Sedgwick, *Billy Budd* revealed paranoia to be the paradoxical logic that underwrites the unchecked expansion of forms of control, discipline, and oppression that would destroy every human through its impulse to imagine threats in order to prevent them. Yet, viewed from our current moment, the essay also seems pulled into a paranoid apocalyptic vision in which the only way to combat the homophobic forces that would destroy the species is to remain unceasingly aware and suspicious: "how can it fail to be all the more necessary that the avenues of recognition, desire, and thought between minority potentials and universalizing ones be opened and opened and opened?"[11]

A decade later, Sedgwick, perhaps unsurprisingly, became one of the first critics to remark on the limits of what she calls "paranoid reading," a form of inquiry that has come "to seem entirely coextensive with critical theoretical inquiry rather than being viewed as one kind of cognitive/ affective theoretical practice among other, alternative kinds."[12] In this later essay, "Paranoid Reading and Reparative Reading," Sedgwick worries about paranoia's shift from being "a privileged *object* of antihomophobic theory" in the mid-1980s to "being its uniquely sanctioned *methodology*" in the late-1990s, and she undertakes a study of her own earlier work to "retrace that transition – one that seems worthy of remark now but seemed at the time, I think, the most natural move in the world." She identifies two possible causes of the transition, the first structural, involving the character of paranoia itself: "paranoia tends to be contagious; more specifically, paranoia is drawn towards and tends to construct symmetrical relations, in particular, symmetrical epistemologies." The second cause is historical, and it has to do with the cultural milieu of the baby boomer generation and the spread of paranoid reading beyond the boundaries of queer studies: "because it is less easy to account on structural terms for the frequent privileging of paranoid methodologies in recent nonqueer critical projects such as feminist theory, psychoanalytic theory, deconstruction, Marxist criticism, or the New Historicism."[13] Read today, Sedgwick's worry about paranoia's shift within disciplinary practice suggests reconsidering her prior essay on *Billy Budd*, which itself escalates from an analysis of paranoia as an object in the novel to the diagnosis of a systemic homophobia that is not only genocidal but, as she terms it, omnicidal in its fantasy of the annihilation of the human. The present essay takes this occasion to read *Billy Budd* as about this very extrapolation of paranoia, its compulsory and escalating logic, thus providing insight on the challenges that face post-critique.

My hypothesis is that *Billy Budd* is not only a special text within debates about paranoid reading and critique, but that it actually takes the problem, the spread of paranoid reading practices and the loss of anything like an earnest posture, as its central theme. Reconsidering the novel as such, we may consider how it links the paranoid nature of ironic critique to a political and technological historical moment. What Melville describes, in lapsarian terms, is the advent of modern ironist interpretation, arising not as a corrective to hidden regimes of control, but rather as their cause and viciously cyclical effect. At the root of this paranoia is nature and the non-human – the material forces of the world itself. That is, paranoia in *Billy Budd* turns out to be not an aberrant psychological disorder particular to individuals but a historically distinct variant of the universal condition of suffering (in a Buddhist sense) responsible for existence itself. Such a tone, pessimistic and melancholic, may at first seem like a quietist capitulation, unable to deliver a prescription for the future of post-critique as it would seem to suggest that the spread of paranoia and paranoid reading is ineluctable and natural. However, the second part of this essay considers Melville's own philosophical interest in pessimism, particularly his reading and annotating of Schopenhauer, as instructive of a possible non-paranoid way to reconceive our relation to interpretation. For pessimism releases the critic from those heroic obligations based on the ideal of a just world and replaces them with an ethical imperative based on a compassion without hope. Rather than take the improvement of the world as the final motive of its work, post-critique could gain from pessimism stakes such as fellowship and love, not as instrumental towards some end, but rather as desirable in themselves in a world of strife and suffering. A sophisticated version of pessimism, I suggest, could answer some of the most difficult issues facing post-critique, though it would necessarily raise others.

I

Billy Budd begins by making the handsome sailor, the type of naïve and earnest reader that Billy Budd will exemplify, an historical figure, only seen in "the time before steamships, or then more frequently than now" (BB 43), and it closes with the sailors' sympathies for Billy Budd being "deepened by the fact that he was gone, and in a measure mysteriously gone" (BB 131). The historical disappearance of the handsome sailor, and with him the possibility of non-ironic earnestness, becomes the source of mystery for the novel. The Dansker's interest in Billy Budd is a version of the story's own: a "speculative query as to what might eventually befall a nature like that, dropped into a world not without some mantraps and against whose subtleties simple courage lacking experience and address, and without any touch of defensive ugliness, is of little avail" (BB 70). What happened to the handsome sailor? What happened to earnestness?

Following the chain of cause and effect, two key moments of irony stand out as turning points in Billy's doomed career upon the *Bellipotent*. The first is Billy's farewell to the ship from which he had been impressed: "And good-bye to you too, old *Rights-of-Man*." Though the narrator explains that Billy could not have meant the statement ironically, being "by no means of a satirical turn," it is still read that way by the lieutenant who asserts discipline: "instantly assuming all the rigor of his rank, though with difficulty repressing a smile" (BB 49). This initial ironic misreading becomes a cause of suspicion that careens through paranoid interpretations eventuating in Billy's execution. Claggart tests Billy's character by having his cat's-paw, Squeak, lay traps for him. Squeak, on his part, catches the ironist strain of interpretation, reading in Claggart's orders an assumed meaning: "the corporal, having naturally enough concluded that his master could have no love for the sailor, made it his business, faithful understrapper that he was, to foment the ill blood by perverting to his chief certain innocent frolics of the good-natured foretopman" (BB 79). And Claggart, a committed paranoid reader, "never suspected the veracity of these reports, more especially as to the epithets, for he well knew how secretly unpopular may become a master-at-arms" (BB 80). Paranoid tests lead to ironic readings which lead to confirmations underwritten by paranoid assumptions. These culminate in Claggart's reference to the *Rights-of-Man* incident as an "adroit fling" when alleging conspiracy against Billy, the "good-humored air" being the chief cause of suspicion: "You have but noted his fair cheek. A mantrap may be under the ruddy-tipped daisies" (BB 94). Extending irony's career through the narrative, Claggart's taking good humor as the sign of secret resentment becomes the cause of Vere's own suspicion of Claggart, and impels Vere's withdrawal of the scene into secrecy, because the allegation itself might "undesirably affect the ship's company" (BB 96). After the introduction of ironic reading, the deepening of secrecy and suspicion follow, eroding the very human rights over which the ironic readers worry. If Billy says goodbye to the ship, and his superiors think he is saying goodbye to human rights, it is a second-order irony that it is the suspicion itself that brings about the ironic reading's fulfillment.

The second key moment in the text, when Billy spills his soup into the path of Claggart, shows how the tautological energy of paranoid reading draws from a reversal of handsomeness's own tautological structure. Claggart's ironic insult at Billy's spill – "Handsomely done, my lad! And handsome is as handsome did it, too!" (BB 72) – is predictably misunderstood by Billy. But the logic of the statement, in which Claggart suggests that Billy is not handsome because the spilling of the soup was not handsome, works by referring to the adage "Handsome is as handsome does" – a tautological saying in which handsomeness is taken as a self-same quality, without internal difference between outward action and internal character. Using handsomeness against itself, Claggart's ironic deployment of that proverb "let escape an ironic inkling . . . as to what it was that had first moved him [Claggart] against Billy, namely, his significant personal beauty" (BB 77). Yet this beauty is not mere surface, but rather the quality of handsomeness itself as consistency between outward and inward nature: "If askance he eyed the good looks, cheery health, and frank enjoyment of young life in Billy Budd, it was because these went along with a nature that, as Claggart magnetically felt, had in its simplicity never willed malice or experienced the reactionary bite of that serpent" (BB 78). The ironic inkling that escapes from Claggart is that he *does* believe that Billy is handsome, which is ironic only because Claggart's own statement is ostensibly ironic in the first place. Claggart stumbles into earnestness for a moment, but that earnestness flips back into irony because Claggart is, by nature, an ironic reader. The loss of the earnest reading does not seem to be directed in any personally malicious way, in fact it would seem to be shouldered out of the picture by the self-replicating circular reversals within Claggart's ironic position: "a nature like Claggart's, surcharged with energy as such natures almost invariably are, what recourse is left to it but to recoil upon itself and, like the scorpion for which the Creator alone is responsible, act out to the end the part allotted it" (BB 78). Irony emerges as an inhuman engine, built into Claggart's nature, driven by a self-sustaining mechanics of reversal.

Subject to such mechanics, Billy's earnest position becomes the site of most suspicion, primarily because in the grip of a hermeneutics of suspicion, the most superficially innocent will be seen as the most successful in hiding something. Paranoid reading parallels what is understood as Claggart's "evil"; the practice, in other words, is a subtler depravity that not only hides itself behind prudence and respectability, but cuts off all routes to verification: "in case of an injury but suspected, its secretiveness voluntarily cuts it off from enlightenment or disillusion; and, not unreluctantly, action is taken upon surmise as upon certainty" (BB 80). On a structural level, the loss of the handsome sailor is caused by the symmetrical, reversible, and self-sustaining logic of paranoid reading and ironic interpretation, a kind of virus that Claggart carries but for which he is not responsible.

Such a structural description of the problem necessarily requires an historical account. For if paranoid reading emerges from the imputation of irony and would make earnest readings unavailable through its unchecked spread, then what is being described is not a discrete moment, but rather a world-historical one. Melville's placement of *Billy Budd* in the "time before steamships" and during the Napoleonic wars situates the disappearance of the Handsome Sailor within the historical moment of technological innovation and European political revolution. The fears of mutiny aboard the *Bellipotent* are described as contagiously contracted, from the French Revolution, and bear the same accelerating, contagious, description: "[r]easonable discontent growing out of practical grievances in the fleet had been ignited into irrational combustion as by live cinders blown across the Channel from France in flames" (BB 54). Moreover, this escalation generates the conditions for irony: "The event [the *Nore* mutiny] converted into irony for a time those spirited strains of Dibdin" (BB 55). Irony becomes a symptom or signal of revolution and mutiny, and earnest statements are made to stand for something else, for their reverse: "British colors with the union and cross wiped out; but that cancellation transmuting the flag of founded law and freedom defined, into the enemy's red meteor of unbridled and unbounded revolt" (BB 54). Melville's story suggests that irony bears a special relation to revolution, and refers to its oppositional and negative logic (it "converts" and "transmutes" by cancellation) as forming the basis for irony and its quality of escalation-through-reversal responsible for its aggressive epidemiology in a post-revolutionary context. Moreover, because revolutionary symbology in *Billy Budd* is not itself positive, does not have its own flag, and is only the negative of the reigning structure, the cancellation of another's flag, then it bears resemblance to the methodology of critique, especially in its deconstructive guises. As a procedure of splitting and doubling, turning words and symbols and power against themselves from within, ironic reading is an exceptionally powerful tool. But, *Billy Budd* seems to suggest, for the same reasons, it is difficult to control or to stop.

It is a tool, moreover, that Melville aligns with technological development, in particular the development of the steam engine. For in the first sentence of the novel, Melville locates the Handsome Sailor in the "time before steamships." When Melville paints the portrait of the Handsome Sailor as a type, he focuses on the physical engagement of the sailor with the sails, those technologies made obsolete by the steamer: "Close-reefing topsails in a gale, there he was, astride the weather yardarm-end, foot in the Flemish horse as stirrup, both hands tugging at the earing as at a bridle, in very much the attitude of young Alexander curbing the fiery Bucephalus" (BB 44). The "less prosaic time" to which the Handsome Sailor belongs is not simply before the Napoleonic wars but a time in which there existed a direct relation between the sailor's body, the equipment of the ship, and the natural elements. The loss of the Handsome Sailor would seem to be linked to the loss of sailing in general. But Melville's recreation of this moment is more than just a nostalgic exercise, because handsomeness, that transparent relation between surface and content, is related to a bodily engagement with the world, one that is lost with the advent of steam power and the corresponding rearrangement of material forces and structures of power.

Sailors in *Billy Budd* are an older class, both disappearing and associated with a frankness that opposes the irony of the paranoid reader, who reads "the fairness of appearance" as evidence of the necessity for "distrust." It is this direct relation, the sailorness of Billy Budd, that Melville indicates is responsible for his naïve innocence:

> And what could Billy know of man except of man as a mere sailor? And the old-fashioned sailor, the veritable man before the mast, the sailor from boyhood up . . . The sailor is frankness, the landsman is finesse. Life is not a game with the sailor, demanding the long head . . . Every sailor, too, is accustomed to obey orders without debating them; his life afloat is externally ruled for him; he is not brought into that promiscuous commerce with mankind where unobstructed free agency on equal terms – equal superficially, at least – soon teaches one that unless upon occasion he exercise a distrust keen in proportion to the fairness of appearance, some foul turn may be served him. (BB 87)

The sailor here is not free; he belongs to a rigid hierarchy. Distrust and finesse are actually generated by "unobstructed free agency" and re-echoes the sense that revolutionary liberalism creates the conditions for paranoid reading. Removing visible structures of power leads to subterranean versions, this in turn paralleling the substitution of an adversarial relationship between human and nature into one between human and human. In tracking the question of what has happened to the Handsome Sailor, we sense that there have been two interrelated developments: the loss of authority that enables a freedom which leads ineluctably to distrust, and the birth of modern technologies that change the relation of body to world.

The logic of paranoia (and of technology) always picks up steam. When Billy Budd is sentenced to death, Melville returns to the steamer motif in illustrating the motive power of the officers' fears: "The greater the fog the more it imperils the steamer, and speed is put on though at the hazard of running somebody down. Little ween the snug card players in the cabin of the responsibilities of the sleepless man on the bridge" (BB 114). The officers, obeying an ever-vigilant paranoia, actually accelerate the dangers. The "snug card players" are released by the technology of the steam engine into a comfortable free play, ignorant of the paranoid acceleration of the ship at the hands of the centralized power of the captain which steam power has allowed. Melville uses the difference between sail and steam in order to chart the maturation of a modern paranoid condition, one that proceeds from symmetrical to asymmetrical expression in both material technologies and structures of power. That transformation is underlined when the narrator notes that the loyalty of sailors under Nelson, impressed by "his mere presence and heroic personality," are replaced by a "new order" of "martial utilitarians" endowed with "personal prudence" and steam-powered ironclads that are "unsightly, unavoidably lacking the symmetry and grand lines of the old battleships" (BB 57). The asymmetry of the ironclads models the asymmetry of power in the grip of the paranoid imaginary: demanding more men, demanding more prudence, desiring to be free of the fog of threat, paranoia develops out of its symmetrical logic an asymmetrical escalation of defensiveness.

The loss of the Handsome Sailor and the corresponding question of what has happened to the earnest position is attributed in *Billy Budd* to the advent of irony and paranoia, not simply as a psychological phenomenon but as a world-historical event associated with both political and technological change. This may seem at first a deeply pessimistic conclusion, suggesting that the modern world has fallen into an irretrievable state of constant paranoia. Melville invites such a lapsarian reading by suggesting that the alienness of Billy's good nature corroborates "the doctrine of man's Fall, a doctrine now popularly ignored" (BB 52) and considers his virtues to be "exceptionally transmitted from a period prior to Cain's city and citified man" (BB 53). But if the conclusion is politically pessimistic, it may not be for all that an ethical dead end. Melville's late reading in pessimism, particularly his annotations in Schopenhauer, provides context for a richer understanding of how *Billy Budd* reframes the problem of paranoid reading. Rather than try to redeem or reverse irony's sink into paranoia and interpersonal conflict, attempts that would by the very recoiling architecture of ironic reading be just as likely to extend rather than curtail it, Melville's interest in pessimism may offer an alternate vision of how to imagine post-critique. For pessimism, through its denial of a utopic possible future, would reframe our ethical obligations towards one another as a species of compassion in hopeless distress, an analog of hospice care, rather than revert, as in some contemporary defenses of post-critique, back to the obligation to pursue a just, fair, and egalitarian society conforming to those ideals of liberalism that, in *Billy Budd* at least, may be partially responsible for the turn to paranoia in the first place.

2

Melville's interest in pessimism is evident in his repeated references to the pessimistic poetry of Leopardi in *Clarel*, and it appears to mature during his final years, most conspicuously in his annotations on Schopenhauer, an outspoken philosophical defender of pessimism. Melville checked out volumes of Schopenhauer in early 1891, and then purchased a set of Schopenhauer's works later in the year, which he marked liberally.[14] Judging by the notes, it is likely that Melville found in Schopenhauer echoes and parallels with the themes of slander and tragedy in the work he was still completing. Melville's recommendation of "The City of Dreadful Night," a pessimistic poem in a distinctly Schopenhauerian vein, several years earlier also suggests that some version of philosophical pessimism was influential during the course of *Billy Budd*'s composition.[15] In pessimism, suffering is the inexorable reality of experience. There is no attempt, in pessimism, to redeem or salvage an inherently flawed world; rather, pessimism's posture is stoic, accepting the inevitability of the fallen world and offering as its only comfort the acknowledgement of shared and necessary suffering. Although this may seem a dour and cheerless philosophy, it attracted Melville in his later years, and could present a novel response to the tireless defensiveness of paranoia. Rather than rejecting it, pessimism acknowledges paranoia and describes its functions while still remaining agnostic about the possibility of escaping its grip.

Melville's interest in Schopenhauer during the composition of *Billy Budd* has been productively analyzed by Sharon Cameron. Cameron, arguing for the influence of Schopenhauer's *The World as Will and Idea* on *Billy Budd*, connects the apparent loss of individuality in the novel to Schopenhauer's theory of the world as immanent will. Focusing on Schopenhauer's lack of distinction between persons and things, Cameron reads the novel as effacing distinctions until achieving a state of ascetic neutrality: "a beauty not compromised by possession or adaptation – in something clear, 'smooth,' and all-encompassing," a "state – without the sun's glorification (or a God's), and equally without the bright constraint of personal will (which Benjamin called 'the sun of individuality')."[16] Read along these lines, *Billy Budd* portrays a fulfillment of Schopenhauer's quest for an ascetic withdrawal from individuation and a cognizance of the world as fundamentally undifferentiated.

Cameron's reading leads us to Schopenhauer's material immanence, yet in order to describe the functioning of paranoia and irony within *Billy Budd*, we need also to incorporate Schopenhauer's unrelenting and sophisticated sense of pessimism. For if we take Schopenhauer's will as only a blind essence into which the problems of distinction melt at the end of *Billy Budd*, we may miss the crucial differences between Schopenhauer's pessimistic ontology and similar philosophies. Leibniz and Spinoza also describe an undifferentiated essence uniting phenomenal experience, but for Schopenhauer these philosophies are flawed by their ego-soothing optimism. Schopenhauer's pessimism, drawn from Buddhism and explicitly opposed to Leibniz and Spinoza, touches every point of his philosophical system. And Melville's marginal scoring confirms that it is this aspect – the inescapable suffering of the world and the folly of optimism – that draws him to Schopenhauer. In his copy of *Studies in Pessimism,* among his liberal marginal markings, Melville scored Schopenhauer's description of the three main differences between his philosophy that of Leibniz and Rousseau: "(1) the recognition of the preponderating magnitude of the evil and misery of existence with which he is deeply penetrated; (2) that of the strict necessity of the acts of will; (3) that of the truth of Locke's principle, that what thinks may also be material."[17] Evil and misery are ubiquitous and real, the will is not free, and cognition is material: these three points give us an immanence that is wholly bound to the conditions of the world, both as will and as idea, and offer no possible liberation or escape. To understand the pessimistic origin of Schopenhauer's immanent materialist philosophy helps us to understand how the physical materials of Billy's environment could become elemental agents within the fable of the birth of paranoid and ironic reading. For if, as Cameron points out, *Billy Budd* attempts to portray a state of undifferentiated, characterless being as any way desirable, that is because the very conditions of differentiation that create the physical world are also responsible for the suffering suffusing it. Paranoid reading, it may turn out, is the natural outcome of the constitution of the world as will: it is as much the physical state of the world as it is a psychological state of the individual.

Structurally, Schopenhauer's pessimism is based upon a Buddhist-inspired understanding of the experienced world as comprised of adversarial relations or limits. Melville's reading of Schopenhauer would thus have afforded him a philosophy in which the strife of the world in its physical manifestations is directly related to misanthropy, paranoia, and suspicion in its social phenomena. Individuation, the very constitution of difference upon which all experience and existence depends, is first and foremost for Schopenhauer a recursive and endless struggle: "everywhere in nature we see strife, conflict, and alternation of victory, and in it we shall come to recognize more distinctly that variance with itself which is essential to will. Every grade of objectification of will fights for the matter, the space, and the time of others."[18] This primal strife and conflict within the will manifests itself outwardly through the material individuation of the physical universe and the psychological individuation of human consciousnesses, both of which continue to exist within the unceasing adversarial context which gives them being.

The will's inherent property of turning against itself, constantly generating experience out of suffering, is thus not merely analogical but actually identical with the psychological torment of the will as objectified in the body. In a long passage of Schopenhauer's marked by Melville, we can hear a version of Claggart's mysterious "natural depravity" that surmounts egoistic motives and recoils upon itself:

> For all suffering is simply unfulfilled and crossed volition; and even the pain of the body when it is injured or destroyed is as such only possible through the fact that the body is nothing but the will itself become object. Now on this account, because much intense suffering is inseparable from much intense volition, very bad men bear the stamp of inward suffering in the very expression of the countenance; . . . From this inward torment, which is absolutely and directly essential to them, there finally proceeds that delight in the suffering of others which does not spring from mere egoism, but is disinterested, and which constitutes *wickedness* proper, rising to the pitch of *cruelty*.[19]

The inward torment of the world is thus responsible for the inward torment of "very bad men" seen in facial expressions, like Claggart's "involuntary smile, or rather grimace" (BB 72), or the more ambiguous "expression less guarded than that of the bitter smile, usurping the face from the heart – some distorting expression" (BB 73). Read through Schopenhauer, Claggart's natural depravity is the internal variance of the will turned against itself, "self-contained" (BB 76), driven by a psychology determined at top by intense volition rather the conscience: "Claggart's conscience being but the lawyer to his will" (BB 80). The peculiar symmetry of Claggart's paranoia would thus be explained by pessimism as an exacerbated case of the internal strife endemic to the world as will. The symmetrical oppositions of paranoid reading, which enable Claggart to use reason "as an ambidexter implement for effecting the irrational," derive from the fundamental constitution of the world as self-contained, self-opposed, internal strife. His evil, therefore, is not "engendered by vicious training or corrupting books or licentious living, but born with him and innate, in short 'a depravity according to nature'" (BB 76).

On a structural level, then, pessimism would explain the contagious and self-confirming feature of paranoid reading to be a load-bearing beam within the architecture of the world. Although this does not radically alter Sedgwick's understanding of paranoid logic, it does reorient its origin and trajectory. Rather than being a unique individual pathology that has mysteriously run rampant across social relations, paranoia becomes a universal pathology, originating out of the variance of the will, and, as I read *Billy Budd* to say, developing in the ripe conditions of a superficial freedom from hierarchical limitations in liberal revolution and from natural limitations in technological progress. The echoes of this second, historical condition for paranoia's ascendance may also be found in Schopenhauer.

In *The Wisdom of Life* (the Schopenhauer volume that Melville read prior to purchasing a set of his works), Schopenhauer's pessimism takes an historical turn, finding a current source of strife in the growth of "modern honor" and the force of slander in the "civilized" world of superficially free, liberal urbanity. For Schopenhauer, the modern individual is under constant distress because one's identity, or honor, is dependent upon the esteem of others, and thus is always open to verbal attack. In many ways, Schopenhauer's description of the escalation of slander to violence in such an environment parallels the route of Claggart's false testimony to Billy's strike. Melville scored Schopenhauer's section on honor liberally, and following these clues, we may restore the context of Schopenhauer's description of the modern dilemma to the drama of Billy and Claggart.

The climactic moment in *Billy Budd*, when Claggart slanders Billy and Billy strikes him because he cannot respond in language – "Could I have but used my tongue I would not have struck him" (BB 106) – plays out the description of slander's itinerary that Melville scored in Schopenhauer: "His honor is thus at the mercy of every man who can talk it away on the tip of his tongue; and if he attacks it, in a moment it is gone forever – unless the man who is attacked manages to wrest it back again."[20] To wrest it back requires violence: "If a fellow likes to insult any one, attribute to him, for example, some bad quality, this is taken as *prima facie* a well-founded opinion true in fact; a decree, as it were, with all the force of law; nay, if it is not at once wiped out in blood, it is a judgment which holds good and valid to all time."[21] Melville marked these two sentences, as well as another that shows how slander leads, in the current context of a social world built upon interpersonal reputation, to violence: "the code implies that the highest court to which a man can appeal in any differences he may have with another on point of honor is the court of physical force, that is, of brutality." Read in this context, Billy's strike against Claggart is the expression of the utter lack of alternate defenses available to earnestness within a world of duplicity. Melville also scored Schopenhauer's description of the escalation from insult to violence: "My opponent has truth, right and reason on his side. Very well. I insult him. Thereupon right and honor leave him and come to me, and for the time being, he has lost them – until he gets them back, not by the exercise of right or reason, but by shooting and sticking me."[22] Yet when Melville draws a similar symmetrical arrangement of slander and violence in Billy's strike, he reverses the polarity: "innocence and guilt personified in Claggart and Budd in effect changed places" (BB 103). In the action of Billy's strike, Billy may take the only non-verbal, non-ironic route left open to him but it paradoxically enmeshes him within the very binary adversarial structure to which his nature was opposed from the start.

In Schopenhauer's account of the escalating and paradoxical nature of modern honor and slander, he considers it a recent and unique variation on the basic structure of adversity central to pessimism's philosophy. Given the less structurally codified nature of social hierarchy in "Cain's city," one's identity and worth are even more dependent upon the fickle esteem of others: "the sphere of what we are for other people is their consciousness, not ours; it is the kind of figure we make in their eyes, together with the thoughts which this arouses."[23] This displacement of social identity onto the minds of others, exacerbated by the growth of urban populations, gives redoubled power to slander. As Schopenhauer writes, in a passage that Melville scored in part:

> There are two things which more than all else serve to make the social arrangements of modern life compare unfavorably with those of antiquity, by giving our age a gloomy, dark and sinister aspect, from which antiquity, fresh natural and, as it were, in the morning of life, is completely free; I mean modern honor and modern disease – *parcnobile fratrum*! Which have combined to poison all the relations of life, whether public or private ... From the time that poisoned arrows have been found in Cupid's quiver, an estranging, hostile, nay devilish element has entered into the relations of men and women, like a sinister thread of fear and mistrust in the warm and woof of their intercourse; indirectly shaking the foundations of human fellowship, and so more or less affecting the whole tenor of existence.[24]

What began as a discourse on the evils and causes of dueling in the modern age, becomes a much broader indictment of a deep historical and social change, a "modern" fall into paranoia that has fundamentally changed not only society but "the whole tenor of existence." Melville, marking this passage, may have adopted from it the epochal character of his own narrative of the fall from premodern innocence into modern paranoia.

Schopenhauer's pessimism can thus be seen as an influence upon Melville's construction of the dilemma of paranoid reading's recursive spread. Structurally, the reversible symmetries at the base of irony and paranoid reading are the immanent mechanics of a seething, self-adverse world. Historically, the conditions of late eighteenth-century modernity, in particular the twinned advent of social revolution against orthodox hierarchies and technological innovation that shifted adversarial context from the natural to the social world, generate a new, recursive and escalating expression of those mechanics in paranoia and suspicion. To return to the question of post-critique, *Billy Budd* does not necessarily point a way forward towards some optimistic future in which post-critical thought saves the day. In fact, pessimism would suggest that not only is critique a kind of virus of thought, endemic to both our ontological and social situation, but also that it is inescapable and tends naturally towards injurious forms of strife and suffering. Rather than the plethora of "alternate" forms of engagement with the text, promoted by Felski, pessimism would predict that all alternate forms of reading would, when thrown into the adversarial and paranoid environment of the academic market and the scarcity of resources, be forced into either a defensive or a heroic position, justifying itself along the same grounds of necessity and political or social melioration that informs critique. So what, finally, can pessimism offer?

The answer is only a deep and empathetic bond of fellowship between sufferers and an acknowledgement of the inescapability of one's own suffering. As Schopenhauer writes, "In fact, the conviction that the world and man is something that had better not have been, is of a kind to fill us with indulgence toward one another. Nay, from this point of view, we might well consider the proper form of address to be, not 'Monsieur, Sir, mein Herr,' but 'my fellow-sufferer,' *Soci malorum, compagnon de miseres*!"[25] This defense of pessimism from the point of view of fellowship is even more pronounced in the opening to James Thompson's pessimistic poem, "The City of Dreadful Night," which Melville read and praised during the composition of *Billy Budd*. It opens with the question of pessimism's purpose – "why evoke the scepters of black night / To blot the sunshine of exultant years?"[26] – and comes to the conclusion that it is only for a "sad Fraternity":

Yes, here and there some weary wanderer
In that same city of tremendous night,
Will understand the speech and feel a stir
Of fellowship in all-disastrous fight;
"I suffer mute and lonely, yet another
Uplifts his voice to let me know a brother
Travels the same wild paths though out of sight."[27]

For Thompson's poem, the only positive outcome for pessimism is a sympathetic bond that doesn't collaborate towards victory but rather shares in defeat.

Melville closes *Billy Budd* with "Billy in the Darbies," a poem in which Billy's execution is depicted as relieved, at several points, by Billy's anticipation of fellowship ("a messmate will reach me the last parting cup," "Donald he has promised to stand by the plank; / So I'll shake a friendly hand ere I sink") and his memory of friends ("I remember Taff the Welshman when he sank. / And his cheek it was like the budding pink" [BB 132]). The turn towards fellowship, both imagined and anticipated, is not a reprieve from pessimism; it doesn't, in the end, loosen the bindings, both human (the darbies) and natural (the weeds), in which Billy twists. But it also doesn't valorize the heroic critic, which may be seen as versions of Vere, intending to save and behave responsibly, but nevertheless always open to suspicion and always capable of exacerbating the very evils one seeks to cure. Instead, pessimism would suggest a mode of co-existence and acceptance of the world in spite of its unjustness. It would suggest rethinking our assumption of the ameliorative potential of ideological critique.

These may seem hollow comforts and are not likely to win advocates from any quarter. To scholars who argue strongly for a diversity of alternative forms of textual engagement, pessimism will mostly likely sound like a version of the quietism of which post-critique has been accused by its detractors. And to read Melville's novel as depicting paranoia as a modern lapsarian condition would reproduce the very assumptions of epochal difference that Latour identifies as underpinning critique in the first place. Yet perhaps pessimism may accord with Sedgwick's own suggestion for redrawing our critical methodology, closer to what she prefers as a Melanie Kleinian "depressive" position over the reigning "paranoid-schizoid" position. In this depressive position, as in pessimism, we are not animated above all to protect ourselves from threats real and imagined in the world outside of us. Rather, we acknowledge the shared precarity of our existence and we fear, above all, our capacity to harm others. In such a position, we would be capable of empathy and care of others, and could assemble out of our shared condition the conditions for fellowship. As Sedgwick notes, "Among Klein's names for the reparative process is love."[28] Can an academic methodology in the current budgetary and political environment survive with such a non-technical, sentimental rationale as fellowship and love? Especially when it is not claimed as instrumental for justice or freedom? Rather, according to pessimism, such fellowship and such love would blossom in the absence of hope, rooted in the soil of a universal struggle that we will all lose, and shared even with those who doom us: "God bless Captain Vere!"

CHAPTER 12

Melville, Mardi, *and Materialism*

Michael Jonik

> "What, ho! Babbalanja!" cried Media from under a tree, "don't be a duck, there, with your bill in the air; drop your metaphysics, man, and fall to on the solids. Do you hear?"
>
> –Melville, *Mardi*

The recent "material turn" in literary studies has opened new modalities for understanding Melville's corpus. Whether engaging new materialist, neovitalist, and posthumanist perspectives, analyses of Melville's materialism have prompted inquiries into how questions of human and nonhuman physicality, agency, and ontologies of life are animated by his work. Perhaps this is not surprising, and indeed overdue, given Melville's manifold and penetrating depictions of the material world. From the planetary to the particular, from the wide expanse of the "inhuman sea" to the press of Babo's razor against Benito Cereno's neck, from the flesh and the fury of *Moby-Dick* to the silent stones of his later poetry, Melville's work is a study in material relations. However, despite this renewed attention to the varieties of materialism in Melville's work, little of it has addressed the meaning and prominence of matter in Melville's third novel, *Mardi* (1849). This is partly attributable to *Mardi's* unpopularity: the novel has long been seen as a Neoplatonic reverie or metaphysical voyage across the uncharted world of the mind – in short, Melville at his most idealist. To be sure, Melville's characters frequently discourse on the soul and allude to passages from Plotinus and Proclus. They declare the immanence of the god Oro, and proclaim that the "universe is all of one mind" (M 428). Influential early critics such as Cesare Pavese thus took *Mardi* as evidence that Melville "drank most deeply" of the "current of Platonizing rationalism"; similarly, Merton Sealts saw in Babbalanja, Melville's tropical philosopher, a considerable debt to Plato and Neo-Platonism.[1] Other critics have read the novel as a latter-day Spenserian spiritual journey across the wandering isles of the Mardian chain, or as a political allegory for Melville's contemporary United States.[2]

Despite its frequent idealist and allegorical conceits, the world of *Mardi* is a world materially alive. Objects in *Mardi* burst with meaning, and its characters repeatedly explore the origins and qualities of particular substances in a series of rich, heteroglossic meditations. They debate how pipe bowls appear to be "petrifactions of roses," and whether they, like skulls, will "endure till broken" (M 375). They discuss how "farnoo" is an "unctuous, argillaceous substance"; whether amber might be the "congealed tears of broken-hearted mermaids" or "gold-fishes' brains, made waxy, then firm, by the action of the sea"; and, if ambergris indeed forms out of the "honey-comb of bees, fallen from flowery cliffs into the brine," or is a "morbid secretion of the Spermaceti whale" (M 375). *Mardi* is a book of stones, much like *Pierre* or *Clarel*: we find "sculptured stones" (M 525) and "Runic-looking stones" (M 336), "mossy" stones (M 338) and "sharp, tusk-like stones" (M 236), "the petrified gall-stones of crocodiles" (M 375) and "vitreous stones fallen from the skies in a meteoric shower" (M 236). Melville also explores diverse forms of archipelagic and oceanic materialities. In the chapter "The Sea on Fire," after dismissing the cause of "marine phosphorescence" to be an irradiation of the disheveled hair of mermaids, Melville's narrator seeks a materialist explanation: "Faraday might, perhaps, impute the phenomenon to a peculiarly electrical condition of the atmosphere; and to that solely. But herein, my scientific friend would be stoutly contradicted by many intelligent seamen, who, in part, impute it to the presence of large quantities of putrescent animal matter, with which the sea is well known to abound" (M 123). In contrast to Faraday, who posited the cause of such phenomena as the Aurora Borealis to be charged particles illuminating the earth's atmosphere, "intelligent seamen" attribute to the bioluminescent spectacle of the sea a biological, not electromagnetic, causality. However, when the seawater is poured across a ship's deck and agitated into a "stream of flame," the dead matter alone does not "kindle a fire in the brine." Rather, living and "putrescent matter" are rendered all but indistinguishable as "myriads of microscopic mollusca," and other organisms striving to be "a beacon to love," glow together with decaying ones (M 123). Throughout *Mardi*, debates about materiality such as these proliferate and multiply, transforming the novel into an extended inquiry into the sources and boundaries of matter itself, in all of its states and forms.

Melville's materialism, however, is not merely set in opposition to idealism. Given the co-presence of idealist and materialist philosophies, the question, perhaps, is not whether *Mardi* is *either* idealist or materialist; the question is how the two relate – an issue that remains far from settled. The Western philosophical tradition has tended to present the material-ideal relation through persistent dualisms of matter and mind, body and soul, or, analogously, instinct and reason. But in *Mardi,* Melville, instead of recapitulating these dualities or collapsing them into a reductive monism, stages dramatic dialogues that reveal their mutuality and co-generative strife, their contiguity as well as their disparity. For Melville, I will argue, the complex entanglement of the material and the ideal is particularly evident in experiences of sensation and vibration; in the causal order of material events; in manifestations of free will (i.e., the mental power to affect these events); and in the relation between instinct and moral sense. To establish these connections, Melville draws on debates about materialism and idealism that he found in eighteenth-century British philosophy, a largely underexplored philosophical context for his writing. Certainly, much has been said about the German contexts of Melville's metaphysics – his reading of Goethe or, later, Schopenhauer; his interactions with German Romanticism and German Idealism via Coleridge and Carlyle; or, his famous trans-Atlantic conversation with the nineteenth-century Germanist George Adler as he was *en route* to London to market *White-Jacket* in 1849. But even before Melville had met Adler or conducted his more extensive reading in German thought – or, indeed, finished writing *Mardi* – he had encountered a series of lively and unsettled philosophical debates about the matter-mind relation in the work of George Berkeley, David Hume, Joseph Priestley, David Hartley, and Samuel Taylor Coleridge.

Crucially, as he was revising *Mardi* in the winter of 1848, Melville borrowed Hartley's 1749 *Observations on Man: His Frame, His Duties, and His Expectations* from the New York Society Library and purchased Coleridge's *Biographia Literaria.*[3] Although Melville was reading other writers at the time – Rabelais, Browne, Montaigne, Seneca – Hartley and Coleridge were especially important to Melville's revisions, informing and shaping his understanding of the relationship between mind and matter. This is not to say that Melville adopts a settled philosophical position on materiality or ideality or its related terms, or that he present his positions in the manner of Berkeley or Hume, who use the form of the philosophical dialogue to dialectically legitimate their own positions. Rather, as Paul Hurh has argued regarding Melville's use of philosophy in *Mardi,* we find Melville's collocation of "contrary voices" and "dialectical musings" in a perpetually "uneven balance."[4] Given the novel's expansive and digressive style, such dialogues are often left unresolved, or they veer into other directions, "talk[ing] round a Subject without getting at it" (M 491). These philosophers nonetheless provided Melville with tempting ways to rethink the mind-matter duality, and collectively offer us a new and multi-textured context for understanding Melville's materialism within his notoriously elusive and elliptical early novel.[5] My aim, therefore, is two-fold: I want to reconsider Melville's materialism in light of the material-ideal relation in *Mardi*, and, at the same time, posit that Melville's exploration of sensation, vibration, causality, and instinct in the novel point to an interest in how ideality and materiality were developed in eighteenth-century British philosophy.

Throughout the novel, Melville juxtaposes ideal and material philosophies in ways that either satirize or recapitulate the standard, dualistic picture of matter and mind. In the chapter "Some Pleasant, Shady Talk In The Groves," even as Babbalanja flirts with "a composite" understanding of matter and mind, he adds "matter and mind, though matching not, are mates; and sundered oft" (M 597). After Media accuses him of being once again "incoherent," Babbalanja's replies by reasserting the dualist position: "My lord Media, there are things infinite in the finite; and dualities in unities. Our eyes are pleased with the redness of the rose, but another sense lives upon its fragrance" (M 597). Babbalanja often seems to propound a pure idealism, holding that "things visible are but conceits of the eye" (M 284). But such Berkeleyan pronouncements regularly prompt more materialist-inclined characters to try to bring him back to earth – or, as I cited in the epigraph, to make Babbalanja "drop [his] metaphysics and fall to on the solids" (M 387). As Media objects, at another point: "Babbalanja, your philosophy is but a dream that seems true while it lasts; but waking again into the orthodox world, straightway you resume the old habit" (M 370). For Media, the material realities of life and habit ground Babbalanja's idealist flights on fancy (perhaps like the proverbial Johnson who claimed to refute Berkeley by kicking a large stone). At other times, Melville indulges the risible implications of the material-ideal duality. In "Noises and Portents," the Skyeman Jarl, while pondering the "phantom-like qualities" of the ship after purportedly hearing a "supernatural sneeze," resembles Bishop Berkeley, who, "metaphysically speaking, [held] all objects to be mere optical delusions." Yet Melville's narrator is quick to add that the burly Norseman is nonetheless "extremely matter-of-fact in all matters touching matter itself. Besides being pervious to the points of pins, and possessing a palate capable of appreciating plum-puddings: – which sentence reads off like a pattering of hailstones" (M 63).

The metaphysical idealism of Berkeley, in which *esse est percipi*, and the "matter-of-fact" materialism of the sensory world of painful pins and pleasurable puddings are co-present in the character of the Skyeman. As if to emphasize the materialist tendencies of Jarl, the narrator, in a metafictional aside, comments how the repeatedly alliterated "p" sounds enact the material patter of letters.

Melville's juxtaposition of metaphysical idealism (even if conflated with optical delusions or superstition) and materialism (even if whimsically treated) is one way in which he explores the viewpoints as distinct. But he also troubles this distinction, rejecting both a brute materialism and a pure idealism, and thereby begins to chart an uncertain middle passage between the two. Not only is the question of whether the soul is primary to the body or the body primary to the soul never answered; Melville ultimately undoes the traditional, dualistic ontology of mind and matter. We can begin to see this undoing in the novel's treatment of sensations, which dialogue, in both explicit and implicit ways, with eighteenth-century modes about thinking about the subject. In the chapter "Wherein Babbalanja Discourses of Himself," Melville charts how Babbalanja's sensation of life unsettles any coherent sense of his self-identity:

> To you, perhaps, I seem Babbalanja; but to myself, I seem not myself. All I am sure of, is a sort of prickly sensation all over me, which they call life; and, occasionally, a headache or a queer conceit admonishes me, that there is something astir in my attic. But how know I, that these sensations are identical with myself? For aught I know, I may be somebody else. At any rate, I keep an eye on myself, as I would on a stranger. There is something going on in me, that is independent of me. Many a time, have I willed to do one thing, and another has been done. I will not say by myself, for I was not consulted about it, it was done instinctively. My most virtuous thoughts are not born of my musings, but spring up in me, like bright fancies to the poet; unsought, spontaneous. Whence they come I know not. I am a blind man pushed from behind; in vain, I turn about to see what propels me. (M 456)

If we read Babbalanja as adopting the method of Cartesian doubt, we find that he fails to arrive at any foundational, stable identity. All he can be certain of is an immanently "prickly sensation," an ensemble of staccato stimuli – the proprioceptive pins and needles of feeling alive. If we read him as following the path of Humean skepticism, we find that doubt likewise undoes any certainty that these sensations will associate into a self-identical "I." How can he know that he is who he appears to be to others? Like the revenant Rip Van Winkle who questions whether he both is and is not himself, Babbalanja simultaneously "seems" and "seems not" to be himself. This sensation also provokes in Babbalanja the uncanny recognition of a strange life within him, a force that compels him to act otherwise than he would. This sensation is likened to the material sensation of an instinctual prompting. He feels an unnamed, unsought agency working in and through him. What he does is "done instinctively" (M 456); or, as Bardianna puts it, "[w]hat we do, we do blindly . . . Many things we do, we do without knowing" (M 459). Instinct here is not merely a biological stimulus; it is a form of knowing without knowing, a nonconscious thinking that acts though us, if not *for* us. It is worth noting that "prickly," whether intentionally or not, plays off the etymological origins of instinct as an *instigation*, as if pricked with a stick and incited to act.[6] (Or as William James writes in his *Principles of Psychology*, "Every instinct is an impulse."[7]) Instinct becomes a material if impersonal force: an impulse that "propels" us. But at the same time that sensation refers to a material experience, however strange or disconcerting, it also points to the source of our ideational life. Not only are Babbalanja's physical actions involuntary; his very thoughts "spring up" unbidden and "spontaneously."[8] Thus, even "virtuous thoughts" (not merely ones related to instinctual appetites), and also imaginative thoughts ("like bright fancies to the poet"), become indistinguishable from the seat of instinctual action, since immaterial ideas and material instincts arise from a common, if mysterious, source.

Later in the same chapter, Melville reprises the drama of sensation and identity. Ironically borrowing from Hume's associationist account of the self as a "bundle of different perceptions,"[9] Babbalanja proclaims, "[w]e are bundles of comical sensations; we bejuggle ourselves into strange phantasies: we are air, wind, breath, bubbles; our being is told in a tick" (M 460). Like his description of the rose as a concatenation of different sensory data (the smell and color and other qualities are assembled by the mind into a unitary object), the "self" is likewise an association. The self we think we know is just a collection of fantasies or comic sensations. Therefore, in Babbalanja's discourse on himself, sensation moves between material and ideal ontological coordinates as it traverses the feeling of self-estrangement. What is more, the bundle of comical sensations of our being, like the uncanny, prickly sensations of our life, not only denote a dissociation of identity, they also mark processes of becoming other or becoming inhuman. As the feeling of life is a feeling of disindentification, our being, insofar as "we are air, breath and bubbles," is given to an inhuman, material otherness.

Melville sketches "Mardi" itself as an ecology of material sensations: endosensations and exosensations, animal-sensations and tree-sensations, rock-sensations and water-sensations, all given to a collective "throbbing" across its surfaces.

> There are more things alive than those that crawl, or fly, or swim. Think you . . . there is no sensation in being a tree? feeling the sap in one's bough's, the breeze in one's foliage? think you it is nothing to be in a world? . . . In the sight of a fowl, that sees not our souls, what are our own tokens of animation? That we move, make a noise, have organs, pulses and are compounded of fluids and solids. And all these are in this Mardi as a unit. Daily the slow, majestic throbbings of its heart are perceptible on the surface in the tides of the lagoon. . . . Mardi is alive to its axis. (M 458)

"Mardi" is brimming with life. Plants "feel" and have a proprioceptive vitality – of sap flowing through their branches as blood through an animal organism, or wind through their leaves like a breeze through a person's hair. For Geoffrey Sanborn, this passage evinces *Mardi* as another example of Melville's "exclamatory" celebration of the incessant material processes of nonhuman life.[10] Indeed, it could be read as an expression of *Mardi*'s vital materialism: the pulse of the human's animate heart is one with the "majestic throbbings" of all of nature. The passage revolves around an understanding of sensation that is both material and ideal. On the one hand, the sap, the wind, and the waters reveal the creative self-organization of matter into the forms of the perceiving and self-perceiving world. Yet at the same time, Mardi's ecology of sensations aspires to an ideal unity of "life": "all these are in Mardi as a unit." At both the level of the microcosm (the singular tokens of animation, the pulses and individuated sensations) and in the impersonal and inhuman ensemble of shared sensations, the world of the mind and the living world of Mardi are shown to overlap.

Melville further elaborates on this immanent life-sensation in the chapter "They Converse of the Mollusca, Kings, Toad-Stools and Other Matters." Here, Babbalanja offers an analogy between the political structure of Vivenza (a "mystic league" held "intact" despite the internal strife and divisions of its constituent tribes) and the "mysterious federation" of "the mollusca [sic] of the Tunicata order" (M 536).[11] In both Vivenza and the mollusk colonies, he asserts, "the model, whence they derive their union, is one of nature's planning" (M 536). That is, the constituent individuals confederate through the creative self-organizing processes of life itself. As Babbalanja explains: "They live in a compound structure; but though connected by membranous canals, freely communicating throughout the league – each member has a heart and stomach of its own; provides and digests its own dinners; and grins and bears its own gripes, without imparting the same to its neighbors. But if a prowling shark touches one member, it ruffles all" (M 537). The implications of the political allegory notwithstanding (Vivenza as Melville's United States), the "mystery of federation" of the mollusks could be explained on biological grounds as the result of teleonomy or instinct: all the members of a colony of mollusks emerge as distinct individuals, with distinct hearts and digestive systems, yet, despite their individualities, they respond in unison to dangerous stimuli. Key to their federation is an inhuman semiotics of sensation: when a shark touches one mollusk, it "ruffles all." As the characters discuss Babbalanja's "human" sensations, they likewise describe them as an impersonal and inhuman ensemble. Queried as to what sort of sensations conspire to form him, he reroutes the question: "what sort of a sensation, think you, life is to such creatures as those mollusca?"; "what sort of a sensation life is to a toad-stool?" He concludes by positing a non-anthropocentric, monistic ontology of life in which for "kings, mollusca, and toad-stools, life is one thing and the same" (M 537). Although animated in a plurality of forms, life is for Babbalanja a univocal sensation that permeates all things and creatures. If Babbalanja here gestures toward an ideal or transcendental oneness, the material sensation of life – its feeling – is set within and not in opposition to this ideality or ontological sameness. It is all sensation, whether the sense of danger or the feeling of being alive, and it traverses all of nature, bringing about innumerable "mysterious federation[s]." In the islands of Mardi, the ideal unity of life is thus effected through its material economies of sensation.

But, as with most topics in Melville's Polynesian symposium, philosophical matters regarding life are perpetually open to further debate. As "Mollusca, Kings, Toad-Stools and Other Matters" continues, Babbalanja invokes the definitions of life given by the philosophical authorities, "Dumdi" and "Bardianna":

> The Philosopher Dumdi pronounces it a certain febrile vibration of organic parts, operating upon the vis inertia of unorganized matter. But Bardianna says nay. Hear him. "Who put together this marvelous mechanism of mine; and wound it up, to go for three score years and ten; when it runs out, and strikes Time's hours no more? And what is it, that daily and hourly renews, and by a miracle, creates in me my flesh and my blood? What keeps up the perpetual telegraphic communication between my outpost toes and digits, and that domed grandee up aloft, my brain? – It is not I; nor you; nor he; nor it. No; when I place my hand to that king muscle my heart, I am appalled. I feel the great God himself at work in me. Oro is life." (M 538)

For Dumdi, life is a fevered "vibration," a *vis viva* that works "upon" the self-resistance (*vis inertiae*) of chaotic matter, and lends form or organization to it.[12] Yet Dumdi's position is quickly disclaimed by Babbalanja, who cites the pantheistic vitalism of the ancient authority Bardianna, who held that matter is mechanistic, passive, and imbued with an external agency. For Babbalanja, echoing Bardianna, it is the force of God himself working through all things: "It is not I; nor you; nor he; nor it . . . I feel the great God himself at work in me. Oro is life." Media, as is often the case in the novel, offers a materialist rejoinder, demanding: "And what is death?" Babbalanja flatly responds: "Death, my lord! – it is the deadest of all things" (M 538).

This passage, Paul Gilmore argues, enlists the figure of a "telegraphic/electric body" that enables Melville to "restage the Vitalist debate."[13] To be sure, the passage could be a pastiche of Erasmus Darwin's *Zoonomia,* or of another late eighteenth- or early nineteenth-century expression of vitalism. But the phrase "febrile vibration" points more specifically to David Hartley's 1749 *Observations on Man,* a work that Melville was reading while rewriting *Mardi.* In *Observations,* Hartley develops a physiological psychology to explain the interconnection of matter and mind, and in doing so inaugurates a materialist approach to the brain that is still being carried out by contemporary neuroscientists. Hartley begins *Observations* by insisting, along Cartesian lines, "Man consists of two parts, Body and Mind,"[14] and throughout the book he retains a mechanistic understanding human and animal bodies. Hartley uses the Lockean term "impression," as well as other elements of Locke's theory of the mind. He endeavors to stay true to the Newtonian laws of physics, including Newton's controversial postulation regarding the existence of an aether (i.e., an elastic substance or medium that permeates all things and through which bodies communicate impulses to one another).[15] However, he adapts Descartes, Locke, and Newton to provide a new way of understanding how the materiality of the physical world is translated into ideas in the human brain. This is his "theory of vibrations": first, "when external Objects are impressed on the sensory Nerves, they excite Vibrations in the Aether residing in the Pores of these Nerves, by means of the mutual Actions interceding between the Objects, Nerves, and Aether."[16] These vibrations are impressed in the "white medullary substance of the brain," giving rise to ideas and leaving, in their wake, an after-impression of themselves, called tiny "vibranticules," which associate with other impressions to form complex ideas, memories and habits.[17] For Hartley, our brains are what we would now term "plastic." As Jess Keiser explains, "[o]nce enough vibrations have joined themselves together in the mind, one cannot help but follow certain trains of thought or see complex ideas where simpler ones once stood distinct. . . . [F]or Hartley we simply wouldn't have complex ideational lives if vibrations didn't actively link together and determine thought."[18] By joining the materiality of sensations with the associations of ideas, Hartley provides a corporeal explanation for neuropsychology: the matter of the world comes to act on the matter of the brain, and the resulting associations "generate" ideas.[19] Although Hartley's theory relies on a mechanistic understanding of matter and brain, he denies that he is asserting that matter itself is "endued" with sensation, and is at pains not to reject the "immateriality" of the soul.[20] But by positing a "certain Connexion . . . between the Sensations of the Soul, and the Motions excited in the medullary Substance of the Brain,"[21] as Charles Wolfe argues, he nonetheless "propos[es] a causal, associative, naturalized account of mental process,"[22] and thus articulates a strong account of the connection between mind and matter.

Melville responds to Hartley's theory in several ways in *Mardi*. In the passage about "febrile vibrations," Melville describes the body along Hartleian lines as a "marvelous mechanism" which functions through the "perpetual telegraphic communication" of nerves from the toes to the brain; likewise we must keep up "the nervous communication between our eyes, and our cerebellums" (M 537). Later Babbalanja characterizes minds in similar terms, describing them as "cunning, compound mechanisms; and one spring, or wheel, or axle wanting, the movement lags, or halts" (M 593). As if to make light of the corporeal residue left in the brain by our sensations, or perhaps of the brain's stubborn resistance to its own plasticity, the characters joke that crania, like pipes, become stuffed with "concretions." Profound thinkers, however, experience an "unpleasant vibration" in withholding their innermost thoughts, one which is "ever consequent upon striking a new vein of ideas in the soul" (M 581). In the early chapter, "A Calm," to anatomize the psychological effects of a seemingly eternal and inescapable oceanic doldrum which arrests the voyagers, Melville's narrator again draws on Hartleian language: "by certain nameless associations revived in me my old impressions upon first witnessing as a landsman this phenomenon of the sea." Taji notes that the calm "not only revolutionizes [the sailor's] abdomen, but unsettles his mind" and himself encounters indistinct feeling of "existence where existence itself seems suspended" (M 9). The calm, barely tolerable, sets in motion a series of strange interior sensations:

> The stillness of the calm is awful. His voice begins to grow strange and portentous . . . It keeps up a sort of involuntary interior humming in him, like a live beetle. His cranium is full of reverberations . . . But more than all else is the consciousness of his utter helplessness . . . Even his undoubted vested rights, comprised in his glorious liberty of volition, become as naught. (M 10)

The "cranium full of reverberations" again alludes to Hartley's theory of mind. But in this passage Melville also begins to test out the implications of Hartley's account of vibrations for human volition. Hartley, for his part, links the two. As he writes at the conclusion of his first volume of *Observations*, "According to the Theory here laid down, all human Actions proceed from Vibrations in the Nerves of the Muscles, and these from others, which are either evidently of a mechanical Nature, as in the automatic Motions; or else have been shown to be so in the Account given of the voluntary Motions."[23] At the same time, Hartley takes his theory to be a defense of the doctrine of necessity insofar as the causes of these exogenous vibrations and sensations can be traced back to God and thus support the idea of Providence. In "A Calm," as Melville limns the "involuntary interior humming" that sailors feel in their heads amidst the stillness, he draws together Hartleian notions of sensations, vibration, and volition. Like Babbalanja's prickly sensations, this involuntary humming bespeaks another uncanny otherness within the sailors: a "live beetle" living in their crania. Yet, interestingly, to explicate the implications of the calm in terms of free will and necessity, Melville does not name Hartley, but Joseph Priestley, who decades after Hartley's work became a strident defender of Hartley's materialist picture of the mind. (Hartley's *Observations*, indeed, was later re-edited by Priestley, and added as an appendix to his *Doctrine of Philosophical Necessity*.) As Melville writes, if a sailor is "a reader of books, Priestley on Necessity occurs to him; and he believes in that Sir Anthony Absolute to the very last chapter" (M 9).[24] In *The Doctrine of Philosophical Necessity Illustrated* (1777), Priestley, after Hartley, rejects the "two-substance view"[25] of body and soul and seeks to reconcile materialism and metaphysical determinism. As Priestley writes, "every thing belonging to the doctrine of materialism is, in fact, an argument for the doctrine of necessity, and, consequently, the doctrine of necessity is a direct inference from materialism."[26] Later invoked by the lawyer in "Bartleby" to explain to himself the scrivener's famous passivity, Priestley's text here indicates the impotence of the will in the face of overpowering material conditions. Taji's utter helplessness during the dead calm is figured as a nullification of his "liberty of volition": he can merely accede to the necessary order of material events.

Melville further explores the implications of Hartley's and Priestley's materialist philosophies throughout the novel. When another calm falls in the chapter "Babbalanja Discourses in the Dark" (the dark, as it were, of instinctual action), the characters debate the causality of an accident that occurs on the boat. Vee-Vee, "impatient of the calm," lifts his conch and "sound[s] a blast which ran in and out among the hollows, reverberating with the echoes." The sound startles the paddler and he falls, nearly breaking his arm. This prompts Babbalanja to debate with Media whether the accident was a necessary or willed event: "My lord Media, was there any human necessity for that accident?" Media, ascribing it to Vee-Vee's carelessness, inadvertently develops, in Babbalanja's estimation, a "doctrine of Philosophical Necessity" in which "every thing takes place through absolute necessity" (M 424). For Media, Vee Vee's carelessness was hereditary, a result of the carelessness that found its germ in the generations of his forebears. But Babbalanja distinguishes his account from any fatalist or occasionalist account of causality, insofar as fatalism "presumes express and irrevocable edicts of heaven concerning particular events" and necessity "holds that all events are naturally linked, and inevitably follow each other, without providential interposition, though by the eternal letting of Providence" (M 425).

In these passages, we find Melville, after Hartley and Priestley, essaying the adverse consequences of the doctrine of necessity by dramatizing how the material circumstances and the order of events – the stultifying calm and the unfortunate accident – circumscribe the power of thinking. (Or as Emerson would have it, the power of intellect to "annul" fate.) As Hartley writes (and Melville's becalmed sailors would agree), "if by Free-will be meant a Power of beginning Motion," then "Man has no such Power."[27] However, if free will means the "voluntary or semivoluntary Powers of calling up Ideas," then, for Hartley, the liberty of volition does not contradict the theory of vibrations, but indeed "even flows from it."[28] After all, consciousness is part of mechanical causality, and human volition can therefore be said to be made possible by necessity, not in spite of it. There is not space to develop it here, but Hartley devotes much of his *Observations on Man* (especially volume two) to the broader implications of the reliance of human life on the mechanisms of sensation, attributing even phenomena such as culture, theology, art, and child-raising to the associative forms of matter. Melville too is attuned to these significances. Mohi recollects that as a boy, he once heard "a sage" claim that "Necessity and

Free Will" are "reconcilable" (M 429). In "Some Shady, Pleasant Talk," Babbalanja shows how Lombardo acts in a way beyond his volition until his consciousness and ambition are awakened within him: "ere Necessity plunged spur and rowel into him, he knew not his own paces. That churned him into consciousness; and brought ambition, ere then dormant, seething to the top, till he trembled at himself" (M 593).[29] The causality of moral sense is more ambiguous: in some people, says Babbalanja, "moral sense bridles their instinctive passions," while in others, "the instinctive passions" have "supremacy over the moral sense." It is easier, Babbalanja argues, "for some men to be saints, than for others not to be sinners" (M 457).

Although *Mardi* brings Hartley and Priestley's materialist causalities to life, it does not mean that Melville entirely accepts their mechanist worldview. As Melville adopts their materialist language or integrates materialist concepts into the fabric of *Mardi's* philosophical debates, he often couples them with idealist philosophical positions, exploring their contiguities and disparities. Babbalanja asserts an idealist take on events, even within dialogues that take their cues from materialist causalities. As we have seen, his thoughts arise from an unknown source, and the vital force of Oro maintains the "perpetual telegraphic communication" between his body and brain. Thus, rather than enforcing a reason/instinct duality, Melville composites "instinct with mind" and rethinks human reason as a "noble instinct" (M 426). The "right use of our reason," it would seem, involves using it as an instinctual tool. After describing how the minds of profound thinkers such as Bardianna are given to Hartleian "unpleasant vibrations," Babbalanja adds a pastiche of Neoplatonic, Spinozist, and Coleridgean notions of oneness to name the secret dynamisms of their innermost thoughts: "the profoundest ponderer seldom tells us all he thinks; seldom reveals to us the ultimate, and the innermost; seldom makes us open our eyes under water; seldom throws open the totus-in-toto; and never carries us with him, to the unconsubsistent, the idea immanens, the super-essential, and the One" (M 581). Babbalanja traces the impersonal source of Lombardo's genius in idealist terms: the "essence of all ideas is infused. Of ourselves, and in ourselves, we originate nothing" (M 595). In pulling forth a few crumbling sheets of the ancient manuscript of Bardianna's "Thoughts, by a Thinker," Babbalanja recognizes how the causal order of both bodies and souls are intertwined: "Here, perhaps, thou didst dive into the deeps of things, treating of the normal forms of matter and of mind; how the particles of solids were first molded in the interstices of fluids; how the thoughts of men are each a soul, as the lung-cells are each a lung; how that death is but a mode of life." Both the matter and soul of Bardianna's living voice seem given over to the Ozymandian forces of material dispersion: "If the fogs of some few years can make soul linked to matter naught; how can the unhoused spirit hope to live when mildewed with the damps of death" (M 385). Against the loss of matter and soul, Melville often speaks of a material-ideal transmission or resurrection of ideas in *Mardi*, in which future generations of people give old ideas new embodiments and trajectories.

Furthermore, Melville's characters remain open to idealist causalities as well as mystical explanations of human thought and action. Indeed, Melville found an idealist picture of causality in Coleridge's *Biographia Literaria*, which he was reading while revising *Mardi*, and which offers a riposte to Hartley's robust materialism. Following Priestley, the young Coleridge was intensely interested in Hartley, and even named his first-born son after the philosopher. Later on, Coleridge turned toward German Idealism and altered his thinking, switching from Hartleian materialist associationism to a more organic idealism.[30] In *Biographia Literaria*, Coleridge tries to dismiss the materialist causality of Hartley's neuropsychology and its "phantasmal chaos of association."[31] As Coleridge writes, "It is a mere delusion of the fancy to conceive the pre-existence of the ideas, in any chain of association, as so many differently coloured billiard-balls in contact."[32] This leads Coleridge to critique the materialist position as "utterly unintelligible":

> But how any affection from without can metamorphose itself into perception or will, the materialist has hitherto left, not only as incomprehensible as he found it, but has aggravated it into a comprehensible absurdity. For, grant that an object from without could act upon the conscious self, as on a consubstantial object; yet such an affection could only engender something homogeneous with itself. Motion could only propagate motion. Matter *has no Inward*. We remove one surface, but to meet with another.[33]

Coleridge takes issue with Hartley's theory of the will because it makes reason and the understanding the "creatures" rather than "the determining causes of association."[34] Coleridge's idealist account of the will reverses the direction of Hartley's mechanical-materialist causality: the mind, in its organic union, is ontologically and causally primary to material effects.

Seeking a transcendental, spiritual unity leads Coleridge to break away from Hartley's associationst psychology to move toward the German idealism of Schelling, as well as older, Neoplatonic philosophies of oneness.

In *Mardi's* disquisitions, Babbalanja often follows Coleridge to probe such depths. This is particularly evident in the late chapter "A Book From the 'Ponderings of Old Bardianna,'" in which Melville draws on Coleridgean language to describe reason, the soul, and the limits of human understanding:

> Let us hear our own thoughts. The soul needs no mentor, but Oro; and Oro, without proxy . . . Undeniably, reason was the first revelation; and so far as it tests all others, it has precedence over them. It comes direct to us, without suppression or interpolation; and with Oro's indisputable imprimatur . . . But if this our first revelation stops short of the uttermost, so with all others . . . Fellow-men; the ocean we would sound is unfathomable; and however much we add to our line, when it is out, we feel not the bottom. (M 576–577)

For Babbalanja, citing Bardianna, the voyage of knowing is endless and the depths are abyssal: "[y]et so far as, in our theories, we dwarf our Mardi; we go not beyond an archangel's apprehension of it . . . But as the atom to the animalculae, so Mardi to us. And lived aright, these mortal lives are long; looked into, these souls, fathomless as the nethermost depths." Like Coleridge, he seeks an ideal, organic, if not divine unity, and appeals to a revelatory notion of reason that transcends the finite human mind. The ocean is unfathomable and we feel not the bottom. But the last word goes again to Media, who, in another materialist rejoinder, calls on him to "cease," telling him "I do not observe, oh, Sage! that for all these things, you yourself are practically the better or wiser." Babbalanja can merely babble in response: "Gogle-goggle, fugle-fi, fugle-gogle-orum!" (M 578). Similarly, in "Mohi Tells Of One Ravoo, And They Land To Visit Revaneva, A Flourishing Artisan," Babbalanja defends the "world of wonders insphered within the spontaneous consciousness," and describes himself as "intent upon the essence of things"; but Media interrupts his "subtle cogitations" to cynically implore him to "when aught is found, cry out, that we may run to see" (M 352). Such exchanges highlight how Melville uses his characters in *Mardi* as conceptual personae to act out an unresolved drama of idealism and materialism. They seek to articulate the profundities and pretenses of the idealist and materialist worldviews, opting exclusively for neither of them, but nevertheless underscoring the fundamental nature of both.

In *Mardi's agon* of matter of mind, there is perhaps the possibility of the "composite" that Babbalanja hints at. But at the same time, matter and mind, even as non-matching mates, are "sundered oft." Just as the Lawyer in "Bartleby" finds few answers to the enigma of passivity in either Priestley's materialist understanding of the will or Edwards's idealist defense of necessity, Babbalanja and company never find a final answer to the enigma of matter and mind. They do not endorse in any systematic way Hartley's physical reductionism, Priestley's materialism, or Coleridge's idealism, or any of the other philosophies they incorporate. Characters ventriloquize their philosophical musings through multiple voices (Babbalanja serves as "mouthpiece" for Bardianna, and Azzageddi "stirs" within him). Philosophers are given ambiguous Polynesian pseudonyms (Hartley might be "Dumdi," Coleridge "Bardianna," or Proclus "Doxodox"), and still others form a dissonant chorus: "Zeno murmurs maxims beneath the hoarse shout of Democritus; and though Democritus laugh loud and long, and the sneer of Pyrrho be seen; yet, divine Plato, and Proclus, and, Verulam are of my counsel" (M 367). Babbalanja, as if reprising Emersonian aversive thinking, celebrates the virtues of his philosophical inconsistency: "the sum of my inconsistencies makes up my consistency" (M 459). But far from a philosophical farrago and by no means a boring book, *Mardi* engages eighteenth-century debates around matter and mind in ways that are important not only for interpreting the novel; *Mardi* also provides a sobering corrective to how the "material turn" has been effected in Melville's work, cautioning critics interested in Melville the materialist to not elide or dismiss his idealism. Elizabeth Grosz, in her recent *The Incorporeal: Ontology, Ethics, and the Limits of Materialism*, charts ideality as neither identical to materiality (as in a reductive monism) nor as opposed to materiality (as in a substance dualism), but one which "informs" materiality. Grosz endeavors to think the material-ideal relation rather "in terms of their thorough interplay and accompaniment, their transversal or perpendicular relations."[35] *Mardi's* dispersed ruminations already offer a powerful series of instances of such "interplay and accompaniment." *Mardi* thus shows Melville "sailing on" from his earlier romances *Typee* or *Omoo* to his experimental philosophical fictions of the 1850s. Melville, of course, will continue to explore the material-ideal relationship, from Ahab's soliloquies on materiality and immateriality, to the narrator's uncertainty in "The Apple-Tree Table" whether to trust Democritus or Cotton Mather, to the "running battle of the star and clod" in *Clarel.* But it is in *Mardi* that Melville first truly ventures out into the trackless seas of both the world of the mind and the world of matter. It is a "rich" book whose depths, as Hawthorne characterized it, would "compel a man to swim for his life."[36] It is a book of "fiery yearnings" that would, across Melville's later writing, "their own phantom-future make" (M 557).

CHAPTER 13

Popular Networks in Melville's Battle-Pieces

Eliza Richards

It is no longer possible to accept Hershel Parker's declaration that when writing *Battle-Pieces and Aspects of the War* (1866), "as far as we know, Melville seems not to have been influenced by any of the war poems which peppered collections like the *Rebellion Record* and appeared in newspapers and magazines (such as *Harper's Weekly*, to which he subscribed)." For Parker, Melville simply ignored his contemporaries, favoring the "older British poets such as Milton, Scott, and Wordsworth."[1] Flatly countering this assessment, Faith Barrett claims that "Melville is responding both to popular poetry and popular song throughout this collection," and she goes on to demonstrate several strong engagements.[2] For Barrett, Melville's response to popular poetry is ambivalent. She finds that he "mixes high literary and more popularly oriented voice-effects in the collection, not only to broaden his audience but also because he is torn between a desire to critique nationalist poetry and a desire for the consolations that a nationalist poetry might offer."[3] Addressing the issue on the level of form, Timothy Sweet argues that "Melville often engages critically with such forms, disrupting the ways in which vernacular poetics have been vehicles for discourses that legitimate violence, such as glory, patriotism, or religion." He goes on to say that the "volume's baseline form is that of the hymn, ballad, or epitaph in the process of becoming something else."[4] For Sweet, Melville experiments with vernacular form in order to encourage his readers to think more profoundly about national ideology: "Developing a poetics of supplement to the vernacular tradition, Melville hoped that enough would remain of familiar forms to transact the people's self-recognition, while enabling deeper, critical reflection and national reconstitution on an enlightened foundation."[5]

Melville's contemporary reviewers also contextualized his poetic response to the war in relation to his peers, though they often identified an affinity where more recent critics would perceive difference. Noting that war is a daunting subject, one reviewer regretted that "Mr. Melville must take his place with the herd of recent versifiers" who fail to meaningfully address the conflict.[6] This reviewer also found *Battle-Pieces* oddly redundant:

> It is a misfortune that the special events which had moved Mr. Melville to write are the same, in several instances, which have already been put into verse by other writers, and those earlier poems, already more or less familiar to the public, are necessarily brought into comparison with his. Thus his brief verse entitled "Shiloh: A Requiem" almost inevitably suggests, by contrast, the very striking poem of Mr. Forceythe Wilson's (sic), of which a great part of the scene is laid on the battle-field of Shiloh, called "The Old Sergeant."[7]

The reviewer is so intrigued by Forceythe Willson's poem – in which a dying soldier has a vision of the entrance to Heaven ("Headquarters"), tries to orient himself by recalling the details of the battle where "the grape-shot took me, just as we began to win," briefly returns to his senses, and then dies just after his son arrives – that he devotes the rest of his discussion to it, concluding that "we doubt that the war has inspired a narrative poem more imaginatively conceived."[8] Comparing Melville to Willson, Henry Howard Brownell, Ralph Waldo Emerson, and Walt Whitman, among others, reviewers did not doubt that Melville was familiar with the poets of his period who were writing about the war. I don't believe these perspectives should be dismissed out of hand as evidence that his reviewers could not recognize the brilliant difference in Melville's war poems that more recent critics have perceived. Emerson, Whitman, Willson, and Brownell were all celebrated (or condemned) for their originality, and Emerson and Whitman still bear that stamp today. When comparing Melville with others, reviewers could also find Melville gifted or unusual; they simply did not find him to be singular in his endeavors, and they often did not distinguish his work from more popular poets.

When considering Melville in relation to his peers, Barrett, Sweet, and others generalize the "popular," creating an undifferentiated, abstract category of conventional poetry. It was "the popular poetic ground against which his formal innovations took place," in Sweet's words.[9] Virginia Jackson claims that "unlike the popular poetry that circulated outside books, Melville's verse incorporated genres rendered practically unrecognizable by their alienations from their expected contexts."[10] For Peter Coviello, "where Melville's poetic form is concerned, the incongruity, it seems, is all."[11] Critics also see a relation of critique or surplus: Melville's poetry surpasses or builds on the popular but is not part of it. Although "the popular" has come to signify the merely generic or conventional, critics of Melville's time often differentiated among popular poets, identifying similarities and differences among individual writers. I take a cue from Melville's contemporary reviewers, so often charged with a lack of comprehension, in order to think of the popular as variegated, multiplicitous, and difficult to consolidate meaningfully into a homogenous whole. I argue that Melville engages with a popular poetry he thinks of as heterogeneous and elusive, a poetry that escapes his or anyone's ability to comprehend fully because of its ability to carry and appeal to a vast range of public feelings and attitudes. He is, moreover, interested in developing a theory of popular poetry's relation to national sentiment, or public knowledge. Melville's relation to the popular, in other words, is something to be posed as a question to explore, as is the nature and constitution of "the popular." Melville's interest in the popular may be one of the reasons his war poems are indeed belated in relation to his peers, "originat[ing] in an impulse imparted by the fall of Richmond" (PP 3). He seemed to have been "moved to write" about topics which had already appeared in earlier poems because he wanted to think about what earlier poems – not popular poetry as a mass noun – could do for readers and for writers, including himself.

The contemporary reviewer who characterizes Melville's poems as belated raises a significant question. Why indeed would Melville be moved to write about the same "special events" that have "already been put into verse by other writers," so that "those earlier poems, already more or less familiar to the public, are necessarily brought into comparison with his"? Could this be part of Melville's design, to establish a comparative relation between his own poems and other well-known poems of the war period? There are, after all, an uncountable number of "aspects" of the war about which someone could write, and Melville underscores this variety at the outset of his volume when he says he "placed a harp in the window, and noted the contrasted airs which wayward winds have played upon the strings" (PP 3). Even given the indisputable political importance or emotional weight of some of the events he treats – John Brown's hanging, the New York Riots, the Battle of Antietam, Lincoln's assassination – why would the wayward winds bring so many of the same events to his mind that other poets have treated memorably, especially when Melville stresses that "but a few themes have been taken" (PP 3)? The figure of the harp in the window is remote from Melville's individual mind: rather than playing a part in the compositional process, he "noted" the activity, leaving open the possibility that the "contrasted airs" may have come from other writers, were carried by the winds in the way a telegraph carries messages through a wire, and played upon the strings once they arrived. Melville hints that his topical selections were more than arbitrary, that some of the themes that "chanced to imprint themselves upon the mind" may have arrived via the poems of his peers and other earlier mediations of events. In the preface, he doesn't claim the memories, moods, and meditations as his own, which are all convoluted in the following phrase: "The aspects which the strife as a memory assumes are as manifold as are the moods of involuntary meditation." Melville strangely depersonalizes these subjective states, leaving open the possibility that they could belong to anyone who lived through the war. Even more explicitly, he says that he offers feelings "not inspired from any one source exclusively" (PP 3). Given that he mentions various sources and textual associations in his notes to the volume, Melville could well be encouraging readers to identify the source materials that ghost the poems, even those materials he does not explicitly mention. What the preface foregrounds, more than anything else, is Melville's collage-like compositional practice.

I suggest that in *Battle-Pieces*, Melville places his poems in oblique, retrospective relation to the poems of his peers, not against them, nor alongside them. He may aggregate their poetry into a heterogeneous collection, but he does not, or does not only, abstract them into a homogenous idea of "popular" or "nationalist" poetry, nor does he merely critique these abstractions. Rather, he works at establishing poetic networks that extend the fabric of utterance beyond his own character or personality. "Obscure as the wood, the tangled rhyme / But hints at the maze of war," Melville says in "The Armies of the Wilderness" (PP 76). He does not claim that the "tangled rhyme" is limited to his own productions. The tangle is made up of many perspectives, Northern and Southern, grieving and victorious, civilian and soldier, officers and enlisted men, dead and alive (in part via what Barrett calls "voice-effects").[12] Melville finds the maze of war so complex that it is unnavigable by the most extensive tangle of rhymes, and it does not seem to be his aim to simplify or distill it: no single source – and, more to the point, no single poem or collection of poems – can gain a truthful vantage point on the conflict. Opening spaces for the work of others to interact with his own, Melville extends his battle-pieces beyond himself: he summons the work of his peers and opens historical routes toward them, fashioning a maze so intricate that it begins at least to suggest how partial is any knowledge of the war, and how it relies on parts, or "pieces" of multiply mediated information. Melville tried to collect these pieces, in part by sifting through the poetry of his peers and engaging with it in an individuated, but not in a personalized way.

Melville's "The Portent" proves a useful test case for these ideas, in part because critics have often juxtaposed it to popular poems to bring out its difference. As Jackson puts it, it is a "weird poem"[13]:

Hanging from the beam,
Slowly swaying (such the law),
Gaunt the shadow on your green,
Shenandoah!
The cut is on the crown
(Lo, John Brown),
And the stabs shall heal no more.

Hidden in the cap
Is the anguish none can draw;
So your future veils its face,
Shenandoah!
But the streaming beard is shown
(Weird John Brown),
The meteor of the war. (PP 5)

Critics have tended to see Melville's deviations from popular verse practices as reflections of his position on the war. For Sweet, "the question of political authority emerges in the volume's opening poem, 'The Portent,' formally in its address to the reader's expectation of ballad stanza," which is then frustrated immediately by the inversion of the first two lines. Generating this frustration with form, according to Sweet, is part of Melville's plan to encourage his readers to think more deeply about "enlightened" terms for reconstruction.[14] Even more radically, for Peter Coviello, Melville expresses his ambivalences toward the "nation-form" through a complete departure from readers' expectations, which have been conditioned by popular form: "Melville is not, then, merely varying widely from the expected patterns of stress. Nor is he merely extending and contracting the number of feet in each line, in ways that echo while departing from ballad meter." Refusing "to allow any pattern of metrical expectation to solidify behind and beneath the lines," Melville writes "a sort of metapoetic music – that is audible in the tense relation between the expectation of pattern and the offered language's simultaneous invitation and refusal of it."[15] Reading the poem within the history of nineteenth-century lyricization, Jackson also distinguishes between Melville's poetry and popular verse: "Unlike the popular poetry that circulated outside books, Melville's verse incorporated genres rendered practically unrecognizable by their alienation from their expected contexts." For Jackson, "The Portent" brings home the fact that Melville's is a poetry of despair: "In 1866, Melville invoked a lyricism that, even when belatedly recognized, could not save the dead."[16] In spite of their differences, these critics have based their arguments on the idea that Melville's work is defined by its incongruity with his peers.

But some of the poems that are most closely related to *Battle-Pieces* – via inspiration, borrowing, formal echoes, and intertextual allusion – also have incongruous elements, elements that Melville seems to have absorbed and adapted. One of those poems is Edmund Clarence Stedman's "How Old Brown took Harper's Ferry. A Ballad of the Times (containing ye true history of ye great Virginia fight.)," which first appeared in the *New York Daily Tribune* on November 12, 1859, after Brown's court trial, but before his hanging.[17] Stedman's massively popular and influential poem heads a full page of news about Brown. In eighteen stanzas, the poem tells the mytho-history of Brown's anti-slavery activism from the time he fought in Osawatomie, Kansas, through his raid on Harper's Ferry, through his court conviction.

Though the poem is dramatically different from Melville's, the difference makes the similarities all the more striking. The emotional registers of the two poems emphatically diverge – Stedman's is enraged while Melville's is taciturn and withdrawn. But Stedman, like Melville, shows a self-consciousness of form, archaicizing the ballad and drawing attention to its news-carrying, broadside traditions: though inaccurate, Stedman's poem purports to convey true information about the events. More significant, the form of the ballad is unusual, and the refrain resembles Melville's not only in the repetition of Brown's name but also in the strange way it is embedded within the stanzas rather than coming at the end. Here are the last two stanzas, depicting the end of the trial and a warning to Southerners of their future doom:

How the conquerors wore their laurels; how they hastened on the trial;
How Old Brown was placed, half-dying, on the Charlestown Court-House floor;

How he spoke his grand oration, in the scorn of all denial;
What the brave old madman told them, – these are known the country o'er.

"Hang Old Brown,
Osawatomie Brown,"
Said the judge, "and all such rebels!" with his most judicial frown.

But, Virginians, don't do it! for I tell you that the flagon,
Filled with blood of Old Brown's offspring, was first poured by Southern hands;
And each drop from Old Brown's life-veins, like the red gore of the dragon,

May spring up a vengeful Fury, hissing through your slave-worn lands!
And Old Brown,
Osawatomie Brown,
May trouble you more than ever, when you've nailed his coffin down![18]

The poem is a reminder of how often popular nineteenth-century ballads don't fit the 4–3–4–3 iambic pattern we attribute to them: many readers were quite familiar with metrical variation and were highly sophisticated in their understandings of formal experimentation, which was not as unusual as we might imagine. Though certainly not as "weird" as Melville's, Stedman's verse form is unusual in ways that parallel "The Portent." The first four lines recall Poe's "The Raven," alternating between trochaic octameter and trochaic octameter catalectic (the first four lines of Melville's stanzas are also trochaic). The meter is loose, with extra syllables that make it hard to parse, but that suggest singability, for the 8-beat line stays steady, and the reader has to alter the length of the syllables accordingly to fit the beat (a quality of ballad form). The final line, breaking the expectation of a quatrain, is also octameter catalectic, suggesting that it is part of the stanza (now revealed to be a cinquain), and that the refrain intervenes in the stanza's coherence. Stedman's two-line refrain, like Melville's, is embedded within the stanza. The first line of the refrain is highly resonant with Melville's. "Hang old Brown," or "And Old Brown" (also, even more similarly, in stanza ten, "Mad John Brown") are three stressed syllables ending in Brown's last name, like Melville's "(Lo, John Brown)" and "(Weird John Brown)." The combination of Brown's name in the second line of the refrain with a place name – "Osawatamie" – suggests Melville's first refrain, "Shenandoah!" Both names summon a well-known place of wartime violence, both are multisyllabic and highly localized in their reference. And there is another, even more direct suggestion that Melville relied on Stedman's poem. In the fifteenth stanza, we learn that Brown "received three bayonet stabs, and a cut on his brave old crown." Melville's "The cut is on the crown" condenses the phrase, keeps key words, and intensifies the symbolic valence.

Another difference that draws the two poems into relation is the form that prophecy takes. Stedman's last stanza introduces an impersonal "I" for the first time – the story had been told in a third-person omniscient balladic style before that – a style that Helen Vendler associates indirectly with Melville's *Battle-Pieces.*[19] Over a year before the war begins, Stedman's speaker prophesies a war of retribution where the South will suffer; he summons the story of Cadmus, who slayed a dragon. Athena instructed Cadmus to bury the dragon's teeth, and fierce warriors sprang from them.

The speaker suggests that by sowing the blood of Brown's children, the Southerners will reap "hissing" monsters that will destroy them. With the image of Brown's children's blood (one son was killed in the Bleeding Kansas fights, while two others were killed in the Harper Ferry's raid), Stedman summons Brown's final speech: "Now, if it is deemed necessary that I should forfeit my life for the furtherance of the ends of justice, and mingle my blood further with the blood of my children and with the blood of millions in this slave country whose rights are disregarded by wicked, cruel, and unjust enactments, I submit; so let it be done!"[20] The poem channels Brown's righteous rage and alchemizes the sacrifice of the blood of sons, slaves, and abolitionists into the blood of slaveowners. Many years later, statesman John Hay (himself a poet, and an assistant to President Lincoln during the Civil War) wrote: "I remember how in an hour Stedman grew famous with that Tyrtaen ballad which rang like a reveille in the troubled and clouded morning of the great war, where the poet's voice gave forth the deep inspiration of the prophet. It was when the scaffold was building for John Brown. I have not lost the sonorous refrain in forty years."[21] In "The Portent," Melville recalls Stedman's poem from a postwar distance, summoning the fury yet signifying an overlay of time through his muted refrain and emotionally neutral language.

Stedman's prophecy could not be more violently partisan, of course. Melville takes the idea of prophecy and renders the outcome both ambiguous and inevitable by combining retrospective and prospective viewpoints. This dual perspective – both anticipating and confirming the violence of the war – renders it difficult to imagine a human speaker, or perhaps any speaker at all. Jackson asks: "But does 'The Portent' represent any subjective experience at all? If so, who is the subject? And is that subject the speaker of these lines?".[22] Just as in many ballads, there is no individual speaking subject: no person or persona. Even in Stedman's profoundly emotional poem, the emotion is not lyric, and the subject is not personalized: the poem expresses an outsized collective sense of righteous rage. Perhaps the biggest difference between Melville's poem and Stedman's is the emotionlessness of "The Portent." Melville's purging of the emotion while retaining and intensifying the idea of an omen fulfilled tends to render the poem relatively impersonal: not nonpartisan, but beyond partisanship. I will develop this idea further, but first I want to discuss another poem about John Brown that bears a relation to "The Portent."

Henry Howard Brownell was one of the most popular and widely acclaimed poets of the war – Oliver Wendell Holmes, Sr. dubbed him "The Battle Laureate" in an essay of that title in the *Atlantic*

Monthly.[23] Brownell's "skillfully rhymed version of Farragut's 'General Orders' to his fleet before the attack on New Orleans" led to Admiral Farragut's invitation to serve as his personal secretary aboard the flagship *USS Hartford*, where Brownell observed the Battle of Mobile Bay and wrote an eyewitness poem about it, supposedly on the spot.[24] In Brownell's "The Battle of Charlestown (December 2, 1859)," a poem about John Brown's hanging published during the war, an enthusiastic Southerner is eager to torture John Brown and see him hanged; the Southerner is an ironic creation of a Unionist poet who makes his dramatic persona bloodthirsty and deeply cruel. Here is the fourth stanza:

> 'Tis a right smart chance to test him –
> (Here we are at the gallows-tree,)
> So knot the noose – pretty tightly –
> Bandage his eyes – and we'll see,
> (For we'll keep him waiting a little,)
> If he tremble in nerve or knee.[25]

Like Stedman's, Brownell's meter is again notable: a trimeter made halting by the varying location of anapests, dactyls, and iambs. But most striking are the odd parenthetical comments. Parentheticals are repeatedly mentioned as an aspect of Melville's innovation in "The Portent." Though not as dislocated as Melville's, Brownell's parentheticals place the speaker between two forms of address: to the participants in the hanging (outside the parentheses), and to another group, including the reader, who is not present, or who does not understand what is happening. Apparently an outsider to the violence, the parenthetical addressee needs to be told he is at the gallows-tree, and to be informed of the intentions behind making Brown stand so long: it is a sadistic challenge, to allow time for the fear to grow and unman him. Brownell's parentheses precede and echo Melville's split address, though the division is along different lines.

The gruesome attention to the details of the hanging – "knot the noose pretty tightly," "Bandage his eyes" – recalls Melville's clinical attention to shocking details: the hanging beam, the cut on the crown, the stab wounds, the cap, the streaming beard. Brownell's fourth stanza resembles Melville's most closely in the specific detail:

> Look hard in the blindfold visage,
> (He can't look back,) and inquire,
> (He has stood there nearly a quarter,)
> If he doesn't begin to tire?

Asking a blindfolded man about to be hanged whether he is tiring foregrounds the hangman's cruelty. But looking at a hanged man whose face is "Hidden in the cap" with "the anguish none can tell," surely assumes the same vicarious, disturbing position to the violence. Brown "can't look back" in either case, and his "anguish" is indiscernible, untransmittable, though indisputably present. In Brownell's case, Brown is living, and the emotion of the hangman is almost hysterical in his strange glee over the killing. But Melville's evacuation of emotion that leaves clinical description alone is also bizarre.

In "The Portent," Melville seems to have engaged directly with these works, borrowing features of poems published in the heat of a moment – unusual features – and adapting them to a cooler, retrospective perspective. He treats the poems as individual, not mass or generic productions. The poems, though popular, are unconventional in a number of ways. Rather than a critical viewpoint, I see something more like an associative logic: a play between these violent expressions of outrage and Melville's clinical detachment. The latter would be incomplete without the former, even incomprehensible. Stedman's poem certainly, and Brownell's poem likely, were firmly ingrained in the public's mind when they turned to read Melville's poem, and they were most likely reading comparatively. Rather than condemning or critiquing these fiery statements, Melville folds them in noncommittally as part of the broader tangle of rhyme he creates to explore the "maze of war." There are places in *Battle-Pieces* that warn of excess emotions, as in the elegy to Lincoln, where mourning can turn to vengeance ("Beware the People weeping / When they bare the iron hand."), but this is not the only response (PP 104–5). "The Portent" takes for granted the intense emotions on both sides that the raid and hanging gave rise to, and mounts his poem in oblique, unspoken relation to that emotion that informs, shapes, and gives rise to his work.

Hsuan Hsu's brilliant analysis of ekphrasis in Melville's war poems suggests a related dynamic in Melville's deep engagements with contemporary visual practices. Hsu brings out the range of ways Melville attends to disparate materials, from Salvator Rosa's *Battaglia* (1642) to Alfred Waud's illustration for *Harper's Weekly* of "General Custer Presenting Captured Battle-Flags at the War Department" (1864), to paintings Melville saw at the Spring Exhibition of the National Academy, in 1865. Rather than simply explaining the mimetic effects of Melville's poetic renditions, Hsu makes a complex argument about the canceling, "elliptical" relation between Melville's interest in panoramic effects and his attention to fragmenting detail. According to Hsu, this "dual vision" frustrates "every attempt at ekphrasis" in a way that indicates a troubling absence of viewpoint at the heart of war: "*Battle-Pieces* presents poetic ekphrases only to turn away from them – only to turn toward the unfathomable core, the 'silent vision unavowed' at the bare foundation of society."[26] Hsu's idea of "turning away" is related to my suggestion that Melville invites popular poems to ghost his own productions, gesturing toward "aspects of the war" that he does not resolve into a whole, or even fully incorporate. If Melville is so deeply interested in paintings, maps, and newspaper illustrations, and if these materials generate such a complex relation with his attempts to comprehend the war, why would his interest in intertextuality stop there?

Though Parker finds no evidence that Melville was touched by the sea of poetry that surrounded him, critics have indicated too many resonances for coincidence to account for, especially for those readers familiar with the popular poetry of the war. In his study of Melville's use of the *Rebellion Record*, Frank Day identifies two poems that directly inform Melville's work: "The Swamp Angel" by T.N.J., with its accompanying note, shares words and phrases with Melville's "The Swamp Angel" and its note; and "The Eagle of the Eighth Wisconsin," by an anonymous poet, carries details noted in Melville's "The Eagle of the Blue."[27] A contemporary reviewer compares Melville's "Sheridan at Cedar Creek" with Thomas Buchanan Read's "Sheridan's Ride," and this connection has been explored by Aaron Shackelford in a recent dissertation. The same reviewer compares Melville's "The Cumberland" with Longfellow's "The Cumberland," and Faith Barrett compares Longfellow's exuberant hopes for reunification with Melville's more muted response.[28] Barrett also compares Will Hays' "The Drummer Boy of Shiloh" with Melville's "Shiloh."[29] In a forthcoming book, I argue for Melville's sustained engagement with Henry Howard Brownell's "The Bay Fight" in his "The Battle for the Bay"; one could also compare Brownell's "The River Fight" with Melville's "The Battle for the Mississippi."[30] In addition to Melville's "The Portent," there are numerous poems published before and during the war about John Brown's hanging, by Stedman, Brownell, John Greenleaf Whittier, Rose Terry Cooke, and others. Melville's elegy to Lincoln is part of a wave of tributes, by Whitman, Brownell, Richard Henry Stoddard, Stedman, William Cullen Bryant, and others. These are just some of the possible points of comparison within my own, limited range of knowledge.

Melville encourages this sort of proliferation of association because his poems both gesture toward other well-known poems in their titles and topics, and veer away toward a sense of encryption or encoding. "Storms are formed behind the storm we feel" (PP 7) in Melville's war poems. There is a sense of thick, underlying, and only partially accessible knowledge in his terse, iconic poems which can have the effect of encouraging the reader to seek access to historical events by reading newspaper reports, poring over the *Rebellion Record* and *Harper's Weekly*, studying Civil War poetry, and bringing this proliferation of materials into relation with Melville's poems in a sort of reverse process of how the poems seem to have been composed, in a meticulous, textually layered way.

This haunted quality of the poems (and their often cryptic, partial notes) does not derive solely from their visual and verbal intertextuality. It is also a function of their elusive engagements with history. Summoning what was the recent past in 1866, and is now a distant past, the poems are full of lost and partially lost resonances.[31] In the penultimate paragraph of the "Supplement," Melville says: "These thoughts are sincere ones; they seem natural – inevitable. Here and there they must have suggested themselves to many thoughtful patriots. And, if they be just thoughts, ere long they must have that weight with the public which already they have had with individuals" (PP 187). These lines needn't refer to the prose supplement alone. They offer an impersonal theory of language and thought that pervades the volume. If ideas are "sincere" and "just" – one might even venture "true" – then they "suggest themselves" to "many thoughtful patriots," and they outweigh other thoughts and gain ground with "the public." This model of spreading thought, not rooted in individual introspection but flowing through people like an impersonal current, governs Melville's poetic practice. For Melville, poetry is a crucial medium for the transmission of thoughts and feelings, one that plays an important role in forming ideas before, during, and after events. He thinks of poetry as a commonly shared practice of building a reservoir of thoughts and feelings about the war, to be distilled and discerned only in the future.[32] It was not uncommon during the Civil War for writers to feel as if their thoughts and feelings were not exclusively their own. Emily Dickinson said that "Sorrow seems to me more general than it did, and not the estate of a few persons, since the war began; and if the anguish of others helped with ones own now would be many medicines."[33] Brownell said of his poems that "They are spray, as it were, flung up by the strong Tide-Rip of Public Trouble, and present the time, perhaps, more nearly than they do the writer."[34] Melville accessed this public emotion via the poetry of his peers. Sharon Cameron writes that "one way of approaching impersonality is to say it is not the negation of the person, but rather a penetration through or a falling outside of the boundary of the human particular. Impersonality disrupts elementary categories we suppose to be fundamental to specifying human distinctiveness."[35] Brownell and Dickinson evoke a sense of interpenetration of persons that defies human distinctiveness, and so does Melville.

Unlike others, however, Melville gives the impression of working at a remote distance as he gathers and amalgamates common feelings. Again, his contemporary reviewers noticed this attribute:

> We read his songs, if we may call them such, and wonder while we read, first, that the events should have presented themselves to his mind in the shape that they did, and, second, that, with his genius, he has not succeeded in placing us more *en rapport* with them. Mr. Brownell has this last power in many of his patriotic pieces, while Mr. Walter Whitman, the most shapeless of all our versifiers, possesses it in a remarkable degree. We fail, however, to sympathize with the mass of Mr. Melville's poems, which are scarcely intelligible, as he has handled them.[36]

The reviewer identifies Melville's project with Brownell's and Whitman's: all are trying to convey a sense of the war to their readers. Brownell and Whitman forge emotional connections with their readers; Melville does not. William Dean Howells' assessment is more familiar: "Here lies the fault. Mr. Melville's skill is so great that we fear he has not often felt the things of which he writes since with all his skill he fails to move us ... Indeed the book is full of pictures of many kinds, – often good, – though all with an heroic quality of remoteness, separating our weak human feelings from them by trackless distances."[37] Again, Melville "fails to move us," but Howells declines to speculate about the reasons for these "trackless distances." Why would Melville work with popular materials saturated with emotion, and re-present them from a muted, distant viewpoint? Many critics have noted this quality in *Battle-Pieces*. Milette Shamir has recently argued that Melville is foregrounding "the problem of the civilian author, whose distance allows a broad vision of the war even as it undermines that vision's access to truth and ethical viability."[38] Melville certainly notes the difficulty or even impossibility of achieving a truthful and ethical viewpoint, not least by presenting highly partial, emotional perspectives from a chilling distance, Sherman's "glorious glad" soldiers in "The March to the Sea," for example, or the rioters in "The House Top," or Lincoln's mourners in "The Martyr." By keeping his distance I believe Melville is trying to serve as a conduit to distill or temper wartime emotions into postwar "thoughts": "natural – inevitable," "just." The thoughts emerge from emotions in a process that leads toward reconciliation. In "A Canticle: Significant of the national exaltation of enthusiasm at the close of the War," Melville describes a convergence of the waters that flow through the collection: it is one of the more obscure pieces in the volume and certainly the most exuberant (one critic says he "out-Whitmans Whitman" here):[39]

> The Nation, in her impulse
> Mysterious as the Tide,
> In emotion like an ocean
> Moves in power, not in pride;
> And is deep in her devotion
> As Humanity is wide. (PP 101)

Brownell's "Tide-Rip of Public Trouble" resonates with this fathomless image of national "emotion like an ocean," something beyond any one's ability to know. But as a poet, Melville finds that one way of writing about experiences as "mysterious as the tide" is to draw from the meditations of others, who channel others in turn. Stedman, for example, gives voice to "the deep inspiration of the prophet," according to John Hay.[40] By entering the massive tangle of popular poetry, Melville can navigate, indicate, and sublimate, even if he cannot explain, the maze of war. Engaging with popular poetry in singular terms, mining poems for diverse reactions to varied events, Melville collects "feelings not inspired by any one source" and amalgamates them into a collection of pieces that urge readers to move beyond his poems and look to the complexities of what can be found and what is lost in the historical record of the war. His impersonal, retroactive retelling suggests that finding thoughts that are "sincere" and "just" is a process that is "natural – inevitable." That process entails entertaining oceanic emotions of the war period and distilling them into thoughts which, if they endure, prove their public value.

CHAPTER 14

The Biographical Re-Turn
Writing Melville Biography and the Example of Women

John Bryant

> [I]n strict speech there can be no biography of an Indian-hater *par excellence*, any more than one of a sword-fish, or other deep-sea denizen; or, which is still less imaginable, one of a dead man. The career of the Indian-hater *par excellence* has the impenetrability of the fate of a lost steamer. Doubtless, events, terrible ones, have happened, must have happened; but the powers that be in nature have taken order that they shall never become news.
>
> —Melville, *The Confidence-Man*

Let's begin with the impossibility of biography. In *The Confidence-Man*, Melville's narrator reckons with the problems a biographer must confront: the elusiveness of the subject and the ungraspability of a consciousness. The "Indian-hater *par excellence*" is a curiously apt case with universal applications. This serial killer, who randomly ambushes innocent Native Americans, strikes savagely in darkness then returns to normal living. He is a gruesome, unknowable consciousness hiding out in civil society. How do we grasp this "deep-sea denizen," track the traumatic sources of his pathology, and comprehend his wretched inner life? And yet writing the life of such a deadly man is no different from writing the biography of any "dead man." Living or dead, we are all deep-sea Bartlebys and isolatoes in one way or another, and what life is ever fully witnessed or knowable? What documents or life facts fully supply the link between the workings of a mind and that mind's deeds, or writings on a page? Writing "a life" is like trying to penetrate "the impenetrability of the fate of a lost steamer." We know events "happened, must have happened," but what we imagine having happened can never be taken as "news," if by news we mean actual fact. Melville is one such "lost steamer," and our only record of this wreck is the jetsam of his writings ejected before he went down in 1891 and the flotsam of his daily and family life that, even before his birth in 1819, has floated only randomly to the surface for us to gather. Even so, despite the impossibility of biography and despite Melville's arguments cogently urging me not to do his biography, I am writing a comprehensive, two-volume work anyway, titled *Herman Melville: A Half Known Life*.

If, "in strict speech," there can be "no biography," then why attempt one? What is the critical, gravitational pull that biography has on us? Some literary biographies are little more than romantic hagiography; others are more archival and sedulously avoid speculation into the writer's inner life. What pulls me into biography is neither bardolatry nor mere record-keeping – though I will admit to occasional lapses into these sins – but rather a twofold gravity. First is the historicist impulse to investigate how Melville's multistranded consciousness evolved from childhood to old age, and how that evolving consciousness shaped his writing. Second is the desire to find openings in our research that will enable us to bring Melville's life experience and creative process more fully into our critical thinking about his written work. In writing *A Half Known Life*, I want to see if biography can be a reliable approach to interpretation.

The profession of literary studies remains resistant to biographical criticism, but if we want to understand the dynamics of an evolving consciousness as it plays out in the example of a writer engaging a layering of cultures, we will need biographical research to clarify a lifespan of interpretive possibilities in the reading of texts and a culture. Because the traumas of everyday life – at home, in social settings, on the road, in the hunt for whales, at work in customs, in confronting a blank sheet of paper, in making countless revisions – are identifiable moments in a life that erupt into written self-expression, these life events are concrete resources enabling us to link those moments in the evolution of a consciousness to moments, sometimes obsessively repeated, in a writer's fluid text.

Melville's encounter with the black sailor John Backus on his first whaleship *Acushnet*, who, according to marginalia in another shipmate's copy of *Moby-Dick*, was bumped, traumatically, from a whaleboat, is the undeniable source for the nearly-drowned and maddened Pip whose fictionalized experience is repeated by the "third man" Ishmael, who is also bumped from a whaleboat. This confluence of an actual black sailor, a fictional black cabin boy, and Ishmael replaying Pip, is an early instance of Melville's persistent "black consciousness," an experience of black people in life that erupts, in various repetitive ways, into his writing. These versions of Pip and Ishmael-as-Pip are replayed later, in a different register, as Babo in "Benito Cereno" and later again as an African sailor witnessed on the docks of Liverpool, recalled in *Billy Budd*, and written late into Melville's manuscript during a time in which lynching peaked in the US. In turn, *Billy Budd*'s black Liverpool sailor recalls the mulatto Lavender in *Redburn*, strolling the streets of Liverpool, arm-in-arm with two white women, an image that evokes Frederick Douglass's escorting of two white women on Broadway, in May 1849, just as Melville was writing *Redburn*, and just a week before the Astor Place riot. If we are to pursue both the textual and cultural ramifications of Melville's use of black figures in his writing, we have little recourse but to situate this suite of imaginative replays in the context of Melville's demonstrable proximity to black people in his domestic sphere, in the streets of his urban neighborhoods in Manhattan and Albany, on board ships, and in his experience of the everyday trauma of American racism throughout his century, and reverberating into ours.

Out of this kaleidoscopic swirling of life traumas and imaginative versions of such traumas replayed in fiction, biographical criticism can discern a thread of development in which memory transforms life events into an evolving sense of a personal past, and in which compositional events recast that past into writing, so that the linearities of these reconstructions of past memory and present writing become for us the warp and woof of an evolving creative life. Such biocritical openings will float to the surface in Melville studies, or for that matter literary studies in general, only when biographers take on the role of critic in order to "see" those biocritical openings, and only when critics adapt their interpretive skills to include the reading of imaginative texts biographically.

But biographers and critics tend to keep to their separate spheres of inquiry. The reluctance of both groups to adjust their interpretive optics into a shared biocritical vision is rooted in an understandable skepticism of the role that speculation must play in the analysis of the growth of an artist. What, indeed, is evidence of a growing imagination other than the imaginative texts? But these texts require speculative interpretation. Melville is an imaginative writer who wrests fiction out of life-writing, creative nonfiction, auto-fiction. Whatever name suits what we may call Melville's autobiographical approach, his written works are inventions from life; they are not documents of a life. At the same time, much of Melville's writing is not merely occasionally drawn from life but fundamentally responsive to life moments. Melville looked into his past in order to look inward, in order to see himself more clearly and to see more than himself. To gain some purchase on Melville's personal acts of intro-retrospection, we search for plausible biographical features in his written work. His relation to John Backus and Pip, for instance. Moreover, his process of writing, not only in the works he published and relentlessly revised in print, but also more evidently in the unpolished manuscripts that survive, is an ongoing biographical event worth studying as an opening into Melville's relation to himself and his various audiences. While we may be content to examine the surface of Melville's imaginative texts and go no further into their making and revision, we risk losing sight of the phenomenon of the process of writing as both a personal and cultural event and as a way of reading Melville.

Our biographical investigations into the link between consciousness and the imaginative writings of "a dead man" and "deep-sea denizen" enrich our critical reading of Melville's interaction with his culture. As an approach to literary and cultural analysis, biographical criticism is ready for a return to critical legitimacy. But biography is fraught with critical anxieties, and, as we shall see, the history of Melville biography has certain blindnesses worth correcting, in particular its neglect of women in the shaping of Melville's writing. How a return to biography might be effected depends on a more fluid conception of both life and text, on how vigilant we are in looking for biocritical openings, and on how we allow ourselves to see new openings beyond our blindnesses.

The Anxiety of Biographical Criticism

The New Criticism sounded the death knell of literary biography as an approach to critical interpretation. In the formative years of literary study in the nineteenth century, biography played a significant role in establishing the *bona fides* of a writer, elevating that person – typically male – from writer to "author." That process of validation was in play in 1919 when Columbia University scholar Carl Van Doren asked his junior colleague Raymond Weaver to submit a biographical essay on a once-celebrated but now obscure writer. The essay was meant simply to acknowledge the centennial of Herman Melville's birth, but it achieved the added effect of returning Melville to the status of an Author, and, more importantly, a writer for the world.

In his research, Weaver found enough new information and texts to write his 1921 biography, *Herman Melville: Mariner and Mystic.* During the ensuing Melville Revival, scholars engaging in the practice of descriptive bibliography, which determines the sequence and extent of a writer's work and publication, tracked the writer's creative life and provided a grounding for Michael Sadleir's standardized Constable edition of Melville's works (1922–1924). Publishing records, letters, journals, manuscripts, family materials, collections of associates, maps, official documents, and statistics from government, industry, and business – dispersed in archives worldwide – added flesh to the bones of Melville bibliography. And with these biographical materials, textual scholars – some of them students of Stanley Williams at Yale, including Walter Bezanson, Merrell Davis, Elizabeth Foster, William Gilman, Harrison Hayford, Merton M. Sealts Jr., and Nathalia Wright – were better equipped in the 1940s to establish more reliable editions of the writer's texts, and, more to the point, more reliable representations of the variant versions of a writer's fluid text.[1] Biography and critical edition, expertly combined in the magisterial Northwestern-Newberry *Writings of Herman Melville* (1968–2017), spans three generations of scholarship.

Even though these disciplinary necessities of bibliography, archive, and scholarly edition were at mid-twentieth century still evolving, a golden age of Melville biography emerged in and around 1951. Jay Leyda's *The Melville Log* – a curated timeline of personal, familial, professional, historical facts, and excerpts from selected letters, documents, and Melville texts – provided a two-volume archive, a still-indispensable framework for anyone wanting to write a biography. In that same year, Leon Howard created one such narrativizing of the *Log* in his *Herman Melville*, which also offered bracing forays into Melville's creative process. Though Howard Vincent's earlier study, *The Trying-out of Moby-Dick* (1949), had gone deeper into Melville's sources for *Moby-Dick*, both Vincent's and Howard's books avoid diving too deeply into the motives or interpretations of Melville's creativity. William Gilman's *Melville's Early Life and Redburn* (1951) and Merrell Davis's *Melville's Mardi: A Chartless Voyage* (1952) integrated the life and works more effectively through the lens of a single work, using additional biographical details of Melville's "exterior" life to inform his "interior" creativity. While Newton Arvin's slimmer 1952 critical biography went eloquently inward, it sometimes sacrificed accuracy of detail.[2] Given the New Critical focus on text and text alone, these foundational biographies of the mid-century reflect that era's reluctance to bring biography and interpretation together. In the half century that followed, the caveat against biographical criticism had not abated despite, or in part because of, the literary Freudianism of Edwin H. Miller's audacious 1975 biography, which, though stimulating, proved reductive and a caution against the kind of critical excess a biography might commit.

By the mid-1990s, new generations of scholars increased the demand for Melville biography, and a spate of new biographies, with new approaches, emerged. These works – stimulated, in part, by the discovery in 1983 of the so-called Augusta Papers, including the *Typee* manuscript – reflect decades of biographical research that had transpired during the transition in literary study from New Criticism to the poststructuralist and New Historicist era.

Hershel Parker's two-volume *Herman Melville: A Biography* (1996, 2002) is a capacious rendering of facts, drawn from foundational archives and augmented by the aforementioned Augusta Papers.[3] Rarely mentioning Herman Melville, these documents nevertheless disclose the lives of Melville's relatives – mother, siblings, cousins, in-laws – and numerous family friends. Parker's interweaving of old and new archives relates the fabric of Melville's domestic life and includes discussions of Melville's creativity – his jocund treatment of revisions in *Typee*, his finding that Melville had titled a work *The Isle of the Cross*, and his moving assessment of Melville's late pencilings in the *Billy Budd* manuscript are particularly memorable – but like its predecessors, it offers little guidance in how to transform the facts of Melville's creative process, lodged in letters and manuscripts, into a critical understanding of the growth of Melville's consciousness in the context of his family and culture. For Parker, influences on texts detected in sources outweigh the influence of life experiences – Melville's travel and work – on the evolution of a consciousness. In general, he disparages the "following in the writer's footsteps" approach.[4]

Laurie Robertson-Lorant's *Melville: A Biography* (1996) is also a comprehensive study informed by research into old and new archives, though not as accurate as Parker's. The volume's primary contribution is its attempt to situate Melville's life, creativity, and works in the context of slavery and other primal sins of politics, war, and economy. Andrew Delbanco in his *Melville: His World and Work* (2005) makes no claim to offer new discoveries in the life but grounds sensitive readings in reliable archival research in the context of nineteenth-century American politics and culture. While his biography minimizes Melville's later works, from *The Confidence-Man* to the late poetry, his treatment of Melville's "restlessness" as it evolves in both the life and writings is an effective yardstick for measuring Melville's politics and aesthetics. In tone, insight, and concision, Delbanco's biography is a model of excellence in biographical criticism.

For myself, attempting a Melville biography in light of these forebears, I am humbled by the impossibility of any biography to achieve a perfect balance between archival rigor and interpretive application, between accuracy in reporting and the pull of one's critical imagination, between an allegiance to the small detail of an event or in a text and a social commitment to the larger picture of cultural movements within a democracy. In striving for some kind of balance beyond the scope of previous biographies, my aim in writing *Herman Melville: A Half Known Life* is to document moments of growth in Melville's evolving consciousness concerning his father-anger, his god-hunger and desire for transcendence, his black consciousness and empathy for the underclasses, his various masculinities, his love of women and love of men, his ability to tell a story, his wresting of the picturesque out of the sublime. But in pursuing these distinguishing features in what I presume to call Melville's consciousness, I risk using Melville's text as biographical fact; I risk making my biography of Melville a mirror of my own desire. These two fundamental problems, which the New Criticism rightly skewered, question the limits of biographical speculation in interpretation of imaginative texts. They get to the heart of our anxiety over biocriticism and require our focused attention.

Autobiography as Biography

The first problem is what appears in retrospect to be the remarkably naïve assumption that apparently autobiographical details in a writer's text are reliable records for writing a writer's life. Melville scholarship played a significant role in both committing and exposing this autobiographical fallacy. In his pioneering biography, Raymond Weaver made the mistake of assuming that Melville's claim in *Typee* of having spent "four months" on Nuku Hiva was factual, when, as Charles Roberts Anderson revealed in his 1939 *Melville in the South Seas*, Melville had spent only "four weeks" on the island.[5] Anderson contributed abundant new evidence of Melville's life at sea and of Melville's borrowings from numerous travel narratives, setting a high standard for fact-finding scholarship. In its wake, Wilson Heflin's dissertation (edited posthumously into a book by Mary K. Bercaw Edwards and Thomas F. Heffernan) contributed even more facts regarding Melville's whaling years and his seafaring books. William Gilman's biography of Melville's adolescence in upstate New York separated fact from fiction in *Redburn*. Walter Bezanson's reading of *Clarel* placed that epic poem in light of Melville's travels and sources. Nathalia Wright's *Melville's Use of the Bible* provided categories for following Melville's lifelong reading of scripture, and Elizabeth Foster's edition of *The Confidence-Man* contextualized the comedy in light of high and lowbrow culture.

As a biographical subgenre, these source studies are a healthy deterrent to the autobiographical fallacy, if only because they allow us to distinguish

Melville's often fallacious statements of fact from facts garnered externally in other resources. Biographical source study also demystifies Melville's habits of appropriation. Like his siblings, with whom he learned to write, Melville was a voracious reader, inveterate researcher, and instinctual absorber of detail. His prose fictions are, in many places, a collage of pirated facts and borrowed texts, with each borrowing a link to an external source, and each link representing an act of reading these separate textual identities and a strategy of appropriation. By delineating the various source identities within Melville's collage, we begin to discern the workings of a writer writing: a blatant plagiarism here, an artful paraphrase there, then on to an inventive digression, an unanticipated application in fiction, and then a "return" to the interrupted narrative. With these boundaries established, we can ground biographical criticism in more reliable acts of imaginative reconstruction of the dynamics of Melville's appropriation and achieve a more fully informed interpretation of the absorptive and transformative functions of his creativity. Some will call Melville a thief, and so he was, but source studies need not condemn; they are openings into a consciousness.

Reluctant to engage in such a biocritical analysis of Melville's texts, Anderson and other source hunters have been content to expose rather than interpret Melville's appropriations, but the thrill of exposure also led Anderson into critical missteps of his own. Concluding his study of Melville's sources for *Typee*, Anderson writes: "it can be said almost without exaggeration that, with these sources open before him and with a lively imagination to body them forth, Melville might have written *Typee* without ever having seen the Marquesas Islands."[6] Despite his disclaimer of exaggeration, Anderson exaggerates wildly and never retracts, giving readers the impression that *Typee* is little more than a cobbling of sources. Anderson's misstep forestalls a deeper analysis of a crucial moment in Melville's creativity, his first unfolding at the age of twenty-five, when in writing *Typee* the writer learned that he could be an author. Instead Anderson takes appropriation as a misdemeanor rather than an inherent part of the creative process and minimizes Melville's creativity to a dismissive "lively imagination." Once we recuperate from the news that the writer has feet of clay, we are given no instruction on how Melville molded the clay. *Typee* is undeniably a collage of facts, thefts, and fictions. But this kind of collage, evident in all of Melville's prose writings and most of his poems, reveals a pattern of writerly behaviors that link text back into experience: Melville's recollection of moments lived, his passion for research, his identification with, then revision of, researched texts, his transformation of personal and formal research into fiction, in short his patterns of creation and deception. The study of *Typee* did not recover from Anderson's dismissal until the discovery in 1983 of the *Typee* manuscript.

Which brings us back to the dilemma of using Melville's published writings as any kind of evidence for telling the multistranded stories of his life. In speaking of the fallacy of relying on "Melville's books" as "straight biography," Hershel Parker offers this rumination: "breaking that reliance . . . requires heroic discipline, and disciplined judgment of another sort is required in acknowledging that *Typee* and others of Melville's books are in fact, in passages, something like straight autobiography."[7] The autobiographical fallacy – the presumption that fictions contain biographical truths – is itself fallacious. Melville revealed as much in a letter to Lemuel Shaw. We are most familiar with Melville's revealing characterization of *Redburn* and *White-Jacket* as two "jobs," which rightly registers his resistance to the literary marketplace. But he also wrote of these two texts: "I have not repressed myself much . . . ; but have spoken pretty much as I feel" (L 138–39). Readers of books like *Typee, Redburn*, and *White-Jacket* are free, in fact encouraged, to ask, Who is this person within the text? Following suit, biographers freely ask, What had been "repressed" within this "self" and what had he "pretty much" felt?

Melville's writings are so deeply rooted in documented personal experience that biographers would be remiss in ignoring Melville's apparent invitation to use them as a biographical resource. But which "person" is in the text: the boy, the adolescent, the sailor? or the writer recalling a past self but writing "pretty much" as he felt during the present moment of re-memory, or the revised self, revealed in later revisions of the text? Is the haiku-like "Pebble VI" in *John Marr*, Melville's late collection of nostalgic but also *avant garde* poems, a snapshot of the sailor bodysurfing on the Peruvian coast in July 1842, or of Melville's memory of that event in later years, or of Melville's "compositional present" (to borrow John Wenke's apt term) when he wrote and rewrote the short poem in 1888? The person in this poem is all of these selves, of course, and more. To say biography is incidental to the poem as text only precludes any discourse on the critical reconstruction of how poets transform experience, memory, and self into words. Like any mode of interpretation, that discourse requires "disciplined judgment" of one sort or another, which begins with a characteristically Melvillean mediation of fact and fiction. The biographer's task is to find a middle way between Weaver's too confident reliance on Melville's fiction and Anderson's too triumphant disbelief.

No matter how much a writer takes writing as an escape from selfhood, readers invariably wonder about how that writerly self escapes into a text. The agenda of modernism and many postmodernisms is to honor the privacy of the escape and ignore the meaning of the writer-as-writer's process of disappearance, but Melville's modernity lies in the self-conscious disruption of his fictions that expose the "strange" emotion within the escapee failing to escape. "Who ain't a slave," asks Ishmael. Accordingly, the dynamic between Melville's life and writing – that factor we denominate Melvillean, which is so useful in critiquing American culture in general – calls for a rigorous form of biographical criticism that invites readers to draw upon autobiographical reportage, representations of actual events delivered in bursts of transformative memory, strategic appropriations of sources, textual revisions, and fictive self-inventions. One of Melville's many tricks in writing is that he blends versions of fact, versions of self, and versions of invention to make us think we have access to his ungraspable consciousness. Risk-taking biographical criticism helps us wonder more responsibly about how Melville plays this game and discern more fully his strategies of private and social identity formation. These discernments in measuring how a life hides out conspicuously within a text are worth pursuing because they are vital exercises for anyone attempting to survive the deceptions of modern democracies.

Author, Historicism, and Fluid Text

The autobiographical fallacy is an important caution but should not be taken as a proscription against using fiction judiciously in the study of a life. A corollary concern is that a biography will mirror the biographer's own autobiography. Such subjective colorations are inevitable and best announced openly, but the more insidious risk is that a biographer might transform the subject into the hero (or villain) of a narrative arc imposed upon the life. No life has an arc: a life is a series of events, and then you die. Certainly, all lives have an easily discernible beginning and end; but it is the time between birth and death that makes us want to shape it into a narrative arc, and readers expect such arcs. By these lights, biographers are doubly-damned. They need to devise a good story; they need to resist The Arc of their own devising. If we want to guess at why Melville, at twenty-one, went whaling, we can record the random circumstances leading up to that event, but when we assert these circumstances are causes, we impose an arc on the randomness of life. Biographers need a better metaphor than "arc." Melville's early life seems like a marble let loose in the warp of time and space. It is drawn toward and pulled away from other spheres of influence – family, politics, sex – by one gravitational pull or another. But Einstein's continuum may be too complex a metaphor for a genre so Newtonian as biography: readers want to follow Melville riding a simple inevitable curve, and biographers inevitably bend to the curve.

As a genre, biography insists upon a narrative, but biographers are also obliged to resist biography's generic expectations and, in particular, lurid voyeurism, stagey dramatizations, and reductive theories of character. No one wants to reduce Melville to a single note, though plenty of "legends in Melville scholarship"[8] exist to suggest that readers give credence to such reductions: Melville the randy heterosexual; Melville the homosexual lover of Hawthorne; Melville the alcoholic wife beater; Melville the Puritan believer, or atheist; Melville the reclusive failure and *poète maudit.* By reducing the dynamics of anger, family, sexuality, work, trauma, race, religion, spirituality, god-hunger, and creative process in Melville's life to a single label, the biographer misses an opportunity to engage readers more fully in the complexity of human identity. On the other hand, a biography that does not theorize intelligibly on authorship and culture will be annoyingly inconsequential.

These tendencies toward subjectivity, voyeurism, dramatism, reductionism are the bane of critical biography and have consigned the genre to the periphery of literary studies since the era of the New Critics. New Historicists have also resisted biography even though their agenda to contextualize is an obvious invitation to biographical criticism. The focus on text and cultural discourse presents a field of study wherein theories of an individual's life and work might fruitfully merge with broader theories of ideology and social forces. But a full synthesis of life and discourse analysis is rarely attempted in biography, or in biographical criticism. One possibility for synthesis, as we shall see, is a focus on creative process in the interpretation of texts, even though that approach also has yet to achieve acceptance in literary criticism.

Writing fifty years ago when "the author as solitary genius" still prevailed in literary studies, Michel Foucault dismissed the notion that the author and a writer's "work" were the only sources of signification in cultural analysis; he recognized a multiplicity of agents performing that function in a culture. Even so, he considered how we might reconceive of the author in relation to various cultural discourses. In "What is an Author?" he posed several provocative questions:

> How, under what conditions, and in what forms can something like a subject appear in the order of discourse? What place can it occupy in each type of discourse, what functions can it assume, and by obeying what rules? In short, it is a matter of depriving the subject (or its substitute) of its role as originator, and of analyzing the subject as a variable and complex function of discourse.[9]

Some will lament the seeming loss of the "subject" personality as a romantic "originator" in Foucault's theory, but I detect a liberation in it for biographical study. Rather than affirming Roland Barthes's announcement of the "death of the author," Foucault resituates the subject author, from the role of "originator" of culture to a "function of discourse." If the new historicist agenda is to consider the "conditions" in which a subject like Herman Melville might "appear in the order of discourse" – to locate this evolving writer's "place" either within or apart from differently evolving fields of discourse – then the biographer's job is to facilitate cultural interpretation by narrating the contingencies of the dynamics of subject and "place." How, for instance, might Melville's persistent replaying of versions of Pip expose not only Melville's evolving sense of self but also the discourses of Pacific colonialism in *Moby-Dick*, the slave trade in "Benito Cereno," and the beauty of blackness in *Billy Budd*?

Foucault's definition of the author as a function of discourse will strike us as bloodless and lacking in the specificity of personality, and surely a biographer will want to represent the flesh and blood of the human. But the historicist's seeming dehumanizing of the subject reads to me like a reasonable caution. In writing biography, I have learned to refrain from minor-league dramatizations that might encourage hagiography: the humidity of Melville's tobacco breath, the rectitude of his social bearing, the faraway-ness of his blue eyes, and other characterizations that seem consequential but tell us nothing. Though Foucault's abstraction of the living, breathing writer to a "functional principle" might err in its austerity, I nevertheless find validation for biography in this construct and in Foucault's questions for determining how the "variable and complex" functionalities collectively known as "Melville" might actually function. Rather than dramatizing or reductively theorizing a personality, the biographer can show readers whatever drama there might be in the intellectual, artistic, and discourse functions a writer performs. Here is where the subject function can come alive, and in writing biography I do not prevent myself from representing emotions, anxieties, joys, and depressions in both the everyday exasperations with living with mother and siblings and the private passions of pursuing an idea in the process of writing. One discourse functionality that permits a synthesis of biography and historicism is revision.

Revision is rarely studied systematically, in part because the material evidence of revision in a writer's work is often only fortuitously preserved, randomly dispersed in multiple archives, unevenly edited, or not transcribed at all. More to the point, revision is not validated by traditional notions of textuality: revision is *avant texte*, which is to say it is not yet text at all. Going against the grain of the editorial theories of his day, Foucault was open to including a writer's working drafts, even laundry lists, as part of the writer's "work," that is, "oeuvre." In my own editorial theorizing about textuality and access, I consider "work" to be more verb than noun, an experience best understood in the present progressive than past tense. That is, a writer's *work* is not final intentions reified in a singular publication; rather, it is the persistent energy put into the writing and revisionary processes, extending up from genesis, through drafts and versions, to and even after the published product. Revision is crucial to a writer's identity and our best evidence of how a writer grows. To meet the challenges of revision, we also need a broader conception of textuality. A written work put out into a culture, say *Moby-Dick*, is the product of relentless revision. It is never static; it is a fluid text.

A fluid text is any work that exists in multiple versions, due to acts of revision by an author, editor, or adaptor.[10] We read Melville in published form, but the fuller story is that Melville was an insistent reviser as is abundantly clear in his working draft manuscripts; and with *Typee*, for instance, we can discern at least three manuscript versions spread out over eight stages of composition. Once published, Melville was not immune to further revision, as is evident in the American expurgations of *Typee* and the British expurgations of *Moby-Dick*. Even after the author's death in 1891, especially with the ascendency of his posthumous reputation starting in the 1920s, translators and adaptors (in various media) continued to revise Melville's work. The originating author (Melville), his publishing editors (Evert Duyckinck, John Murray, Richard Bentley, the Harper Brothers, George Putnam, John Wiley, and others), and his subsequent adaptive revisers (among them, Cesare Pavese, Ray Bradbury and John Huston, E.M. Forster and Benjamin Britten, Jake Hegge and Gene Scheer, just to name a few) are the multiple, sequential, editorial, and adaptive performers of Melville's fluid texts. Melville's borrowing of sources – his quotation and plagiarisms – also contribute to the textual fluidity of his works since any of his appropriations functions as a revision: it is Melville's version of another writer. To this extent, biography is a natural history of the revision of self and text. The biographer's challenge is to integrate our revision narratives of a writer with the evolving versions of a culture.

Revision texts are biographical moments. Just as fluid texts evolve through various textual identities, Melville's revisions are a working through of various versions of selfhood, a "replaying" of himself as he wrote. In the *Typee* manuscript, his revision of the word *savage* to *native* or *islander* is a pattern of textual revision that signifies a shift in Melville's awareness, triggered by the very act of rewriting, not simply because he plays games with these culturally loaded terms but because the direction that his revisions take indicate an erasure of *savage*, signifying an evolution in his political consciousness. Melville was himself a fluid text. In this regard, textual fluidity is a useful resource for integrating biography and cultural studies. Revision is the kind of "variable and complex function of discourse" that Foucault takes as the "author," and biography is or can be, in Foucauldian terms, a research into the functionality of the author function.

If we are to engage in a return to biographical criticism, we need to address our critical anxieties about the nature of biographical evidence – the use of imaginative texts and revision texts – and about the function of writers writing within a culture. To the extent that literary biography tracks the evolution of a consciousness in relation to a concurrently evolving culture, the biographer records a writer's private performances of cultural discourse. But this risky word "consciousness" prompts another biographical anxiety. With Melville, we recognize that a consciousness is an ungraspable "lost steamer"; we acknowledge its existence, but only indirectly and through the muddied optics of our own subjectivity. Melville argues for the impossibility of writing a biography of the Indian-hater, but that did not prevent him from characterizing Captain John Moredock. In devoting ten years and more to writing a Melville biography, I embrace this paradox and give flesh and blood renderings (though not dramatizations) of Melville's evolving consciousness. It is the complex functions of this consciousness that we critically desire: the how of creativity and the cultural meaning of creative acts. How, then, do we manage the risky business of studying a consciousness? How, too, do we avoid certain blindnesses of our subjectivities, in particular the past neglect of women in our understanding of Melville's growth?

Biography and Consciousness

"What place can it occupy in each type of discourse": Foucault is careful to suggest that the "it" – the author function, a subject writer, a Melville –

does in fact have a "place" in different types of discourse. For Melville, these discourses include, at the very least, slavery and race, sexuality and gender, work and economy, trauma and disability, masculinity and anger, transcendence and nihilism. From a biographer's perspective, the challenge is how to spell out the dynamics of each discourse in terms of Melville's lived life and how to narrate the continued development of these multiple discourses as they evolve in the context of the culture. The biographer's task is to locate the earliest recorded moments in Melville's boyhood, adolescence, and young manhood when some frequency of awareness began vibrating within his evolving consciousness. What are the earliest events that trigger later resonances with the familial, racial, sexual, intellectual, spiritual dynamics evident in his mature but always exploratory writing? Melville did not fully comprehend urban poverty, independent of African American poverty, until he walked the streets of Liverpool; he did not know the prairie until he rode a horse through Illinois scattering rabbits out of the tall grass before him; he did not feel the strange emotions he associated with whales until he went whaling. Asking when and under what circumstances these events occurred allows us to plot the growth of one person's awareness and how memory triggers invention and symbol in the writing process. Symbolizing is itself a mode of consciousness.

When did Melville grow sexually, in the absence of his father, in the presence of brothers, in his attachments to boyfriends he travelled with, and in his longings for the girlfriends he courted? How might his performance on a high school stage inflect his writing or his later attendance at theatrical readings shape his understanding of Shakespeare? To what extent was this white, privileged urban youth exposed to recently manumitted slaves, on the streets of New York and Albany and in his own family? How was his evolving political consciousness shaped by his awareness of underclass Jews, free and freed African Americans, emotionally vexed sailors, loving and threatening Polynesians, and missionaries, both inspiring and corrupt? How was his sense of time, space, matter, and language altered by his shifting relation to the economy, first as a bank and store clerk, and then when he climbed into the rigging of a ship, and then again when he negotiated the literary marketplace? What moments inland or at sea occasioned his sense of the sublime, and then the picturesque? When did he touch the flesh – living or dead – of a whale and make contact with the consciousness of "other beings than man" (MD 79)? Apart from momentous losses in his life – a father, beloved cousins and siblings, a son – how did he endure everyday traumas as a farmhand, teacher, debater, or lover; in school, at work, at sea? Where did he get his anger? his sense of nothingness but his hunger for god? his obsession with materiality yet openness to transcendence?

For the biographer, these when-and-where questions of consciousness require a cultural context. We begin with the assumption that a writer's workshop is not entirely private but operates within domestic and public spheres. The challenge lies in supplying a reliable narrative – one that is conditional not "arched" – that connects the formative moments of a private *past* to the creative *then* of Melville's transformations of memory to the public *now* of composition, revision, and publication. To find meaning in these layered moments, we look for recurring practices: his staged intrusions of memory interrupting a narrative; his deployment of accident despite probability and necessity in plot and his bafflement over "strange emotions" in characters; his pushing of materiality into symbol as if to mimic transcendence; his replaying of scene, image, and phrase as if writing were a working through of traumas sourced in everyday alienations; his incessant revision in manuscript and changes in print; his growth out of first-person into third-person narration; his transformation from a prose writer to a poet and back. And what of his play with his most public tool: language? Melville imagined himself – or at least Ishmael does – as a "smuggling verbalist." Melville's verbalism was nurtured early on, at home, among his highly verbal siblings: how might we read Melville as both a maritime loner and a cosmopolitan and yet a domestic homebody, always awash in words?

Even though a consciousness is ungraspable, we continue to grasp at it, and biography is a critical grasping. Two episodes in my biography – abstracted in my retelling of them here – narrativize moments in Melville's family life that shaped his literary practice. They involve two women – a sister and an actress.

A Sibling Coterie of Writers: The Example of Augusta

Language was a central feature in the Melville parlor, and after the death of their ebullient father, Herman's equally effusive older brother Gansevoort took the father's place, trained himself in oration, and facilitated his siblings' absorption into language by proctoring, correcting, and nurturing them in their school compositions. Gansevoort's revisions appear on rough drafts of ten essays that Herman's younger sister Augusta submitted to instructors at the Albany Female Academy in 1836–38 when she was sixteen. Augusta Melville's compositions show the growth in sophistication of an already talented writer, from her jejune "History of a Hat" to deeper expressions of loss and yearning, in her essays on grief, the passing of fathers, the Sabbath, and Jesus on Mount Olive. Her essay on the poetry of Felicia Hemans also reveals a promising literary critic and her aspiration to be a poet. Her quotations from Hemans in this and other compositions disclose a family respect for this generally dismissed poet, whose bridal poems were echoed decades later in Melville's Rose Poem, "Under the Ground." Augusta brought an appreciation for Hemans into the Melville family parlor and a broadening of poetic perspective for her otherwise Byron-soaked older brothers.

On some of Augusta's compositions, a proud twenty-year-old Gansevoort had ornately inscribed "Corrected by GM," as a seal of validation and, incidentally, as his claim of his shared ownership of the piece he edited. Augusta's 1838 term paper on the uses and abuses of power throughout history – only half of it survives – is riddled with his revisions; it is, as Augusta puts it, "my composition with my dear Gansevoorts corrections." In her framing of the sibling collaboration, her claim of textual possession ("my composition") precedes her acknowledgment of her brother's editing. This fluid text of layered writings – Gansevoort's revisions inscribed atop Augusta's original expression – records a conflict of political and religious ideas. But in this manuscript version, the conflict is frozen in mid-struggle. Since no fair copy of the term paper exists, we cannot know to what degree Augusta adopted or rejected her brother's revisions.

Nor can we be certain how Augusta and Herman negotiated with their older editor brother. In 1835, sixteen-year-old Herman was also composing "themes" at the Albany Classical School, earning the praise of his instructor, Charles E. West (Gilman 71; Log 1.64). Since Melville's school papers no longer exist, we can only assume that, like his sister during this same period, he also submitted his rough drafts to Gansevoort for "correction." However, solid evidence that Herman was in the similar family habit of seeking Gansevoort's editing does not emerge in the record until ten years later. In Melville's 1845 working draft manuscript of *Typee*, we find Gansevoort's deletion of several lines of sexual content that do not appear in print. In all probability, Herman had, like his sister Augusta, submitted to Gansevoort's editing during his teenage school years and returned to the habit in his drafting of *Typee*. Interestingly, though, while Herman agreed to tone down his sexualized rhetoric, Augusta may have been more resistant to Gansevoort's editing of her term paper since some of her brother's revisions add wordings that flatly contradict her original arguments. Whereas Gansevoort's revisions of Herman are sexual expurgations, his revisions of Augusta attempt to change her ideas. Her egalitarian philanthropist John Howard, for instance, becomes, in Gansevoort's editing, a Christian elitist. Since a final draft of Augusta's term paper does not survive, we cannot know if she accepted or resisted Gansevoort's changes. But it is enough to know that these possibilities existed in the Melville family of writers and editors. Whatever the scenario, the dynamics of writing, revision, and textual ownership in this sibling coterie – an embryonic stage in the development of Melville as an "author function" – suggest that the collaborative nature of Melville's creative process was nurtured in the family parlor.

In addition, Augusta's 1838 term paper reveals a pattern of research and appropriation, typical of Melville's own creative process. She transforms source materials through clever mixings of quotation, plagiarism, paraphrase, and invention, a pattern in her brother's process familiar to most Melville researchers and many readers. One heavily used resource in the Melville coterie was *The Carcanet*, an anthology of inspirational writings and love poems. Curiously, Herman received this literary volume as an award for "ciphering," that is arithmetic, at the Albany Academy in 1831. Over the years, this prize book became a public document for family use, and the marginalia on almost every page attests to its heavy use as a resource by at least two of the siblings. Augusta quoted from it in her compositions, and Herman used it to court girls. On a flyleaf, he inscribed a sensual duet from John Gay's *The Beggar's Opera* and allowed girlfriends to add their names there as well. Given Augusta's research into death and grief over deceased fathers – evident in two of her weekly compositions – and given Herman's research into love, the *Carcanet* marginalia are a remarkable mingling of variant sibling longings.

Another coterie resource is Augusta's notes based on a series of school lectures on how historical research into ancient Jewish practices can demystify otherwise obscure biblical scriptures. Augusta's glossing of an odd passage from the Gospel of Matthew about sticking to your "house top" during the apocalypse resonates with Melville's *Battle-Pieces* poem "The House-top," which presumes an understanding of the apocalyptic implications of the biblical vantage point of Judaean roofs. Augusta's bible study is generally dismissed as a sign of her piety in light of her brother's skepticism. But in all likelihood Melville's bible study profited from parlor discussions with his sister. At any rate, biblical research (not just Bible reading) was a family affair.

While I believe I am the first biographer to identify this sibling coterie of writers, I have to wonder why. I did not "discover" the relevant documents hidden in some bread box; they are not a part of the recently discovered Augusta Papers. These documents have been available for inspection since the 1940s. Leyda excerpted some of Augusta's compositions in the 1951 *Melville Log*, and yet decades of scholars have ignored them. They have been hiding in plain sight. What, then, has impeded the disclosure of this family dynamic? Granted, the relevant documents are dispersed. Augusta's compositions and lecture notes are at the New York Public Library; Herman's *Carcanet* at Yale's Beinecke Library. Because these documents are not fully transcribed or edited, they remain "coded," so to speak. Putting these documents together on a single desktop requires digitization and the decoding of manuscripts and marginalia through transcription, fluid-text editing, and contextual annotation.

But a more serious impediment involves a certain blindness in the culture of Melville studies. The tendency in Melville biography has been to minimize the role that the "Melville women" played in shaping Melville's language and discourse. Augusta is perceived to be a scrivener not a poet, a believer not a doubter, a lover of female writers not Byron. But as Wyn Kelley shows, Augusta's "literary thirst" was profound,[11] and she was a respected model of thought and expression within the family. Still, we have yet to comprehend her critical impact on Melville's writing, largely because of an implicit misogyny in Melville biography that has marginalized Melville's female siblings.[12] We do not read Augusta's essays, because we have chosen not to see them, or her.

Reading Shakespeare: The Example of Fanny Kemble

This blindness extends to women on the periphery of the Melville family. The actress Fanny Kemble, who electrified audiences in Britain and America, was a Melville family acquaintance. In Summer 1833, Kemble brought her first tour of America to Albany, and Herman's oldest sister Helen was in attendance, probably escorted by Gansevoort and Herman. Soon after, Melville's mother Maria met the actress while visiting Elizabeth Sedgwick in Lenox, MA. Helen, who attended Sedgwick's School for Young Ladies in 1835, observed Kemble closer at hand when the actress sought refuge from her failing marriage, at the Sedgwick home. In later years, Kemble returned to the Berkshires, led Sedgwick's students on field trips and outings, coached them in their weekly Shakespeare memorizations, bought a house in Lenox, shared meals with the Melvilles at the Sedgwicks' house, and is credited with initiating, in the 1840s, the practice of hiking up nearby Monument Mountain to read William Cullen

Bryant's poem of that title, a tradition more memorably re-enacted when Sedgwick's nephew Harry led Melville, Hawthorne, and others on the same hike in 1850.

In response to custody proceedings stemming from her divorce from the American slaveholder Pierce Butler, Kemble began her second tour of America in fall 1848. But she returned to the stage with a difference. Kemble had always abhorred the histrionics of her "unpoetical craft": the strutting, fretting, and "wretched, tawdry, glittering rages" of the stage; in particular, Juliet's "fumbling for [Romeo's] dagger." Eschewing performance altogether, she would now offer programs of selected readings that permitted audiences to absorb the poetry of Shakespeare's lines, without the distractions of stagecraft. She appeared alone, at a desk on stage, without other actors and without "acting!" In letters to her friends, she stated that "The happiness of reading Shakespeare's heavenly imaginations is so far beyond all the excitement of acting them."[13]

When Kemble arrived in Boston, in February 1849, Melville was in town with his pregnant wife Elizabeth to assist in the birth of their first child Malcolm. Melville assisted by making himself absent: he attended two of Kemble's performances. Though Melville found fault with Kemble's too-sweet interpretation of Desdemona, he deemed her Lady Macbeth to be "glorious." That week he also purchased the six-volume Hilliard and Gray edition of Shakespeare, began reading, and fired off his 24 February letter to Evert Duyckinck, claiming: "Dolt & ass that I am I have lived more than 29 years, & until a few days ago, never made close acquaintance with the divine William." While Melville's earlier, random "acquaintance" with Shakespeare had included the intimacy of his own performance of Shylock in high school, attendance at performances, and the memorization of lines for classroom oration, he was now ready for "closer," more systematic reading. His 1850 review essay of "Hawthorne and his Mosses" registers this new absorption that he had begun to acquire in 1849, triggered by Kemble's staged readings. His revelations about Shakespeare resemble Kemble's. Like Kemble, Melville disdains the "Richard-the-Third humps, and Macbeth daggers" of stagecraft. He echoes Kemble's equation of Shakespeare's poetry to scripture: what she calls "heavenly imaginations," he attributes to the "Divine William." What makes "Shakespeare, Shakespeare," Melville writes, are "those deep far-away things in him; those occasional flashings-forth of the intuitive Truth in him; those short, quick probings at the very axis of reality" (PT 244). Kemble and Melville are spheres of equivalent gravity revolving around one brilliant star, and we have yet to acknowledge the pull that the actress had on the novelist.

February 1849 was a turning point in Melville's thinking about Shakespeare, literary genius, and writing; and Fanny Kemble was center stage for Melville's turning. And yet, as with Augusta, Melville biographers have been blind to Kemble. Once again: why? In addition to her protracted and notorious divorce, Kemble enjoyed scandalizing Victorian society on both sides of the Atlantic by wearing bloomers, fly-fishing from rowboats, and riding horseback *comme les garçons*. Kemble's masculine bearing had more to do with her forthright, "manful" character than her sexual orientation, and she was for many men who observed her as appealing in her manliness as she was unconventional. Although Melville's jokey disparagement of Kemble's masculine femininity in his letter to Duyckinck is ungracious, the letter's revealing critique of Kemble's performances of Shakespeare is a recognition of her genius. Conceivably, Kemble merits as much attention as Hawthorne during this transitional moment in Melville's thinking. Even so, an early critical speculation that Melville based his negative characterization of the manly Goneril in *The Confidence-Man* on Kemble – an argument debunked by Elizabeth Foster – remains one of the few studies we have of Kemble's influence on Melville, and it is a study of rejection.[14]

Given her presence among the Melvilles as a performer, teacher, and neighbor, Kemble was a "sister" in an extended version of the Melville family coterie. Apart from her shared perspective on Shakespeare, Kemble's transgendered identity resonates with Melville's range of masculinities. Kemble is an opening into the study of the role of women in Melville's evolving consciousness and aesthetic sensibility, but only if we choose to see her.

For some, my apologia for biography will seem obvious, and I apologize if I belabor the need for a return to biographical criticism. Even so, my point is not to demand that you compose a biography of your own, though I join with Jay Leyda in encouraging critics to read Melville biographically, which implies certain acts of biography. Rather, I want to imagine a return to a more effective form of biographical criticism in our aesthetic and historicist approaches to the study of writing and culture in general, and Melville in particular. By grounding biographical criticism in representations of the evolution of a writer's multistranded consciousness, biographies can model approaches to the interpretation of texts, approaches that clarify how the strategies of individual creative processes function within cultural discourses. Such a return permits a closer inspection of "the

Melville function": How the description of the brow of a whale swimming in the Pacific evokes prairie grasses; or how travels in Egypt and Rome recall Kentucky and the Ohio; or how, in Melville, place is a collocation of thought and feeling that permits place to recall place, or how materiality gestures toward the immaterial; or how a sister or an actress can trigger deeper investigations into poetry. In this and many other ways waiting to be tried, biography is an opening into the critical fusion of experience and interpretation.

CHAPTER 15

Afterword
"New," "Old," and "With"

Robert S. Levine

The New Melville Studies offers stimulating critical essays on Melville as a philosopher, theorist, poet, cultural critic, and artist, paying close attention to Melville's style, humor, and experiments with form and genre. The interest in form and genre points to a related contribution: an emphasis on Melville as a "transbellum" writer whose career is much longer and more considerable than the novel writing years – 1846 to 1857 – that critics typically focus on.[1] Several essays make the case not only for the value of Melville's poetry, which he published between 1866 and 1891, but for the importance of considering the poetry and fiction together as parts of an unfolding career in which different phases are in conversation with one another (see the essays by Otter, Duquette, Osborne, and Yothers in particular). But is any of this really "new," or might we concur with the narrator of *Moby-Dick* "that for the millionth time we say amen with Solomon – Verily there is nothing new under the sun" (MD 209)? Perhaps with that Solomonic injunction in mind, I found that I was intrigued by the volume's claim to be doing "The New Melville Studies." Without a "new" in the title, are other books on Melville, whether collections or monographs, by default doing the old Melville studies? The question is worth some investigation. I'll say up front that I believe there is something new about this volume, and that the newness pivots on editor Cody Marrs's use of the word "with" in the section titles of the two parts of his anthology: "Feeling with Melville" and "Thinking with Melville."

What does it mean to be "with" Melville and how does the "with" in this volume differ from more traditional approaches to Melville? I would suggest that reckoning with tensions between the old and new remains a crucial part of doing critical work on Melville. In order to address those tensions, and as a way of framing the essays in this collection, I want to return to the 1990s and consider a seminal moment in Melville studies: the publication in 1994 of a special issue of *American Literature* titled "New

Melville." That issue can be usefully compared to a book published just two years earlier, Brian Higgins and Hershel Parker's *Critical Essays on Herman Melville's Moby-Dick*, which contributors to the *American Literature* issue would no doubt have regarded as an exemplary instance of the old Melville.

Higgins and Parker's book, it should be said, is an essential reference work, one that I continue to consult. It collects reviews, articles, and chapters ranging from 1851 to 1992, mostly working with excerpts so that there are over 100 selections, including three in a concluding section called "New Essays." Newness is important not only to the volume's concluding section but also to the introduction, where the editors celebrate "the beginning of a new era in Melville scholarship." But as they quickly make clear, that new era only further develops the work that Parker and other scholars associated with the Northwestern-Newberry edition of Melville had been doing for the past twenty years. Thus their introduction hails the publication of the 1988 Northwestern-Newberry *Moby-Dick* as the scholarly achievement ushering in the new era. The introduction points to other new developments as well, but they all involve Northwestern-Newberry editors and scholars, particularly Parker, whose then forthcoming two-volume biography of Melville, we're told, promises to be the capstone of the new era. For the editors, the "new" means better textual editions, a more comprehensive understanding of literary influences and affinities, and an overall more capacious appreciation of Melville's greatness. What the new does not mean is reading Melville in relation to critical theory, which seems clear when the editors lament that "*Moby-Dick* has been subjected to every fashionable academic approach, Freudian, Jungian, Marxist, neo-Christian, existential, New Critical, myth, structuralist, poststructuralist, reader-response, deconstruction, New Historicist, in addition to a multitude of thematic studies."[2] Significantly, Higgins and Parker have nothing to say about feminist approaches, and in that regard it's worth pointing out that of their over 100 selections, only three are by women. They ignore the key contributions of Joyce Sparer Adler, Ann Douglass, Carolyn Karcher, and many others, while choosing not to commission a woman critic for the volume's concluding section of "New Essays."

That section consists of an essay by David Reynolds on *Moby-Dick* and popular culture, an essay by John Wenke on "Melville's Learning," and an essay by Parker on "*Moby-Dick* and Domesticity." The first two essays are consistent with the volume's emphasis on literary sources and influences. Parker's essay is of particular interest for its effort to say something new about Melville and women from a biographical perspective. Still, there is something old about this new essay. As Parker tells the biographical story, Melville appreciated the women of his household for providing "the comfortable and comforting domesticity he had grown used to," which allowed him to be "absolutely free to read and write." Parker then shares Melville's anger when, right around the time he began *Moby-Dick*, the women's work on "household chores did not end abruptly at the projected time" and Melville's "working conditions degenerated." This was especially true after his wife, Elizabeth Shaw, became pregnant. Melville, who loved domestic comforts, now began to see the women of the house (who were also charged with copying his nearly illegible drafts) as distracting nuisances, and so in his imagination he decides to leave port (home) and go to sea. *Moby-Dick*, Parker concludes, is at least in part "about the rival – and incompatible – claims of creativity and marriage." According to Parker, Melville heroically chose creativity.[3]

Such was Higgins and Parker's Melville of 1992. Two years later, the editors of *American Literature* presented a very different Melville in a special issue called "New Melville." The unsigned preface, presumably by the journal's editors, Cathy N. Davidson and Michael Moon, asserts that "new critical concerns" can play a significant role in the effort to offer insights into "such recurrent Melville questions as sexuality, textuality, violence, the pastoral, innocence, authorship, and canon formation." Unlike Higgins and Parker, the editors offer an almost utopian embrace of theory as something that revolutionizes the field, enabling critics to "augment our understanding of Melville's work and investigate the interconnections between Melville's texts and aesthetic, social, cultural, and political preoccupations of the day."[4] The issue includes Paul Lauter on Melville's place in the canon (a study which is not especially theoretical), Caleb Crain on the anxious place of homosexuality in Melville's writings (a reading influenced by the emergence of queer studies), Samuel Otter on landscape and ideology in *Pierre* (a piece influenced by postcolonial studies), and Nancy Ruttenberg on directness and indirectness in *Billy Budd* (a fairly traditional approach, though she does invoke Foucault). To my mind the "new" is best exemplified by the two concluding essays: Julian Markels's "The *Moby-Dick* White Elephant" and Elizabeth Renker's "Herman Melville, Wife Beating, and the Written Page." Markels works with textual theory and Renker with a feminist, biographical, and textual approach. But the newness of these essays is less about theory than about critical positioning within the field of Melville studies.

To be blunt: Operationally speaking, in 1994 (and even before) "New Melville" meant working with Melville in a manner different from the Northwestern-Newberry editors and the scholars associated with their textual project. This is not to say that doing new Melville required rejecting the extraordinary achievements of those editors and scholars. But it did mean raising questions about the critical practice of those scholars who, at the time, often served as the gatekeepers of Melville studies. In his essay, Markels takes on the Northwestern-Newberry *Moby-Dick*, the very work that Higgins and Parker had celebrated for inaugurating a new era in Melville studies. That volume is quite an achievement, but is it beyond critical investigation? The volume includes nearly 500 pages of textual, biographical, bibliographical, and historical material. That material, Markels argues in his essay, "monumentalizes a deeply compromised ideology of scholarship peculiar to these editors," an ideology that saw Melville's texts as corrupted by his "editors, printers, and proofreaders." Convinced of the existence of such corruption, the textual editors' stated goal for their edition of *Moby-Dick* was to somehow recover what Melville "intended" to publish, thereby creating a text that was not published in Melville's lifetime. According to Markels, the editors also used their appendices to call attention to the existence of a "metatext" that would support co-editor Harrison Hayford's idea that there are two *Moby-Dick*s (the novel we know and the adventure novel Melville may have initially begun to write). Hayford's bibliographical overview, Markels asserts, seeks "to obscure the dynamic process of *Moby-Dick* scholarship and to valorize as if it were definitive the fifty-year history of activity by those who share his [Hayford's] quasi-positivist assumptions." Hayford and his co-editors, Markels concludes, use "this edition both to promulgate and at the same time insulate their interpretations from engagement with rival interpretations that can be as knowledgeable as theirs."[5] In effect, the editors of the Northwestern-Newberry *Moby-Dick* sought to marginalize the new.

Markels has equally strong concerns about Hershel Parker's 127-page historical note, which in 1988 anticipated (or actually set forth) the arguments of his essay on Melville and domesticity in the "New Essays" section of his 1992 coedited collection. In this historical note, which Markels says is informed by "methodological misogyny," Parker tells the story that he would tell four years later about how Melville was the victim of the very women who nurtured him and helped to prepare his manuscripts. Parker, to quote from his historical note, indicts Melville's mother, wife, and sisters (all of whom were living with him at the time) for having "imperfectly understood his [Melville's] needs as a writer." Parker notes, as he would in his 1992 essay, that while Melville worked on the manuscript of *Moby-Dick*, he and his wife conceived their son Stanwix, and that the pregnancy added to the disruptions of the household. As Markels sums up from his reading of Parker's historical note, which by its placement in an MLA-approved volume canonized a particular way of thinking about Melville and women: "Evidently the women who loved Melville could have understood his needs more perfectly if they could have managed to be seen and not heard except when they were called on to copy or copulate."[6]

Women as copyists is one of the central concerns of Elizabeth Renker's "Herman Melville, Wife Beating, and the Written Page," an essay which, at least in part, is also positioned against scholars associated with the Northwestern-Newberry edition. An admirer of Melville's writing, Renker asks probing questions about Melville treatment of the women in his family, and she does so in the service of better understanding his writing. Taking as her starting point the evidence that Melville's possible violent outbursts against his wife had long been ignored or covered up by the Melville establishment, she presents fairly convincing evidence that Melville either beat or threatened or was just plain cruel to his wife. She discloses that there was a family plot to "kidnap" Elizabeth Shaw during the 1860s as a way of liberating her from her husband. For Renker, this evidence needs to be aired, and just as importantly, she argues, scholars need to further explore Melville's "tortured relationship to his writing and his simultaneous dependence on and resentment of the Melville women whose labor he needed to produce his texts." Back in 1994, when I first read the essay, I thought that Renker offered a genuinely new way of thinking about how Melville tended to "associate women with blank pages and textual production." But from the point of view of many Melvilleans, Renker had committed a primal sin in working against the notion of Melville as victimized by the women of his family. The editors of *American Literature* were brave to print the essay; Renker, for intrepidly developing a new perspective on Melville, was vilified in Melville circles for years to come.[7]

Twenty-five years after the special issue on "New Melville," Cody Marrs, in his introduction to *The New Melville Studies*, suggests that the "pull between the old and new" contributes to the vitality of Melville studies. I would agree, which is why I've spent some time discussing the moment during the 1990s when the old and new were in direct conflict. But here is where Marrs's "with" provides us with a way past the impasse between the old and new. As he elaborates in the introduction, one of the goals of the volume is to read Melville as a writer who could critique his culture and raise some of the same theoretical issues about art, politics, and culture that we're engaging right now. In the essays in the collection, Marrs states, critics do not situate themselves outside of Melville in an ironic or diagnostic fashion, but instead read him "horizontally, immanently, from positions within or next to Melville's works." To some extent, it could be argued that the desire to be "with" Melville is precisely what characterized the old Melville studies, the idea that the critic could, in Marrs's words, follow Melville's "thoughts as they rise, fall, ripen, or jolt." But there is an important difference between the old and new Melville scholarship in terms of the "with": the idea that, as Marrs puts it, "Melville's writings also vivify an important axiom: how we interpret something – including whether and to what extent we critique it – depends on one's perspective, and the best interpretations are based on multiple, juxtaposed perspectives." In this sense, the critics in this volume try to take account of and even inhabit the "myriad viewpoints" immanent in Melville's writings.

I am especially interested in the way the "with" works in relation to critical theory, and along these lines it is worth recalling the dismissal of critical theory in the introduction to Higgins and Parker's volume. That dismissal fails to consider that Melville himself might have worked, at least in part, as a critical theorist. After all, to focus just on *Moby-Dick*, it doesn't take too much effort to read Melville as a sort of reader-response critic ("And what are you, reader, but a Loose-Fish and a Fast-Fish, too?"); queer theorist (see Ishmael and Queequeq and "A Squeeze of the Hand"); eco-critic (see the entire novel); proto-deconstructionist (see Pip in "The Doubloon" chapter); and a Marxist or class-oriented critic (see the paean to the "meanest mariners, and renegades and castaways"). These are of course selective examples from a novel that insistently foregrounds issues of interpretation. By regarding Melville himself as a critical theorist, we can begin to see him as a writer who deepens and enriches our own critical enterprise.[8] There is something new about that.

An effort to think about Melville in relation to critical theory, and as a critical theorist himself (and thus to think "with" Melville) can be seen in numerous essays in the volume. As I discuss below, there is also theoretical cross talk that links a number of the essays across the somewhat arbitrary division of "Feeling with Melville" and "Thinking with Melville" (another strength of the volume is that this two-part division is presented in terms of emphasis; the sections constitute a dualism rather than a binary).

Jennifer Greiman's "Melville and the Conceits of Theory" is definitely well placed in the "Thinking with Melville" section, as this is a theoretically dense discussion of Melville's *Pierre* in relation to such philosophers and critical thinkers as Bruno Latour, Gilles Deleuze, and Jacques Rancière. One might ask how Melville could be thinking "with" critics working approximately 100 years after his death, but right from the start Greiman does a fine job of linking the concerns of these theorists to Melville's representation of "the crisis that wrecks the moral and intellectual life of Melville's Pierre Glendinning" as he explores such theoretical issues as "the processes of figuration and fabulation that are central to both literature and philosophy." Overall, this is less a Latourian, Deleuszian, or Rancièrian reading of Melville's sometimes baffling novel than a Melvillean reading of recent theory. Greiman makes her case about the importance of philosophy to the novel through a trenchant reading of "Chronometricals and Horologicals," the fragment from Plinlimmon's theoretical text that Pierre unknowingly wears in the lining of his coat. As Greiman wittily puts it, Pierre "does not know that he is theorized by his own coat," and she concludes that theory "fails when it does not recognize that it shares a common hermeneutic plot with literature itself – a plot in which the very thing we try to read slips between a surface and a lining to be carried unwittingly everywhere." Pierre, as Greiman put it, is "failed by both the surfaces and depths of his reading." Even in this complex essay on "thinking," there is "feeling" as well, for there is something wrenching about what Greiman terms Pierre's "unknowing comprehension" of his fate as he hurtles toward his death.

Greiman's reference to surfaces and depths leads me to Justine S. Murison's "Paranoid Reading, Surface Pleasures, and Deadpan Humor in *The Confidence-Man*." Like Greiman, Murison deftly uses current debates about critical theory to illuminate Melville's elusive novel of 1857 (which, too often, is read allegorically as having a single meaning).[9] By reading with Melville, Murison deploys *The Confidence-Man* to raise questions about the very theoretical works she adduces; she thus creates a conversation between Melville and our own contemporary critics that illuminates both. Specifically, she deploys Stephen Best and Sharon Marcus's work on "Surface Reading" to help us better understand a novel in which the characters seem little more than surfaces, while at the same time calling attention to the ways that Melville's ironical deadpan humor underscores "the depth of surfaces and the perversities of a joke."[10] Humor, she points out, tends not to be part of debates about surfaces and depths or paranoid/reparative reading as elaborated by Eve Sedgwick. However, in her close reading of the novel, Murison shows how Melville's humor works both to develop and undercut the novel's paranoid structure of misdirection and conspiracy. The essay significantly contributes to debates about surface reading, showing how Melville's deadpan "undoes the surface-depth model" and presciently illuminates "the role of pleasure in our own hermeneutics of suspicion." Ultimately, Murison's approach encourages the reader to enjoy *The Confidence-Man* as sheer textual fun.

In contrast with Murison's description of the "intense pleasure" of reading *The Confidence-Man*, Elizabeth Duquette, like many readers of the novel, regards it as "a tedious but important slog." Duquette's fascinating reading of "*The Confidence-Man* between Genres" analyzes the novel's "relationship to both philosophy and Melville's turn to poetry." She sees *The Confidence-Man* as "on a trajectory toward poetic form" as it addresses "problems inherent to the poetic process as rigorously as it rejects those associated with the narrative one." Duquette, like Murison and Greiman, reads Melville with the theorists. Influenced by Sianne Ngai's notion that *The Confidence-Man* is more sonorous than semantic, that "anaphora [word repetitions in various forms] overtakes analogy as the book's "defining feature," Duquette nonetheless locates Melville within a philosophical tradition of writings about analogy going back to Plato. Her reading of anaphora helps to explain Melville's move toward poetic form, but it also leads to a better understanding of how analogies "provide the basic mechanism for sympathetic identification and create the equality celebrated in the nation's founding documents." Analogies, in other words, can be approached philosophically and politically, and in *The Confidence-Man*, she declares, Melville shows how analogies, like the nation's institutions, can be "easily perverted and manipulated."

The idea of Melville as both a reader of philosophy and a philosopher himself informs other essays in the volume. Michael Jonik's "Melville, *Mardi*, and Materialism" examines Melville in relation to philosophic theory with a vengeance, but the theorists he focuses on are not those that Melville was anticipating but actually reading on materialism and idealism: Berkeley, Hume, Priestly, and especially Hartley and Coleridge. As an essay on the philosophical underpinnings of *Mardi*, this reminded me (in a good way) of the approach to Melville that can be found in the Northwestern-Newberry editions. But Jonik does develop a fresh perspective on a novel that continues to frustrate many of Melville's readers. Rather than approach the novel in relation to metaphysical and particularly Neoplatonic idealism, Jonik makes the case for understanding the novel's world as "materially alive," even as it "moves between material and ideal coordinates." I have to say that Jonik does not make this difficult book any easier to read, but he does open up new aspects of the novel as a work of philosophical exploration. Philosophy is also important to Dominic Mastroianni's "Perfectionist *Pierre*." Like Jonik, Mastroianni is interested in the novel's engagement with materialist philosophies, but as in a number of the volume's theoretically oriented essays, he sees Melville anticipating new critical approaches, such as posthumanism. Over the course of his analysis, Mastroianni identifies an aspect of *Pierre* that, as far as I know, no one has previously explored: the various ways that it plumbs the question of "how do bodies move?" Mastroianni adduces numerous moments in the novel of sliding, stepping, and other forms of movement (which he discusses in relation to Calvin, Kant, Emerson and Frederick Douglass), and shows how Melville links posture and gait to cognition in the manner of Wittgenstein. As in Murison's essay, there is much fun in the critical brio here, which, to Mastroianni's credit, seems adjacent to Melville's own perspective in his weird and wonderful novel. However strange the novel might seem, Mastroianni concludes, it wants to teach us the disturbing truth "that in the world as we find it, we may be most unfree, and inflict harm most thoughtlessly and insensibly, most casually, just where it feels easiest to move."

Arguably, this is a terrific way of talking about US and European imperialism as it developed during the nineteenth-century, and that is the subject of Edward Sugden's "Marginal States: Herman Melville in the Marquesas, 1842." I'm not sure that this essay is truly "with" Melville, but Sugden does an excellent job of challenging sometimes overly optimistic notions of the border as "a place of permeable interchange between different cultures." He proposes as an alternative or supplement to border studies the concept of the "marginal state," which "marks the point between the edge of the world-system and an area as yet unincorporated into it." His reading of *Typee* as a work that challenges the easy comforts of transnational exchange is bracing. My concern is that the seriousness of Sugden's subject – the unidirectional force of imperialism and capitalism – leads him to neglect the role of what Murison terms deadpan humor in the work's cultural thematics. There are a number of comic exchanges in the novel, with the humor of those exchanges pivoting on the way Melville ironically depicts Tommo's failed efforts to makes sense of his situation. Sugden claims that Tommo experiences "the vertiginous and dizzying experience of being outside of a power structure, outside of a community, outside of a polis," but in my reading Tommo is never outside and his entire experience is mediated by his western literary and cultural perspectives. Melville's emphasis on the limits of the perspectives that most readers bring to the novel contributes to the humor of a book that, as we can see from Mastroianni's essay, also charts how people(s) move.

Movement of course is absolutely crucial to the crisis moments in *Billy Budd*, a novella that Paul Hurh reads as "about the loss of an earnest, non-ironic position within a world full of hidden motives and powers." Irony is central to my reading of *Typee* and to Murison's reading of *The Confidence-Man*. In "*Billy Budd*: Pessimism for Post-Critique," Hurh raises questions about ironic ways of reading, both in the novella and in the history of criticism of the novella, arguing that the novella suggests "a structural and historical account of the rise of ironist reading that implicates the liberal ideals that often justify our own work." In a tour de force discussion that takes into account the history of the critical debate on the novella, the novella's formal workings, and recent work on paranoid and reparative reading, Hurh places his greatest emphasis on Melville's turn to pessimism as influenced by his reading of Schopenhauer. Hurh maintains that Melville saw in pessimism "an ethical imperative based on compassion without hope." Read through Schopenhauer, whom Melville was reading at the time, "Billy's strike against Claggart is the expression of the utter lack of alternative defenses available to earnestness within a world of duplicity." According to the pessimism of Melville, Schopenhauer, and, it seems, Hurh himself, all that we are left with in a world lacking in hope and ultimate meaning is "a deep and empathetic bond of fellowship between sufferers." That bond of fellowship is most profoundly conveyed in the novella through its concluding poem, "Billy in the Darbies."

As mentioned in the opening of this Afterword, one of the volume's major contributions is the approach to Melville's poetry. Instead of presenting Melville as having two careers – that of a novelist and then that of a poet – various contributors make a case that the poetry and prose should be read together (as at the end of *Billy Budd*). Duquette's essay, I should note, seems a bit more like the "old" Melville in the way it argues for *The Confidence-Man* as a transitional work in terms of genre. But consider the challenge to the notion that there is a significant transition from "the earlier exuberant prose" to the supposedly "exhausted poetry" in Samuel Otter's "Melville's Style." Otter's essay focuses on the close connections between the 1846 novel *Typee* and the 1876 epic poem *Clarel*, which Otter regards as Melville's rewriting of the Marquesan encounters in *Typee*. Otter develops his argument through close attention to diction, syntax, and figure in an effort to present Melville's career as Melville may have understood it in 1876. After all, as Otter points out, the Marquesas have a key role near the end of *Clarel* in the canto titled "The Prodigal." Just as importantly, both works make use of a verbal style that disorients and makes alien that which might seem familiar, and in both works Melville asks such question as, "What does it mean to see sights? To keep time? To encounter strangers?" As Otter illustrates, Melville's poetry is as exuberant, disorienting, and surprising as his prose. And the key to reading all of Melville's writing, he says, is reckoning with the "peculiar verbal sensuousness and strenuousness" of what we can understand as Melville's trans-generic style.

Gillian Kidd Osborne's "Melville and His Flowers" develops a similar perspective on the connections between the later poetry and Melville's earlier writings. Concentrating on the relatively little-known poetry volume *Weeds & Wildings: Chiefly with a Rose or Two*, which Melville left unfinished at his death, she argues in the vein of Otter for reading the late poems as "continuous with Melville's earlier work in its examination of what literature makes of life." She builds a strong case for reading the love poems in *Weeds & Wildings*, which many believe are directed at Elizabeth Shaw, as in fact directed at Hawthorne. In that sense, the poems Melville wrote shortly before his death in 1891 can be linked to the 1850s. But in her study of what she terms the poems' "intimacy effect," an effect which can also be read across Melville's career, Osborne does more than examine Melville's expression of feelings about Hawthorne. By focusing on the importance of flowers to that volume, and to Hawthorne's writing as well, she revises our understanding of gender in Melville's writing across the decades. Melville, she asserts, in this and other of his works "adopts the floweriness of nineteenth-century American women's writing: he writes *like* a woman." This claim leads her to remark on "the instabilities of feminized qualities in nineteenth-century writing by male authors, including Melville," an insight that suggests new ways of reading such works as *Pierre*.

Unlike Otter and Osborne, Eliza Richards in "Popular Networks in Melville's *Battle-Pieces and Aspects of the War*" addresses Melville's poetry not across his career but across the time and space of the American Civil War. Like Otter, Richards studies Melville's style, but instead of emphasizing its uniqueness, she discusses the poetry in relation to that of popular Civil War poets. Challenging the "old" Melville studies, particularly Parker's claim that Melville was a transcendent genius who was not influenced by supposedly conventional contemporary Civil War poets, Richards identifies literary "networks" that help to illuminate Melville's connections to a wide range of experimental and formally innovative Civil War poets. Edmund Clarence Stedman and Henry Howard Brownell are particularly compelling examples of such poets. On the basis of her comparative readings, Richards concludes that Melville during the Civil War sought to establish "poetic networks that extend the fabric of utterance beyond his own character of personality." This view of a networked Melville is not all that different from the Melville of Christopher Freeburg's "Pip and the Sounds of Blackness in *Moby-Dick*." Just as Richards reads Melville in close relation to Civil War poets of the period, Freeburg, in the tradition of Sterling Stuckey, situates *Moby-Dick* in relation to black expressive culture.[11] Freeburh's compelling take on sound in the novel links his essay to Duquette's and Jonik's, which address sound in *The Confidence-Man* and *Mardi*, respectively, and his fine reading of Pip's existential crisis offers further support to Hurh's argument on the connections between pessimism and companionship in Melville's writings.

For Brian Yothers, whose "Melville after Secularism" gives a big-picture overview of an integrated career, any study of pessimism or existentialism in Melville's writings needs to attend to tensions between the religious and the secular in his poetry and prose from the 1840s to the time of his death in 1891. According to Yothers, Melville is a "writer whose work probes the possibilities and the limits of the secular." The striking image of Ishmael at the end of *Moby-Dick* nicely captures the tensions that Yothers limns in his essay. Ishmael in Queequeg's coffin, he says, can be regarded as "a religious orphan on a secular sea – or a secular orphan borne up by a sea of faith." Yothers studies similar tensions across Melville's long career. Again, there is something new in the vision of an integrated, unfolding career in which the later works help to illuminate the earlier, and vice versa. But there is something admirably old here, too, for the portrayal of Melville as a religious writer in an increasingly secular market seems reminiscent of the Melville depicted in Ann Douglass's *The Feminization of American Culture* (1977).[12]

The tension between the new and old Melville studies can be considered one more time with respect to the volume's concluding essay, John Bryant's "The Biographical Re-Turn: Writing Melville Biography and the Example of Women." In 1992, Higgins and Parker hailed the forthcoming publication of Parker's two-volume biography of Melville as the culmination of what the contributors to the 1994 special issue of *American Literature* would have called the old Melville studies. John Bryant is currently working on a new two-volume biography of Melville. Both Parker's and Bryant's biographical enterprises depend on an additive or incremental method of finding new facts about Melville's life, and both follow a chronological trajectory. The two biographers also make clear that they believe their work allows them to know Melville, which is to say that both claim to be with Melville. But there are differences. Parker focuses on Melville's family and professional relations, literary sources and influences, and struggles to get his writings into print as he intended them. Bryant, arguably even more "adjacent" to Melville than Parker, aspires to tell the story of the emergence of Melville's art, with an emphasis on helping us to better understand Melville's artistic consciousness. Parker of course also seeks to illuminate Melville's artistic consciousness. Maybe the old and new, at least in terms of a standard biography, aren't so different after all.

Yet Bryant positions himself as different by stating that one of the goals of his biography is to address the "neglect of women in the shaping of Melville's writing." This announced goal suggests that his biography will be probing the specific conflict between the old and new Melville studies as exemplified in 1992 and 1994: Parker's insistence that the women in Melville's family let him down by not fully attending to his needs (1992) versus Renker's claim that Melville expressed rage against the women who nurtured him (1994). Where does Bryant fit in here? What sort of intervention is he making? In the brief excerpts from the biography, Bryant gives us two instances where we can consider the influence of women on Melville's artistic consciousness. First, we learn that the young Herman during 1836–1838 composed themes for the Albany Classical School along with his sister Augusta. Their older brother, Gansevoort, looked over the papers. This information leads Bryant to conclude that these three Melvilles constituted a "sibling coterie of writers." From the positivistic, chronological perspective of the biography, Augusta thus had a shaping influence on Melville's writing, and Bryant chides biographers for having been blind to this influence. But I wonder, as someone who once shared school writing with a younger sister, whether such sharing is as important as Bryant suggests. He depicts Augusta as having a strong literary bent, but questions remain about Melville's attitude toward her in 1850–1851. Is she still part of a coterie or now a beleaguered copyist who is one of the objects of Melville's rage? And what about other influences on Melville's writing from 1838–1850? We'll need to see the fuller biography to learn more.

Bryant similarly attacks biographers for their alleged blindness to the impact of the actress Fanny Kemble on Melville's imagination. (Kemble gets a brief mention in Parker's biography.) This takes us to Bryant's second instance of the impact of women on Melville's artistic consciousness. In 1849, Melville chose to attend performances of *Macbeth* instead of assisting his wife during the birth of their first child (a fact that Bryant mentions but chooses not to address). Bryant asserts that it was

Kemble's dynamic performance of Lady Macbeth that most profoundly led Melville to appreciate Shakespeare. That performance, Bryant claims, was even more important to Melville than his emerging relationship with Hawthorne. Melville may well have been electrified by Kemble, but he had already been passionately reading Shakespeare (see his annotations of Shakespeare editions), and in Hawthorne he seemed to have found a version of his darker authorial self (see the 1850 "Hawthorne and His Mosses"). Again, Bryant's claims probably can best be assessed in the context of the fuller biography. What I admire about his work is the effort to develop a more positive view of the influence of women on Melville's artistic consciousness; such an effort over a two-volume biography would certainly add to our understanding of Melville.

Marrs begins his introduction by commenting on the near-exhaustion of Melville studies. Part of that exhaustion has to do with how successful the old and new Melville studies together have been in recovering information about Melville's life and art. Much information can be found in the Northwestern-Newberry editions, and recently even more has become available via electronic media, such as in the superb "Melville's Marginalia Online," edited by Steven Olsen-Smith and Peter Norberg. One of the great virtues of the essays in this collection is that the contributors make excellent use of the information about Melville that scholars over the years have managed to track, compile, and present in a variety of formats. Another of the collection's virtues is the way that so many of the contributors use the newer criticism to reposition themselves in relation to Melville without the mediation of the old. True, we can say with Solomon and the narrator of *Moby-Dick* that there is nothing new under the sun, but under the sun (a key metaphor in Emerson for insight) everything is new when viewed with fresh eyes. And yet how difficult it is, Emerson and Melville both insist, to achieve such a perspective. If the new Melville of this volume can help us to re-envision and re-energize the old Melville, then there is both nothing new under the sun and, inevitably, something new that illuminates like the sun. With the help of contributors who are "with" Melville, *The New Melville Studies* lives up to the promise of its title.

Notes

1 Introduction

1. Christopher Castiglia, "Cold War Allegories and the Politics of Criticism," in *The New Cambridge Companion to Herman Melville*, ed. Robert S. Levine (Cambridge: Cambridge University Press, 2014), 220.
2. Robert S. Levine, "Introduction," in *The New Cambridge Companion to Herman Melville*, ed. Robert S. Levine (Cambridge: Cambridge University Press, 2014), 2.
3. Jennifer Fleissner, "After the New Americanists: The Progress of Romance and the Romance of Progress in American Literary Studies," in *A Companion to American Literary Studies*, eds. Robert S. Levine and Caroline Levander (London: Wiley-Blackwell, 2011), 174.
4. See Stephen Best and Sharon Marcus, "Surface Reading: An Introduction," *Representations* 108.1 (Fall 2009): 1–21.
5. See Eve Sedgwick, "Paranoid Reading and Reparative Reading; or, You're So Paranoid, You Probably Think This Introduction Is about You," in *Novel Gazing: Queer Readings in Fiction*, ed. Sedgwick (Durham: Duke University Press, 1997), 1–38.
6. This work is too rich and varied to responsibly summarize. But some representative studies include: Faith Barrett, *To Fight Aloud Is Very Brave: American Poetry and the Civil War* (Amherst: University of Massachusetts Press, 2012), 251–80; Hershel Parker, *Melville: The Making of a Poet* (Evanston: Northwestern University Press, 2008); Timothy Sweet, "Melville's *Battle-Pieces* and Vernacular Poetics," in *Literary Cultures of the Civil War*, ed. Timothy Sweet (Athens: University of Georgia Press, 2016), 99–118; Paul Hurh, "*Clarel*, Doubt, Delay," in *Melville's Philosophies*, eds. Branka Arsić and K. L. Evans (New York: Bloomsbury, 2017), 79–106; Elizabeth Renker, "Melville the Realist Poet," in *A Companion to Herman Melville*, ed. Wyn Kelly (London: Wiley-Blackwell, 2006), 482–96; Illana Pardes, "Melville's Song of Songs: *Clarel* as Aesthetic Pilgrimage," in *Melville and Aesthetics*, eds. Samuel Otter and Geoffrey Sanborn (New York: Palgrave, 2011), 213–34; Sanford Marovitz, ed., *Melville as Poet: The Art of "Pulsed Life"* (Kent: Kent State University Press, 2013); and the special issues of *Leviathan: A Journal of*

Melville Studies on "Late Melvilles" (October 2016), "Reading and Teaching *Clarel*" (October 2017), and "Melville the Civil War Poet" (October 2015).

7. Bruno Latour, "Why Has Critique Run Out of Steam?: From Matters of Fact to Matters of Concern," *Critical Inquiry* 30 (Winter 2004): 225–48; Rita Felski, *The Limits of Critique* (Chicago: University of Chicago Press, 2015), 1; Joseph North, *Literary Criticism: A Concise Political History* (Cambridge: Harvard University Press, 2017), 160.
8. Carolyn Lesjak: "Reading Dialectically," *Criticism* 55.2 (Spring 2013): 233–77; Timothy Bewes, "Reading with the Grain: A New World in Literary Criticism," *differences: A Journal of Feminist Cultural Criticism* 21.3 (2013): 2.
9. See Branka Arsić and K. L. Evans, eds., *Melville's Philosophies* (New York: Bloomsbury, 2017); Corey McCall and Tom Nurmi, *Melville Among the Philosophers* (Lanham: Lexington Books, 2017); Paul Hurh, *American Terror: The Feeling of Thinking in Edwards, Poe, and Melville* (Stanford: Stanford University Press, 2015). The quote comes from Arsić's Introduction to *Melville's Philosophies*, 3.
10. My thinking about Melville's thinking has been influenced by Elizabeth Heinz Swails and her dissertation-in-progress, "The Thinking Animal: Nonhuman Movement in American Romanticism."
11. As James puts it, "Toussaint L'Ouverture [was] one of the most remarkable men" from a "period rich in remarkable men ... [B]etween 1789 and 1815, with the single exception of Bonaparte himself, no single figure appeared on the historical stage more greatly gifted than this Negro." C. L. R. James, *The Black Jacobins: Toussaint L'Ouverture and the San Domingo Revolution* (New York: Vintage Books, 1989), x.
12. C. L. R. James, *Mariners, Renegades, and Castaways: The Story of Herman Melville and the World We Live In* (Hanover and London: University Press of New England, 1985), 69.
13. Elizabeth Foster, "Melville and Geology," *American Literature* 17.1 (March 1945): 50–65; Walter Bezanson, "Historical and Critical Note," in the Newberry-Northwestern edition of *Clarel*.
14. My thanks to Dominic Mastroianni for suggesting this comparison.
15. Henry David Thoreau, *Walden*, ed. William Rossi (New York: Norton, 1992), 64.

2 Paranoid Reading, Surface Pleasures, and Deadpan Humor in *The Confidence-Man*

1. Elizabeth Renker, "'A–!': Unreadability in The Confidence-Man," in *The Cambridge Companion to Herman Melville*, ed. Robert S. Levine (New York: Cambridge University Press, 1998), 118.

2. Maurice Lee, "Skepticism and *The Confidence-Man*," *The New Cambridge Companion to Herman Melville*, ed. Levine, 118.
3. See Rachel Cole, "At the Limits of Identity: Realism and American Personhood in Melville's *Confidence-Man*," *Novel* 39.3 (Summer 2006): 384–401; Zach Hutchins, "Herman Melville's Fejee Mermaid, or A Confidence Man at the Lyceum," *ESQ* 60.1 (2014): 75–109; Susan M. Ryan, *The Grammar of Good Intentions: Race & the Antebellum Culture of Benevolence* (Ithaca: Cornell University Press, 2003), chapter 1.
4. Jennifer Greiman, "Theatricality, Strangeness, and the Aesthetics of Plurality in *The Confidence-Man*," in *Melville and Aesthetics*, eds. Otter and Sanborn, 178.
5. "Unsigned review, *New York Dispatch*," *Melville: The Critical Heritage*, ed. Watson G. Branch (London: Routledge & Kegan Paul, 1974), 369.
6. "Unsigned review, *Literary Gazette*," *Melville: The Critical Heritage*, 373; "From an unsigned review, *London Illustrated Times*," *Melville: The Critical Heritage*, 380.
7. Best and Marcus, 9.
8. It would be beyond the scope of this essay to provide an exhaustive view of the responses to Best and Marcus but several distinct approaches have emerged. One, exemplified by Elizabeth Weed and Caroline Lesjak, points to a fundamental misunderstanding and reifying of "symptomatic reading" in these accounts. See Weed, "The Way We Read Now," *History of the Present* 2.1 (2012): 95–106, and Lesjak, 233–77. A second, which we can see with Timothy Bewes, is to read this through genre theory as a way to explain the history of symptomatic reading and offer a new approach rooted in the particular form of the novel. See Bewes, "Reading with the Grain." A third approach, exemplified by Kathryn Bond Stockton, is to playfully reimagine the depths (sexual and queer) of supposed surfaces through an action like a kiss, which touches a surface but also "goes deep," so to speak. See Stockton, "Surfacing (in the Heat of Reading): Is It Like Kissing or Some Other Sex Act?," *J19: The Journal of Nineteenth-Century Americanists* 3.1 (Spring 2015): 7–13.
9. Lesjak, 251.
10. In bringing together the question of surface reading and Melville's humor, this essay charts a different course from Michael T. Gilmore's *Surface and Depth: The Quest for Legibility in American Culture* (New York: Oxford University Press, 2003) and John Bryant's *Melville and Repose: The Rhetoric of Humor in the American Renaissance* (New York: Oxford University Press, 2003). Gilmore's book, written before the current debate about surface

reading and paranoid reading, attempts to resuscitate visibility and legibility from Foucauldian suspicion, but he does not have a particular reading of *The Confidence-Man*. Bryant argues that Melville's humor is essentially genial rather than, as mine pursues, about the mechanics of a deadpan joke.

11. Eve Kosofsky Sedgwick, *Touching Feeling: Affect, Pedagogy, Performativity* (Durham: Duke University Press, 2003), 125, 141, 146.
12. Ibid., 135–136.
13. Sianne Ngai, *Ugly Feelings* (Cambridge: Harvard University Press, 2005), 51.
14. Sacvan Bercovitch, "Deadpan Huck: Or, What's Funny about Interpretation," *The Kenyan Review* 24.3/4 (2002): 90–134 at 123.
15. Jennifer A. Greenhill, *Playing it Straight: Art and Humor in the Gilded Age* (Berkeley: University of California Press, 2012), 5.
16. Mark Twain, "How to Tell a Story," in *How to Tell a Story and Other Essays* (New York: Oxford University Press, 1996), 4.
17. Twain, 9.
18. Jonathan Elmer, "'Bartleby,' Empson, and Pastoral Pleasures," *J19: The Journal of Nineteenth-Century Americanists* 2.1 (Spring 2014): 25.
19. Twain, 5.
20. Renker, 121.
21. Sedgwick, 130.
22. Lauren Berlant and Michael Warner, "Sex in Public," *Critical Inquiry* 24.2 (1998): 547–66.
23. Beverley A. Hume, "Of Cuttle-Fish and Women: Melville's Goneril in The Confidence-Man," *Melville and Women*, eds. Elizabeth Schultz and Haskell Springer (Kent: Kent State University Press, 2006), 203, 199.
24. For arguments that privacy is really another form of publicity, and depends on a transparency of identity, see Berlant and Warner, "Sex in Public"; Katherine Adams, *Owning Up: Privacy, Property, and Belonging in U.S. Women's Life Writing* (New York: Oxford University Press, 2009); Jeffrey Insko, "The Logic of Left Alone: *The Pioneers* and the Conditions of U.S. Privacy," *American Literature* 81.4 (2009): 659–85; and Stacey Margolis, *The Public Life of Privacy in Nineteenth-Century American Literature* (Durham: Duke University Press, 2009).

3 Melville and His Flowers

1. John Bryant, "Melville's Rose Poems: As They Fell," *Arizona Quarterly* 52.4 (Winter 1996): 49–84; Bryant, "Ordering the Rose: Melville's Poet's Revisions," *Melville Society Extracts* 117 (1999): 17–18; Lyon Evans, "'Tears of the Happy': The Design of Darkness in 'To Winnefred' and 'The Year,'" *Leviathan* 9.3 (October 2007): 79–94; Robert Milder, "Old Man Melville:

The Rose and the Cross," in *New Essays on Billy Budd.* ed. Donald Yannella (New York: Cambridge University Press, 2002), 83–113.

2. Ann Douglass, *The Feminization of American Culture* (New York: Alfred A. Knopf, 1978), 325.
3. Nathaniel Hawthorne, *The Centenary Edition of the Works of Nathaniel Hawthorne*, vol. 17, ed. William Charvat (Columbus: Ohio State University Press, 1962–1997), 304.
4. See Dorri Beam, *Style, Gender, and Fantasy in Nineteenth-Century American Women's Writing* (New York: Cambridge University Press, 2010).
5. Eliza Richards, *Gender and the Poetics of Reception in Poe's Circle* (New York: Cambridge University Press, 2004).
6. Virginia Jackson, "The Poet as Poetess," in *The Cambridge Companion to Nineteenth-Century American Poetry*, ed. Kerry Larson (New York: Cambridge University Press, 2011), 54–75.
7. Fanny Fern, *Fern Leaves: Fanny's Portfolio* (Buffalo: Miller, Orton, and Mulligan, 1853), v.
8. John Keats, *The Selected Letters of John Keats*, ed. Lionel Trilling (New York: Farrar, Straus, and Young, 1951), 13.
9. E. W. Wirt, *Flora's Dictionary* (Baltimore: Fielding Lucas, Jr., 1831), np; Sarah Josepha Buell Hale, *Flora's Interpreter: Or, The American Book of Flowers and Sentiments* (Boston: T.H. Webb, 1833), iv–v.
10. Paula Bernat Bennett, *Poets in the Public Sphere: The Emancipatory Project of American Women's Poetry, 1800–1900* (Princeton: Princeton University Press, 2003); on flower language, see Beam, 37–38.
11. Alex Calder, "Blubber: Melville's Bad Writing," in *Melville and Aesthetics*, eds. Samuel Otter and Geoffrey Sanborn (New York: Palgrave, 2011), 31.
12. Susan Howe, *The Birth-Mark: Unsettling the Wilderness in American Literary History* (Hanover: Wesleyan Press, 1993), 179–80.
13. On Isabel, see James Creech, *Closet Writing / Gay Reading: The Case of Melville's Pierre* (Chicago: University of Chicago Press, 1993), 88, 119; John D. Seelye, "'Ungraspable Phantom': Reflections of Hawthorne in 'Pierre' and 'The Confidence Man,'" *Studies in the Novel* 1.4 (Winter 1969): 436–43. On Urania, see Robert K. Martin, *Hero Captain, and Stranger: Male Friendship, Social Critique, and Literary Form in the Sea Novels of Herman Melville* (Chapel Hill: University of North Carolina Press, 1986), 99–100; Elizabeth Schultz and Haskell Springer, "Melville Writing Women/Women Writing Melville," in *Melville and Women*, eds. Schultz and Springer (Kent: Kent State University Press, 2006), 6.
14. Eve Kosofsky Sedgwick, *Epistemology of the Closet* (Berkeley: University of California Press, 1990), 115–16, 101.
15. Hawthorne, Vol. 10 of *Works*, 150–51.

16. M. H. Abrams, *The Mirror and the Lamp: Romantic Theory and the Critical Tradition* (New York: Oxford University Press, 1953), 201–12.
17. Walter E. Bezanson, "Historical and Critical Note," in *Clarel* (Evanston and Chicago: Northwestern University Press and The Newberry Library, 1991), 601.
18. Hawthorne, Vol. 10 of *Works,* 150–51.
19. This classification has remained consistent from the nineteenth century to today. Dennis W. Magee and Harry Ahles, *Flora of the Northeast* (Amherst: University of Massachusetts Press, 1999), 619–920.
20. Richard Bridgman, "Melville's Roses," *Texas Studies in Literature and language* 8 (Summer 1966): 239; Bryant, "Melville's Rose Poems," 63.
21. On roses as intertext, see Bridgman, 235; Milder, 16; Bryant, "Ordering the Rose," 18; Richard Ryan, *Weeds and Wildings, Chiefly: With a Rose or Two by Herman Melville. Reading Text and Genetic Text,* 1967 Dissertation, xxiv–xxv.
22. Hawthorne, Vol. 10 of *Works*, 38, 39.
23. Hawthorne, Vol. 1 of *Works,* 48, 110, 112.
24. Hawthorne, Vol. 3 of *Works*, 47, 234.
25. On Melville's later reading generally, see William B. Dillingham, *Melville and His Circle: The Last Years* (Athens: University of Georgia Press, 2008); on Melville's reading of Schopenhauer, see Sharon Cameron, *Impersonality* (Chicago: University of Chicago Press, 2007), 184, 196–204, and Cody Marrs, *Nineteenth-Century American Literature and the Long Civil War* (Cambridge: Cambridge University Press, 2015), 114–20.
26. Bridgman, 239.
27. *Melville's Marginalia Online* records that both these books were inscribed to Herman from Lizzie: Johnson in 1882, and Aldrich in 1883.
28. Rossiter Johnson, ed., *Poems Narrative* (Boston: Houghton Mifflin, 1881), 107.
29. Thomas Bailey Aldrich, *The Poems of Thomas Bailey Aldrich* (Cambridge: The Riverside Press, 1882), 38, 46, 47.
30. See also Jay Leyda, *The Melville Log: A Documentary Life of Herman Melville, 1819–1891*, Vol. 2 (New York: Harcourt, Brace and Company, 1951), 782.
31. Hawthorne, Vol. 4 of *Works*, 454.
32. Hawthorne, Vol. 10 of *Works*, 117.
33. Eliza Richards, "The Civil War Language of Flowers," in *A History of Nineteenth-Century American Women's Poetry*, eds. Jennifer Putzi and Alexandra Socarides (Cambridge: Cambridge University Press, 2016), 5.
34. Hawthorne, Vol. 1 of *Works*, 48.
35. Samuel Reynolds Hole, *A Book about Roses: How to Grow and Show Them* (New York: William S. Gottsberger, 1883), 65, 178–80.

36. James Andrews, *Floral Tableaux* (London: David Bogue, 1846), np. The poem is a translation from Frederic Adolphus Krummacher, *Parables*, trans. J. H. Agnew (Philadelphia: Hooker and Agnew, 1841), 18–19.
37. Wirt, np.
38. Andrews, np.
39. On Melville's interest in Khayyám and Sa'di, see Dorothy Finkelstein, *Melville's Orienda* (New Haven: Yale University Press, 1961).
40. Wirt's *Flora's Dictionary* is one of several guides to the language of the flowers beginning with a quote from Percival that grounds the language of flowers in "eastern lands" (*np*).
41. Edward Fitzgerald, trans, *The Rubáiyát of Omar Khayyám* (Boston: Houghton, Osgood, 1878), 25.
42. Washington Irving, *The Sketch Book of Geoffrey Crayon, Gentleman* (New York: Heritage Press, 1939), 50.
43. Hawthorne, Vol. 10 of *Works*, 150–51.
44. John Ingram, *Flora Symbolica* (London: F.W. Warne, 1869), 114–15; Sarah Carter (Edgarton) Mayo, *The Flower Vase; Containing the Language of Flowers and Their Poetic Sentiments* (Lowell: Powers and Bagley, 1844), 89; Wirt, np.
45. Hawthorne, Vol. 10 of *Works*, 153.
46. Hershel Parker, *Herman Melville: A Biography*, vol. 2 (Baltimore: Johns Hopkins University Press, 2005), 412.
47. Wirt, np; Hale, 177; Mayo, 123.

4 Pip and the Sounds of Blackness in *Moby-Dick*

1. There are exceptions, however. See, for example, Robert S. Levine and Samuel Otter, eds., *Melville and Douglass: Essays in Relation* (Chapel Hill: University of North Carolina Press, 2008); Robert K. Wallace, *Douglass and Melville: Anchored Together in Neighborly Style* (New Bedford: Spinner, 2005); and Eric Sundquist's chapter on "Benito Cereno" in *To Wake the Nations: Race and the Making of American Literature* (Cambridge: Harvard University Press, 1993).
2. See Sterling Stuckey, *African Culture and Melville's Art: the Creative Process in Benito Cereno and Moby-Dick* (New York: Oxford University Press, 2008).
3. Fred Moten, *In the Break: The Aesthetics of the Black Radical Tradition* (Minneapolis: University of Minnesota Press, 2003).
4. Toni Morrison, *Playing in the Dark: Whiteness and the Literary Imagination* (Cambridge: Harvard University Press, 1992).
5. Stuckey, *African Culture*, 32.
6. Ibid., 31–32.
7. Sterling Stuckey, *Slave Culture: Nationalist Theory and the Foundations of Black America* (New York: Oxford University Press, 1987), 12.

8. Albert Raboteau, *Slave Religion: The "Invisible Institution" in the Antebellum South* (New York: Oxford University Press), 70.
9. Stuckey, *African Culture*, 91.
10. Edward Glissant, *Poetics of Relation* (Ann Arbor: University of Michigan Press, 1997), 8.
11. Vincent Brown, *The Reaper's Garden* (Cambridge: Harvard University Press, 2008), 77.
12. Donald Pease, "Pip, *Moby-Dick*, Melville's Governmentality," *Novel: A Forum on Fiction* 45.3 (2012): 335.
13. Moten, *In the Break*, 253.

5 Melville after Secularism

1. See *The New Testament of our Lord and Saviour Jesus Christ: Translated out of the Original Greek; and ... The Book of Psalms, Translated out of the Original Hebrew* (New York: American Bible Society, 1844) at *Melville's Marginalia Online*, Steven Olsen-Smith, Dennis Marnon, and Peter Norberg, eds., at http://melvillesmarginalia.org.
2. In the *Melville's Marginalia Online* edition, see Matt. 5–7 and 26.45, Acts 17.28, Titus 1.12, and Rev. 22.19.
3. See Charles Taylor, *A Secular Age* (Cambridge: Harvard University Press, 2007); John Lardas Modern, *Secularism in Antebellum America* (Chicago: University of Chicago Press, 2011); and Tracy Fessenden, *Culture and Redemption: Religion, the Secular, and American Literature* (Princeton: Princeton University Press, 2007).
4. Benjamin Franklin, *The Autobiography and Other Writings*, ed. Kenneth Silverman (New York: Penguin, 1986), 80.
5. On Melville's use of biblical models, see Jonathan A. Cook's *Inscrutable Malice: Theodicy, Eschatology, and the Biblical Sources of Moby-Dick* (DeKalb: Northern Illinois University Press, 2013).
6. Franklin, 116–17.
7. On the "nova effect," see Taylor, 300. Jonathan A. Cook's *Satirical Apocalypse: An Anatomy of Melville's The Confidence-Man* (Westport, CT: Greenwood Press, 1996) shows that *The Confidence-Man* can be read as a Mennippean satire (pp. 16–17).
8. Cody Marrs, "A Wayward Art: Melville's *Battle-Pieces* and the Poetic Turn," *American Literature* 82.1 (March 2010): 91–119.
9. See Stan Goldman, *Melville's Protest Theism: The Hidden, Silent God in Clarel* (DeKalb: Northern Illinois University Press, 1993); William Potter, *Melville's Clarel and the Intersympathy of Creeds* (Kent: Kent State University Press, 2004).

10. See Grant E. L. Watson, "Melville's Testament of Acceptance," *New England Quarterly*, 6.2 (1933): 219–27; Phil Withim, "*Billy Budd*: Testament of Resistance," *Modern Language Quarterly* 20.2 (1959): 115–27; Joseph Schiffman, "Melville's Final Stage, Irony: A Re-examination of *Billy Budd* Criticism," *American Literature* 22.2 (1950): 128–36; Lawrance Thompson, *Melville's Quarrel with God* (Princeton: Princeton University Press, 1952); Hershel Parker, *Reading Billy Budd* (Evanston: Northwestern University Press, 1991).
11. See Harrison Hayford and Merton M. Sealts, "Introductory Essay," in *Billy Budd, Sailor: A Reading Edition* (Chicago: University of Chicago Press, 1962); Elizabeth Renker, "Melville as Postbellum Poet," in *The New Cambridge Companion to Herman Melville*, ed. Robert Levine (New York: Cambridge University Press, 1998); William H. Shurr, *The Mystery of Iniquity: Melville as Poet, 1857–1891* (Lexington: University of Kentucky Press, 1972); William Bysshe Stein, *The Poetry of Herman Melville's Late Years: Time, History, Myth, and Religion* (Albany: State University of New York Press, 1970); and William Spengemann, *Three American Poets: Walt Whitman, Emily Dickinson, and Herman Melville* (South Bend: University of Notre Dame Press, 2008).
12. Herman Melville, *Collected Poems*, ed. Howard P. Vincent (Chicago: Packard, 1947), 300.
13. *Collected Poems*, 411.

6 Marginal States: Herman Melville in the Marquesas, 1842

1. See Arjan Appadurai, *Modernity at Large: Cultural Dimensions of Globalization* (Minneapolis: University of Minnesota Press, 1996); Gloria Anzaldúa, *Borderlands/La Frontera: The New Mestiza* (San Francisco: Aunt Lute Books, 2012); Homi Bhabha, *The Location of Culture* (London: Routledge, 1994); Gilles Deleuze and Felix Guattari, *A Thousand Plateaus*, trans. Brian Massumi (Minneapolis: University of Minnesota Press, 1987); Paul Gilroy, *The Black Atlantic: Modernity and Double Consciousness* (London and New York: Verso, 1993); Michael Hardt and Antonio Negri, *Multitude: War and Democracy in the Age of Empire* (London: Penguin, 2004); and Mary Louise Pratt, *Imperial Eyes: Travel Writing and Transculturation* (London: Routledge, 1992).
2. Paul Giles, *The Global Remapping of American Literature* (Princeton: Princeton University Press, 2011), 2.
3. There are now too many transnational works to list all of them. For those beginning to explore transnationalism, several anthologies and edited collections provide a useful set of methods, influences, and readings. See for instance, Caroline F. Levander and Robert S. Levine, *Hemispheric American*

Studies (New Brunswick: Rutgers University Press, 2008); Wai Chee Dimock and Lawrence Buell, *Shades of the Planet* (Princeton: Princeton University Press, 2007); and Hester Blum, *Turns of Event: Nineteenth-Century Literary Studies in Motion* (Philadelphia: University of Pennsylvania Press, 2016), especially chapters 3, 5, 7, and 8.

4. Paul Giles, in *The Global Remapping of American Literature*, makes this argument particularly forcefully: for him, the national phase of the United States takes place only within the 100 years between 1865 and the 1970s and early 1980s.
5. For studies with a transatlantic emphasis, see Elisa Tamarkin. *Anglophilia: Deference, Devotion, and Antebellum America* (Chicago: University of Chicago Press, 2008); Christopher Hanlon, *America's England: Antebellum Literature and Atlantic Sectionalism* (New York: Oxford University Press, 2013); and Karen Ordahl Kupperman, *The Atlantic in World History* (New York: Oxford University Press, 2012).
6. For an introduction to world-systems theory, see Immanuel Wallerstein, *World-Systems Analysis: An Introduction* (Durham: Duke University Press, 2004).
7. Cesare Casarino, *Modernity at Sea: Melville, Marx, Conrad in Crisis* (Minneapolis and London: Minneapolis University Press, 2002); Jason Berger, *Antebellum At Sea: Maritime Fantasies in Nineteenth-Century America* (Minneapolis: University of Minnesota Press, 2012).
8. Karl Marx, *Capital: A Critique of Political Economy*, vol. 1, trans. Ben Fowkes (London: Penguin, 1990), 506.
9. Wendy Brown, *Walled States, Waning Sovereignty* (New York: Zone Books, 2010), 24.
10. Jeremy Adelman, "What is global history now?" *aeon* (2 March 2017); Jared Hickman, "On the Redundancy of Transnational American Studies," in *The Oxford Handbook of Nineteenth-Century Literature*, ed. Russ Castronovo (New York: Oxford University Press, 2014), 269–90; Nan Z. Da, "Intransitive Encounter," paper delivered at King's College London; and "Formality in the C19 Transpacific," delivered at "Terminal Transnationalisms" panel at C19 conference in March 2016. The above analysis in particular has benefitted greatly from Da's concept of transnational intransitivity – scenes of cross-cultural interaction in which nothing is learned, gained, or exchanged – even if the brute physicality of the obstructions literalizes and extends such an intransitivity.
11. Marx, *Capital*, 873–942.
12. Some histories of the Pacific that I have found particularly useful include Matt K. Matsuda, *Pacific Worlds: A History of Seas, Peoples, and Cultures* (Cambridge: Cambridge University Press, 2012); David Igler, *The Great*

Ocean: Pacific Worlds from Captain Cook to the Gold Rush (New York: Oxford University Press, 2013); Paul Lyons, *American Pacificism: Oceania in the U.S. Imagination* (New York and London: Routledge, 2006); Rob Wilson, *Reimagining the American Pacific: From South Pacific to Bamboo Ridge and Beyond* (Durham: Duke University Press, 2000); and Stuart Banner, *Possessing the Pacific: Land, Settlers, and Indigenous People from Australia to Alaska* (Cambridge: Harvard University Press, 2007).

13. See Edward Sugden, *Emergent Worlds: Alternative States in Nineteenth-Century American Culture* (New York: New York University Press, 2018).
14. Hannah Arendt, *The Origins of Totalitarianism* (London: Penguin, 2017), 398.

7 Perfectionist *Pierre*

I am grateful to Cody Marrs, Paul Hurh, Michelle Neely, Samuel Otter, and Elisa Tamarkin for their generous contributions to the work presented in this essay.

1. Stanley Cavell, *Conditions Handsome and Unhandsome: The Constitution of Emersonian Perfectionism* (Chicago: University of Chicago Press, 1990), 5.
2. In *Little Did I Know*, Cavell writes of reading, in 1953, "almost at random – warhorse novels I had not been through (of Melville, Dostoevsky, Stendhal, Balzac, etc.)." *Little Did I Know: Excerpts from Memory* (Stanford: Stanford University Press, 2010), 311–12.
3. Cavell, *Conditions*, 4.
4. Ralph Waldo Emerson, *The Collected Works of Ralph Waldo Emerson*, vol. 2, ed. Joseph Slater et al. (Cambridge: Belknap Press of Harvard University Press, 1979), 5.
5. But see Cavell, *Conditions*, 3, 12. Stanley Cavell, *Cities of Words: Pedagogical Letters on a Register of the Moral Life* (Cambridge: Belknap Press of Harvard University Press, 2004), 329.
6. Cavell, *Conditions*, 4.
7. Ibid., 2.
8. Stanley Cavell, *In Quest of the Ordinary: Lines of Skepticism and Romanticism* (Chicago: University of Chicago Press, 1988), 9.
9. Cavell, *Conditions*, 9.
10. Sharon Cameron, *The Corporeal Self: Allegories of the Body in Melville and Hawthorne* (Baltimore: Johns Hopkins University Press, 1981), 4.
11. Colin Dayan, "Melville's Creatures, or Seeing Otherwise," in *American Impersonal: Essays with Sharon Cameron*, ed. Branka Arsić (New York: Bloomsbury, 2014), 52.
12. Cameron, *The Corporeal Self*, 15.
13. Nancy Ruttenburg, *Democratic Personality: Popular Voice and the Trial of American Authorship* (Stanford: Stanford University Press, 1998), 348.

14. Ludwig Wittgenstein, *Philosophical Investigations*, 3rd edn., trans. G. E. M. Anscombe (Malden: Blackwell, 2001), II, iv.
15. Emmanuel Levinas, *Otherwise than Being or Beyond Essence*, trans. Alphonso Lingis (Pittsburgh: Duquesne University Press, 1981), xlviii.
16. Plato, *Symposium*, trans. Robin Waterfield (Oxford: Oxford University Press, 2008), 211c.
17. Plato, *Republic*, trans. G. M. A. Grube, revised by C. D. C. Reeve (Indianapolis: Hackett, 1992), 515c.
18. Wittgenstein, *Philosophical Investigations*, §107. I adopt Cavell's rendering of Wittgenstein's "dann" as "then." *This New Yet Unapproachable America: Lectures after Emerson after Wittgenstein* (Albuquerque: Living Batch Press, 1989), 55.
19. Stanley Cavell, *Philosophy the Day After Tomorrow* (Cambridge: Belknap Press of Harvard University Press, 2005), 197.
20. Merton Sealts, *Pursuing Melville 1940–1980* (Madison: University of Wisconsin Press, 1982), 264.
21. Ralph Waldo Emerson, *The Collected Works of Ralph Waldo Emerson*, vol. 3, eds. Alfred R. Ferguson and Jean Ferguson Carr (Cambridge: Belknap Press of Harvard University Press), 29, 28.
22. Ibid., 27.
23. As Cindy Weinstein argues, Pierre does marry Isabel, or forms a union that is "just as good (or bad) as the real thing." Weinstein, "Sentimentality," in *The Cambridge History of the American Novel*, eds. Leonard Cassuto, Clare Virginia Eby, and Benjamin Reiss (New York: Cambridge University Press, 2011), 214.
24. Elsewhere "the thought of Lucy" is called "serpent-like" (P 104).
25. Cameron, *Corporeal Self*, 19.
26. Ralph Waldo Emerson, *The Collected Works of Ralph Waldo Emerson*, vol. 4, eds. Joseph Slater, et al. (Cambridge: Belknap Press of Harvard University Press, 1987), 121.
27. See Sharon Cameron, *Impersonality: Seven Essays* (Chicago: University of Chicago Press, 2007), 182.
28. Frederick Douglass, "*The Heroic Slave*," *The Norton Anthology of American Literature*, 9th ed., vol. B, ed. Robert S. Levine (New York: Norton, 2017), 1261.
29. Henry David Thoreau, *Walden*, ed. Jeffrey S. Cramer (New Haven: Yale University Press, 2004), 37.
30. So does Emerson. In the last chapter of the book of essays that includes "Experience" he writes: "We are weary of gliding ghostlike through the world, which is itself so slight and unreal. We crave a sense of reality, though it come in strokes of pain." *Collected Works*, vol. 3, 161.

31. Dayan, 54.
32. Melville was baptized in a "strictly Calvinistic" manner. T. Walter Herbert characterizes his family as embracing a "theocentric religiousness … a mixed tradition in which Calvinistic orthodoxy was important but not supreme." T. Walter Herbert, *Moby-Dick and Calvinism: A World Dismantled* (New Brunswick: Rutgers University Press, 1977), 28.
33. On Melville and Adler, see Paul Hurh, *American Terror*, 177–90.
34. Sarah Austin, trans., *Fragments from German Prose Writers. With Biographical Sketches of the Authors* (New York: D. Appleton and Company, 1841), 289. I use Austin's incomplete translation of Kant's title, "Beantwortung der Frage: Was ist Aufklärung?"
35. Ibid., 228.
36. Ibid., 230.
37. Ibid., 229, 230.
38. See Dominic Mastroianni, *Politics and Skepticism in Antebellum American Literature* (New York: Cambridge University Press, 2014), 69.
39. Emory Elliott, "The Problem of Authority in *Pierre*," in *Ideology and Classic American Literature*, eds. Sacvan Bercovitch and Myra Jehlen (Cambridge: Cambridge University Press, 1986), 347.
40. Jonathan Edwards, *The Works of President Edwards*, vol. 6 (London: James Black, 1817; reprint, New York: Burt Franklin, 1968), 464.
41. The narrator of "Bartleby, the Scrivener" (1853) claims to have "slid" into a Calvinist view (PZ 37).
42. Edwards, *Works*, 453–54.
43. Ibid., 451.
44. Perry Miller, *The New England Mind: From Colony to Province* (Cambridge: The Belknap Press of Harvard University Press, 1953), 55.
45. William Perkins, *A Graine of Musterd-Seede or, the Least Measure of Grace that is or can be Effectuall to Saluation* (London: Iohn Legate, Printer to the Vniuersitie of Cambridge, 1611), 5.
46. Emerson, *Collected Works*, vol. 2, 182.
47. Andrew Delbanco, *The Puritan Ordeal* (Cambridge: Harvard University Press, 1989), 2.
48. Cavell, *Philosophy the Day After Tomorrow*, 121.
49. Cavell, *Conditions*, xix.
50. F. O. Mattheissen, *American Renaissance: Art and Expression in the Age of Emerson and Whitman* (London: Oxford University Press, 1941), 473.
51. Cameron, *Corporeal Self*, 15.

52. Stanley Cavell, *Emerson's Transcendental Etudes*, ed. David Justin Hodge (Stanford: Stanford University Press, 2003), 223.
53. Thoreau called Ethan Allan a "ranger [. . .] in a lower and less important field" than the one occupied by John Brown. Henry David Thoreau, *Essays*, ed. Jeffrey S. Cramer (New Haven: Yale University Press, 2013), 192.

8 *The Confidence-Man* between Genres

1. Jennifer Greiman, *Democracy's Spectacle: Sovereignty and Public Life in Antebellum American Writing* (New York: Fordham University Press, 2011), 30; Robert Milder, "Herman Melville," in *The Columbia Literary History of the United States* (New York: Columbia University Press, 1988), 440.
2. Nina Baym notes Melville's bitterness in "Melville's Quarrel with Fiction," *PMLA* 34 (1979): 909–23. See also Cecilia Tichi, "Melville's Craft and Them of Language Debased in the *Confidence-Man*," *ELH* 39.4 (December 1972): 657, and Maurice Lee, "Skepticism and The Confidence-Man," in *The New Cambridge Companion to Herman Melville*, ed. Robert S. Levine (New York: Cambridge University Press, 2014), 114.
3. Milder, 440; Sianne Ngai, *Ugly Feelings* (Cambridge: Harvard University Press, 2005), 50.
4. "The Contemporary Reviews," London *Literary Gazette* (11 April 1857).
5. Plato, *The Collected Dialogues of Plato*, eds. Edith Hamilton and Huntington Cairns (New York: Bollingen Series of Pantheon Books, 1961), 17.
6. Ngai, 37.
7. William Spengemann, "Melville the Poet," *American Literary History* 11:4 (1999), 569–609 at 574; F. O. Matthiessen, *American Renaissance*, 386.
8. Ngai, 76, 65, 67.
9. Johann Herder, "On the Cognition and Sensation of the Human Soul" (1778), in *Philosophical Writings*, ed. Michael N. Forester (Cambridge: Cambridge University Press, 2002), 188.
10. In *Poetics*, Aristotle lists analogy as one of the four kinds of metaphor.
11. Hugh Blair, "Figurative Language," in *Lectures on Rhetoric and Belles Lettres* (London: Thomas Tegg, 1845), 158.
12. Paul Bartha, *By Parallel Reasoning: The Construction and Evaluation of Analogical Arguments* (New York: Oxford University Press, 2010), 1.
13. Ibid., 3.
14. Seeking alternatives to arguments about identity and difference, scholars have returned to the possibilities offered by analogy's similitudes. See

Andrew Cole's *The Birth of Theory* (Chicago: University of Chicago Press, 2014), and Kaja Silverman's *The Miracle of Analogy* (Stanford: Stanford University Press, 2015).

15. Victor Harris, "Allegory to Analogy in the Interpretation of Scriptures," *Philological Quarterly* 45 (1966): 1–23 at 1.
16. Devon Griffiths, *The Age of Analogy: Science and Literature between the Darwins* (Baltimore: Johns Hopkins University Press, 2016), 267. In 1740, for example, George Cheyne posited that the "*natural* Language" of God depended on analogy (cited in Harris, 20).
17. David Hartley, *Observations on Man, His Frame, His Duty, and His Expectations*, 2 vols. (London: J. Johnson, 1801), II: 165, I: 295.
18. Griffiths, 34.
19. David Simpson, *Irony and Authority in Romantic Poetry* (New York: Palgrave Macmillan, 1979), 139; John Stuart Mill, *A System of Logic Ratiocinative and Inductive*, 2 vols. (London: Longmans, Green, Reader, and Dyer, 1868), II: 86.
20. Rachel Cole, "At the Limits of Identity: Realism and American Personhood in Melville's Confidence-Man," *Novel* 39.3 (Summer 2006): 384–401 at 389.
21. For a contrasting reading, according to which Pitch relies on deduction (starting with a premise and generating its implications across evidence) rather than induction (moving from evidence to conclusion), see Lee, "Skepticism and *The Confidence-Man*."
22. Plato, 590 (340e).
23. Jonathan Culler, *On Puns: The Foundation of Letters* (New York: Blackwell, 1988), 5.
24. On January 17, 1848, Melville withdrew works by Hartley from the New York Society Library; Hershel Parker, *Herman Melville: A Biography. Volume 1, 1819–1851* (Baltimore: Johns Hopkins University Press, 2005), 577.
25. Hartley, I: 296–97.
26. George Campbell, *The Philosophy of Rhetoric* (New York: Harper and Brothers, 1868), 76.
27. Simpson, 139; Ngai, 60.
28. Ngai, 51, 59.
29. Goethe, *Maxims and Reflections*, trans. Elisabeth Stopp (New York: Penguin, 1999), 70.
30. Baym, 921.
31. Renker points in this direction when, after noting Melville's "frustrations with the page," she suggests that "his experiments with character in *The Confidence-Man* laid the ground for [the] important but still little-understood shift in Melville's writing career" to poetry. Elizabeth Renker, "' A—!': Unreadability in The Confidence-Man," *The Cambridge Companion*

to Herman Melville, ed. Robert S. Levine (New York: Cambridge University Press, 1998), 132.

32. Theo Davis, *Ornamental Aesthetics: The Poetry of Attending in Thoreau, Dickinson, and Whitman* (New York: Oxford University Press, 2016), 38, 29, 50.
33. Davis's project echoes one of Ngai's claims about *The Confidence-Man*, that "the world of the novel's story *runs on a feeling that no one actually feels*" (69). For both critics, an affect and the attitude it creates – attention for Davis, tone for Ngai – is dependent on the formal attributes of a literary text.
34. Spengemann, 589.
35. Michael Cohen, *The Social Lives of Poems in Nineteenth-Century America* (Philadelphia: University of Pennsylvania Press, 2015), 13.
36. J. A. Cuddon, *The Penguin Dictionary of Literary Terms and Literary Theory* (New York: Penguin, 2015), 721.
37. Cleanth Brooks and Robert Penn Warren, eds., *Understanding Poetry* (New York: Henry Holt and Company, 1938), xxxiii, xxxviii.
38. Melville completed a prior book of poems, but its manuscript has not been found. Scholars surmise that some of its contents may be gathered in *Timoleon* (1891). See Milder, 442.
39. Milder, 442.
40. W. K. Wimsatt, "Imitation as Freedom, 1717–1798," *New Literary History* 1.2 (Winter 1970): 217.
41. Tichi, 640.
42. Claudia Stokes, "The Poetics of Unoriginality: The Case of Lucretia Davidson," *Legacy: A Journal of American Women Writers* 32.1 (2015): 31.
43. Lara Langer Cohen and Jordan Stein, *Introduction to Early African American Print Culture* (Philadelphia: University of Pennsylvania Press, 2012), 15.
44. Cole, 387.
45. Timothy Sweet, "Melville's *Battle-Pieces* and Vernacular Poetics," in *Literary Cultures of the Civil War*, ed., 100.
46. Edmund Wilson, *Patriotic Gore* (New York: Norton, 1994), 479.
47. William Dean Howells, *Atlantic Monthly* 19 (February 1867): 252.
48. Sweet, 103.

9 Melville's Style

1. John Freeman, *Herman Melville* (New York: The MacMillan Co., 1926), 170–188; Lewis Mumford, *Herman Melville* (New York: The Literary Guild of America, 1929), 181–187; F. O. Matthiessen, *American Renaissance*, 421–431; Newton Arvin, *Herman Melville* (New York: William Sloane Associates, 1950), 143–193, 253–299; Warner Berthoff, *The Example of Melville* (Princeton:

Princeton University Press, 1962), 208; Eric J. Sundquist, "Suspense and Tautology in *Benito Cereno*," *Glyph* 8 (1981): 103–126; James Creech, *Closet Writing/Gay Reading* (Chicago: University of Chicago Press, 1993), 91–179; Elizabeth Renker, *Strike Through the Mask: Herman Melville and the Scene of Writing* (Baltimore: Johns Hopkins University Press, 1996), 69–100; Sharon Cameron, *Impersonality*, 180–184; William C. Spengemann, *Three American Poets: Walt Whitman, Emily Dickinson, and Herman Melville* (Notre Dame: University of Notre Dame Press, 2010), 167–177; Alex Calder, "Blubber: Melville's Bad Writing," 11–31. For examples of recent critics who have asserted the unfashionability of style, see Robert Alter, *Pen of Iron: American Prose and the King James Bible* (Princeton: Princeton University Press, 2010), 20–41 (his second chapter is on *Moby-Dick*), and Jeff Dolven, "Style," in *The Princeton Encyclopedia of Poetry and Poetics*, 4th edn., eds. Roland Greene, et al. (Princeton: Princeton University Press, 2012), 1369–1370. Early in the twentieth-century's "Melville Revival," Arthur Johnson audaciously linked the "crude and stark" Melville (citing excerpts from *Pierre*) and the "master" James in terms of their "thoroughness" and "philosophers' painstakingness"; see "A Comparison of Manners," *New Republic* 20.251 (August 27, 1919): 113–115.

2. Susan Sontag, "On Style" (1965), *Susan Sontag: Essays of the 1960s and 70s*, ed. David Rieff (New York: Library of America, 2013), 40; Charles Altieri, "Style," in *The Oxford Handbook of Philosophy and Literature* (New York: Oxford University Press, 2009), 421.
3. Nelson Goodman, "The Status of Style," *Critical Inquiry* 1.4 (June 1975): 811.
4. Andrew Harrison, "Style," in *A Companion to Aesthetics*, ed. David Cooper (Cambridge: Blackwell, 1992), 405–406; Richard Neer, "Connoisseurship and the Stakes of Style," *Critical Inquiry* 32.1 (Autumn 2005): 17. "Salience" is also the term used by Stephanie Ross, who argues that stylistic perception depends both on the features of the artwork and the contexts in which it is experienced; see "Style in Art," in *The Oxford Handbook of Aesthetics*, ed. Jerrold Levinson (New York: Oxford University Press, 2005): 228–244; "salience" appears on 243. Art historical approaches to style are summarized by E. H. Gombrich, "Style," in *The International Encyclopedia of the Social Sciences*, vol. 15, ed. David L. Sills (New York: Macmillan, 1968), 352–363, and Meyer Schapiro, "Style," in *Anthropology Today: An Encyclopedic Summary*, ed. A. L. Kroeber (Chicago: University of Chicago Press, 1953), 287–312.

5. Colin Dayan, "Melville's Creatures, or Seeing Otherwise," in *American Impersonal*, 56.
6. For critical associations of Melville's Pacific with a desired equanimity, see William H. Shurr, *The Mystery of Iniquity: Melville as Poet, 1857–1891* (Lexington: University of Kentucky Press: 1972), 96–98; Gavan Daws, *A Dream of Islands: Voyages of Self-Discovery in the South Seas* (New York: W. W. Norton, 1980), 125–26; and James Duban, "From Bethlehem to Tahiti: Transcultural 'Hope' in *Clarel*," *Philological Quarterly* 70.4 (Fall 1991): 475–483.
7. Melville's spelling for the places and peoples he describes in *Typee* differs from present-day usage: Nukuheva (for Nuku Hiva), Typee (for the Taipi or, as they refer to themselves, Vai'i'i), Happar (for the Ha'apa'a), the Typee valley (for Taipivai or Taipi or Vai'i'i), and Tior (for Tai'oa or Haka'ui).
8. Noah Webster, *An American Dictionary of the English Language*, rev. and enl. Chauncey A. Goodrich (Springfield: George and Charles Merriam, 1851), s.v. "interval"; *Oxford English Dictionary Online*, s.v. "intervale."
9. Editorial concerns about the book's veracity (held by its British publisher John Murray) and about its propriety and politics (held by its American publisher John Wiley) altered the composition of Melville's book and resulted in three early editions, all published in 1846: the first British (under the title *Narrative of a Four Months' Residence Among the Natives of a Valley of the Marquesas Islands; or, a Peep at Polynesian Life*); the first American (under Melville's preferred title of *Typee: A Peep at Polynesian Life*), with several alterations; and then a heavily revised and significantly cut American edition. See Leon Howard, "Historical Note," in the Northwestern Newberry *Typee*, 282–288, and Hershel Parker, *Herman Melville: A Biography*, 2 vols. 1 (Baltimore: Johns Hopkins University Press, 2005), vol. 1: 405–461. Howard speculates that the author, rather than his editors or typesetters, was most likely responsible for the return of "inter-vales" in the Revised American edition (290). With the exception of the change from "inter- / vales" to "intervals" and then back to "inter-vales," the passages from *Typee* that I quote in this essay remained unaltered in the early editions of Melville's book.
10. Captain David Porter, *Journal of a Cruise Made to the Pacific Ocean, in the United States Frigate Essex, in the Years 1812, 1813, and 1814*, 2nd ed., 2 vols. (New York: Wiley and Halsted, 1822; reprinted Upper Saddle River: Gregg Press, 1970), vol. 2: 94; Porter describes the journey from Taioha'e Bay to the valley of the Ha'apa'a (or Happah) in vol. 2: 93–99. Charles S. Stewart, *A Visit to the South Seas, in the U.S. Ship Vincennes, during the Years 1829 and 1830*, 2 vols. (New York: John P. Haven, 1831; reprinted New York: Praeger, 1970),

vol. 1: 225, 348, 217, 342. We do not know which specific editions of Porter and Stewart Melville consulted as he was writing *Typee*. As Charles Roberts Anderson observed in his pathbreaking 1939 study of Melville's reliance on sources such as Porter and Stewart in writing his Pacific narratives, questions about the authenticity of *Typee* date back to its original publication; see *Melville in the South Seas* (New York: Columbia University Press, 1939; reprinted New York: Dover, 1966), 179–195. Hershel Parker describes *Typee* as "true in much of its substance and grand items," but "truth a good deal varnished," in *Herman Melville: A Biography*, vol. 1: 214. Debates about fact and fiction in *Typee* have ebbed and flowed over the decades, cresting most recently in a special issue of *ESQ: A Journal of the American Renaissance* 51.1–3 (2005), edited by G. R. Thompson, under the title "Melville in the Marquesas: Actuality of Place in *Typee* and Other Island Writings." In this issue, the archaeologist Robert C. Suggs maintains that Melville overstated the insularity of the valleys and the vacancy of the ridges, which, during Melville's visit in 1842, housed a system of Marquesan forts. Skeptical of the factual basis for the narrator's description of his several days of wandering with Toby between Taioha'e Bay and the Taipi valley, he argues that no actual features of the terrain on the high plateau between the two locations correspond to those depicted by Melville. He suggests a resemblance to Stewart's descriptions of Taioha'e Bay and to the series of perpendicular ridges at Haka'ui ("Melville's Flight to Taipi: Topographic, Archeological, and Historical Considerations," 63–65, 70). In the same issue, John Bryant counters such skepticism and questions Suggs's evidence, and Mary K. Bercaw Edwards surveys Melville's debts to Porter. In terms of language and detail, Stewart seems an even more prominent influence on Melville's portrayal of the trip across the highlands. A few critics have attended to the significance of the topographical details in the early chapters of *Typee*. See Rod Edmond, *Representing the South Pacific: Colonial Discourse from Cook to Gaugin* (New York: Cambridge University Press, 1997), 85–86; Vanessa Smith, "Crossing the Beach at Taipivai: The Psychogeography of Islands," *ESQ* 51.1–3 (2005): 105–113; Geoffrey Sanborn "Purple Haze: Making Sense of Uncertainty (and Uncertainty of Sense) in *Typee*," *ESQ* 51.1–3 (2005): 129–135; Ian S. Maloney, *Melville's Monumental Imagination* (New York: Routledge, 2006), 26–28; and David Farrier, *Unsettled Narratives: The Pacific Writings of Stevenson, Ellis, Melville, and London* (New York: Routledge, 2007), 138–140.

11. Melville's point-of-view inquiries in *Typee* are trenchantly analyzed by T. Walter Herbert, *Marquesan Encounters: Melville and the Meaning of Civilization* (Cambridge: Harvard University Press, 1980) and by

Mitchell Breitwieser, "False Sympathy in Melville's *Typee*," *American Quarterly* 34.4 (Autumn 1982): 396–417.

12. Alex Calder argues that Tommo and the Typee negotiate different, but not exclusive, metaphors that give shape to their cross-cultural understandings, in "'The Thrice Mysterious Taboo': Melville's *Typee* and the Perception of Culture," *Representations* 67 (1999): 27–43. The terms and figures of the skin mercer scene are intensified, and the caress perceived as an assault, in *Typee*'s pivotal chapter 30, when the Nuku Hivan artist Karky demonstrates his eagerness to tattoo the narrator's face.
13. Viktor Shklovsky, "Art as Technique" (1917), in *Russian Formalist Criticism: Four Essays*, trans. and intro. Lee T. Lemon and Marion J. Reis (Lincoln: University of Nebraska Press, 1965), 22; Cleanth Brooks, *The Well Wrought Urn: Studies in the Structure of Poetry* (New York: Harcourt, Brace, 1947), 180; Theodor Adorno, *Minima Moralia: Reflections from a Damaged Life* (1951), trans. E. F. N. Jephcott (New York: Verso, 2005), 247.
14. Warwick Wadlington, *The Confidence Game in American Literature* (Princeton: Princeton University Press, 1975), 33. Wadlington centers his analysis on three writers: Melville, Mark Twain, and Nathaniel West.
15. Peter Coviello, *Intimacy in America: Dreams of Affiliation in Antebellum Literature* (Minneapolis: University of Minnesota Press, 2005), 14.
16. Berthoff, *Example of Melville*, 208; Paul Lyons, "Language, Vision, and the Trope of Federation in Herman Melville's *Moby-Dick*" (Ph.D. diss., University of North Carolina at Chapel Hill, 1990), 14, 131; Jennifer Greiman, "Theatricality, Strangeness, and the Aesthetics of Plurality," in *Melville and Aesthetics*, eds. Otter and Sanborn, 189; Calder, "Melville's Bad Writing," 28, and see also his analysis of Melville's "style of not knowing . . . a style in which things can be said," in "Thrice Mysterious Taboo," 29–30.
17. Parker identifies Melville's penchant for overlapping images in *Herman Melville: A Biography*, 1: 356–357, 454. I am grateful to Brian Yothers for sharing his insights on this canto.
18. Rolfe's thoughts take a similar turn back to the South Pacific later in the poem: "From Bethlehem here my musings reach / Yes – frankly – to Tahiti's beach . . . Tahiti should have been the place / For Christ in advent" (CL 445). See also Melville's entry on a page in the journal of his trip to Europe and the Levant in 1856–1857, probably made after his return home, where he suggests that "J. C. should have appeared in Taheiti [sic]" (J 154). A source for passages in *Clarel*'s, the 1856–1857 journal serves as a pivot for Melville's joining of Palestine and the Pacific. The journal's compressed, measured, and often fragmentary lines suggest Melville's increasing interest in poetry, also evident in his frustrated efforts to publish a volume of poems in 1860.

19. The palm also calls to the despondent exile Mortmain, once a Swedish revolutionary leader: "While bright he saw the angel-tree / Across the gulf alluring sway: / *Come over! be – forever be / As in the trance*" (CL 371). Mortmain is found dead the following morning, his eyes fixed on the palm.
20. Walter E. Bezanson, "Explanatory Notes" to *Clarel*, 630.
21. The connection between "Ned Bunn" and Richard Tobias Greene is asserted by Leon Howard, in *Herman Melville: A Biography* (Berkeley: University of California Press, 1951), 321, and by Howard P. Vincent, in his notes to *Collected Poems of Herman Melville* (Chicago: Packard, 1947), 472. The notes in the Northwestern-Newberry *Published Poems* are more circumspect (740).
22. Robert Louis Stevenson, *In the South Seas* (1896), ed. and intro. Neil Rennie (New York: Penguin Books, 1998), 23–36; Jack London, *The Cruise of the Snark* (New York: Macmillan, 1911), 154.
23. Melville figures the ocean as containing "hollows" not only in "Rolfe and the Palm" but also in "Pebbles," the concluding sequence of poems in *John Marr and Other Sailors*, and in the unpublished poem "The Old Shipmaster and his Crazy Barn." See *Published Poems*, 245, and *"Billy Budd, Sailor" and Other Uncompleted Writings*, vol. 13 of *The Writings of Herman Melville*, ed. Harrison Hayford, Alma A. MacDougall, Robert A. Sandberg, and G. Thomas Tanselle (Evanston and Chicago: Northwestern University Press and The Newberry Library, 2017), 133. In *Typee*, as well as in *Clarel* and "To Ned," Melville seems to have deliberately simplified his portrayals of Nuku Hiva; social arrangements of greater complexity on the island are detailed in one of the main sources for *Typee*, Porter's *Journal of a Cruise Made to the Pacific Ocean*. On the speaker's implication in "To Ned," see Shurr, *Mystery of Iniquity*, 142–143; Parker, *Herman Melville*, vol. 2: 882; and Hsuan L. Hsu, *Geography and the Production of Space in Nineteenth-Century American Literature* (New York: Cambridge University Press, 2010), 159–162.
24. Jenny Franchot, "Melville's Traveling God," in *The Cambridge Companion to Herman Melville*, ed. Levine, 160–162, 180–183. A few critics have scrutinized the persistence of Polynesia in Melville's later work. Warren Rosenberg argues that Melville drew on his Marquesan experience in shifting from prose fiction to what Rosenberg views as the balanced contraries and quest for transcendence that for Rosenberg distinguish his poetry; see "Poem as Palm: Polynesia and Melville's Turn to Poetry," *"Whole Oceans Away": Melville and the Pacific*, eds. Jill Barnum, Wyn Kelley, and Christopher Sten (Kent: Kent State University Press, 2007), 239–252, and also "Melville's Turn to Poetry: A Genre Approach to *Clarel*" (Ph.D. diss., City University of New York, 1981). Robert Milder describes the effects of

Melville's experiences in Polynesia as both a "constant" and a "variable" across his career (6), providing him with "an outsider's perspective on matters of race, class, sexuality, social organization, progress, and history"; see *Exiled Royalties: Melville and the Life We Imagine* (New York: Oxford University Press, 2006), 3–26; I have quoted from pages 5 and 6.

25. Ilana Pardes argues that Melville sustains both allegorical and literal interpretations of the Song of Songs; see "Melville's Song of Songs eds. Otter and Sanborn, 213–233.

26. The tangle of Clarel's desires includes not only Ruth and the Lyonese but also the young Italian Celio and the middle-aged American Vine. Martin Kevorkian analyzes the encounter between Clarel and the Lyonese, speculating about the effect of the young Frenchman's lyricism on Clarel's development, in "Clarel and the Prodigal: The Caesuras of Melville's Iron Age," *Leviathan: A Journal of Melville Studies* 18.3 (October 2016): 31–46.

27. The Epilogue has become an interpretive crux for readers. On the side of continuity and conclusion are, among others, Ronald Mason, *The Spirit Above the Dust: A Study of Herman Melville* (London: John Lehmann, 1951), 242–244; Stan Goldman, *Melville's Protest Theism: The Hidden and Silent God in Clarel* (DeKalb: Northern Illinois University Press, 1993), 125–129; James Duban, "From Bethlehem to Tahiti," and "'The Oracle of God Within': Human Nature and Personal Faith in the Epilogue to Clarel and Melville's Annotated Bible," *Literature & Theology* 28.4 (December 2014): 425–437; Brian Yothers, *The Romance of the Holy Land in American Travel Writing, 1790–1876* (Burlington: Ashgate Publishing, 2007), 134–135; and Martin Kevorkian, *Writing beyond Prophecy: Emerson, Hawthorne, and Melville after the American Renaissance* (Baton Rouge: Louisiana State University Press, 2013), 172–177. On the side of irresolution are Shurr, *Mystery of Iniquity*, 120–123; Bryan C. Short, "Form as Vision in Herman Melville's *Clarel*," *American Literature* 50.4 (January 1979): 567–569; and Edgar A. Dryden, *Monumental Melville: The Formation of a Literary Career* (Stanford: Stanford University Press, 2004), 144–145. Hilton Obenzinger describes the Epilogue as "a final benediction of sorts," a "small consolation, a flourish of stoic counterpoint at the very coda of textual instability"; see *American Palestine: Melville, Twain, and the Holy Land Mania* (Princeton: Princeton University Press, 1999), 77–79.

28. Biblical allusions in the Epilogue are analyzed by Goldman, *Melville's Protest Theism*, 164–165 (for whom the various allusions are synthesized); Dryden, *Monumental Melville*, 145 (for whom the allusions clash); and Pardes, "Melville's Song of Songs," 230–232.

29. Goldman, *Melville's Protest Theism*, 164; Nathaniel Hawthorne, *The Scarlet Letter (1850)*, vol. 1 of *The Centenary Edition of the Works of Nathaniel Hawthorne*, eds. William Charvat, et al. (Columbus: Ohio State University Press, 1962), 258.
30. Goldman, 153–165.
31. Hershel Parker, agreeing with those who contend that Melville rejected Unitarianism, views him as rebuking a facile optimism and a denial of evil and suffering that he associated with Orville Dewey and Ralph Waldo Emerson; see Parker, *Herman Melville*, vol. 2: 65–68, 501–502, 896. Recently, several critics have argued persuasively for Melville's deeper interest in Unitarian ideas. See Duban, "The Oracle of God Within"; Yothers, Sacred Uncertainty, 164–166, 187–188; and Dawn Coleman, "Melville and the Unitarian Conscience," in *Visionary of the Word: Melville and Religion*, ed. Jonathan A. Cook and Brian Yothers (Evanston: Northwestern University Press, 2017), 129–157.
32. Shurr considers the ambivalences of "prove," in *Mystery of Iniquity*, 123. Dryden connects the last line of the Epilogue to Paul and Isaiah and observes the peculiarity of death's "routing" life, in *Monumental Melville*, 145.
33. Dryden, *Monumental Melville*, 145.

10 Melville and the Conceits of Theory

1. Bruno Latour, "Why Has Critique Run Out of Steam?," 225–48.
2. William Spanos, "Pierre's Extraordinary Emergency: Melville and 'the Voice of Silence,' Part 1," *boundary 2* 28.2 (Summer 2001): 112.
3. Szendy's italics. Peter Szendy, *Prophecies of Leviathan: Reading Past Melville*, trans. Gil Anidjar (New York: Fordham University Press, 2010), ix, 10.
4. For Marcus, "just reading" is a practice that "accounts for what is in a text 'without construing presence as absence or affirmation as negation.'" Stephen Best and Sharon Marcus, "Surface Reading," 12.
5. Giorgio Agamben separates the "literary constellation" that contains Melville's "Bartleby" (and includes Dostoevsky's Mishkin and all of Kafka's clerks) from the "philosophical constellation" that, he argues, "alone contains the figure merely traced by the literary constellation to which Bartleby belongs." Giorgio Agamben, "Bartleby; or, On Contingency," in *Potentialities: Collected Essays in Philosophy*, trans. Daniel Heller-Roazen (Stanford: Stanford University Press, 1999), 243–71; Gilles Deleuze, "Bartleby; or, the Formula," in *Essays Clinical and Critical*, trans. Daniel Smith and Michael Greco (Minnesota: University of Minneapolis Press, 1997), 68–90;

Jacques Rancière, "Deleuze, Bartleby, and the Literary Formula," in *The Flesh of Words: The Politics of Writing*, trans Charlotte Mandell (Stanford: Stanford University Press, 2004), 146–64.

6. The bibliography of work on Melville and philosophy is extensive, with Branka Arsić and K.L. Evans' volume, *Melville's Philosophies*, collecting essays by scholars who have developed a range of readings, not just of Melville's engagement with philosophical traditions but of "the philosophical arguments themselves – often very strange and quite radical – that Melville never stopped articulating and reformulating." Branka Arsić and K. L. Evans, "Introduction," in *Melville's Philosophies*, eds. Arsić and Evans, 3.
7. Kevin Attell, "Language and Labor, Silence and Stasis: Bartleby among the Philosophers," in *A Political Companion to Herman Melville*, ed. Jason Frank (Lexington, KY: University of Kentucky Press, 2013), 194.
8. Ibid., 225.
9. Nancy Ruttenburg, "'The Silhouette of a Content': 'Bartleby' and American Literary Specificity," in *Melville and Aesthetics*, eds. Otter and Sanborn, 139; Michael Jonik, "Murmurs, Stutters, Foreign Intonations: Melville's Unreadables," *The Oxford Literary Review* 33.1 (2011): 30–31. Both Cameron and Arsić explicitly read against the grain of Americanist criticism on Melville's work in order to describe a long American literary and philosophical tradition of impersonality. See Sharon Cameron, *Impersonality*, 180–204; Branka Arsić, *Passive Constitutions; or, 7–1/2 Times Bartleby* (Stanford: Stanford University Press, 2007); and Arsić, ed., *American Impersonal.*
10. Attell, "Language and Labor," 222.
11. Ruttenburg, "The Silhouette of a Content," 137, 139, 144.
12. Ibid., 147.
13. Jonik, "Murmurs, Stutters, Foreign Intonations," 41, 35.
14. Deleuze, "Bartleby; or, The Formula," 68, 73, 78.
15. In Deleuze's triangular system, Bartleby stands at one pole ("the nothingness of the will") with Ahab at the other ("the will to nothingness"), while the lawyer looks on as "a representative of secondary nature." Ibid., 79–80.
16. Rancière, "Deleuze, Bartleby, and the Literary Formula," 146, 148, 153.
17. Jonik makes a similar point concerning how Rancière reads Deleuze's claim for the sounds made by Isabel's guitar: "it would seem that Rancière expects something of a grander, modernist gesture" through which form is ruptured by the murmur of her guitar (37). Jonik offers the most sustained reading of Rancière's critique of Deleuze, taking seriously

Rancière's final point in "Deleuze, Bartleby, and the Literary Formula" that the wall of uncemented stones is just that – a barrier to shared fabulation – while also seeking to preserve the power of the inhuman murmur within human language (40–41).

18. See Jacques Rancière, *Dissensus: On Politics and Aesthetics*, trans. Steven Corcoran (Stanford: Stanford University Press, 2010), especially 152–83.
19. Ranciére, "Deleuze," 155, 156, 158.
20. Ibid., 157, 159, 161, 162.
21. Rancière, *Dissensus*, 182; Deleuze, "Bartleby," 77.
22. Michael Snediker, "*Pierre* and the Non-Transparencies of Figuration," *ELH* 77.1 (2010): 223.
23. Rancière, *Dissensus*, 180; Snediker, "Pierre," 223.
24. Rancière, "Deleuze," 153.
25. Rancière, *Dissensus*, 164, 167.

11 *Billy Budd*: Pessimism for Post-Critique

1. E. L. Grant Watson, "Melville's Testament of Acceptance," *New England Quarterly* 6.2 (June 1933): 319–27.
2. William V. Spanos, *The Exceptionalist State and the State of Exception: Herman Melville's Billy Budd* (Baltimore: Johns Hopkins University Press, 2011), 79.
3. See Spanos, *The Exceptionalist State,* 76: "Every reading I refer to in the previous chapter, especially those associated with the 'testament of acceptance,' has been, in fact, a symptomatic (and ideological) reading."
4. Barbara Johnson, "Melville's Fist: The Execution of *Billy Budd*," *Studies in Romanticism* 18.4 (Winter 1979): 567–99 at 573.
5. Latour, "Why Has Critique Run Out of Steam?"
6. See Rita Felski, *The Limits of Critique* (Chicago: University of Chicago Press, 2015); Eve Kosofsky Sedgwick, "Paranoid Reading and Reparative Reading" in *Novel Gazing: Queer Readings in Fiction*, ed. Eve Sedgwick (Durham: Duke University Press, 1997); Stephen Best and Sharon Marcus, "Surface Reading: An Introduction."
7. See "On Rita Felski's *The Limits of Critique*," *PMLA* 132.2 (March 2017): 331–91.
8. Felski, *The Limits of Critique*, 186.
9. Eve Kofosky Sedgwick, *Epistemology of the Closet* (Berkeley: University of California Press, 1990), 97.
10. Ibid., 100, 127, 107.
11. Ibid., 127, 128, 130.
12. Sedgwick, "Paranoid Reading," 126.

13. Ibid., 126, 127.
14. Merton M. Sealts Jr. *Melville's Reading: A Check-List of Books Owned and Borrowed* (Madison: The University of Wisconsin Press, 1966), 91.
15. See Herman Melville's letters to James Billson and Henry Stephens Salt. As he writes to Billson, "one can hardly overestimate" the poem, "massive and mighty as it is, – its gloom is its sublimity" (L 514). To Salt, he writes: "The '*City of Dreadful Night*' is the modern Book of Job, under an original poem duskily looming with the same aboriginal verities" (L 522).
16. Sharon Cameron, *Impersonality*, 2007, 204.
17. Arthur Schopenhauer, *The World as Will and Idea*, vol. 3, trans. R. B. Haldane and J. Kemp (London: Kegan Paul, Trench, Trübner & Co., 1906), 397.
18. Schopenhauer, *The World as Will and Idea*, 191.
19. Ibid., 469.
20. Arthur Schopenhauer, "The Wisdom of Life," in *Essays of Arthur Schopenhauer*, trans. T. Bailey Saunders (New York: A. L. Burt, N.D.), 1–92 at 59.
21. Ibid., 60.
22. Ibid., 63, 62.
23. Ibid., 42.
24. Ibid., 77.
25. Arthur Schopenhauer, "Studies in Pessimism," in *Essays of Arthur Schopenhauer*, 394.
26. James Thompson, *The City of Dreadful Night and Other Poems* (London: Methuen & Co., 1932), 19.
27. Ibid., 20.
28. Sedgwick, "Paranoid Reading," 128.

12 Melville, *Mardi*, and Materialism

1. Cesare Pavese, *American Literature: Essays and Opinions*, trans. Edwin Fussell (Berkeley: University of California Press, 1970), 60; Merton M. Sealts, Jr., *Pursuing Melville, 1940–1980: Chapters and Essays* (Madison: University of Wisconsin Press, 1982), 278–97.
2. See for example, Paul Gilmore, *Aesthetic Materialism: Electricity and American Romanticism* (Stanford, CA: Stanford University Press, 2009), 88–89.
3. For a record of Melville's book borrowings and purchases while writing *Mardi*, see Merton M. Sealts's essential *Melville's Reading*, 15–18.
4. Paul Hurh, *American Terror*, 170–71.

5. Here, I would disagree with Jordan Stein's argument that the novel performs an undoing of context. Rather, we find a superfluity of contexts held, to again use Paul Hurh's phrase, in "uneven balance." See Jordan Stein, "Are 'American Novels' Novels? *Mardi* and the Problem of Boring Books," in *The Oxford Handbook of Nineteenth-Century American Literature*, ed. Russ Castronovo (Oxford and New York: Oxford University Press, 2012), 42–58.
6. "instinct, n." *OED Online*, Oxford University Press, January 2018, www.oed.com/view/Entry/97085. Accessed January 31, 2018.
7. William James, *Principles of Psychology*, Vol. 2 (New York: Dover, 1950), 404.
8. Cf. David Hume's assertion in his Treatise that "reason is nothing but a wonderful and unintelligible instinct in our souls, which carries us along a certain train of ideas, and endows them with particular qualities, according to their particular situations and relations." Hume, as, quoted in John Yolton, *Thinking Matter: Materialism in Eighteenth-Century Britain* (Oxford: Basil Blackwell, 1983), 32.
9. David Hume, *Treatise of Human Nature* (1739), ed. L. A. Selby-Bigge (Oxford: Oxford University Press, 1962), 252.
10. Geoffrey Sanborn, "Melville and the Nonhuman World," in *The New Cambridge Companion to Herman Melville*, ed. Levine, 12.
11. Melville, here, misclassifies tunicates as molluscs.
12. See also William Paley, who notes in his *Natural Theology*, "In the civil world, as well as in the material, it is the *vis inertiæ* which keeps things in their places." William Paley, *Natural Theology: or, Evidences of the Existence and Attributes of the Deity* [1809], 12th ed. (London: Printed for J. Faulder), 513.
13. Gilmore, *Aesthetic Materialism*, 88–89.
14. David Hartley, *Observations on Man: His Frame, His Duty, and His Expectations* (1749) (Cambridge: Cambridge University Press, 2013), i.
15. "ether, n." *OED Online*. Oxford University Press, January 2018. www.oed.com/view/Entry/64728. Accessed January 30, 2018.
16. Hartley, 21.
17. Ibid., 8.
18. Jess Keiser, "Plastic Matters," in *The New Politics of Materialism: History, Philosophy, Science*, eds. Sarah Ellenzweig and John H. Zammito (London and New York: Routledge, 2017), p. 74.
19. As Hartley writes, "sensations are conveyed to the mind, by the efficiency of corporeal causes . . . [therefore] it seems to me, that the powers of generating ideas, and raising them by association, must also arise from corporeal causes, and consequently admit of an explication from the subtle influences of the small parts of matter on each other." *Observations*, 1.

20. Ibid., 512.
21. Ibid.
22. Charles T. Wolfe, "Varieties of Vital Materialism," in *The New Politics of Materialism: History, Philosophy, Science*, eds. Sarah Ellenzweig and John H. Zammito (New York: Routledge, 2017), 44–65 at 61.
23. Hartley, *Observations*, 503.
24. Melville alludes to Sir Anthony Absolute, the protagonist of Richard Sheridan's comedy of manners *The Rivals* (1775), a work roughly contemporary to Priestley's *Doctrine*.
25. Yolton, *Thinking Matter*, 111.
26. Joseph Priestley, *The Doctrine of Philosophical Necessity Illustrated* (London: J. Johnson, 1777), xix–xx.
27. Hartley, *Observations*, 501.
28. Ibid.
29. See Keiser, "Plastic Matters," 74–75.
30. For a discussion of Coleridge's philosophical development, see Tim Milnes, *The Truth about Romanticism: Pragmatism and Idealism in Keats, Shelley, Coleridge* (Cambridge: Cambridge University Press, 2010), 154–55.
31. Samuel Taylor Coleridge, *Biographia Literaria: Or, Biographical Sketches of My Literary Life and Opinions* (1817) in *The Collected Works of Samuel Taylor Coleridge*, eds. James Engell and W. Jackson Bate (Princeton: Princeton University Press, 1983), 117.
32. Ibid., 108.
33. Ibid., 133.
34. Ibid., 110.
35. Elizabeth Grosz, *The Incorporeal: Ontology, Ethics, and the Limits of Materialism* (New York: Columbia University Press, 2017), 251.
36. Cited in F. O. Matthiessen, *American Renaissance*, 188–89.

13 Popular Networks in Melville's *Battle-Pieces*

1. Hershel Parker, *Melville: The Making of the Poet* (Evanston: Northwestern University Press, 2008), 199–200.
2. Faith Barrett, 325n5.
3. Ibid., 252.
4. Timothy Sweet, "Melville's *Battle-Pieces* and Vernacular Poetics," in *Literary Cultures of the Civil War*, ed., 100.
5. Ibid., 101.

6. "More Poetry of the War," *Nation* (September 6, 1866), 187–88, *The Contemporary Reviews*, 515.
7. Ibid., 516.
8. Forecythe Willson, *The Old Sergeant, and Other Poems* (Boston: Ticknor and Fields, 1867), 7–18. The review states that the poem was originally published in *The Louisville Journal* during the war.
9. Sweet, "Melville's *Battle-Pieces*," 155n6. For a treatment of Melville's critique of conventional pastoral ideals, see Timothy Sweet, *Traces of War: Poetry, Photography, and the Crisis of the Union* (Baltimore: Johns Hopkins University Press, 1990).
10. Virginia Jackson, "Who Reads Poetry?," *PMLA* 123.2 (2008): 181–87 at 185.
11. Peter Coviello, "Battle-Music: Melville and the Forms of War," in *Melville and Aesthetics*, eds. Otter and Sanborn, 196.
12. Barrett, 10.
13. Jackson, 184.
14. Sweet, "Vernacular Poetics," 102.
15. Coviello, 198.
16. Jackson, 185–86.
17. Edmund Clarence Stedman, "How Old Brown took Harper's Ferry. A Ballad of the Times (containing ye true history of ye great Virginia fight.)," *New York Daily Tribune* (November 12, 1859), 6; the poem later appeared under the simpler title "How Old Brown Took Harper's Ferry," in Edmund Clarence Stedman, *Poems, Lyrical and Idyllic* (New York: Charles Scribner, 1860), 169–79.
18. Stedman, *New York Daily Tribune*, 6.
19. In a discussion of "The March into Virginia": "The speaker is Melville as omniscient narrator – a personage not often found in nonballad lyric, though regularly present in epic. The storyteller of a ballad, however, does not philosophize like Melville's persona." Helen Vendler, "Melville and the Lyric of History," in *Herman Melville, Battle-Pieces and Aspects of the War*, ed. James M. McPherson (Amherst: Prometheus Books, 2001), 257.
20. John Brown, "Last Address to the Virginia Court," *The Tribunal: Responses to John Brown and the Harper's Ferry Raid*, eds. John Stauffer and Zoe Trodd (Cambridge: Belknap Press of Harvard University Press, 2012), 55.
21. John Hay, *Putnam's Magazine* 1 (October 1906): 16. At "eserver antislavery," https://antislavery.eserver.org/poetry/john-brown-poetry/john-brown-poetry. Accessed January 6, 2018.
22. Jackson, 184.
23. Oliver Wendell Holmes, Sr., "Our Battle Laureate," *Atlantic Monthly* (May 1865): 589–91.

24. M. A. DeWolfe Howe, "Introduction," in Henry Howard Brownell, *Lines of Battle and Other Poems* (Boston and NY: Houghton Mifflin Company, 1912), 15. Brownell says that "all these poems have been printed heretofore – mostly in the daily papers," in his "Preface" to *Lyrics of a Day; or Newspaper Poetry. By a Volunteer in the US Service* (New York: Carlton, 1864), iii. "The Battle of Charlestown" is included in this volume (57–58). I haven't found the original publication, but it was reprinted in *Littel's Living Age* (January 17, 1863): 142.
25. Brownell, "The Battle of Charlestown," *Lines of Battle*, 54.
26. Hsuan Hsu, "War, Ekphrasis, and Elliptical Form in Melville's *Battle-Pieces*," *Nineteenth-Century Studies* 16 (2002): 52, 65. Hennig Cohen was perhaps the first to draw attention to Melville's interest in visual materials in his edition of *Battle-Pieces*. Herman Melville, *The Battle-Pieces of Herman Melville*, ed. Hennig Cohen (New York: Thomas Yoseleff, 1963). See also Christopher Sten, *Savage Eye: Melville and the Visual Arts* (Kent: Kent State University Press, 1991).
27. Frank Day, *Melville's Use of The Rebellion Record in His Poetry* (Clemson: Clemson University Digital *Press*, 2002), 54, 58.
28. *New York Independent* (January 10, 1867), 525; Aaron Shackelford, "Unfamiliar War: Literature and Trauma in the US Civil War," PhD dissertation, University of North Carolina Chapel Hill, 2013 (see, in particular, chapter two); Barrett, 255–57.
29. Barrett, 270–74.
30. Eliza Richards, *Battle Lines: Poetry, Media, and the US Civil War* (Philadelphia: University of Pennsylvania Press, 2019). I make other comparisons between Melville's poetry and popular poetry of the war as well.
31. In reference to Melville's *Billy Budd*, Sharon Cameron formulates this relevant idea: "What is in excess of personality is not only an action, and not even a content, but also a set of expressions. In this way Melville renders individuality and its undoing coterminous. The effect is not a neutralization but a bafflement or haunt." Sharon Cameron, *Impersonality*, xiii.
32. Cody Marrs argues that Melville's idea of conflict is cyclical; violence repeats, with a difference, rendering temporality periodic. Marrs asserts that "Melville is actively searching history for patterns." This search leads to an interest in prospective retrospect, retrospective prospect, and other temporal overlays such as the one I am positing here. Cody Marrs, 94.
33. Emily Dickinson, *The Letters of Emily Dickinson*, ed. Thomas Johnson (Cambridge: Belknap Press of Harvard University Press, 1958), L298.
34. Brownell, "Preface" to *Lyrics of a Day*, iii.

35. Cameron, *Impersonality*, ix.
36. *Albion* (September 15, 1856), in *Reviews*, 518.
37. William Dean Howells, *Atlantic Monthly* (February 19, 1867), in *Reviews*, 527.
38. Milette Shamir, "Herman Melville and the Civilian Author," in *A History of American Civil War Literature*, ed. Coleman Hutchison (Cambridge: Cambridge University Press, 2015), 222–23.
39. *New York Independent* (January 10, 1867), in *Reviews*, 526.
40. John Hay, *Addresses* (New York: The Century Co., 1906), 232.

14 The Biographical Re-Turn

1. For assessments of early Melville biography, bibliography, and editions, see James Barbour, "Melville Biography: A Life and the Lives," and G. Thomas Tanselle, "Melville and the World of Books," in *A Companion to Melville Studies*. ed. John Bryant (New York: Greenwood Press, 1986).
2. Harrison Hayford registers his disappointment in Arvin's unrevised treatment of Owen Chase, which Arvin subsequently knew to be untrue; see Harrison Hayford, *Melville's Prisoners* (Evanston, IL: Northwestern University Press, 2003), 133–35.
3. Named for Melville's younger sister who preserved them, these materials, formerly catalogued as the Melville Family Additions, are now catalogued at NYPL as the Augusta Melville papers. The four boxes include hundreds of family letters and the three-chapter *Typee* manuscript. The foundational collections of Melville materials are Harvard's Houghton Library, New York Public Library, Boston Public Library, New-York Historical Society, Newberry Library, the Beinecke Library, and the Berkshire Athenaeum.
4. Hershel Parker, "Biographer and Biography: Melville and the Footsteps Theory of Biography," in *Melville Biography: An Inside Narrative* (Evanston: Northwestern University Press, 2013).
5. Charles Roberts Anderson, *Melville in the South Seas* (New York: Columbia University Press, 1939), 70.
6. Ibid., 191.
7. Parker, *Melville Biography*, 515n9.
8. Bryant, "A Melville Renaissance," in *A Companion to Melville Studies*, ed. Bryant, xxi.
9. Michel Foucault, "What is an Author?" in *Contemporary Literary Criticism*, eds. Robert Con Davis and Ronald Schleifer (2nd edn.; New York: Longman, 1989), 274.
10. In *The Fluid Text* (Ann Arbor: University of Michigan Press, 2002), I devised a critical vocabulary for identifying kinds of versions and revision and

developed print and digital protocols for editing works in revision. In fluid text analysis, sequential versions are "textual identities" and by narrativizing the sequence, we can make arguments about the rhetoric of Melville's evolving texts in relation to audience and culture. See also John Bryant, "Witness and Access: The Uses of the Fluid Text," *Textual Cultures* 2.1 (Spring 2007): 16–42; *Melville Unfolding* (Ann Arbor: University of Michigan Press, 2008); and "Textual Identity and Adaptive Revision: Editing Adaptation as a Fluid Text," *Adaptation Studies: New Challenges, New Directions*, eds. Jørgen Bruhn, Ann Gjelsvik, and Eirik Frisvold Hanssen (London: Bloomsbury, 2013), 47–67.

11. Wyn Kelley, "'My Literary Thirst': Augusta Melville and the Melville Family Correspondence," *Resources for American Literary Study* 25.1 (1999): 45–56.
12. Since the 1990s, critics have focused more on Melville's reading of women writers, the influence of women in Melville's writing, and issues regarding gender and domesticity. For an overview, see Charlene Avallone, "The Company of Women Authors," in *A Companion to Herman Melville*, ed. Wyn Kelley (Malden, MA: Blackwell, 2006). For specific studies, see *Melville and Women*, eds. Elizabeth Schultz and Haskell Springer (Kent: Kent State University Press, 2006), especially Laurie Robertson-Lorant's chapter on "Melville and the Women in His Life," pp. 15–37. Even so, Augusta receives barely a passing reference.
13. Catherine Clinton. *Fanny Kemble's Civil Wars* (New York: Simon & Schuster, 2000), 144–45.
14. Elizabeth Foster, ed., *The Confidence-Man* (New York: Hendricks House, 1954), 311–14.

15 Afterword

1. Cody Marrs develops the notion of the "transbellum" in his *Nineteenth-Century American Literature and the Long Civil War*; see Ch. 3 for his discussion of Melville's career.
2. *Critical Essays on Herman Melville's Moby-Dick*, ed. Brian Higgins and Hershel Parker (New York: G. K. Hall, 1992), 29.
3. Hershel Parker, "*Moby-Dick* and Domesticity," in *Critical Essays on Herman Melville's Moby-Dick*, eds. Brian Higgins and Hershel Parker (New York: G.K. Hall, 1992), 545–62 at 551, 555, 560, 561.
4. Cathy N. Davidson and Michael Moon, "Preface: New Melville," *American Literature* 66.1 (March 1994): v, vi.
5. Julian Markels, "The *Moby-Dick* White Elephant," *American Literature* 66.1 (March 1994): 105, 111, 109–110, 113. On the limits of the Northwestern-Newberry edition's principle of attempting to recover Melville's original

intention, see also Robert S. Levine, "Why We Should Be Teaching and Writing about *The Literary World*'s 1850 'Hawthorne and His Mosses,'" *J19: The Journal of Nineteenth-Century Americanists* 5.1 (Spring 2017): 179–89.

6. Markels, "The *Moby-Dick* White Elephant," 119; Hershel Parker, "Historical Note," to *Moby-Dick; or, The Whale*, vol. 6 of *The Writings of Herman Melville*, eds. Harrison Hayford, Hershel Parker, and G. Thomas Tanselle (Evanston and Chicago: Northwestern University Press and The Newberry Library, 1988), 581–762 at 628.
7. Elizabeth Renker, "Herman Melville, Wife Beating, and the Written Page," *American Literature* 66.1 (March 1994): 123, 133. On Renker and the Melville establishment, see Philip Weiss, "Melville Mystery Cannot Be Stifled by New Biography," *Observer*, June 17, 2002. Web. Accessed February 12, 2018.
8. Melville, *Moby-Dick*, 398, 117, 6. On approaching Melville and other American writers as theorists, see Joel Pfister, *Surveyors of Custom: American Literature as Cultural Analysis* (New York: Oxford University Press, 2016). Pfister calls for a new way of doing critical theory in relation to American writers that "reverses the usual literary historical trajectory . . . by consciously bringing literature to our understanding of what constitutes – and can constitute – cultural theory and history" (9).
9. In her influential modern edition, Elizabeth S. Foster helped to initiate scholarship on the novel by arguing from an allegorical perspective that the Confidence Man was the devil himself in various disguises; see Herman Melville, *The Confidence-Man: His Masquerade*, ed. Foster (New York: Hendricks House, 1954).
10. See Best and Marcus, "Surface Reading," 1–21.
11. On Melville and black expressive culture, see Sterling Stuckey, *American Culture and Melville's Art*.
12. See Ann Douglass, *The Feminization of American Culture* (New York: Alfred A. Knopf, 1977), ch. 9.

Select Bibliography

The following bibliography is a compilation of selected material referenced in the previous chapters.

Agamben, Giorgio. "Bartleby; or, On Contingency." In *Potentialities: Collected Essays in Philosophy*, trans. Daniel Heller-Roazen. Stanford: Stanford University Press, 1999.

Anderson, Charles Roberts. *Melville in the South Seas*. New York: Columbia University Press, 1939.

Arsić, Branka and K. L. Evans, eds. *Melville's Philosophies*. New York: Bloomsbury, 2017.

Barrett, Faith. *To Fight Aloud Is Very Brave: American Poetry and the Civil War*. Amherst: University of Massachusetts Press, 2012.

Baym, Nina. "Melville's Quarrel with Fiction," *PMLA* 34 (1979): 909–23.

Berger, Jason. *Antebellum At Sea: Maritime Fantasies in Nineteenth-Century America*. Minneapolis: University of Minnesota Press, 2012.

Berlant, Lauren and Michael Warner. "Sex in Public," *Critical Inquiry* 24.2 (1998): 547–66.

Best, Stephen and Sharon Marcus. "Surface Reading: An Introduction," *Representations* 108.1 (Fall 2009): 1–21.

Bewes, Timothy. "Reading with the Grain: A New World in Literary Criticism," *differences: A Journal of Feminist Cultural Criticism* 21.3 (2013): 1–33.

Bryant, John. *The Fluid Text*. Ann Arbor: University of Michigan Press, 2002.

"Melville's Rose Poems: As They Fell," *Arizona Quarterly* 52.4 (Winter 1996): 49–84.

Calder, Alex. "Blubber: Melville's Bad Writing." In *Melville and Aesthetics*, eds. Samuel Otter and Geoffrey Sanborn. New York: Palgrave, 2011.

Cameron, Sharon. *Impersonality: Seven Essays*. Chicago: University of Chicago Press, 2007.

Casarino, Cesare. *Modernity at Sea: Melville, Marx, Conrad in Crisis*. Minneapolis and London: Minneapolis University Press, 2002.

Castiglia, Christopher. "Cold War Allegories and the Politics of Criticism." In *The New Cambridge Companion to Herman Melville*, ed. Robert S. Levine. Cambridge: Cambridge University Press, 2014.

Cavell, Stanley. *Conditions Handsome and Unhandsome: The Constitution of Emersonian Perfectionism*. Chicago: University of Chicago Press, 1990.

Cohen, Michael. *The Social Lives of Poems in Nineteenth-Century America*. Philadelphia: University of Pennsylvania Press, 2015.

Cole, Rachel. "At the Limits of Identity: Realism and American Personhood in Melville's *Confidence-Man*," *Novel* 39.3 (Summer 2006): 384–401.

Coleman, Dawn. "Melville and the Unitarian Conscience." In *Visionary of the Word: Melville and Religion*, eds. Jonathan A. Cook and Brian Yothers. Evanston: Northwestern University Press, 2017.

Coviello, Peter. "Battle-Music: Melville and the Forms of War." In *Melville and Aesthetics*, eds. Samuel Otter and Geoffrey Sanborn. New York: Palgrave, 2011.

Intimacy in America: Dreams of Affiliation in Antebellum Literature. Minneapolis: University of Minnesota Press, 2005.

Creech, James. *Closet Writing / Gay Reading: The Case of Melville's Pierre*. Chicago: University of Chicago Press, 1993.

Davis, Theo. *Ornamental Aesthetics: The Poetry of Attending in Thoreau, Dickinson, and Whitman*. New York: Oxford University Press, 2016.

Dayan, Colin. "Melville's Creatures, or Seeing Otherwise." In *American Impersonal: Essays with Sharon Cameron*, ed. Branka Arsić. New York: Bloomsbury, 2014.

Deleuze, Gilles. "Bartleby; or, the Formula." In *Essays Clinical and Critical*, trans. Daniel Smith and Michael Greco. Minnesota: University of Minneapolis Press, 1997.

Dillingham, William B. *Melville and His Circle: The Last Years*. Athens: University of Georgia Press, 2008.

Douglas, Ann. *The Feminization of American Culture*. New York: Alfred A. Knopf, 1977.

Elmer, Jonathan. "'Bartleby,' Empson, and Pastoral Pleasures," *J19: The Journal of Nineteenth-Century Americanists* 2.1 (Spring 2014): 24–33.

Felski, Rita. *The Limits of Critique*. Chicago: University of Chicago Press, 2015.

Finkelstein, Dorothy. *Melville's Orienda*. New Haven: Yale University Press, 1961.

Fleissner, Jennifer. "After the New Americanists: The Progress of Romance and the Romance of Progress in American Literary Studies." In *A Companion to American Literary Studies*, eds. Robert S. Levine and Caroline Levander. London: Wiley-Blackwell, 2011.

Franchot, Jenny. "Melville's Traveling God." In *The Cambridge Companion to Herman Melville*, ed. Robert S. Levine. New York: Cambridge University Press, 1998.

Giles, Paul. *The Global Remapping of American Literature*. Princeton: Princeton University Press, 2011.

Goldman, Stan. *Melville's Protest Theism: The Hidden, Silent God in* Clarel. DeKalb: Northern Illinois University Press, 1993.

Greiman, Jennifer. *Democracy's Spectacle: Sovereignty and Public Life in Antebellum American Writing*. New York: Fordham University Press, 2011.

Grosz, Elizabeth. *The Incorporeal: Ontology, Ethics, and the Limits of Materialism*. New York: Columbia University Press, 2017.

Hurh, Paul. *American Terror: The Feeling of Thinking in Edwards, Poe, and Melville*. Stanford: Stanford University Press, 2015.

"*Clarel*, Doubt, Delay." In *Melville's Philosophies*, eds. Branka Arsić and K. L. Evans. New York: Bloomsbury, 2017.

Hutchins, Zach. "Herman Melville's Fejee Mermaid, or A Confidence Man at the Lyceum," *ESQ* 60.1 (2014): 75–109.

Jackson, Virginia. "Who Reads Poetry?," *PMLA* 123.2 (2008): 181–87.

James, C. L. R. *Mariners, Renegades, and Castaways: The Story of Herman Melville and the World We Live In*. Hanover and London: University Press of New England, 1985.

Johnson, Barbara. "Melville's Fist: The Execution of Billy Budd," *Studies in Romanticism* 18.4 (Winter 1979): 567–99.

Jonik, Michael. "Murmurs, Stutters, Foreign Intonations: Melville's Unreadables," *The Oxford Literary Review* 33.1 (2011): 21–44.

Kelly, Wyn, ed. *A Companion to Herman Melville*. London: Wiley-Blackwell, 2006.

"'My Literary Thirst': Augusta Melville and the Melville Family Correspondence," *Resources for American Literary Study* 25.1 (1999): 46–56.

Latour, Bruno. "Why Has Critique Run Out of Steam?: From Matters of Fact to Matters of Concern," *Critical Inquiry* 30 (Winter 2004): 225–48.

Lee, Maurice. "Skepticism and *The Confidence-Man*." In *The New Cambridge Companion to Herman Melville*, ed. Robert S. Levine. Cambridge: Cambridge University Press, 2014.

Lesjak, Carolyn. "Reading Dialectically," *Criticism* 55.2 (Spring 2013): 233–77.

Levine, Robert S., ed. *The Cambridge Companion to Herman Melville*. New York: Cambridge University Press, 1998.

The New Cambridge Companion to Herman Melville. New York: Cambridge University Press, 2014.

Leyda, Jay. *The Melville Log: A Documentary Life of Herman Melville, 1819–1891*. 2 Vols. New York: Harcourt, Brace and Company, 1951.

Markels, Julian. "The *Moby-Dick* White Elephant," *American Literature* 66.1 (March 1994): 105–22.

Marovitz, Sanford, ed., *Melville as Poet: The Art of "Pulsed Life."* Kent: Kent State University Press, 2013.

Marrs, Cody. *Nineteenth-Century American Literature and the Long Civil War*. Cambridge and New York: Cambridge University Press, 2015.

Mason, Ronald. *The Spirit Above the Dust: A Study of Herman Melville*. London: John Lehmann, 1951.

Mastroianni, Dominic. *Politics and Skepticism in Antebellum American Literature*. New York: Cambridge University Press, 2014.

McCall, Corey and Tom Nurmi. *Melville Among the Philosophers*. Lanham: Lexington Books, 2017.

Melville, Herman. *Billy Budd, Sailor*, eds. Harrison Hayford and Merton M. Sealts. Chicago: University of Chicago Press, 2001.

Clarel. Vol. 12 of *The Writings of Herman Melville*, eds. Harrison Hayford, et al. Evanston and Chicago: Northwestern University Press and The Newberry Library, 1991.

The Confidence-Man. Vol. 10 of *The Writings of Herman Melville*, eds. Harrison Hayford, Hershel Parker, and G. Thomas Tanselle. Evanston and Chicago: Northwestern University Press and The Newberry Library, 1984.

Correspondence. Vol. 14 of *The Writings of Herman Melville*, ed. Lynn Horth. Evanston and Chicago: Northwestern University Press and The Newberry Library, 1993.

Israel Potter. Vol. 8 of *The Writings of Herman Melville*, eds. Harrison Hayford, Hershel Parker, and G. Thomas Tanselle. Evanston and Chicago: Northwestern University Press and The Newberry Library, 1988.

Journals. Vol. 15 of *The Writings of Herman Melville*, eds. Howard C. Horsford and Lynn Horth. Evanston and Chicago: Northwestern University Press and The Newberry Library, 1989.

Mardi. Vol. 3 of *The Writings of Herman Melville*, eds. Harrison Hayford, Hershel Parker, and G. Thomas Tanselle. Evanston and Chicago: Northwestern University Press and The Newberry Library, 1970.

Moby-Dick. Vol. 6 of *The Writings of Herman Melville*, eds. Harrison Hayford, Hershel Parker, and G. Thomas Tanselle. Evanston and Chicago: Northwestern University Press and The Newberry Library, 1988.

Omoo. Vol. 2 of *The Writings of Herman Melville*, eds. Harrison Hayford, Hershel Parker, and G. Thomas Tanselle. Evanston and Chicago: Northwestern University Press and The Newberry Library, 1968.

The Piazza Tales and Uncollected Prose. Vol. 9 of *The Writings of Herman Melville*, eds. Harrison Hayford, Hershel Parker, and G. Thomas Tanselle. Evanston and Chicago: Northwestern University Press and The Newberry Library, 1987.

Pierre. Vol. 7 of The *The Writings of Herman Melville*, eds. Harrison Hayford, Hershel Parker, and G. Thomas Tanselle. Evanston and Chicago: Northwestern University Press and The Newberry Library, 1992.

Published Poems. Vol. 11 of *The Writings of Herman Melville*, eds. Robert C. Ryan, et al. Evanston and Chicago: Northwestern University Press and The Newberry Library, 2009.

Redburn. Vol. 4 of *The Writings of Herman Melville*, eds. Harrison Hayford, Hershel Parker, and G. Thomas Tanselle. Evanston and Chicago: Northwestern University Press and The Newberry Library, 1969.

Typee. Vol. 1 of *The Writings of Herman Melville*, eds. Harrison Hayford, Hershel Parker, and G. Thomas Tanselle. Evanston and Chicago: Northwestern University Press and The Newberry Library, 1968.

Weeds and Wildings, ed. Robert C. Ryan. Evanston: Northwestern University Press, 1967.

White-Jacket. Vol. 5 of *The Writings of Herman Melville*, eds. Harrison Hayford, Hershel Parker, and G. Thomas Tanselle. Evanston and Chicago: Northwestern University Press and The Newberry Library, 1970.

Milder, Robert. *Exiled Royalties: Melville and the Life We Imagine*. New York: Oxford University Press, 2006.

Ngai, Sianne. *Ugly Feelings*. Cambridge: Harvard University Press, 2005.

North, Joseph. *Literary Criticism: A Concise Political History*. Cambridge: Harvard University Press, 2017.

Olsen-Smith, Steven, Dennis Marnon, and Peter Norberg, eds. *Melville's Marginalia Online*: http://melvillesmarginalia.org/

Otter, Samuel and Robert S. Levine, eds. *Melville and Douglass: Essays in Relation*. Chapel Hill: University of North Carolina Press, 2008.

Otter, Samuel and Geoffrey Sanborn, eds. *Melville and Aesthetics*. New York: Palgrave, 2011.

Pardes, Illana. "Melville's Song of Songs: *Clarel* as Aesthetic Pilgrimage." In *Melville and Aesthetics*, eds. Samuel Otter and Geoffrey Sanborn. New York: Palgrave, 2011.

Parker, Hershel. *Herman Melville: A Biography*. 2 Vols. Baltimore: Johns Hopkins University Press, 2005.

Herman Melville: The Making of a Poet. Evanston: Northwestern University Press, 2008.

Potter, William. *Melville's* Clarel *and the Intersympathy of Creeds*. DeKalb: Northern Illinois University Press, 2004.

Rancière, Jacques. "Deleuze, Bartleby, and the Literary Formula." In *The Flesh of Words: The Politics of Writing*, trans. Charlotte Mandell. Stanford: Stanford University Press, 2004.

Dissensus: On Politics and Aesthetics, trans. Steven Corcoran. Stanford: Stanford University Press, 2010.

Renker, Elizabeth. "'A–!': Unreadability in The Confidence-Man." In *The Cambridge Companion to Herman Melville*, ed. Robert S. Levine. New York: Cambridge University Press, 1998.

"Melville the Realist Poet." In *A Companion to Herman Melville*, ed. Wyn Kelly. London: Wiley-Blackwell, 2006.

Strike Through the Mask: Herman Melville and the Scene of Writing. Baltimore: Johns Hopkins University Press, 1996.

Ryan, Susan M. *The Grammar of Good Intentions: Race & the Antebellum Culture of Benevolence*. Ithaca: Cornell University Press, 2003.

Sanborn, Geoffrey. "Melville and the Nonhuman World." In *The New Cambridge Companion to Herman Melville*, ed. Robert S. Levine. New York: Cambridge University Press, 2014.

Schultz, Elizabeth and Haskell Springer, eds. *Melville and Women*. Kent: Kent State University Press, 2006.

Sealts, Merton M. *Melville's Reading*. Madison: University of Wisconsin Press, 1966.

Sedgwick, Eve. *Epistemology of the Closet*. Berkeley: University of California Press, 1990.

"Paranoid Reading and Reparative Reading; or, You're So Paranoid, You Probably Think This Introduction Is about You." In *Novel Gazing: Queer Readings in Fiction*, ed. Eve Sedgwick. Durham: Duke University Press, 1997.

Shamir, Milette. "Herman Melville and the Civilian Author." In *A History of American Civil War Literature*, ed. Coleman Hutchison. Cambridge: Cambridge University Press, 2015.

Shklovsky, Viktor. "Art as Technique." In *Russian Formalist Criticism: Four Essays*, trans. and intro. Lee T. Lemon and Marion J. Reis. Lincoln: University of Nebraska Press, 1965.

Shurr, William H. *The Mystery of Iniquity: Melville as Poet, 1857–1891*. Lexington: University of Kentucky Press, 1972.

Snediker, Michael. "*Pierre* and the Non-Transparencies of Figuration," *ELH* 77.1 (2010): 217–35.

Spanos, William V. *The Exceptionalist State and the State of Exception: Herman Melville's Billy Budd*. Baltimore: Johns Hopkins University Press, 2011.

Spengemann, William C. *Three American Poets: Walt Whitman, Emily Dickinson, and Herman Melville*. South Bend: University of Notre Dame Press, 2008.

Sten, Christopher. *Savage Eye: Melville and the Visual Arts*. Kent: Kent State University Press, 1991.

Stuckey, Sterling. *African Culture and Melville's Art: the Creative Process in Benito Cereno and Moby-Dick*. New York: Oxford University Press, 2008.

Sweet, Timothy. "Melville's *Battle-Pieces* and Vernacular Poetics." In *Literary Cultures of the Civil War*, ed. Timothy Sweet. Athens: University of Georgia Press, 2016.

Szendy, Peter. *Prophecies of Leviathan: Reading Past Melville*, trans. Gil Anidjar. New York: Fordham University Press, 2010.

Taylor, Charles. *A Secular Age*. Cambridge: Harvard University Press, 2007.

Vendler, Helen. "Melville and the Lyric of History." In *Herman Melville, Battle-Pieces and Aspects of the War*, ed. James M. McPherson. Amherst: Prometheus Books, 2001.

Watson, Grant E. L. "Melville's Testament of Acceptance," *New England Quarterly* 6.2 (1933): 219–27.

Withim, Phil. "*Billy Budd*: Testament of Resistance," *Modern Language Quarterly* 20.2 (1959): 115–27.

Yothers, Brian. *Sacred Uncertainty: Religious Difference and the Shape of Melville's Career*. Evanston: Northwestern University Press, 2015.

Yothers, Brian and Jonathan Cook, eds. *Visionary of the Word: Melville and Religion*. Evanston: Northwestern University Press, 2017.

Index